I0570846

Dream Maker
A Mystical Tale

Grigor Fedan

All rights reserved by the author. Copyright © 2002

We are the music makers
We are the dreamers of dreams...
We are the movers and shakers
of the world over, it seems

-Arthur O'Shaughnessy

O Body swayed to music,
O brightening glance,
How can we know the dancer from the dance?

-W.B. Yeats

INTRODUCTION

What is real?

I subscribe to the simple answer that if something has an effect, then it's real.

The experiences described in these pages are real to me. They impacted me deeply. I am certain that much of what's in this novel happened in a dream, which I was able to recall in the process of writing. Apparently I had a host of questions that I wanted answered, ranging from *who am I?* And *what am I doing here?* And perhaps the most important one, *why is the world the way it is?* The universe does appear to be cruel and haphazard. Then there were the mundane questions: *I wonder who I was in a past life? Do we meet loved ones again and again?*

This is what I believe happened:

In 1995 I experienced a tremendous personal crisis. At some point I formulated the above questions, with sufficient force and determination to produce a dream. I do think I was helped, that this was an intervention of sorts.

After a few years the images and concepts from the dream started surfacing, and I felt compelled to write. I found myself uncovering a past life and answering the questions I had posed. Writing was in a way like connecting the dots in one of those drawings I did as a child. The outline was generated by the dream, but the blanks I filled using my intuition, creativity and facts I gathered through historical research.

I didn't set out to write historical or spiritual fiction, or for that matter a novel. It just came out that way. Now I realize the wisdom. The format was perfect for what I had to say, how I experienced things and therefore how I told the story. Also, by dropping all preconceived notions of what I should write and how, I was able to tap that part of our mind that can perceive beyond the boundaries of everyday reality.

It was also a lot of fun.

CHAPTER ONE

The cars in front had slowed down to a crawl, a sea of red lights stretching as far as the next rise on the road. Martin's hands slowly twisted around the steering wheel. *Some idiot who can't drive...an old geezer probably.* The rain was now a steady drizzle. He turned the knob to speed up the wipers, but that was only more annoying. Again he looked at his watch. Twenty till. *Damn! A wasted trip home. Where could she be?* So much for trying to patch things up.

He got off at the University Avenue exit and headed along the frontage road paralleling the freeway. Then he saw the jackknifed trailer truck on the freeway, smoke coming from the big rig, and realized it was the cause of the slowdown. Past the truck the place seemed deserted, so Martin got back on at the next on-ramp. In his rearview mirror he could see the accident not quite a city block behind. The front right tire of the big truck was resting on top of a red Honda Accord, completely smashing it. *That's Jenny's car.* A sickening feeling took over his stomach. *Oh God, please let them be alive, I'll do whatever you want.* With his heart racing, Martin pulled over and stopped. He got out and ran towards the wreck, his eyes riveted on the Honda and the patrolman talking on his shoulder mike and occasionally peeking inside the smashed car. When Martin was about two hundred feet away, the cop saw him and turned in his direction. Martin glanced desperately at the license plate: the first three letters were DLC. He stopped. That wasn't his wife's car. He surveyed the scene, the cop looking at him intently.

"There's nothing you can do. Stay away," the patrolman shouted.

Martin assented with his head. He felt his insides release the tension. He stood to catch his breath. *Poor people, poor people, whoever you are.* His relief was someone else's pain. Someone related to whoever had died in that car was perhaps expecting her or him home in a few hours. Then the news would come...and the horrible grief would start.

He tried to regain composure as he drove, but the palms of his hands felt cold and clammy, his brow was covered with sweat, and his heart was still racing. For a moment he had been sure, so sure it was Jenny and Adam in that car. He knew that some days she picked up their son at school, especially when the weather was bad. *In the blink of an eye our lives can be destroyed.*

Martin looked at his watch as he parked the car in the bank's lot. Two fifty-four. Six minutes until closing time. Still shaken by the accident, he rushed across the street to the bank.

He noticed an old, slim black man leaning against one of the columns by the bank's door. As he approached, the man raised a trembling hand to catch his attention. In his other hand he clutched a plastic bag.

"Sir," he heard the man say in a tentative voice, "Can you help me? …please?"

Martin looked at the man. Gentle eyes on a leathery face. He knew he had to stop and listen. As the man started to speak, Martin thought how his wife always accused him of being a pushover. He looked at the bank door. *I still have a few minutes.*

"Look sir," the man said, "I don't mean to trouble you or anything, but could you call me a cab?" The voice sounded weak. He was thin, in his late seventies and appeared to be leaning against the column for support. "A lady in the bank called me one a while back." Then he noticed Martin looking him over, studying his clothes." I need to get to the hospital…I got money, I just need a cab."

"Are you all right? Maybe you need an ambulance."

The old man held up a hand. "No, It's not that bad. I just need to check in, that's all."

"I'll see what I Can do. I've got to go in the bank first. Afterwards I'll take care of you."

The watery eyes smiled at him. "I'll be here."

Once inside the bank, Martin wondered why no one else had helped the old guy. As he approached the teller, he recognized Martha, who often waited on him. When he inquired about the man, she told him she had noticed him out there for at least the past half hour or so. She had no idea whom "the elderly gentleman" was waiting for. Martin had always tried to be nice to the plump, rather homely and apparently lonely teller, and he decided to not press her about it.

His business done, Martin looked for the branch manager. He would help the old man, but first things first. He found the assistant manager instead.

"Yes," the young man said, "I've noticed the old gentleman standing out there."

"Has anyone called him a cab?" Martin asked, knowing what the answer was going to be.

"Oh, is that what he's waiting for?"

Martin felt blood surge to his face. The anger came out in his voice. "The old guy walked into this bank, and someone agreed to call him a cab. That's what he's waiting for. Who the hell was supposed to call him a cab?"

"Mister Devon, I assure you that if we knew he needed a cab we would've called him one. Please, sir, calm down."

Calm down…calm down…my ass.

Standing with his face close to the young man's, Martin was now shouting. "I'm going to find out who the old man talked to, who promised him a cab…and then I'll make sure that jerk gets fired. Understand? The old man is sick, and is waiting for a cab to go to the damn hospital!" The entire bank was now silent, all eyes turned in his direction, but he didn't care. With this he walked out. He knew the old guy had been dismissed from someone's mind as unimportant. *Next time they'll know better, stupid bastards.* His anger spent, now he simply felt bad for the old man.

The man was still there, leaning against the column, clutching his plastic bag.

Martin decided to make things right for him. "Come with me sir. I'll take you to the hospital." *So it will take half an hour out of my life, what the hell.*

Smiling and appearing surprised, the man thanked him Martin guessed that at that point his primary need was to sit down somewhere.

As they walked slowly across the street, Martin became aware that he was still feeling the jolt from the accident in the form of a knot in his stomach. *Now the old guy. Wonder why he has to go to the hospital?* The man carried his grocery bag with care. In it he seemed to have some cans of food and what looked like two apples.

Once in the car, Martin's mind started reviewing the things he had to do that afternoon. He had already wasted enough time. *There's the quarterly report for the Labor contract, two calls to make, the United invoice.* The knot had become a gnawing tension in the pit of his stomach. *First, prepare the draft, then call…*

The old man interrupted him. He was saying that his name was Percy and he had taken the bus to the supermarket to buy groceries. "On my way back, I started feeling poorly and knew it was time for the hospital. I got off the bus to look for a cab, but couldn't see none…and no public phone, neither. So I went to the bank."

Percy continued to talk, and Martin figured it was going to be that way for the rest of the trip. He wondered what he himself would be like when he got to be that age.

The old guy was now saying he had been in the Merchant Marines for most of his life, until they told him to retire. Then he worked for a grocery store, "because a man is no good sitting alone in a room." Then had come the cancer, but at the same time he had met Mojo, and he helped him get better.

But now Mojo had told him the time to die was coming to him. "Get ready to go, Percy, is what he told me the other day." The old man let out a weak chuckle, "I'm not just lying in bed waiting to die, no sir. Mojo is helping me get around, keeps pumping me up." Martin turned to look at him, and noticed a big smile on Percy's face as he stared straight ahead.

Poor old guy is making things up. Guess he has a right. Why not? He's probably lonely.

It was surprising that Percy knew exactly how to get to the hospital. He had directed Martin all the while. Martin drove up to the emergency door, but Percy told him to take him to the main entrance.

"No need," he said, "don't plan to die this very minute."

Martin watched as Percy opened the car door, precariously slid off the seat and stood up outside the car. Then he bent down to say something.

"Could you do me one more favor? Don't mean to impose."

In his mind Martin heard Jenny's voice telling him what a pushover he was. *So here it is, he's going to ask me for money. Oh, boy...*

"Could you tell Mojo I'm here? I sure would like to see him."

Martin looked down at the floorboard. *So maybe there is a Mojo after all.* "OK, Percy, give me his phone number."

"Oh, there's no phone. You find him home."

Home? He thought of the report that needed writing, but the eyes and face looking at him expectantly told him this was important.

"OK Percy. How do I find Mojo?" Martin sighed.

The old man seemed to think about it. "I just have to show you. Can't seem to remember the address." He opened the door and got back in the car. Martin felt trapped.

They drove through Oakland's less appealing streets, what once had been a middle-class neighborhood from a hundred years back. Eventually they came to a white, two-story wooden house, one that like the rest in that part of town had seen much better times.

"So this is Mojo's house?" asked Martin.

"This is my place," Percy said. "Mojo is staying here with me." With these words the old man started getting out of the car, and Martin noticed how difficult it was for him to move; it seemed he had been getting weaker by the minute.

"Stay here, I'll go get Mojo." Martin told him.

Percy smiled back and nodded. "Thank you. Just ring the bell for number four." His voice had also gotten noticeably weaker and he now spoke with difficulty, as someone fighting pain.

Martin went around the car and toward the white building. *So I'll ring the door bell...Right, a strange white man in an all-black neighborhood...just go through with it, what the hell...damn.*

Martin rang the button under the faded number four someone had scribbled on the wood with a pen. In short order he heard heavy footsteps coming down creaky wooden stairs. The footsteps stopped behind the door; then he heard the lock turn, and the door opened wide.

He was now looking at a massive black man, of perhaps forty or so, wearing a white tee shirt and black pants. He was taller than Martin by a few inches, so he was at least six-and-a-half feet tall. His body was heavily muscled, as though he had spent most of his life doing grueling physical labor, or lifting weights. However, the face was gentle and calm.

"And how can I help you, friend?" Two warm eyes looked at him under thick, black eyebrows. Then he glanced around Martin at the car and its passenger.

"Ah, Percy! I've been worried about you," the big man shouted past Martin. He went around him and bounded down the steps to the car.

Martin watched as Mojo reached through the open window and gently stroked Percy's head, as a parent would soothe a hurt child.

"Percy, you're weak, and you're in pain. Let's have the nice man take you to the hospital right now." Without further words, Mojo took the bag of groceries the old man handed him and turned around to face Martin.

"Thank you for what you're doing for Percy," he said as he walked back toward Martin and the building. "I'll put these away and be right back down."

Martin walked over to the car and was surprised at Percy's change. It was obvious he was now revitalized, as though he had been given a magic potion. His eyes shone with new vitality, and he sat erect, his face now reflecting a renewed awareness. Martin wondered whether the man named Mojo had somehow made the old man better just by touching him.

"That's my friend Mojo. He can do anything," he explained, as though reading Martin's mind.

On the way back to the hospital Percy again told him he had served thirty years in the Merchant Marines and had traveled "all over God's green earth." He mentioned two wives. He told Martin that six months before, the doctors had found a cancerous tumor in his head and told him there was nothing they could do for him, that he would have to "lie down and die." He had gone home to pack a few things to take to the hospital when Mojo showed up at his door. The moment he met him, his pain had gone away and he had felt much better. The doctors couldn't explain his recovery, and told him to stay at home for as long as he could. He knew it was Mojo who was keeping him strong until the last. His new friend had moved in and stayed with him ever since. "An angel of the Lord," the old man described him, and there was no doubt in Martin's mind that's what he meant.

As Percy rambled on, Martin glanced at the big man in the rear-view mirror. He was now wearing a crisply ironed white dress shirt. He sat impassively, apparently only half-listening and mostly staring out the window. His face bore a smile and what Martin had decided was the look of someone halfway lost in a very pleasant thought. He had a wide, broad face and strong, well-defined black features on very dark skin. The face could easily have portrayed brutal force; however, kindness seemed to have left its mark, for the feeling Martin got from looking at Mojo was that of gentleness. There was something quite different about the man, Martin thought; it wasn't his appearance, although that was impressive, but the feeling he had around him, which now seemed to fill the car…it was a deep peace.

Martin drove to the hospital's main entrance. The two men got out of the car and Martin watched as Mojo helped Percy through the front door. The big man then turned around and waved goodbye as he mouthed a silent "thank you."

Martin drove off and headed home. It was too late to go to the office. Besides, now he didn't feel the urgency. *Things can wait until tomorrow.* His son would have been home for at least two hours, and there was no telling where his wife was.

As Martin got closer to home, the emptiness started to get hold of him. He could feel it starting in his chest, the soft aching of something missing. He drove on, a part of him musing about the two men he had just met and another part of him thinking about his wife.

Jenny was not at home. Martin found his son Adam reading a book in the living room. The dogs, Sebastian and Toby, were lying on the rug. He watched the scene of the teenager lying prone on the couch with the two snoring dogs by his side. *I am so glad he's safe.*

Adam turned to greet him. "Hi, Dad!"

"Hey kid, how you doing…have you taken those mutts out for a walk?"

"Yeah, they peed, they pooped, they sniffed around…they're happy."

Martin watched as Adam resumed reading his book. His son was growing up to resemble him. At fifteen he was already almost grown into a man, and Martin could see himself at that age: the slim body and wide shoulders, high forehead with straight eyebrows and aquiline nose; although he could also see his wife's Irish features, the strong square jaw and a fairer complexion than his own.

"What're you reading, kid?"

"Oh, some stuff for school. Boring."

Martin walked into the kitchen. While he prepared a snack of tomatoes, cheese, and bread, he heard his wife drive up.

Jenny came into the kitchen with a bag of groceries, and without a word started preparing dinner. Martin looked at her, shrugged his shoulders and went into his study.

Later that evening, as they sat having dinner, Martin told them about his weird encounter with Percy and Mojo. Jenny didn't say anything, but Adam appeared amused by the incident.

"Maybe he's some kind of saint who goes around helping people," Adam said referring to Mojo. "He can probably change bodies and become anyone he wants to be."

His mother grimaced and stood up to pour herself another glass of wine. Martin decided to let her be that evening and keep his distance. He was now feeling a bit remote himself. The empty feeling had now grown in his chest. Everything felt heavy.

Martin watched Jenny eat. Her jaw muscles tightened when she chewed. Her fingers held the fork tightly, and she brought the food to her mouth in choppy movements, her gaze fixed on her plate. It was obvious she couldn't wait to leave the table. She had kept her looks over the years, the silky red hair, well-proportioned petite body and handsome, intelligent face; but it was the look in her eyes that had turned ugly. There was now harshness, and very often anger seemed to be constantly simmering under the surface. He wondered what got into her at moments like that, and whether she didn't care how it made her son feel...and him.

Later, when he came to their bedroom, she was sitting on her side of the bed reading. From the cover he could tell it was another one of those New Age books, someone talking about reincarnation, prophesies, U.F.O's, or some inane thing like that. When he got in bed, she closed her book and looked at him.

"Let's talk, Martin."

Oh no, not tonight. He let out a sigh. He needed quiet and he wanted rest. He had been looking forward to sleep...to letting go.

"I know you find it an imposition, but sometimes married people need to talk."

He tried to pull himself together so at least he could go through the motions. Her voice now seemed distant, disjointed...but then the whole world was starting to feel that way. He became aware of his breathing, and heart beating, but there were no feelings, except a soft aching. In the last few hours it had been an effort just to go through the details of life: washing dishes, a phone call with his brother he had kept short, leaving water out for the dogs, brushing his teeth, undressing. He knew it would be almost impossible for him to appear responsive.

She was saying it was lack of communication that was driving them apart. "Oh, I feel it too, Martin. I'm very sorry to see this marriage go down just because you don't ever feel like talking."

He wondered if that was her original topic, or one that she just dove into on the spur of the moment. He watched her eyes glitter with emotion and her mouth become more expressive, but he was most concerned about his depression and whether he would be able to carry on the next day. However, her words had actually registered and he nodded when she told him there was something wrong with him.

"And you go happily around giving rides to strange people from the ghetto, when you are needed at the office. You know they called three times this afternoon."

He almost told her he drove home that afternoon looking for her, but that would probably just prolong the conversation and maybe lead to a fight. *At some point she must have checked the answering machine...she can do it by calling in...and now she's making it sound like she was home.*

"Helen also thinks you need to see a therapist," she said.

Why would two women sit and talk about me when they could talk about so many other things? Martin momentarily visualized the two sisters sitting around, in his own living room, passionately discussing his problems. The image dwindled and then grew grotesque. He had no energy left. In her mood anything he said would be an opening for a fight. Martin got up with pillow under his arm as she continued talking. While he walked down the stairs to the guest room he could still hear her voice, now louder.

"That's right, walk out on your problems, big man." She was no longer keeping her anger in check; her voice now had that shrill quality he knew so well. He heard words like "failure" and "jerk" as he made it to the bottom of the stairs. He was tired, very tired. He went into the guest room and locked the door.

Tomorrow I'll talk to her; tomorrow I'll go to the office early, and tomorrow I'll be fine. Martin brushed aside the oversized pillows and pulled down the covers. With a sigh he plopped himself down and pulled the blankets over him. *Actually, I miss her; miss the woman she was a few years ago, before...Oh, what the hell, go to sleep.* There was a sullen quiet now, as though their distance was palpable and had spread through the big house, making everything thick, thick and cold.

Martin slept. For a time he fidgeted. Then he went into deeper sleep. After a while he dropped into an even deeper state and his eyes fluttered under his closed lids. His body was now very still. Only a part of him that was always aware, deep down in his subconscious mind, observed a silent being that came into his room and stood by the bed, watching him. An arm reached out and a hand waved across the top of Martin's head. At that very moment he started to dream.

In his dream he was driving along a road on a tropical island, and there was pristine blue ocean and sky, and air that felt clean and warm. Then he came to a gate with a man standing by it. Martin could see him clearly, a heavy-set man with red hair wearing a Hawaiian shirt. He was friendly, and Martin told him he had to get to another world in a parallel universe.

The man told him to go through the gate.

Then there was a curving road and a wooden bridge. He saw a beach, a stretch of sand fringed with trees and black rocks at either end. In the middle of it was a big gold door with white columns on either side. The door appeared to be translucent, because he could see lights shining through it. Martin knew he had to go through to the other side.

An impressive looking old man stood by the door. He had a white beard and hair, with gentle but piercing eyes, and Martin somehow knew he was very wise, had powers, was a magician of sorts.

Martin told him he couldn't go on, he didn't want anything more to do with the world because nothing made sense.

The wise man told Martin he would take him to a place where life made sense, where everything was real.

Then the dream ended.

The being waved a hand across Martin's head again, sinking the memory of the dream into his deep subconscious. He stood watching him sleep, perhaps pondering something or other. Then apparently satisfied, the visitor left.

Martin made it to the office in downtown Oakland by eight in the morning, and as he rode the elevator to his company's floor he thought about Jenny. He had tried to kiss her at the breakfast table but she turned her head away. He made an attempt to explain he wasn't feeling well—the euphemism he used to describe his depression—but she ignored him and kept reading the newspaper. He left after hugging his son and wishing him a good day at school.

The empty feeling was very much there, and would probably be with him the entire day.

Mary was manning the receptionists' desk. She was busy putting together folders for a conference Claudia was coordinating.

"Good morning, Mary. I heard you tried to reach me yesterday."

"Yes, Mister Devon." She told him that Sanchez, the Project Officer for their biggest contract, had called saying it was urgent. Mary handed Martin a fax that had been waiting for her when she opened the office. Martin read it. The contract "was being suspended pending a fiscal investigation." He read the fax several times, digesting its contents after the initial shock. *OK. This is bad…real bad.* Inside he felt as if someone had hit him in the chest, and curiously his first reaction was to think about his partner Ted. *Poor guy, this is going to floor him.* He felt Mary watching his reaction. Martin patted her shoulder as he walked past.

He spent the next hour talking with Sanchez on the phone and getting a feel for what had happened. Martin got a lot of official lingo but no straight answers. Sanchez's voice, ordinarily friendly, was now cold and formal.

Then he received a call from a woman higher up in the Department. Her name was Ms. Gates, and she sounded sympathetic. She had been one of the VIP participants at a training conference he had organized two years before, and now she sounded like a friend. She told him some people in the Department had decided to cancel the contract, and they would do it at any cost.

"Why?" he asked.

"Mainly because they can. They have the power, and you upset one of them." She told him what he had heard many times before: the ones with the money are gods, and you have to treat them as such. This was a way to let him know who was boss. She told him it was useless to fight; her best advice was to forget about it. "Fold your tent and go somewhere else."

The problem was, this was a mainstay contract for his company. Without it they would have to go through hard times for the next few months until they could replace the work. He visualized the long days and nights feverishly writing some ten proposals to obtain maybe two or perhaps three contracts.

His partner Ted walked into his office and sat in a chair facing his desk.

"So what happened, Martin?"

He explained that in all probability he had offended a bigwig.

"How? What did you do?"

"You know what I've been doing, steering the project in the right direction and making it seem as though it's their idea, not mine." Ted knew all about it, as he had been involved in some of the planning sessions. Ted remained silent and Martin filled the uncomfortable void. "Something along the way went wrong, and old man Phillips got his nose out of joint. I don't know, maybe something I said, maybe something I didn't say." The work, he knew, was crucial for the Department, and they were performing well. *Done in by a stupid little man with a fragile ego. When Jenny hears this she's going to lose it.* He dreaded telling her the bad news. Inside, he felt the imprint of recent hardships. He recalled how hard it was on her the last time they had lost a contract…and then…It had been a scant couple of years since the fight with the tenants. *I never get a break.*

"Phillips? the Program Chief ?" Ted sounded incredulous.

"Yes, good old Mark Phillips."

Ted looked at Martin, and Martin knew what was going through his mind. They had gone through difficult times before, but this one was a heavy blow. They would go through a punitive audit that, no matter what, would pile on an excruciating amount of "evidence" they would spend many months and many dollars disproving. It was a terrible thing to happen, at any time, to anyone. One of the horror stories they had heard over the years…now it was happening to them.

The emptiness he had felt in the previous two days had been temporarily obscured by the adrenaline surge with the news. Now the adrenaline was subsiding and the depression was growing…becoming a heavy sense of doom. Nothing mattered at that moment.

"Excuse me Ted, we'll talk later, all right?" With this Martin got up, reached for his jacket, and left the office. He felt his partner's gaze follow him until he closed the front door behind him. Once outside, he realized he didn't feel like driving. It would require a level of effort he didn't have the energy for. He decided to walk instead.

Walking was an activity requiring crossing streets, looking at lights, and navigating among pedestrians. He could do that. Aimlessly he wandered through the busy streets that gave way to less crowded ones. Martin came to a residential neighborhood, and then after some time, he found himself approaching a familiar place. It was People's Park in Berkeley, and he realized he must have walked for many hours. The park, which he had cut across many times before when he and his family lived in the apartment building he owned, was a funky but mellow place to sit if one could manage to avoid the street people who congregated there.

Martin watched a group of homeless men sitting in the middle of a grassy area, some sipping from bottles wrapped in paper bags, others openly smoking pot. They were a multi-racial bunch, perhaps fifteen of them, mostly young, although a few had gray hair.

Martin found a bench and decided to sit. He felt worn, not so much physically, but worn out inside, depleted. He watched the homeless men talk, some laughing out loud, one staring down at the ground, shaking his head, a spiral of smoke coming out of the joint he held in his fingers.

Well, look at them. They seem happy. Martin recalled a conversation with a pastor when he was a teenager. It had been about God and his mysterious will.

You certainly are a joker, you know that? Here I am, working my ass off, and you throw nothing but crap at me. And look at those idiots. They do nothing, contribute nothing, are just parasites. What the hell do you want from me? God? Oh, yeah, Praised be the Lord...alleluia... what a joke! You're nothing but a miserable sadist. You like it when people are in pain, don't you? And this depression...why me? Stupid jerk. Monster. Instead of helping me, you make things worse. Go ahead, see if you can destroy me.

Now he wanted to strike something or someone. Martin looked at the street people, and the thought crossed his mind that he would enjoy fighting one of those men.

He had started to visualize a scenario, when he felt someone sit next to him. It was an old woman who had plopped herself down, oblivious to him. She had a shopping cart in front of her, piled with bags, boxes and clothes. She wore several layers of garments: a sweater and long johns under a frilly pink dress with another sweater over it. Her shoulder-length gray hair framed a wrinkled face. Thin lips and pale blue eyes. She turned her head to meet his gaze, and squinted. Martin could see confusion and pain in those eyes. *Oh, man, poor thing.* Suddenly he felt ashamed of his anger, and sad for a world that would let a woman like her amble aimlessly and alone. He wondered what had happened to her in this life.

Without thinking he reached for his wallet and grabbed the first bill. It was a fifty. *Who cares, you can make more.* He handed it to her and watched her thin hand take hold of the money.

He decided to go somewhere where he didn't have to talk about the failed contract. Martin walked over to nearby Telegraph Avenue to catch a cab. He was going to pay Percy a visit.

CHAPTER TWO

He asked for Percy at the nurse's station, and they all seemed to know whom he was talking about. The nurses looked at each other with a knowing glance; then one got up, smiled and told him to follow her.

He found the old man propped up in his bed. His face was noticeably more shrunken, pain written over the old features, but he offered a smile when Martin walked in. Beside him, apparently reading him a story, sat Mojo, book in hand.

"Good morning, Mister Devon," said Mojo. He wore the same clothes from the day before, black pants and white dress shirt. If he had spent the night at the hospital, he didn't look any worse for the wear. He seemed well rested. Just as in the car the day before, the room was filled with Mojo's essence, or a feeling that made the room…cozy, perhaps even happy.

Martin smiled at the big man. "Good morning, Mojo. And please call me Martin." It felt odd calling him Mojo. The presence of the man seemed to require much more than that.

They appeared surprised he had come, but Martin didn't feel out of place; he felt welcomed by the two. Percy again told him he had been in the Merchant Marines and had then worked for a grocery store. He went on talking, even though Martin could tell he was in pain; he would wince and the voice at times would trail off.

Mojo sat listening intently, apparently following every word.

In between Percy's stories, Martin asked Mojo his real name.

"In this life I was named Joseph."

"And the Mojo?"

"Oh, I started calling him that," replied Percy. "It sort of make sense."

Yes, it made a lot of sense, Martin agreed. The man had a lot of mojo, power…strength. *Strange how he answered though—"in this life"—as though he knows himself by other names.*

Martin wanted to know more about him, but Mojo evaded the questions, shrugged them off as unimportant. "Percy is the one with the interesting life," he said.

And it was interesting. The most fascinating part was that Percy seemed to surprise himself with his recall. Several times he said, "Man, I hadn't thought of that in years!" or, "I thought I forgot that." And in the recounting Martin could tell the old man was reliving episodes of his life…some of them not very complimentary, so Martin knew he was recalling the raw truth. But the overall tone was of a man telling of his past, and making no excuses for it. Percy had become a storyteller, and it was a very entertaining recounting, although sad at times.

Martin didn't know how many hours he spent at the hospital, and it seemed that the nurses didn't care how long he stayed. When he decided to leave, he felt renewed, as though he had taken a vacation somewhere. He looked at the two men and bid his goodbye.

"Goodbye, Mister Devon," Percy said. The words carried a certain finality. Martin looked at Mojo, who seemed to be assenting with his eyes. Martin went over and grabbed the old man's feeble hand.

"Good night, friend," he said, and unexpectedly added, "God bless you." He knew Percy was a Baptist and the words would be meaningful to him.

Percy's face registered surprise, and then he smiled. "And God bless you too, Mister Devon. You are a good man. Don't let nobody try to tell you any different."

Martin smiled inside. He then turned to Mojo and shook his hand by reaching across the bed. The touch was wonderful…it was like the feeling in the room, except magnified many times.

That night at dinner, Martin told Jenny what had happened at the office that morning.

"So what does that mean exactly?" She said, her gaze hard on him.

"It means we'll have less money for some time."

"And how long will that be, Martin?" the cold sardonic voice asked him.

She recalled the last lost contract, as he knew she would. She went over the details, how they had lost a project to a competitor who had apparently bribed a government official into canceling their contract, which months later became a "sole-source" project for the other firm.

"I don't want to go through another reversal," she said. She then brought up the ordeal they had experienced with their apartment building…how they had bought the place when their son was an infant, how much like a family the place was until rent control and the lawyers stepped in…and then, four years of financial hardship, litigation and stress. When she finished, she sat with angry tears rolling down her face.

Angry at whom? The tenants, life, God, me?

"We have gone through so much, Martin. When are the good times going to come?"

Martin was now holding his chin in his cupped hands, elbows resting on the table, his food half-eaten, looking at his wife. He wondered why she felt compelled to revisit those painful episodes…maybe to punish him?

"Look, it was my fault, all right?" he said. "How many times do I have to say that before you let it drop? Yes, I wasn't able to produce all the receipts and records that would have made our case. There may be some people who keep exact records going back ten years, but I'm not one of them. I'm lousy at it. But look, we weathered the damn storm, withstood four years of hardship, and we still own the place. From now on, the building will be fine."

"That's not enough, dammit! I deserve better, you hear me?"

"Hey, I want an easy life as well. But that's how things go sometimes. What do you want from me?"

She stormed off and went to their bedroom, presumably to cry away her agony.

Martin sat looking at their son, who had pretended not to hear anything. Adam now gave him a tentative look. Martin smiled back.

Apparently reassured, the kid went back to his dinner and the book propped in front of him.

When Martin came to bed, she was reading her New Age book again. She kept reading as he got into bed.

That night as Martin slept next to Jenny, the visitor came again, and this time Martin's subconscious welcomed him. Again, the stranger waved his hand and again Martin dreamt. He saw the beach again, this time in great detail. The trees fringing it had thorns, and the rocks at either end were jagged. Martin also saw that it was in a bay and the water changed color from turquoise to a deep dark blue. A couple with a child was at the very far end and a younger couple closer by. A man sat on one of the rocks looking out at the ocean. Then Martin saw the door, and in his dream he remembered his previous dream.

The wise man asked him if he was ready to go through the door.

"Yes," Martin replied, "I'm ready."

"Would you take Jenny with you?" The rich, melodic voice asked him.

"No, no. She's changed…but I do love her…I'm not sure."

"What about your son, would you take him?"

"Yes, of course."

"Maybe Jenny would become her old self if you brought her along."

Again the visitor pushed the dream into Martin's subconscious with a wave of his hand. Then he left.

That following day their cat died. They had found him outside a restaurant a year before, and because it had a leg missing, their son had called him "Gimpy." And Gimpy was a very limber cat, a character that charmed everybody. A neighbor lady had started bringing him treats, and others would inquire about the cat. Then that morning he vanished, and Martin went looking for him in the quiet streets around their house. He found Gimpy's collar and a bloody piece of fur behind a tree. As was the case with many cats he had heard about, a coyote from the nearby state park had apparently killed him.

Back home, Martin found Jenny putting on her make-up in the bathroom. "I found Gimpy—that is, what's left of him. A coyote got him." He felt tears welling up in his eyes.

She looked at him, apparently also saddened by the news, but then she noticed his teary eyes.

"Oh, poor little Martin…does he feel sorry for himself?" Then, dropping the sarcasm, she added, "It was only a cat! Grow up."

"And you are only a bitch!" He stood glaring at her, his breathing now hard and heavy. *What a cold, horrible person she's become.*

"You feel like hitting me, don't you?" She faced him with a clenched jaw, eyes staring him down.

"No, I don't want to hit you." *That's a weird thing to say.*

"Oh, but you do. Just like the last time, except then you pushed me. Don't think I don't know."

With apparent relish she went over her version of the incident. How he had come home with a pizza her sister Helen had wanted and he had been resentful because he saw the pizza as being for her; then they had argued and he had shoved her angrily against a wall. That, according to her support group and her therapist, was without question the preface for a physically abusive relationship.

When she finished with her story, she seemed somewhat satisfied.

She enjoys her anger. It feeds something in her.

What he remembered was coming home and finding the two women bantering in the kitchen. For the previous few days he and Jenny had gotten along, and he joined them. Adam was out visiting friends, so it would be the three of them that evening. He suggested ordering pizza, but Helen declared "Zachary's is the best," and the two women had decided on Zachary's.

He had gone for the pizza and it had ended up being a frustrating ordeal…slow traffic, busy pizza parlor…and it took him almost two hours to get back. By then he was irritated at the two women, and slammed the pizza in front of them. He walked away to shower; except he had incited Jenny and she came after him. They argued and she followed him into the bathroom. Feeling at the end of his rope and trapped, he told her to "leave me the hell alone." She had crossed her arms, refused to leave, and kept on badgering him.

He then pushed her out of the bathroom. Martin remembered placing his open hand on her chest and pushing. To his surprise she was propelled backwards and hit the wall some four feet away. He then closed the door and locked it.

That had happened some weeks before. In the meantime she had joined a support group, and she emphasized, there was no question in anyone's mind in her group that he was a physical abuser, and emotional and psychological. At that point she showed him a book her therapist had written, and invited him to see how he fit the profile. "Of course you'll deny it; that's what they all do," she told him.

He spent the rest of that morning reading the book. He didn't feel like going to work. Maybe because of Gimpy, or because he was troubled by what she had said. At any rate, he decided to read.

The book described unpleasant things he did, but that she did as well. According to the author the husband was always the abuser, and the abusive behavior was meant to control the wife.

Martin sat in the living room staring at the book's cover. To him it sounded like a hate manual, something someone would write who was angry at men, for other women who felt the same. *And sell books in the process, lots of them.* But there were bits of truth in it. He wondered if he could be an abuser and not know it. Maybe he could talk to someone impartial, someone who worked with couples.

He decided to call a therapist he knew, a psychiatrist he had met the year before and seen a few times for his depression. He called Doctor Taylor and talked on the phone for some time. Martin told him of the latest events and his reason for calling. The psychiatrist agreed to see him the following morning at nine.

That night the visitor came once more. Martin's subconscious recalled the two previous dreams, and he was expecting to see the beach and the gold door. And he did, but this time the wise man opened the door and Martin found himself going through to the other side. Everything was made of light, and he was made of light, a blue, scintillating body. He could fly…and then he remembered this was his real body, which somehow he had forgotten, and he became concerned he would forget again.

He saw a huge forest and what looked like a road, then a city by a river with high walls around it. He saw a cave, and it was inviting, warm and nurturing. Then he saw a woman. She had long blond hair and big, blue eyes that looked at him in the softest, sweetest way. He knew that she lived deep in the forest in a small hut, had supernatural abilities, and was teaching Martin her magic. She was also very wise. He loved her…and she him.

Once the images stopped, the visitor again pushed the memory of the dream deep into Martin's subconscious.

The sequence of dreams had an effect. The following morning as Martin drove across the bay to Mill Valley to see the psychiatrist, he felt an overlay of anticipation, of excitement, covering his usual emptiness. It was a welcome addition to his life, but it was perplexing because he had no idea where it came from, or what it was.

He talked with Sam, as the psychiatrist insisted he wanted to be called, for over four hours. Doctor Taylor let him know that he had made the time available because he saw Martin to be in a major crisis. They sat on huge pillows on the floor, facing each other, sipping herbal tea.

Then Sam asked him about suicide, whether he had thought about it.

"No, not really," Martin said, "I've had fantasies about it, but something inside me always told me how unlikely that would be, like taking drugs, or becoming an alcoholic. Although I truly know why people drink, take drugs or kill themselves. I really do."

They talked at length about the latest events, about Jenny and the possibility of a divorce. In the course of the conversation, Martin discovered that Jenny might be unfaithful. He surprised himself with the news, but the evidence was all there: the mysterious calls, the long absences. At least on two occasions when Jenny had told him she was going to her sister's, Helen had called.

Then Sam asked him about the failed contract and how it affected him.

The psychiatrist reiterated his previous diagnosis: Martin suffered from depression, and now he was under great stress. But was he abusive? Following more talk, Martin realized Jenny fit the profile much better, although she didn't have the physical ability to abuse him. But she did seem to want to control him, and there was a lot of aggressive behavior on her part.

Sam then reviewed how Martin had felt abandoned by his mother at an early age and was now recreating the same scenario with Jenny. "Maybe that's why you are depressed, don't you agree? You are afraid Jenny will leave you."

Martin looked at the psychiatrist. "Maybe I am afraid, but this business with my mother…besides, I've been depressed for a long time, way before I met Jenny."

Sam went over to his desk, then looked out a nearby window. "My recommendation at this point," Sam said, "is for you to start taking an antidepressant. It will let you see things clearly, and then you can deal with your problems. You could start taking something this morning." He then turned and fixed his gaze on Martin.

It felt wrong. "No, I can't, I won't take drugs." The thought felt repugnant.

Sam took a deep breath. "In my opinion, Martin, you are reaching a breaking point, but you are not aware of it," he said as he took some slow and measured steps on the thickly varnished wood floor, until he stood in front of Martin. "Without some sort of medication, you run the risk of self-destructing. In some manner or another." Then he kneeled down, placed a hand on Martin's knee and looked him in the eyes. "Take the pills, you can start this morning. Your mind will feel clearer and you can start dealing with your problems."

Martin looked at the hand on his knee and the face way too close to his. "Thank you for your concern. You have already helped me." Martin stood up and Sam backed away. "But no drugs." He knew he wouldn't be back.

As he drove toward his office he thought about Jenny and their latest fights. At that moment he felt sorry for her. He was surprised he wasn't angry. After all, she was cheating on him. *Maybe I already knew that...maybe I've figured the marriage was lost.*

She was partly right when she accused him of being passive, uncommunicative. When depressed he was cold and distant. Martin knew the emptiness well; the ever-present gray which sometimes overtook him. He would be talking, and his words and the words of others would seem meaningless, a sham. Other times it would evolve slowly, over several days, until everything around him was empty, hollow, like the senseless motion of a windup toy. And he had no idea what to do about it. He knew his life was a desperate search for relief...a new contract, a new face, a movie. Sometimes even something new in the mailbox. Was his depression the reason why their marriage was breaking up? Or was it anger—her anger?

He knew something had to happen; things couldn't just go on like this. Where to start? Maybe get the office back in order, get a new contract, and then deal with the marriage...that is, the divorce. What else was there? He felt his chest constricting and desperation tearing him up. He felt on the verge of something.

Poor Gimpy. Hope you didn't suffer, little guy.

Instead of the office, he decided to go to Percy's hospital. He could use another visit.

He was walking past the nurses' station and toward Percy's room, when a nurse asked him whom he was coming to see. He mentioned Percy and the room number. She recognized him now; she was one of the nurses from the day before. He watched as her expression changed. She looked down at the counter, cleared her throat, and told him Percy had passed away that previous night.

"He died in his sleep," she said, "peacefully. The night nurse went to give him medicine, and found he had passed away."

"What about his friend, was he there?" Martin asked.

"He was there when I left last night at the end of my shift at ten, but the night nurse didn't see anyone in his room. We don't know when he left."

Martin was at a loss. He had looked forward to another few hours visiting with Mojo and seeing Percy. So that farewell had been final, after all.

"Can I find out his address?" He explained he had given them both a ride to the hospital, but had paid no attention to the street name or house number.

The nurse told him the hospital didn't give out patient information. Martin tried talking to various people in the hospital, but to no avail.

He decided to drive the streets in the neighborhood where he thought the house was. He wanted to find Mojo; somehow that became very important at that moment, and the thought he had lost his chance to talk to him one more time was surprisingly sad to him.

Martin drove around for several hours, but there were many houses that looked the same. Several times he got out of the car and went to look at the apartment numbers, hoping to see the scribbling he remembered.

After a while he gave up.

He drove back to Berkeley, but this time he took the freeway. He got off at University Avenue and on impulse he turned toward the ocean instead of town. He felt as though something was pulling him in that direction. It felt odd and very compelling. He parked the car on the side of the frontage road and decided to walk along the water's edge looking for a place to sit and watch the water. But the feeling kept pushing him on. He knew he had to go to a place nearby, somewhere, for some reason.

Martin stood looking around, debating where to go. To his left he could see the Bay Bridge and in front of him, in the distance, the towers of the Golden Gate. The water that afternoon was placid, a sheet of pewter-gray. He looked at the old pier, a mile-long thing that used to serve the ferry before they built the bridges. Now it was broken into sections, and a person could walk only about a third of the original length. His heart skipped a beat. *That's it.*

Martin walked by fishermen, most of them retirees casting a line and talking. He picked a desolate expanse of pier and leaned on the railing, facing the water. He had always found old places somewhat appealing and comforting. *Maybe I just need to think, and this is a good place for it…that's all.*

It was too bad he had missed seeing Percy one more time. *One day I'll be that old.* Yes, that was inevitable, save for an accidental death. He was healthy, no chance of dying soon otherwise. *Why would someone create a world like this?*

One time he had watched a colony of ants busily going about their lives, building, creating, and carrying things on a log someone had thrown into a bonfire. There was no way he could pull the log out, so instead he watched in morbid fascination as the fire overtook the ants. How stupid, he remembered thinking—God didn't come to their rescue, did he? No, that's the way he created the world, and that's who we are, ants on a log, knowing the fire is coming but somehow managing to avoid thinking about it.

He felt sorry for Percy; he had died alone, save for Mojo. On the other hand, he envied him. He also wanted to go away to where the old guy had gone, anywhere besides this world. Then he thought of Mojo and how sad it was that he had lost touch with him. There was something about the man he found...healing. He seemed whole, with no parts missing, no open wounds. By contrast Martin found himself a total mess, with his life, his insides a jumble of hurt and emptiness.

"Mister Devon." The voice came from behind him. He turned around to see the now familiar smiling face. He felt a jolt go through his chest.

"Mojo!" That without question was the most welcome sight he could have wished for. He wondered momentarily how Mojo had managed to be at the pier, but it didn't matter. Martin had found him.

"Percy passed away very sweetly last night." Mojo said. "When I felt his spirit go, I left the hospital. There was nothing else I could do for him." He placed his elbows on the railing, his eyes now level with Martin's. "I want to thank you for your kindness towards Percy. He told the nurses about you, how you picked him up by the bank. He said you scolded the bank people for not calling him a cab. He was deeply touched by your concern."

Martin looked at his hands. Fleetingly he felt bad for yelling at the bank manager. Then Percy's face came back to mind. Martin felt a knot in his throat. "I'm sorry Percy died. I wanted to see him again." He looked at the placid water, and at the seagulls landing on the railing. Then he started talking about himself, and the words poured out describing his life and showing his emptiness, his despair. In talking he didn't know what he expected from Mojo, but it felt good to talk. It felt much better, more natural than talking with the psychiatrist. Part of him felt a bit sheepish, unloading to a stranger, but then again it felt...really good.

Mojo seemed to take everything he said in stride, as though he was used to having people tell him their troubles. "Your angst is something every person at some time or another has to go through. It's a rite of passage, but you need to understand what life is trying to tell you. Depression is saying you need to change. Anger is pushing you to move on ahead."

His voice dropped down to a whisper, forcing Martin to listen carefully. "You need to realize that it's you who is creating all of those things you told me; the trouble with your marriage, your company's work being pulled away unfairly, even your cat dying. You are the one doing all that, creating a crisis."

Martin stood up straight. *It doesn't make any sense. People can't do that.* After a moment he decided to assume it was possible. He trusted Mojo. *Being so whole and calm, he must know!*

"Why would I do something like that?" asked Martin.

"Because you want a new life, and are pushing yourself out of your present one."

"So what do I want…what am I searching for?"

The big man looked at him. "Go on a pilgrimage. People have forgotten how to make pilgrimages." After a pause he added, "All you have to do is formulate the intent for self-discovery, and a pilgrimage will manifest itself."

Martin stared at the water, feeling his insides. *Yeah, that sounds good.*

"Mister Devon, empty your mind, just push all thoughts out."

Martin did as directed. He felt happy, full of expectation.

"Now visualize a place, the first place that comes to mind, and tell me what it is."

Almost instantly Martin saw an island and a small beach.

"An island…but that's absurd; pilgrimages are usually to holy places, like Palestine."

"The whole earth is sacred, and you picked your holy site, the place that calls you."

The only place that was an island and entered his mind was Hawaii. Still in half-disbelief he mentioned it to Mojo. "So maybe I should go to Hawaii on my pilgrimage." The moment he uttered the words he felt a pang inside his chest, as if he had uncovered something very good he had been hiding from himself.

They stood for a time in silence, and Martin felt peace, as though he had finally found out how to fix his life. Maybe it was an absurd thought, but the more he let it sit the better it felt. *So perhaps I'm escaping from my troubles…so what? I'll go for a week or ten days. It can't hurt anything.*

He thanked Mojo for his help, and asked him how he had managed to find him, but the big man shook his hand, and appeared to be saying goodbye. There was something in his manner that suggested he needed to go and that the visit was over.

Martin watched him walk away with surprising alacrity. Before he knew it, Mojo had disappeared. One moment he was walking past some fishermen, and then he was completely gone from the pier. It was odd, for the pier stretched for another two hundred feet, but there was no sign of the big black man with black pants and white shirt.

That night the visitor came again. He waited until Martin was in deep sleep to wave his hand over his head.

In the dream Martin recalled his previous dreams. He recognized the beach and the gold door, and he knew he already had gone through the door. Now he was sitting next to the beautiful woman. It was as though they knew each other well.

She asked him if he would come to her, and he told her, yes, he would.

She told him that in order to come to where she was, he needed wings, and the wings would take him to a place where he would find a key. He asked her how he could get the wings, and she said they would come to him if he really wanted them.

Then she looked very sad, and he could feel her deep sorrow. She told him she was being kept prisoner. She couldn't escape and was suffering terribly.

In the dream he was shaken to the core, and he asked if there was anything he could do.

She told him yes; in fact he was the only one who could help her.

He asked how. He was just a simple man, and she was all-powerful. What could he do? Then she raised a hand and pointed ahead of her. Martin looked and saw the beach with the gold door. She told him once he found the key, he would understand.

She asked him again if he would come, and Martin felt an immense love for her. Yes, he told her, and he felt the affirmation come from deep inside his being. "I will do anything for you."

Then the dream ended.

The visitor again buried the dream deep in Martin's mind. He stood for some time looking at Martin as he continued to sleep without dreaming. Then the being left.

CHAPTER THREE

He was aware that he was dreaming; there was that quality to things you only have in that state where you merge one reality with a different one, and are viewing one place with the eyes from another. He wondered when he would wake up, what he would feel, and where he would be.

Martin opened his eyes slowly. The ceiling fan stood motionless, modern beige against the white ceiling. He turned his head to look through the sliding glass door at the balcony outside. Through the table legs of the outdoor furniture and the banister slots he caught a glimpse of blue water. His eyes gratefully rested on the small view of ocean.

Then he remembered; he was in Hawaii, and he was searching for something but hadn't found it yet, and he was afraid he never would.

Oh yes...the beach. From the very first day he arrived, he had looked for a beach, not knowing why, but convinced it was critical to find it. He knew it had something to do with his pilgrimage, perhaps a test he had to go through, or an intervening step to something very big and wonderful. He often questioned where the idea had come from, and couldn't figure it out, except that it was very strong, and it compelled him, a hidden force inside him. Martin had no concrete notion such a place existed, only the conviction that it did, and that it was on this very island. He knew the beach was small and remote, so probably not many people knew about it. He had described the place to tourist guides, hotel clerks and even a waitress; asking about a small stretch of white sand in a small bay with thorny trees fringing it. In between a few strange stares, he had gotten leads, but they hadn't panned out. Somehow by just setting foot on a place, something inside would tell him that wasn't it.

It crossed Martin's mind that this too could turn out to be the elusive something he had chased all his life...the escape, the wondrous or magical thing he desperately wanted but didn't exist. Maybe he was becoming obsessed. *Stress can do that.* Perhaps he should just take it easy and relax, maybe let go. Perhaps he was just supposed to have a good time, and this was the way the universe conspired to make him take a break.

Still in bed, Martin closed his eyes for a moment and an image appeared. There it was, the small expanse of beach as real as any memory of any place he remembered.

At that moment a feeling inside told him that today he would find the place. He was sure; it was strange, but he was all of a sudden very certain. Now, looking at the small piece of ocean beyond his balcony, he felt a wave of excitement go through him that literally made him spring out of bed.

He skipped showering and got dressed. Breakfast would have to be fast.

The road was mostly straight, easy to drive. The few clouds in the sky were perfectly white, small tufts. The lava rock on the side of the road varied in texture and color, from charcoal, hard and shiny, to a soil-brown. People had used white rocks to write graffiti against the black surface. Scraggly vegetation grew here and there, but the landscape was still pretty, inviting to the eye.

Martin passed a sign for a beach park, with a handful of cars driving in. Then he passed another beach he had already gone to the previous day. If nothing else he could drive for a while. The sea, down a gentle slope a mile or so away on his left, was a deep blue, without a single whitecap. The sun shone through clean, crisp air that felt warm and silky.

Five days had already gone by. What if nothing happened this day? *Oh well. Then a day of sun would have to do....No, something has to happen! But what if nothing happens, what if Mojo was wrong?*

As though in response, his heart told him otherwise: he was on the right track, and the image of the beach came back to him.

It has to happen, or I am not going back.

Thoughts of Adam came to him. He wished the kid were with him. Martin couldn't wait to see him swimming in the clear, warm water. *And snorkeling. He would love it.*

But that wasn't what this trip was about.

Then there was his job.... That could wait; he'd think about it later, he had time.

In his mind he pictured his son and held his image for a while. Adam was fine, he was sure the kid was fine. At the very least Jenny knew how to take good care of their son.

Back home it would be close to noon. Jenny would have taken Adam to her mother's for Sunday brunch.

The day before he left for Hawaii, she had asked him to walk the dogs together in the park. For days she had been critical of his trip to Hawaii, but then she seemed to accept that he needed some time off by himself.

He saw her trying to strike a friendly note, so he went along for the walk.

The talk at first had been relatively pleasant, with both of them trying to be friendly, making safe, trivial comments.

Then she started talking about her sister; and maybe the talk about Helen had done it, because suddenly she was angry and everything in her eyes was wrong, her life was a horrid mess. Without pausing, she again accused him of abuse and told him what a grave mistake she had made in marrying him.

At that moment he had wondered at what point they would divorce and what would it take.

Going by the entrance to one of the big resorts, he instinctively looked in. Fleetingly, he saw the gatekeeper's booth, and standing beside it, a stocky figure in a Hawaiian shirt. This was the kind of place to avoid, he thought; but as he drove past, the scene, like a photograph, persisted in his mind, somewhat familiar, compelling.

Martin drove on for a while, mesmerized by the image—then on impulse, turned the car around, drove back and pulled into the hotel's entrance. He came up to the booth and stopped short of the mechanical arm blocking the entrance. The man stood a few feet away looking at him expectantly.

Martin blurted out, "I'm looking for a beach around here." He felt foolish, and wondered how he should have framed the question.

"Yes sir, the public is allowed to use the hotel beach."

"Are there any places around here, out of the way, with fewer people?"

The man smiled, perhaps knowing exactly what Martin wanted, and why. Maybe many other people also asked. It was probably all in vain, and there were no such beaches for tourists.

"Yeah, matter of fact I know of a place. There is one that few people know about and it's a little harder to get to."

Is this it? Apparently he had asked the right person the right question. His heart skipped a beat as he felt a distinct feeling of déjà vu. He couldn't wait to see the place, but at the same time there was a nagging trepidation that once again he would be disappointed.

The gatekeeper explained that the beach was part of the hotel complex, not owned by them, but they managed it. Martin never expected the beach he had pictured would be part of a well-manicured resort, but somehow it felt right.

The man pointed down the road. He was a heavy-set man, in his mid-to-late sixties, with reddish hair, and a kind face. The Hawaiian shirt hung loosely around his rotund torso.

"But the hotel beach is real nice. We have a very popular Sunday brunch, you know."

The words barely registered as Martin kept examining the strangely familiar man he couldn't place.

"Well, looks like you want the secret spot, eh?" The man said with his wide smile. "OK, to get to your beach, drive straight and make the second right…"

"Is it nice?"

His eyes crinkled with friendliness. "It's very nice, peaceful and secluded."

Martin followed the directions, past the golf course, right, then down a gravel road.

The road was a validation. Martin drove, mesmerized by the oddly familiar sights, recognizing trees, the bend on the road, the wooden bridge. Then more gravel road and finally, the wide spot on the road the man had described, where people going to the beach parked their cars.

The surroundings were closer to what he had expected, an uneven path made by countless feet, thorny bushes on either side, rough lava rock. Nothing like the resort a short drive behind.

After following the path for a while, he stood at the entrance to a small beach. Martin stood still and took a deep breath as he surveyed the surroundings. The place was exactly as he had pictured it: a small expanse of white sand with thorny trees providing shade, lava rocks at either end of the beach, and an ocean going from turquoise nearby to a deep blue farther away.

He felt a jolt in his heart, his head felt light, and he smiled broadly. Mojo…his feeling inside…everything had been right on target! *What a great sight. All is right, everything is here! Oh, my…amazing, wonderful place.* Martin remained standing for a moment longer, taking in the place. Then he walked on, reviewing the scene several times, each detail telling him he was in the right place. Out on one of the rocks by the water, sat a man looking at the ocean. A couple with a small child had settled under a tree at the far end of the beach; and closer by he could see another couple.

Martin walked slowly to a spot under one of the trees. He sat down on the cool sand and let his body relax. The trees had a quality of belonging, as did the sand and the water. Through the thorny branches, blue, bright sky. From the ocean, the sound of gentle surf on sand. Voices from the couple. The feeling of familiarity persisted. Then he wondered how and when something would happen, and how would he know? Would he meet someone, or find something? Would there be mysterious signs or omens?

He raised his head to look at the sea, absorbing the vast, open blue. The man was still sitting on the rock, motionless, as though carved from stone, and that seemed peculiar—but at the same time natural and fitting, somehow an integral part of the scene. Nothing in particular seemed like a sign; rather he had the sense that the entire place was very special, almost as though it was part of a different world.

OK, Mojo, here I am. Martin tried to sit still but found he couldn't. He was too excited, wanted something to happen.

He decided to go for a long swim. In the five days since his arrival he hadn't gone in the water, as he had been too preoccupied with finding his beach. Now that he had found it, he could celebrate and do something fun. Maybe after his swim he would find a sign, or someone.

He stood up and slowly walked over to the water's edge. For a moment he stood letting the small waves lap against his legs, then walked a little further in to the point where the water reached his thighs.

Martin dove in, opened his eyes under water and propelled himself along the sandy bottom until his lungs craved air. Back on the surface, he swam toward the tip of the bay. He realized his body needed the exercise and swimming felt easy.

He examined the coastline with its harsh lava rocks, and beyond in the distance a mountain that rose in gentle slope to a great height. Everything around him, sky, water, rocks, the trees and the mountain, their colors and texture, seemed still and quiet, easy on the senses.

After a while, Martin turned back toward shore. He could barely distinguish the figures there, but could make out the man sitting on the rock.

The water now felt warmer, caressing. His arms and legs were beginning to tire, but it was still very enjoyable. Slowly he approached the beach. As he got closer, he again felt that exciting feeling of déjà vu and knew something was about to happen. *But what?*

He swam until he reached a spot where he could stand, and he started walking slowly, with the water coming up to his chest.

He was about a hundred feet from the beach when the figure on the rock appeared to wave. *Was it a wave? Maybe he just raised a hand to his eyes.* Martin headed in his direction and somehow knew he had to meet him.

Is that what's supposed to happen? Maybe.

As he got within thirty feet or so he noticed that the man was definitely smiling at him. Martin smiled back. The man was about ten years older than himself, maybe fifty, Martin thought, with olive skin with long black hair just beginning to thin, and black eyes. The man appeared to be Hawaiian. He was heavyset, but not fat, just husky. His face was oval shaped, with thick eyebrows, a generous mouth, wide nose and an ample forehead. Long hair was swept back to reveal a gently curving hairline, adding to the impression of a rounded face. Martin noticed that his smile started in the eyes but the whole face emanated friendliness.

Martin came right up to the rock and the man motioned for him to sit on a promontory some six feet in front of him, on a rock resembling a stool.

It seemed the natural thing to do.

Martin climbed onto the rock, and sat as indicated with his back to the ocean. It was comfortable; his whole body felt very comfortable. He knew something wonderful was happening; he could feel it in his bones, in his heart…without a doubt.

The man asked his name.

"My name is Martin, Martin Devon."

The man smiled broadly. "Welcome to Hawaii, Martin, and welcome to my rock." He paused to look Martin over, then asked, "And how are you?"

The voice was calm, a rich, wonderful voice, a voice of a father, or of an old friend.

Martin was reminded of Mojo. The feeling coming from the stranger was very much what he recalled feeling from the big man; and whatever he was doing, it was taking layers off of Martin, off his shoulders, off his chest; better yet, it was filling his insides, pushing the vestiges of the awful emptiness completely out.

He then realized he carried tension and depression even when he thought he was fine.

"But tell me, sir, what's your name?" Martin could hardly talk; he wanted to study the figure in front of him, while at the same time savor the feeling. His mind raced with questions, and he couldn't figure out what else to say.

Instead of answering, the man asked about his life: where he lived, what he did, how long he was planning to stay in Hawaii…and Martin told him, explaining that he had come alone; had needed a rest. Martin was going to continue, telling the man about Mojo and the pilgrimage, when he cut him off.

"Martin, you are concerned about your life, your marriage, and mostly about the hollow feeling that has pursued you all your life."

At the sound of the words Martin felt a powerful jolt in his heart and he searched for a way to respond. "Yes…yes, I…that's right."

"I can help you Martin, but only if you want me to."

"Yes…thank you. If there is anything you can do for me…please help me." Martin heard his own words and it dawned on him how bizarre everything was. For a moment he wanted to flee, get away. He resisted the impulse and concentrated on the good feeling inside him.

The stranger was still, very still, and looking deep into Martin's eyes.

"First, Martin, will you trust me? I need you to trust me."

"Yes, of course." Martin said without hesitation. But the man continued looking into his eyes, and Martin thought he didn't quite believe him.

"I am going to take you someplace, Martin, that will seem fantastic to you and perhaps a bit unsettling, and is why I need your trust."

"Where will you take me?" *This…this is weird.*

Martin felt the answer in his chest: excitement and happiness…safety… being cared for, protected…and loved, loved deeply. *Of course I'll trust.* He looked at the figure in front of him, and the man didn't seem like a stranger anymore. Somehow Martin knew him, and the love he felt seemed genuine, old, from long before.

Now he meant the words and they came from deep inside him: "Yes, I trust you."

That seemed to satisfy the man. He smiled. "Very good, my friend; you are ready."

Martin leaned closer. *Maybe this man is one of those Hawaiian Kahunas who are supposed to have magical powers…and he's related to Mojo somehow. Do they act as a team?* Martin waited intently for the man to resume talking, for the teaching to begin, but instead he raised a finger, slowly reached across and gently touched Martin's hand.

"It's an adventure, Martin."

Martin saw a flash of light, and felt being propelled through what seemed like a tunnel, a tunnel with a golden light at the end. The light became increasingly bright, to the point where he had to close his eyes. Vibration, a force like thunder—a tremendous sound—it seemed the whole universe was exploding…but the feeling of peace was there…and Martin felt very fine, everything was fine.

Suddenly all was still, quiet, and calm.

Martin felt relieved, whatever it was, it was over and he opened his eyes. Everything had changed. He found himself in the middle of a clearing with a forest of tall trees all around. The air had a different quality to it, as did the light, the smells, and the colors. He realized he was standing beside a road…or perhaps not standing, he didn't seem to have a body.

Martin heard the man's voice. "Yes Martin, this place is unlike anything you have experienced. You have changed as well."

The voice came from behind him, but as he looked there was nothing but trees. His surroundings seemed real—the sky, the wind, the trees, the grass— except there was a halo effect, like a faint light shining behind things. Otherwise it all looked normal.

This is a dream, it has to be.

The road was narrow, made of large stones, and straight. Martin recognized some of the trees as oaks; others were pines, and elms. Birds flew around, chirping and singing. The sun shone brightly, and it appeared to be early morning. Still a bit chilly by the looks of things: dew shone on leaves and fog still clung to the tall grass, but Martin didn't feel the cold.

The overall sensation was of being rather weightless. Martin could feel his body, but when he looked down he could not see where his legs and torso should be. After a short time of staring he began to see something...a bluish light. Where his body should have been there was now a faint glow. He brought his hand up to his face and felt his hand brush his cheek.

"You do have a body, my friend, just one you are not used to."

An outline of the man's figure formed in front of Martin's eyes...a faint light blue figure, becoming more defined as he looked. After a short time Martin could see the man materialized in front of him: the same smiling eyes, the same kind face. His whole body was made of a blue light that became gold as it went out of his body.

"Don't worry, you will become accustomed to this place. The blue light you see where your old body was, is your new body. It will take you some time to get used to the idea you are different, but once you do, you will feel very comfortable." The man observed Martin for some time. "You can have a normal body if you want. You can manifest it at will. Try and visualize your body, Martin."

Martin looked down and did as he was told. He pictured his legs...hips ...torso. At first, there was only the blue shimmering light, without the gold fringe that the man had. But then slowly his familiar body began to emerge. It was odd; he could actually feel himself materialize. At first, he felt rather ethereal, then more defined, seemingly more solid. He looked at his hands and could see his fingers, his knuckles. His body continued to materialize until it was like his own body, except it had a different quality: weightless, vibrant, full of some kind of energy, and it felt...unencumbered. Now he could see details: veins, nails, the curlicues of his fingerprints.

"This is your body as well, my friend; it's been a part of you all along." The man had remained faint, but still visible. "You just have to remember how to use it." He paused. "It's for you to decide how visible and material you want to be."

This is different from a dream...everything has a certain quality of reality to it...which doesn't make sense.

"Where are we? What's this place? And please tell me how we got here."

The man seemed to think. He turned, walked a few paces, then turned around and faced Martin, apparently weighing his words carefully. "You have traveled through space and time," he said slowly. "The only way you could've come here is without your physical body, with your body of light. You may know it as your astral body. Are you familiar with this term?"

The words didn't register at first. It was as though Martin's mind couldn't quite process the concept. He repeated the words to himself until they seemed to sink in. He was in another time and he was in his astral body. Jenny's books talked about the astral body; it was...like the soul. But he hadn't paid much attention to those things; he had always figured when he died he would find out. Now, this was the real thing. It was truly the real thing.

"Am I dead, then? Did I die?" He realized he wasn't afraid, just curious.

"No, Martin, you haven't died. Your physical body is still sitting on that rock, alive. However, this is similar to what people experience when they die. That is, for those who have evolved to that level of awareness."

To Martin it sounded as though the man was trying to bring him out of shock with his gentle words and explanations, and he realized he did feel like he was in shock; but aside from that, he was beginning to feel as if he had just shed a weight, or a disguise.

Martin kept looking at his new body and alternately at his surroundings. As outlandish as it all seemed, something inside him told him this was the right place to be. *Feels so good...to be...once again in this body....Again?*

"Somehow this is familiar. Have I been like this before?"

"Yes, my friend. For the past few incarnations you have been aware of your astral self when you shed your physical body."

Martin looked closely at his new body. *I guess I'm like a ghost.* "So this is the astral world?"

"No, this is still the physical world. You have traveled through space and time, that's all. Everything else is still the same." He was silent for a moment. "This is England, or rather, Britain, and it's the year four hundred sixty-four."

Gone back in time? And to Britain. Why?

For a brief moment he felt afraid the experience was too good to be true, was really nothing but a dream; but then the good feeling inside persisted, reassuring him. It told him everything was all right.

Martin took another look around. He couldn't see any houses or people. The only sign of humans was the road, and it looked like nothing he had ever seen before; big rocks cut so they fit together neatly, stretching in either direction, apparently for miles.

"Why Britain? Why the year four sixty-four?"

"That's for you to find out, my friend. There is something in this time and place calling you." There was hesitation in his voice. "Let me simply say that here you can learn much. Are you interested?" He looked in Martin's eyes. "If not, you can always go back to Hawaii. All you have to do is ask."

It was good to know he could go back at will. With his mind a jumble of thoughts, and his heart racing, he looked around again. Everything was still, except for a light breeze rustling the leaves of the trees. Those were real birds definitely singing. The road was empty, but it appeared well used; he could see where some rocks had been worn smooth. The halo effect on birds, trees, flowers, insects, gave them a new beauty.

"No, I am glad and grateful to be here. Just overwhelmed, that's all." He paused to collect his thoughts. "Yes…I would like to explore this place, experience this body…and learn whatever you say I can learn here." Without question that was the truth, the feeling inside told him that.

"But tell me about the halo effect I see," Martin asked.

"It's what people refer to as auras. All beings have astral bodies, and you can now see them because you are an astral being, and are subject to different laws of physics."

"Why do you have that golden aura and I don't?"

"Astral bodies reflect states of consciousness. I happen to be, let's say, more peaceful, and I show a golden glow. You will notice people's state of mind and emotions reflected in their auras."

The man told him that leaving the physical body was a matter of will power, and given the right conditions any person could do the same. Martin's new state enabled him to do things not possible with the physical body. He would need to experiment, learn how it worked.

The man assured him the knowledge was already his; it was just a question of remembering.

"It all seems like a dream," Martin said.

"Of course. This is very different from what you are used to in your recent memory. Anything that deviates from that physical world would seem 'unreal' to you."

Martin's initial shock had turned into excitement, and apparently the man could sense it. "If you ever need me, come to this glen. I'll be here." He told Martin to explore around, see the place, observe the people. He cautioned him to remain detached from the human drama he would soon witness; his role was that of an observer, and it would be best not to get involved. His new body was not visible to human eyes unless he wanted to be seen.

"I can interact with people if I want to?"

"Please try to remain detached. Becoming involved could be very dangerous. You are here to learn, to experience events. Enjoy it as an adventure, a story in a book. If you do this, you will be highly successful."

"What if I meet someone like me…a ghost?

The man smiled. "Don't worry, what you call ghosts are but shadows; they can't see you."

"What are they, then?"

"Well, to appear in the world in an astral body, the person has to be very advanced, or be helped, just as I'm helping you. Otherwise, strong emotions can bring an otherwise unconscious soul to replay a situation over and over again."

The man's eyes turned grave. "Martin, please focus on what's important: getting over your depression. You can find your answers here. And, please, whatever you do, don't get involved."

He's worried about me. "Then I will just observe and listen. This is England, so they speak English, although an ancient form of the language, I assume."

"No, actually they don't speak English, not yet. Most of the people you will encounter speak Latin. The rest speak a very different language."

"Latin, of course. They were conquered by the Romans for hundreds of years. I took some Latin in college but I don't think I'll be able to understand. Maybe in time, after I listen for a while."

The man nodded. "You will find yourself absorbing the languages very, very quickly. Let's say you will be helped with this."

"What do you mean, 'helped'?"

"Don't worry. I promise you will understand the languages."

Martin pictured himself ambling among blond, blue-eyed barbarians, and Roman soldiers, observing how they lived, and fought....

In the midst of his thoughts a concern arose. "What about my body; what will happen to it while I'm gone?"

"You have nothing to worry about, Martin. No time will pass in Hawaii. Remember we went back in time, and will return at the very moment we left."

Some things he would just have to accept on faith. The thought that his body was somewhere else felt extremely odd. *But the man told me it would be fine. I won't worry about it.* Martin realized he had to focus on the present. *I am really here. And I am in my astral body.* Martin turned around to look for the man, but felt he had left. He was now alone. But he remembered that he could summon him back at any time. *Just come back to this glen and call him.*

What should he do now? He concentrated on his body first, examining his hands, arms, legs. It all seemed the same as his physical body. He was surprised he still had sensations and physical manifestations he equated with emotions: excitement in his chest, where his heart would be; anxiety with a cold feeling on the palm of his hands. Somehow it didn't make sense. If he didn't have a physical body, why would he feel sensations he knew were caused by things like adrenaline?

Martin started to walk on the road. His new body and how it worked was something he would have to explore over time, get used to. For now he wanted to experience his new world as a human.

He found that with his body apparently solid, he could feel the stones under his feet, and the breeze on his face.

He wanted to see what people were like. He was trying to remember what he had read about Britain at this period. He had seen pictures of roads the Romans had built, and this road was much like them.

He wondered why the man had placed him by the road. *There must be a reason, a purpose.* He understood the glen was isolated, so it was safe to assume the man had wanted to drop him in a place far from the sight of people before he learned how to use his body. That had been wise. Also, he could go back to the glen by following this road.

Martin tried to ascertain his location in Britain. He imagined the island as a whole, and tried to picture himself in it. Maybe he should have asked before the man left. And why hadn't the man told him his name? *He's probably a Kahuna, although he doesn't look exactly Hawaiian....Hawaii! So far away.*

Sound of hooves, then voices. Martin continued walking, looked down to make sure his body was not visible. Apparently the blue shimmer was not visible to human eyes.

He could now see two horsemen riding side by side in his direction, with the riders absorbed in conversation. Each man had behind him a spare mount. Martin listened, but could not understand what the men were saying. The language seemed to be very different from the Latin he remembered. It was full of harsh sounds that merged together.

As they drew near, he couldn't help himself and instinctively ran and hid behind a tree. There he stood still. Then gingerly, his heart pounding in his chest, he came out as they walked past him, expecting them to see him, to react to his presence. But they didn't.

He decided to walk beside them.

Obviously neither men nor beasts could detect him. It was very odd, this experience.

He was tempted to materialize, just to make sure he could be seen if he wanted to, but he quickly dismissed the impulse.

Their language was actually more understandable than on his first impression. Martin recognized they were speaking Latin and could make out a few words.

One of the men was older, around forty; the other one much younger, about eighteen or twenty. They both wore a cloak of heavy cloth fastened around their necks. Under it they had a kind of tunic, a one-piece attire covering the torso down to the knees; and they wore sandals strapped up the calf. They each had a sword—short swords Martin associated with the Romans—a rectangular shield, a helmet, and what looked like pieces of body armor tied to the horse's right side behind the rider. The saddles consisted of squares of heavy leather. There were no stirrups. A bow and a quiver full of arrows were slung behind each rider, on the right side. They also had leather bags that appeared to contain provisions and water.

Martin understood the younger man asking how much farther they had to go, but he couldn't make out the answer.

Both men had sandy-colored hair, were about medium height, and had rather squarish faces; they seemed related, maybe father and son.

After a while they rode in silence, more attentive to their surroundings. They proceeded for about another hour until they came to a bridge over a narrow river. There, on the nearest bank, a number of other riders had gathered. There were about twenty of them, and they too were armed; some had short lances, others swords, and a few had both.

As the two riders approached, the men nodded at each other. The two came up to the group and faced them.

The father addressed one who seemed the leader of the group. He was talking in earnest about something on the other side of the mountains. They all looked at the ridge a few miles away. The men dismounted, tied their horses and sat on the grass forming a circle.

Martin noticed that the clothes worn by the father and son and the leader of the other men were finer than those of the others; they fit better and the cloth seemed newer and smoother. Their faces were also clean-shaven, while the other men were bearded.

The father was addressed with deference, as was the leader of the group. Martin learned that the father's name was King Joannes and he was from Isca. The leader of the men was from a place called Lindinus, and he was addressed as King Mateus. The young man with King Joannes was indeed his son, and was called Philippus.

The men talked, with what seemed like great urgency, and Martin noticed that their auras became redder; some seemed to flicker, and others expanded and contracted, as the person's emotions appeared to shift.

Martin was able to understand most of what was said. A few of the words he inferred from the context, but overall their meaning just came to him. Once he heard something, he knew what it meant, like something long forgotten. As the conversation went on he understood more and more, and was surprised at this. He remembered the Kahuna's statement that he would be helped with the language, and wondered if there was some sort of hypnotic directive now operating on his subconscious to unlock knowledge he had all along. Whatever was at play, he did understand the language, even the non-Latin words, the local brogue.

Martin learned that there was an army of primitive people somewhere on the other side of the hills that they could barely see in the distance, and they had attacked a place called Lindum Colonia, a city many miles up the Roman road. They had also attacked several other cities, camps, and farm clusters. The primitive horde had done a great deal of damage everywhere they went, destroying crops, burning down houses with people in them, razing whole towns and villages, killing a large number of people.

Martin felt himself struggling with the feeling that what he was seeing and hearing had to be a dream, but at the same time everything seemed very real…eerily so. When he stood next to the horses he could smell them, and he knew he would be able to touch and feel them if he wanted to. The angst he felt from the group was tangible. When the men talked he could tell they were afraid. He could see a trembling hand, a furtive glance, a vein in a neck popping out when someone got excited and raised his voice.

It became apparent to Martin from the conversation that the men gathered were from all over the place, and not just from the cities of Lindinus and Isca.

They described their farms and villages, tallying the able-bodied men, and those who had been soldiers. Then the talk centered on the enemy. They told tales from the refugees who had streamed down from the attacked towns. They were trying to determine which cities had fallen, and which had withstood the attackers, but mainly they were trying to figure out where the horde was at that point. The men told the stories, some several times as if in disbelief, and they all concerned bloodshed and violence on a scale they had never experienced.

Martin observed the reactions of the men as they heard each other's tales of destruction and carnage. Some grabbed the hilt of their swords, others paced nervously, but mostly they stared down at the ground. Never in their lives had they been threatened like this. They had fought bandits, pirates and the occasional Saxon and Angle raid. That was expected; but these people were threatening to wipe them out. The primitives didn't fear anyone, now that there was no big army, and there was no one to stop them. The enemy numbered in the tens of thousands.

Now Martin understood that he was in fact somewhere in the southern-most part of the island, and for these men there was no escaping. There was no place to go.

"Maybe the Romans can help," said a man with a bushy red beard. "Why don't we ask them?"

"That is right. We hear things are well in Rome," said a heavy-set man. "Ships from Italia have come with stories of more raids by barbarians, but it seems that life goes on there as before."

"Yes," said a man holding a lance, "the Western Empire is recovering and beating back the barbarians. And we all know the Eastern Empire is strong. They have many legions and are not fighting anyone."

"Sorry, friends," Joannes said, "But in the days of the Big Council, we requested help several times from the Emperor, and each time we were turned down. Back in the days of my father, in the year four hundred ten, we sent our first letter for help. Then again in four hundred forty-six, and the last one, some ten years ago. All three had to do with invasions."

"I remember the last two," Mateus said, "Those were Saxons we were fighting, and we beat them back."

"We are free in these parts," said Joannes, "but I heard the Saxons captured some cities in the east."

It became apparent to Martin that both Joannes and Mateus had served in what had remained of the Roman Army, as had several of those present. It seemed The Big Council had been a governing body that took over from the Romans and maintained order for some time, until falling apart because of someone named Vortigern. The council had been in charge of a large army.

Both kings' fathers had been members of the Big Council, and it was Joannes and Mateus who made it clear to the rest that there was no sense in hoping for a rescue by the Romans.

"So what can we do?" asked the man with the red beard.

The men talked among themselves for a while. Martin understood that the enemy came from a land called Caledonia. Their last major invasion had taken place some three years before, after years of laying low, and those present talked about that raid. That previous time the enemy had come into their lands and then, for no apparent reason, turned back.

Martin heard the men talk, and watched them, and it was clear they had little hope of fighting off the Caledonians.

The one with the red beard was apparently of higher rank and not afraid to talk. "Lindum Colonia is as strong as Isca, but I hear they were nearly overrun, and their farms and villages laid to waste; so tell me, King Joannes, why would you fare better?" The man spoke in Latin with just a few words in brogue.

Joannes looked at the man. "I personally know how to fight the Caledonians from two years of serving at 'the Wall,' when Mateus and I fought together." Joannes spoke in what sounded as high-cultured Latin. He then gazed at the whole group. "The Caledonians have no battle strategy, they simply fight head on; and a good disciplined formation would stand an excellent chance of holding them back. Look at my son, Philippus. He has been trained as an archer, and we have many like him. And cavalry troops. All I need are additional fighting men."

Joannes took a few paces around the group, touching a lance here and there, placing a hand on an occasional shoulder. "I have heard the barbarians number in the tens of thousands, but that's rumor. History should tell us how many men we need. Most of the time the Romans had four legions for all of Britannia, and the Big Council did well with three, two in these parts. I have three thousand men, a thousand short of a legion. Without doubt, between all of us, we should be able to come up with two full legions. That should do it. Lindum Colonia and other cities I have heard about, tried to fight the enemy by themselves. I have spoken to many of the refugees coming into Isca, and have not heard of a single instance where cities banded together. So if we pull our men together, there is do doubt we can beat the primitives."

Martin thought the men looked at Joannes with respect, but also with skepticism. They kept repeating how hopeless it was to fight such a large and brutal enemy. The last time the Caledonians came, one pointed out, some villages and farms had escaped being ransacked because the barbarians didn't find them. Maybe this time some of their places would be spared as well.

Joannes insisted that if they banded together they would prevail.

The men appreciated Philippus' bow and arrows, as he went around showing them his weapons. He then demonstrated by shooting a number of arrows at a tree well over a hundred yards away. By the looks on their faces Martin gathered that had been quite a feat.

It could be that Joannes' argument had convinced them; or maybe as Martin gathered, they had no other choice; but at any rate they all agreed to fight.

Some men talked about their farms and villages, how unprotected they were. They knew Isca was well fortified and the city would survive an attack, but their villages and farms would be overrun.

"If I receive the help I need, the enemy will never come close to your homes," Joannes said.

The sun was beginning to set and the group decided to ride in different directions to do their best to assemble as many men as possible.

Martin understood that Joannes and Philippus were going to find the enemy and assess their strength.

Joannes' general, Arcadius, was coming from Isca with their men of war, the three thousand he had mentioned, and they would assemble in the mountains where he expected the enemy to come through. This was to be the place where Joannes intended to hold off the Caledonians.

"Tell us how you plan to fight the Caledonians, King Joannes," said the man with the red beard.

"I have several plans, but which one I use depends on how many men we are able to gather. Bring as many as you can, and no later than by tomorrow night." Joannes said.

Martin had inferred from the conversation that the kingdoms, Joannes' and Mateus', were each loosely held together, and they consisted of the actual city the kings lived in and a few farms around them; but the outlying areas were like a no-man's land, and the men they were meeting came from those places.

They all mounted and departed in different directions.

Martin stood for some time thinking about what he was witnessing. It was interesting, he decided, to be a witness, a shadow or a ghost; but that didn't seem to take away the brutal edge of things. On the other hand, nothing could touch him, he was not being overrun by any enemy, he was not in danger. It all made for a very absorbing experience…or adventure, as the Kahuna had called it.

Martin followed Joannes and Philippus.

He decided there was something very familiar about Joannes and his son, and the distinct sensation made him wonder if it was possible he was witnessing a past life. *So perhaps this is why the Kahuna transported me here! Of course. And maybe that's why I understand the language.*

Martin approached father and son from a new perspective, looking and examining, trying to see if anything would prod long-forgotten memories. It all made perfect sense to him now. *What better way to cure my depression, than to show me I once had a meaningful life.*

He noticed the obvious affection between the two men. For a time they rode with arms entwined, as Joannes comforted his son. He told him hey would be able to beat back the enemy; a strong resistance would make them turn away. As barbaric as they were, the Caledonians were no fools; in the face of strong opposition they would turn around and head for easier targets.

"But what about Isca?" asked Philippus. "With the troops away, won't the bandits from Julius' kingdom take advantage? And what about the barbarians in Gaul?"

Joannes kept his arm around his son's. "Julius' bandits are not strong enough to attack Isca, even with only old men defending her walls. As far as the barbarians raiding from Gaul, they need to cross the ocean to get to us, and they don't seem to have boats."

Martin understood that some people in the north had been expected to defend the Wall, but obviously had not succeeded.

"We are not like the northern people. We know how to fight the Roman way," said Joannes.

Dark descended with a half-moon, and the two riders decided to make camp. They let their horses graze, all four loosely tied together. After watering the animals, the men ate, spread their blankets and lay down to rest.

Martin felt tired as well, and wondered why it was so, if he no longer had a physical body. But he felt like sleeping.

Concerned he would inadvertently materialize when asleep, he floated away further into the forest, until he felt certain no human could see him.

He found a place that appeared as if no man had ever set foot in it. All around him were trees growing close together with thick undergrowth, and the only openings were holes animals had made through the brush. Instinctively he looked around for shelter, half realizing how unnecessary it was.

Behind a clump of trees there was a hill, and as he came closer he saw an opening that looked like a cave—perhaps an animal lair, he thought. He had seen foxes, deer and boar, and he imagined there was also bear around. Well, there was no way a bear could do him harm, not in his present body; so if one was inside, he would simply have a chance to see a bear up close.

CHAPTER FOUR

Martin entered the opening, which was barely big enough for a human body to pass through.

Once inside, he gingerly looked around, half expecting to meet someone. The cave was deceptively big, and surprisingly dry. He had envisioned a damp, musty place smelling of fur, but this place was cozy and seemed quite large.

Martin ambled over to a corner and lay down. Tiredness overcame him, and he was glad to be in this place. Sleep would be good.

He didn't feel hungry, and that was fortunate, because he realized he wouldn't know what to eat, or how to find food. Still, he tried to figure out how his new body replenished itself, what energy or fuel fed him.

Martin thought about his son, and wondered what Adam was doing at that very moment. He tried to estimate the time difference, and caught himself. *There is no time difference, because no time is elapsing back home. He's still doing whatever he was doing when I left.* He smiled. It would take some time to get used to that.

It had been quite a day—if a day it was. He had found his beach, met the Kahuna and made his pilgrimage a reality. Now it seemed he was meant to revisit a past life. Not that he had thought about past lives before. Nor astral bodies. *Yes, quite a day.* He could now comment on Jenny's books. *Man, that's funny. The New Age mumbo-jumbo is real after all!* Martin tried to imagine telling Jenny about his experience so far. The thought of her felt nasty, though. *Best not to think about her.*

So he imagined that his task was going to be finding the passion for life he had lost somewhere along the way, remembering how to live. Judging from what he had seen so far in this one day, that promised to be very interesting…

He became aware of morning light coming through the entrance. For a moment Martin had to remind himself where he was. As he lay gathering his thoughts he had the certainty he was being watched, and glanced down at his body to make sure he was not visible. Then he looked around, but no one was there. He wondered if there was some other being like him around.

He then decided there was no time for that now; he felt a sudden urgency to join Joannes and his son.

As he left he took one last look around the place. He would have to remember the cave, and how to get back.

He retraced his path of the night before and found the Roman road. There was no sign of the two men at the campsite where he had left them.

Martin followed the road, trying to guess the time of day. Judging by the sun, he gauged it was still early. He was sure they couldn't have gotten far, and that he'd see them at any moment.

A mile or so up the road, Martin heard the sound of female voices screaming and of men laughing. He hurried along, a feeling of foreboding coming over him.

At a clearing beside the road, three men were holding two women savagely by the hair and arms, while a fourth one stood in front of a fallen man whom he apparently had just struck with his sword. A large dog, bloodied on the side, was protecting the fallen man, straddling him, while the standing man prepared to finish off the dog.

Martin froze. He didn't know what to do. His impulse was to help the man and the dog, and the women, but with what and how? Another part of him wanted very badly to flee.

A movement to his right, and something swished by—the man slumped and fell. Something had hit him in the side; Martin could see something sticking out. The man screamed, writhing on the ground, and then was still. There was a long arrow going right through him from one side to the other.

Martin turned to look at the three men who had been holding the women. One had been hit with another arrow in the chest and had fallen to the ground. The remaining two men stood stupefied, letting go of the woman they were both holding, then rushed to take cover behind some rocks and emerged with shields and axes.

They nervously faced the direction where the arrows had come from, eyes darting back and forth, both yelling at each other.

Martin barely caught sight of a horse charging past him. He recognized Joannes and his horse.

One man was slammed in the face by Joannes' shield, as the horse spun around in front of them, avoiding a wild ax swing. Joannes jumped from his horse and landed on the remaining man. They struggled on the ground. The man seemed stronger than Joannes, and was overtaking him with one hand clenching Joannes' arm, and the other pushing hard down on his face. He was now on top of him; one arm came up as an arrow flew past his head. He slammed his fist down on Joannes' head.

One of the women picked up a rock and ran with arms raised, stopped behind him, and came down hard with the rock against the man's head. The man bent over, as another arrow hit him in the side.

Joannes pushed the limp body aside.

The fight was over; all was still, with only the sound of heavy breathing. Shocked, Martin stepped back. He had never seen such violence before. Everything had happened so quickly, but at the same time it seemed slow, like slow motion, a dance. His normal awareness slowly returned, and noticed that Joannes had turned his attention to the fallen man with the dog. The dog stood snarling, protecting his master. The man under the dog called his name softly, what sounded like "Achilles," several times. The dog turned, looked at the man and gently licked his face, then his wounded shoulder.

The fallen man stood up shakily. He was tall, thin, and wore a white robe. He bent down to pick up a staff as tall as he. Martin now looked at the women, who had embraced each other sobbing. He now noticed two children, about ten years old, shaken and also crying. Philippus emerged from the forest with his bow. Martin watched as father and son embraced. Philippus, clearly relieved that his father was fine, stood holding the older man and patting him on the back, his face ashen, his voice broken up.

Martin noticed the auras: the tall man's was blue and was slowly turning gold, like the Kahuna's. The women's, Joannes' and Philippus' auras were changing from a reddish hue and slowly becoming blue. The dead Caledonians did not have auras, but the one Joannes had hit with his shield was clearly alive. He showed a red one.

Joannes went from one person to the other, calming the women and the children. With them he spoke a mixture of Latin and a local language. He thanked the woman who wielded the rock. She raised her hand to touch his head where the man had hit him, and he reassured her he was fine. The man in the robe had a serious wound on his shoulder, while his dog had a puncture wound on its side. One of the women had a scraped cheek and a bloody nose. The other two were unscathed, as were the children.

The man who had been hit with the shield lay groaning, apparently unconscious, his face a bloody mess. Joannes and Philippus tied him up with his hands behind his back and a foot tied to the hands. The man stirred, woke, and screamed.

Joannes inspected the tall man's wound. The man, who spoke clear Latin, insisted that Joannes minister to his dog first. He held its head gently in his hands as Joannes put some powder on the wound, sewed it and dressed it. Martin noticed this was no ordinary dog; it was a wolf: thin tall legs, gray coat and shy blue eyes. It was touching to see the affection the man had for his wolf, how he talked to him as its wound was being treated.

The man came next. His wound was sewn as he stared calmly at Joannes and talked.

"I am called Nicolaus Maximus, noble man. How do you call yourself?" the tall man said.

"I am Joannes Patronius, and that is my son Philippus Antonius. We are from Isca."

"Greetings, and my gratitude for your assistance, Joannes of Isca."

"Are you a monk, Nicolaus?"

"I am a monk. Roman, born in Milan. And was initiated as a monk in Greece." He had been a teacher in different places, and had traveled all over the Empire. Two days before, he had run across the women and children fleeing the violence in the north. The women's husbands had stayed to fight, and had sent them to safety, as far south as they could get. They thought the Caledonians were two to three days behind them, until that morning when the four men caught up with them. At first, nothing had happened, as they sat down to share the meager morning meal the women had made. Then at one point, they talked among themselves, laughed, stood up and went for the women; grabbing and trying to throw them down on the ground. The monk had tried to intervene, striking one Caledonian with his staff, but a second one attacked him with his sword. Achilles had defended him by biting the man, slashing his arm. Then the Caledonian struck the wolf, and was about to finish him off when Joannes came on the scene.

Joannes was done dressing the wound. "My apologies for not acting sooner. I could have prevented your injuries. Philippus and I came up on your group and the Caledonians, and they were acting friendly, so we hid in the trees to wait and see what they might do. When they attacked, we acted as fast as we could."

The monk walked over to the fallen men. At first he stood praying, with his hands clasped in front of him; then he raised his hands, apparently blessing them. He turned to the group, his eyes serene and his voice calm. "Please forgive these men. They don't know how to act otherwise; it is in their nature to be violent." The monk walked over to the women and touched them gently, one on the shoulder, one on the head, and the third on a hand. The children he bent down to embrace. He seemed to calm those he touched. The women hugged their children, all still crying, but the women's sobs had given way to gentle words.

Martin noticed how rough the Caledonians looked. They had scraggly beards and long hair, and unlike the men he had seen so far, they seemed unkempt, greasy, and gave off a terrible smell of dirty, sweaty bodies. They were also heavily tattooed on their faces, arms and legs.

The man they had tied up was being interrogated by Joannes, who apparently had a basic knowledge of his language, which he supplemented with signs and drawings on the ground with his knife. The interrogation was not gentle; answers were punctuated with sharp slaps on the wounded face. Joannes stuck his knife under the man's chin and drove the blade in to the point Martin thought would kill him, but Joannes just held the knife there as the captive screamed with pain. Then he broke one of the man's fingers when he refused to answer. Shortly after that, the Caledonian talked in what seemed a deluge, a letting go of what he was being asked. When Joannes had whatever he needed from him, he went over to consult with the women.

Apparently satisfied, he stood thinking, looking at the nearby mountains, as though trying to see through them and into the distance. After some time it seemed he had come up with some sort of answer, or with a plan; for he walked over with a new determination which was reflected in his carriage and the expression on his face.

"Nicolaus, may I press upon your kindness to escort these women and children to Isca?"

"I would be honored, friend Joannes."

"I learned about the Caledonians from refugees such as you, coming to our city. You will be welcomed there." Joannes had taken a piece of parchment from his saddlebag and was writing with what looked like charcoal. "There are soldiers coming this way. I will give you a note of safe passage for you to show. Once in Isca, please ask to see my noble wife, Queen Martigena."

Nicolaus' face registered surprise. Then he bowed at Joannes. "Forgive me my familiarity, your Majesty. I had no idea who you were."

Joannes dismissed his concern with a wave of his hand. "The four men who caught up with you this morning were an advance party sent to scout the area ahead of their army. Their job was to assess the worthiness of the places they encountered, the defenses, and provisions available to supply their men. I estimate their strength at twelve thousand from what I could get from the captive, and what the women told me, and that's good news; for up to now I thought their numbers were much higher. I also now know the enemy is but a day's ride on the other side of the mountains."

"When you meet up with the horse soldiers, see the officer in charge," Joannes said. "Please tell him my findings about the Caledonians, and confirm that we will fight them in the mountains. Once you reach Isca, repeat the information to my wife."

The monk bowed and took the note.

As the group prepared to leave, Martin felt he had to retreat, to go somewhere far from there and away from the group. He had a knot in his stomach, and a sense of grief. He started back on the road, wishing he could talk to somebody. He replayed the events. *What is the purpose of all this…why am I here? This is not an interesting adventure. Real and bad things are happening to real people.* He was greatly relieved Joannes and the rest were alive. It would have been terrible to witness Joannes—or for that matter, the women, the monk, or the wolf—being killed at the hands of the Caledonians. Had the outcome been different, he would have felt very bad for the loss of those beings. He also realized he had been helpless, and that he found disturbing. He had been paralyzed by fear…or maybe just ineptitude, inexperience. He wished he had acted, or at least known that he could.

He stopped on the road and made his body appear, then concentrated on making it solid. When he could see his arm clearly, he bent over to pick up a dry stick on the road. His fingers felt the wood, curved around it and raised it. He then brought the stick down hard on one of the stones. It broke in half with a loud snap. *I can make things happen.* Martin stood looking at the broken stick. Next time, he would certainly do something. Still, there was something else inside him, an ugliness that gnawed. He couldn't quite define it, but he felt it weighing him down. He decided to continue walking, for the comfort it gave him.

Martin was now completely certain that in a past life he had been Joannes. Why else would he find Joannes and Philippus on the road, the first people he met? He was sure the Kahuna had meant it to work out that way; he had picked the exact time and location so Martin would meet those two men in particular. Also, from the start he had felt a very special connection with Joannes. *And the Kahuna said something here beckoned me. Of course, this life must've been very special, otherwise why am I here?*

He decided to talk to the Kahuna. Martin had many questions, and the Kahuna was the only one who could answer them. Martin hurried on down the road toward the glen, no longer walking; he was rapidly skimming along the surface of the road. Soon he recognized the place. He remembered the lay of the land, the trees.

Now what? How do I summon the Kahuna?

He felt the man's presence. It was the good feeling that seemed to come with him. Martin saw a faint shimmering blue outline materialize in front of him, then the familiar gentle, smiling eyes, and the countenance that went with it. Deep peace enveloped him; a sweet feeling that was so reassuring.

"How are you, my friend? Are you having fun?" It seemed a long time since he had heard that voice, seen that face.

"Well, things are very lively. Martin thought for a minute. "Perhaps a bit unsettling, to say the least. I have met some wonderful people, seen some incredible things, and I have many questions to ask you."

The Kahuna motioned for them to sit on the grass.

Martin told him about Joannes and Philippus, the Caledonian invasion, the cave, and what had happened that morning. He heard himself speak admiringly of father and son. Then he couldn't wait any longer. He had to ask him.

"Is this my past life...was I Joannes?"

The Kahuna looked down at the ground, picked up a blade of grass, and stared at it pensively. "Be careful how you perceive this world. Please think about what's important. This translates into how you relate to the people you meet and the events unfolding before your eyes. Your stance can mean the difference between a wonderful, enriching experience, and a nightmare."

Martin realized he was being lectured, that the Kahuna was unhappy with his question.

Then the Kahuna seemed to soften his stance. "I just want you to experience this place as a neutral observer. For now, please stop trying to personalize the experience. Later on, you will find out everything you want to know. At this point let's just say that what you are witnessing here plays a role in who you are today."

That was good enough for Martin. He could wait. He realized the Kahuna was telling him that in fact this was his past life. Maybe at some point he would remember. Maybe that's what he was being told. He would try to play the role of neutral observer from then on. "Well, could you tell me about some things I am curious about? I seem to need sleep, and that doesn't make sense. I don't have a body, so what in me needs to sleep? On the other hand, I'm never hungry; how come?"

"Your body is constantly absorbing energy, a life force that sustains you; so you don't need to eat, but you need sleep because you still have the same mind. Sleep is meant to replenish the body, but it is also needed to rest the mind, to take a break from the human experience. As you progress and become more in harmony with your world, you will need less sleep."

It all makes sense. "How it is that I feel emotions like fear? There is no nervous system, no glandular secretions, so how can there be fear?"

"You have human consciousness, which in turn makes you human. Once you transcend your mind, you will leave behind the emotions and attachments that come with your state of being."

That's interesting. "You said I could interact with people if I chose to do so. Can you make me look and sound like one of the local people?"

He saw the Kahuna's response in his face. He had the look of a parent talking to a precocious child. Now Martin realized his request had been foolish.

"Martin, please think carefully about why you are here." The Kahuna was staring hard into his eyes. "The purpose for it all is to help you find the answers you are seeking. It's a very rare opportunity, but you will throw it all away if you lose your perspective."

Martin agreed to remain detached. He tried to change the topic and talked at length about the people he had met; but then the Kahuna already knew all about them; in fact he knew them by name.

Then the Kahuna told him that soon he would meet a very special person who would open a new world for him.

Martin was going to ask the Kahuna about the person, but then decided not to. He would see how things evolved. He smiled at him. The Kahuna smiled back and then vanished.

The glen was quiet. Serenity seemed to have spread all over the grass, and the trees. Martin knew he hadn't asked all the questions he had, but somehow it didn't matter. He felt peaceful and that was wonderful.

CHAPTER FIVE

Martin started back up the road to where he had left the group. He savored the peace he still carried from the Kahuna. *For him to exude such peace, he must have heaven inside.* He wondered how a person got to be like that.

His thoughts were interrupted by a roaring sound on the road behind him. Martin looked back and noticed many riders coming his way. *They must be from Isca. The three thousand men Joannes mentioned.*

Martin hurried up his pace, to catch up with Joannes and his son. After a while he heard voices and the sound of hooves. He slowed down to a walk and saw riders appear. He recognized Nicolaus and one of the women. The monk had his wolf straddled across his lap, stroking its head gently. The woman was telling him something in a somber tone. As they drew near, Martin saw three other horses behind them, with the two children on one and the two other women on the others. They all seemed tired, worn out and still shaken. He stood still to listen to the conversation between the woman and Nicolaus. She was telling him about her husband, about their life together, how hard he worked and the unending tragedy and hardship. Nicolaus appeared to be listening intently. As they passed Martin, he noticed the wolf's face, seemingly very content, and oblivious to anything else but his master's stroking hand. Martin looked at Nicolaus up close. He appeared to be about thirty, a handsome man with jet-black hair and beard and pale blue eyes, a Roman nose, long face, shrunken cheeks. *The face of an ascetic.*

Martin followed them until the monk and his group encountered the soldiers on horseback. One of the men who rode in front met Nicolaus, who produced something from his pouch. Martin guessed it was the safe pass Joannes had given him. The tone was peaceful, gentle. He was Arcadius, Joannes' general, and he welcomed news from his king. They would be welcomed in Isca and he was certain the Queen would take care of them. Nicolaus asked about any possible dangers ahead of them. Arcadius told him that a good number of foot soldiers from Isca were following close behind; he should show the officer in charge the safe pass from Joannes, and all would be well. The general offered water and food, and ordered his men to depart so the small group could go on their way.

Martin hurried on, wanting to catch up with Joannes and Philippus, who he knew were going to the mountains to look around and make preparations for the upcoming battle. The road became a blur under him as he sped up.

He arrived at the hills, but could see neither rider. The Roman road passed in between two hills. Martin was expecting to see the riders at any time, when he heard a sound from the hill on his left. Looking up, he saw Joannes and Philippus climbing on foot. Apparently they had left the horses tied somewhere, and were now almost halfway up the slope. What about their prisoner? The thought occurred to Martin that they had killed him. Certainly that would be practical, as they would not have to worry about him getting loose and escaping. He felt a knot in his stomach. It would be practical but brutal. Martin went to the foot of the mountain to look for the horses and discovered they had been tied to a tree. There were now three horses, and to his relief, he found the prisoner still alive. He was gagged and securely tied, wiggling and groaning, his eyes darting about, obviously uncomfortable and in pain.

Martin proceeded up the hill to where he had seen the two men. Father and son were climbing quietly, and appeared intent on getting up the hill as quickly as possible. Having reached the top, they scanned the land to the northeast, trying to find any sign of the Caledonians. Everything appeared still and quiet. The road was almost a straight line, with heavy, thick forest on either side, as far as the eye could see. In Joannes' estimate, if the enemy were marching on the road, anywhere within a half-day's march, they would be able to see signs. He pointed out how they could tell that Arcadius and his men were approaching behind them; if you were quiet you could hear the distant sound of hooves on pavement reverberating through the trees' canopy. The forest was being disturbed on their path, with animals scurrying ahead of the troops, birds sounding the alarm. And these were just a thousand men on horseback. No such signs were apparent on the other side of the mountains, he pointed out.

"Maybe they decided not to come this way, " Philippus said.

Joannes' face registered a sad smile. "No, they are coming."

The pair stood on top of the hill, surveying their surroundings. Joannes pointed to the other hill, the tall trees all around them, and told his son of his plan. They would cut trees and build two walls, gather stones from the road, and pile them on top of the hills behind the wooden walls. That's what would defeat the Caledonians. He kept explaining his plan as they came down to wait for Arcadius. Martin didn't quite get the whole strategy, but understood from Joannes' explanation that the rocks and logs would be released on the Caledonians as they came through the pass below.

After a few hours, Arcadius and his riders arrived.

Joannes took his general to the top of one of the hills to survey the surroundings. Where the road came into the mountains, it met a canyon which was wide at the far end and narrow at the other. Joannes pointed out that the place was perfect; the canyon was big enough to fit a large body of men. The wide entrance meant they would come charging in, and the narrow end would slow them down. They estimated the canyon narrowed down in size to half a stadium, which to Martin's eyes was about seventy feet.

The horse soldiers were put to work right away cutting trees. As evening came, the throng of foot soldiers arrived. Two thousand strong, they were orderly, obviously disciplined, but tired from the long march, which apparently had been more like a run all the way from Isca. Arcadius, and ten others congregated around Joannes and Philippus. They appeared somber, tired, but attentive. Joannes gave instructions for the men to join the cavalrymen cutting trees, and to dislodge the rocks that made the road. He pointed to the top of the two hills and explained they were to build walls with the logs, and the rocks were to be piled behind them. Joannes wanted the work to be completed overnight. In the morning, archers were to be posted on the hills, along with men responsible for releasing the logs.

The men lit torches, and set to work. As night fell, more men started arriving. Most were not warriors; they looked like farmers, and carried axes, and poles. A fair number of them came on foot, and there were also horse-drawn carts carrying large numbers of men.

When Mateus arrived, he brought with him some thousand men of war, and more farmers. His soldiers were armed mostly with short spears and swords, and only a handful had bows—unlike the Isca men who all had bows as well as swords. But it was Joannes' cavalrymen who were the best armed. They had long, impressive lances, and also bows and swords.

Martin watched Joannes and Arcadius survey the men.

"We didn't get as many as I had hoped, Arcadius."

"That will have to do," the general said. "At least we have four thousand who know how to fight. The farmers can come down from the hills once the fighting starts, and help the soldiers."

"I hope we won't need them," Joannes said, "but tell them to be ready, just in case."

Martin learned that in Isca, only the cavalry was a standing army; the foot soldiers were civilians with military experience. If Joannes' estimate about the Caledonians was correct, they were outnumbered more than two to one. However, Joannes told Mateus that the cavalry was his secret weapon. It was no ordinary cavalry like the Romans had used, but much more deadly.

As the night wore on, Martin learned that Joannes' idea had been to copy the Greeks' use of cavalry for lightning strikes. The Romans had limited their use for the rapid deployment of troops, and they actually fought on horseback only against undisciplined formations, thinking them useless otherwise. Joannes had a different approach. He was a great admirer of Alexander the Great and his tactics, and had wanted to model his army after the great conqueror's design. Thanks to Arcadius, they had been able to train their thousand men and horses in the previous four years, but up to that day, those soldiers had not fought on horseback. They had mostly manned the walls at Isca. So no one, including Arcadius, from what Martin heard, had quite figured out if the cavalry would be any good against a real enemy.

Martin overhead Mateus and some of his men asking Arcadius how the horse soldiers fought; Mateus' assumption was that the horses were used to try and trample the enemy.

"No," said Arcadius, "they have been trained to fight with a long lance Joannes copied from the Greeks of old."

"I have seen people charge on horseback and swing a sword or throw a lance while riding," said Mateus, "but then the horse gets in the way, and the rider has to dismount. Not a good idea when you are surrounded by the enemy."

Still talking about it, they went to help with the work.

Martin felt tired. The image of the cave where he had spent the previous night came to mind.

He found the cave, and wondered if whoever watched him the night before would return. If someone could see him, it had to be someone like him, an astral being and not a ghost. Was that the special person the Kahuna mentioned who would open another world for him? That would be exciting. Martin entered the small opening, and a wonderful homey feeling enveloped him. He lay down in a corner, against a wall, looking toward the entrance, and fell asleep almost immediately.

Martin woke up with a jolt. He knew he wasn't alone; he felt a presence. Gingerly he looked around, careful not to make sudden movements in case he could be seen. Everything was dark, but almost in front of him, he saw an aura, a blue aura; it was ten feet away by the entrance, and Martin was sure it was facing him. Martin sat up, and it scurried away. He quickly followed, and realized the being was human and was trying to hide from him. Martin stopped a safe distance from the figure, now hiding behind a tree. The being could see him, he was certain. Martin stood for a moment and decided it was best to back away into the cave. He lay down, listening. After a short time he heard soft footsteps going away.

That was fascinating, a human who can see me. But who? Amazing. The thought was more exciting than disconcerting. He was certain the person had been able to see him…somehow. Perhaps the next time, he could approach whoever it was and show him or her that he was harmless. The excitement kept him awake for some time, but eventually he went back to sleep.

He woke up, saw light coming from the cave's entrance and knew it was dawn outside. Martin had slept peacefully in spite of the visitation and he wondered who had come that previous night. Obviously the visitor had been just as interested in him as he was in her….Strangely, now he realized it was a woman. Something about the presence had a female quality to it. That was interesting…but how did he know? At any rate, that would have to wait, now he had to return to the mountains.

Martin felt more optimistic about the possibility that Joannes and his men could persevere against the Caledonians. He still couldn't quite understand the full strategy. He knew Joannes planned to crush a good many of the Caledonians with the rocks and logs, but certainly the enemy was not going to march into the canyon and stand still while he let loose the rocks. And then, how many could he possibly kill that way? Two, three thousand? And then what? That still left some nine thousand he would have to face in combat. *But he seems to know what he's doing.*

When he arrived at the mountains the men were still hard at work. The log walls had not only been finished, but were already halfway filled with rocks, which were huge, and required four men to carry on poles tied in the shape of a cross. They had built thick, solid walls resembling dams. Apparently they had worked without stopping to eat or rest, judging by how much had been accomplished and how haggard they looked. The logs had been laid down one on top of the other, with vertical members every ten feet or so. These, in turn, were held in place by logs set at an angle with one end wedged against the vertical members, and the other firmly embedded in the ground. Thick ropes were tied to the tops of these angled logs, and it appeared they were going to use horses to pull and dislodge them, which in turn would make everything come tumbling down.

Joannes, Arcadius and a few others stood on the road inside the canyon, looking up at the work being accomplished.

"Those walls are too obvious," said Arcadius. "The enemy will notice them, figure out their purpose and climb around them."

"Not if they are too busy giving chase and fighting," said Joannes.

As the men continued the work, Martin heard Joannes call Arcadius, Mateus, Philippus, and eight other officers to discuss his plan.

Joannes was to take five hundred of his cavalry to the other side of the mountains and look for the Caledonians. Once they spotted them, Joannes would send a rider with the news, at which time Philippus, Arcadius and Mateus were to take the men to the top of the two hills, position them, and wait for Joannes and his men to make it through. Joannes was going to make the Caledonians chase him, and once past the canyon, they would position themselves to stop the enemy at the narrow exit.

"Don't worry," said Joannes, "five hundred men will stop the twelve thousand Caledonians long enough for my plan to work. With the enemy in the canyon, the men on top will release the logs and rocks. At this point, the archers on both hills will shoot"—he gravely looked at each man in turn— "with precision, control and total discipline."

All men were to keep working until the walls were filled to the brim with rocks, except for the sentinels. Then they could rest until the rider arrived. Joannes appeared confident, but perhaps it was for the benefit of those around him.

Mateus and the general walked off together.

"Your king's plan is impressive, but the primitives outnumber us two to one, and only four thousand of our men are warriors, Arcadius. From a military perspective we are bound to lose."

"That is correct, your Majesty."

"Then, there's nothing for us to do but try our best. I'm sad when I listen to my men, though. They are sure they're going to die."

Martin saw a quick smirk cross Arcadius' face. "Then we will all die fighting."

They all watched Joannes and his men ride out. Philippus raised a hand at the departing riders, apparently more in blessing than farewell.

Martin decided to accompany Joannes.

The mounted men rode until they came to a rise, a mile or so from the mountains. Joannes gathered his officers around him to go over his strategy. The four men took off their helmets and formed a circle around their king. From where they stood they could see the road for quite a distance, but they were not visible to anyone walking or riding up ahead.

"We are but a short ride at full gallop from the pass, but far enough for our purpose," he told them. "The spot is ideal for an ambush. All we need now is the enemy, and they are probably more than a day's ride up the road. The last I heard they hadn't yet reached Dunum."

This was a town Martin gathered was a day's ride away.

"Once ambushed," Joannes said, "it's important to have the enemy give fast chase, so make them very angry. Angry men are blind and don't think." He drew on the ground with his knife. Two hundred of the riders would form "the wedge." This involved charging on horseback to cut through the enemy's main body, then dismounting and forming a wall with their shields. The rest of the men would shoot five fast arrows each at the Caledonians at either side of the wedge, and each arrow had to hit a target. A hundred men were to remain shooting at the enemy. Two hundred additional men would charge the enemy troops isolated from the main body. Once they were decimated, these riders were to protect the wedge troops while they mounted. "Then ride back to the canyon as fast as your horses can go. Leave the wounded behind." They were to dismount at the narrow end of the canyon and take up a wall formation.

The four officers nodded, stood and went back to their men.

Now it was time to locate the Caledonians. Joannes selected six men to accompany him. They were now scouts and had to shed the extra weight of armor, helmets and supplies from their horses, and keep just enough food and water for two days. Joannes was certain they would locate the Caledonians within a day or so. He instructed the rest of the men to take positions on either side of the road. Then they were to rest, for a hard battle awaited them all.

Joannes and his six scouts rode quietly on the right side of the road. He seemed to be scanning the clouds above, listening intently. Martin noticed they spoke in whispers. They rode in single file, skirting the forest; sometimes going in, and coming out when it became too dense.

After about two hours of riding, they heard sounds from up ahead: yells, hollers, and horses whinnying. The forest opened up to a clearing, and as they approached, they could see what had been a peaceful valley, but was now a chaotic mess of ruined farms, and burnt houses. They had found the Caledonians.

There were campfires all around, and it seemed they were getting ready to break camp and get moving. Apparently they had feasted that previous night; there were signs of slaughtered animals and the smell of roasted meat still hung in the air. It was already close to noon, and it seemed they were in no great hurry to move on.

Martin heard Joannes whispering. He never expected the Caledonians to be so close. They had reached the hills just ahead of this throng, just in time. Only a day later and the enemy would have crossed the mountains. Muttering, perhaps to himself, Joannes reflected that it would have been impossible to stop them in open country.

Martin decided to wander in, to look around and see what these Caledonians were like. Joannes and his men had started to make their way back to rejoin the rest of the advance party.

Martin noticed there were men and women, even some children. The men looked like the ones he had already seen: crude clothes, largely unkempt, and with lots of tattoos. The women were also rough looking, dirty and smelly. He noticed some were wearing finer clothes, presumably taken from the people they had killed, as these women were obviously not used to them. They kept looking at the fabric, feeling it. Martin wandered on, trying to understand the language.

There was a man and a woman, apparently husband and wife, talking. He held her hand and she looked at him with teary eyes. Was she worried about him?

Their campsites were somewhat orderly and most of the tents had been set up in rows. As he neared one of them, he heard a low murmur, a rhythmic sound, the unmistakable sound of prayer. Inside stood a young man, impressively clean by contrast to the rest, staring absently straight ahead. His aura, Martin noticed was blue, with a gold tint.

The sight took him by surprise. Never would he have imagined seeing anyone like that here. The rest of the auras he had seen were mostly red and blue. But here was what looked like a different soul, and a very different person altogether. The man spoke in low tones, repeating the same words over and over again. His gaze became fixed, as his face broke into joyful rapture. His arms rose and opened in front of him, as though ready to receive something. The Caledonian then was silent, and very still, in what seemed like a meditative state, or perhaps a state of grace. *What form of prayer has this man used? Whatever it is, it works. How many more like him are there in this group? If he's so spiritual, why is he a part of this awful bunch?* Martin wished he could talk to him, ask him. Instead he stood looking at the man. The Caledonian was rather handsome, perhaps in his mid-twenties. His hair was reddish-brown just like that of Joannes, and he was about as tall. He let out a sigh, turned to pick up his sword and shield, and walked out. He handled the weapons with familiarity…but, it seemed to Martin, a reluctant familiarity.

Outside, the Caledonians were starting to amass on the road, finally ready to move out. Martin noticed who the leaders were. They shouted the orders, and men obeyed. He saw the young man approach one of the leaders. They seemed to be of equal rank and spoke amiably. A third man now came with a horse for the young man. In a fluid motion he climbed on the horse, his shield on one arm. Martin scanned the throng, observing men getting ready to ride, women washing pots and pans and utensils, children playing. Normal people doing normal things. But then again, they had just destroyed the place around them. He could see slaughtered animals lying in fields; houses still smoldering;

and the bodies of peasants, some of them children, not far from their houses. And here they were, they had spent the night feasting. What about the young man? Had he also slaughtered, and then gone in and prayed?

The camp was dismantled, horses packed. Then the Caledonians assembled and started moving on down the road. Absently, Martin followed them. After some four hours of marching he recognized, up ahead, the rise where Joannes and his men were hiding. He noticed the Caledonians going down the road en masse, no formation, and as many men abreast as the road could hold. They marched about twenty across, with some more riders and foot soldiers spilling over on either side as far as the line of trees.

Men and women and even children were mixed in groups, conceivably clans or extended families. They reached and were passing the rise with nothing happening, and no sign of anyone. Then Martin noticed movement in the forest, the movement became men on horseback, charging the front end of the Caledonians. The attack was swift, and surreal. The Caledonians at first did not appear to realize they were being attacked, as they looked, puzzled, in the direction of the forest. Arrows were hitting men and beasts, as the horsemen from Isca cut a swath through the Caledonians, and were now holding the main body back, while other riders attacked the men in front, maybe five hundred or so. The attackers were deadly on their horses and kept them moving constantly at a fast clip back and forth across the road, mowing down the Caledonians like a knife going through butter. They wielded their long lances expertly, using the momentum of their horses. Some appeared unstable on their mounts, falling off when thrusting with their lances, and others were pulled down, but overall they were effective.

In a moment the attack was over, and the men from Isca escaped at full gallop down the road. It took a while for the Caledonians to regroup, but now they were shouting, circling around their dead comrades on the road. Some men were already in pursuit, while others were yelling at the main group to follow. Anger was heavy in the air. After a pause, the entire group was giving chase; women and children included, those on horseback in front. The young man Martin had seen praying was now riding at full gallop, sword in hand.

As the Caledonians gave chase they seemed to grow angrier, those on horseback frantically beating their horses, trying to catch their attackers. But the riders from Isca kept increasing their lead, better horses and riders, apparently.

Martin saw the Caledonians approach the mountains, and in a relatively short time those on horseback were in between the two hills. Those on foot kept pouring in behind them, and they all were screaming what seemed as fierce battle cries. It appeared the entire horde was amassing between the two hills. Martin heard the sound of battle up ahead. In the back, men were trying desperately to get to the front, pushing and shoving, almost climbing over one another. The men in front were battling furiously, but because of the narrow pass only about eighty could engage the enemy at any one time. The others piled up behind, unable to go any further.

Martin went to the front and saw the Isca men, led by Joannes and Arcadius, holding back the pushing throng, but with difficulty. The Caledonians that were able to fight were doing so with brutal efficiency. They wielded their long, two-handed axes with devastating results, slicing through shields and armor. Some simply slammed themselves against the wall formation, knocking down soldiers. The Caledonians attacked in waves, and it seemed that with each wave they were getting closer to making it through. Martin saw how one group of the attackers managed to make a big gap in the defensive line, but before they could push on through, the gap was quickly filled.

Anxiously, Martin wondered what kept the Isca men on the hills from releasing their boulders.

In the rear the Caledonians kept coming. The men in back were now facing a solid mass of their own men, and realizing they could not get through, were eyeing the mountains, looking for a route over the top.

At that moment a thunderous sound enveloped them, as though the mountains were coming apart. Men and beasts frantically started looking around to escape. The big rocks hurtled down, bouncing, obliterating everything in their path; each rock like a huge cannonball cutting through a solid mass of flesh. Along with the rocks, arrows started pouring down from both sides.

Men were falling down, yelling, some pulling arrows from their shoulders, arms, or legs, and trying at the same time to dodge the big rocks. The place became a heap of men and horses, unable to move in any direction. Martin saw one man wield his ax around at his own men, apparently in desperation. There was dying all around, no place to run, and no one to fight. Chaos gripped the Caledonians. The ones in back were now trying to get away, only to be pierced by arrows while stumbling across the fallen rocks and dead bodies.

Martin noticed how methodical the Isca archers were. They had switched from shooting at the main throng, to picking off the men in the back. The arrows rained from one side, then the other, as the Caledonians vainly tried to protect themselves with their shields. After some time the rocks stopped tumbling, and there was only the piercing sound of horses whinnying, men yelling, metal clashing against metal, and the horrible whistle of arrows coming down in clouds. It was hard to see through the dust that had come down with the rocks, but Martin could sense death and dying. It was a dreadful place of agony. He felt sorry for the Caledonians...sorry for the poor horses. It was a terrible scene. But worse, was the feeling: a pervasive sense of horror and loss, agony and the certainty of death. The feeling tore up Martin's insides; it was intense and somehow familiar. He felt terribly broken up inside, as though the rocks were tearing him up, and the arrows piercing his flesh.

He noticed how people and animals died, some auras fading off slowly, some going off suddenly. And occasionally he saw the blue shimmering images of astral bodies, looking around in amazement. But they didn't seem to see him, apparently too engrossed in their own drama.

There were relatively few Caledonians left standing, maybe five hundred. They appeared to have fallen into a state of shock, dumbly looking around at their fallen comrades. Martin had expected them to retreat, to run into the forest, and some did, but most of them stood silent...some wounded, some protecting their women and children, standing in front of them with their shields. The sound of battle diminished and then stopped. With relief, Martin saw that the deadly arrows also had stopped. The men from Isca and Lindinus descended from the hills, to surround the remaining Caledonians, who threw down their weapons.

It was over.

Martin felt compelled to leave. He started down the road in the direction of Isca. Maybe he was just too soft, he thought. What did he expect? He knew they were going to do battle. The men from Isca and Lindinus had to defend their lands. And the invaders, the aggressors had been defeated. Why did he feel so awful? He should be jubilant, glad Joannes and his men had triumphed. But it had been so violent, too brutal. It wasn't just killing, it was the tearing up of men and beasts who didn't die right away but remained suffering; it was the loss, the grief to come...endless, long grief. Why did the Caledonians have to come? Why invade? If they had just stayed home, they would all be alive. Alive with their families, tending their farms, fishing, and whatever the hell else they did.

A thought stopped him. How were Joannes and Philippus? It hadn't occurred to Martin until now that they might be injured or dead. He knew Joannes' men had sustained casualties. He had seen men lying on the road bloodied. Suddenly worried, he turned around.

At the battle scene the wounded were being gathered and tended. Martin looked for Joannes and Philippus, trying to ignore the carnage all around him.

He looked for the familiar figures, and finally saw both of them in between a group of men. They were both fine. Joannes stood giving orders, organizing the clearing of the battlefield. Martin realized that all Joannes cared about at that moment was his men, the dead and the wounded, and the swift disposal of those whose wounds were fatal—both friend and foe, human and beast.

A group of soldiers were going around with swords in hand, mercifully dispatching the fatally wounded.

Martin saw the release from pain when a sword struck a heart, but he also saw and felt the fear when the wounded saw the man with the sword approach. The fortunate ones were unconscious.

Now that Martin knew that the father and son were fine, he could go. They would probably remain for at least a day, clearing the place of debris and burying the dead. Martin decided to meet up with them later on.

Where would he go? Maybe the Kahuna could help him answer the questions that were pounding in his head. Martin yearned for his peaceful presence, the soft feeling that emanated from him. What would he ask? *Why do men have to do battle? Why the killing, the violence? Why do nice people do terrible things?* His thoughts went back to the young Caledonian, and in his mind Martin saw him praying, his face reflecting devotion and love. Martin was sure the young man had killed. In his mind he saw Joannes and Philippus. They had killed that day as well, and probably quite a few. And what was the difference between them, the men from Isca and the Caledonians? Judging by their auras, absolutely none. In fact he had not seen an aura with gold on the Isca side; but there, among the Caledonians, he knew at least one such person existed, or had existed.

Martin kept on walking for some time, feeling an ever-present rawness. Perhaps the problem was that he wasn't suited for life. He knew people took pride in going to war. Was it the adrenaline rush? He remembered reading about soldiers saying they had never felt more alive than when in combat. He knew people got used to killing. Back at the battle scene just a moment ago, he had seen men from Isca slapping each other on the back, laughing. Some had kicked wounded Caledonians, wanting to inflict more pain, more death. In some, he had seen the relish of victory, and they appeared to be in a state of euphoria. At that moment, Martin thought of hunters. They took pleasure in killing as well. *Maybe hunters make good soldiers.*

He found himself at the meadow. So much suffering—why? For what reason? What did it accomplish? He realized the Kahuna was in front of him, somber eyes studying him intently.

"Hello, Martin."

His voice was gentle, his manner calm as usual. Martin felt enveloped in the man's sweetness. They sat on the grass. There was silence for some time, as Martin let the peace from the Kahuna slowly seep in, clearing his heart and mind. He took deep breaths, and felt his body start to relax. The heaviness lifted somewhat, but its imprint remained in his heart.

"You have discovered a part of yourself, my friend. I am sorry it's painful." The Kahuna's voice was gentle, reassuring. Martin found comfort in his manner, his presence. But his words were wrong.

"A part of myself? It's the world that seems to be awful." Martin's mind was now much clearer, his thoughts felt concise. "All the killing, the suffering. I seem to feel it in my bones, deep inside." He felt his voice get choked up with emotion. "And yes, why is the world like this? Why, if there is a God, and he could have created anything, anything at all, why create a world like this? And why did you bring me here, to witness all that carnage?"

Martin saw compassion in the Kahuna's face, and he saw understanding, but also, surprisingly, there was relief.

"Many lessons are learned in the battlefield, and those souls are learning them. But in your case, you already have gone through many battles like that one."

"Is that why it's so hard on me, because I have been there before?"

"My dear Martin, It's not just the sheer brutality of war that upsets you. The world as you perceive it is crude, cruel and base, and war is just a good example, isn't it?"

Martin didn't know what to say.

"Think about what really bothers you, dear friend. What happened recently? A coyote killed your cat, and someone arbitrarily used his power to dominate you by wiping out your firm's contract. Isn't that true?"

"Yes, but why are you mentioning both incidents as though they were connected?"

"Because they are, in nature and in your heart. Predation in the animal kingdom keeps species evolving by weeding out the weak and keeping populations in check."

"You are saying that the contract…"

"I'm saying that brutality is a cornerstone of creation. And it seems the universe spares no expense in reminding you of it. An accident on the road, your cat dying, the contract taken away, a battle, or just the fact that we grow old."

The Kahuna looked at him with tenderness. "Or how about when the lawyers attacked you when all you did was own a building and try and be a good landlord? They saw weakness and pounced. Money and power are always just a tool. What they were after was dominance. It's the same story everywhere, all around you. Politics, business, everything is permeated by the same element. But don't blame them. Like the coyote, they are just following their nature, their state of consciousness. Eventually, after much pain and misery, their hearts will open and they will change. Just like you."

Just like me?

Apparently able to read his mind, the Kahuna added: "Yes, dear Martin, just like you. Some time ago, you felt no pain because there was nothing for you to feel with. You killed and thought nothing of it. Then you learned to love and your suffering began, but your awakening also began. Then you started to see life as brutal, and you sought diversions, mainly by staying in motion, never stopping to look. Now you can't avoid but face with full awareness how the universe operates. You are at the stage where you want things to be different. And it's all inside you," The Kahuna said.

"What do you mean, inside me? I have to operate in the world the way it is. How can something inside me change the world?"

The Kahuna smiled. "I need to teach you some looking skills."

"Looking skills?"

"Yes, how to look at yourself, and how to look at the world. But not here. There is more for you here, you are not done. But first, we should go back to Hawaii. This place can wait."

The thought of going back made Martin feel relieved. He sighed, and looked at the Kahuna. "Yes, I would like to take a rest from this place. Thank you."

This time the Kahuna took him by the hand. Again Martin felt motion, as if he were in a whirlpool. The motion increased, and the great roaring sound enveloped him. He felt as though he were in a hurricane, except he was the hurricane.

Finally all was still.

Martin's body felt coarse, heavy. At first it seemed too heavy, suffocating. Then he felt his lungs heave and his heart beat. He opened his eyes. He saw the Kahuna's smiling face in front of him, except there was no scintillating light. Everything, including the Kahuna, looked dense, gross in its physicality. Martin looked down and saw his wet body, felt drops of water running down his cheeks, his chest. He had just been swimming, he reminded himself. Waves were lapping up to the rock where he and the Kahuna were sitting. Out on the beach he saw the couple with the child.

The whole world was heavy, thick. It was oppressive, but with each breath he seemed to get better, and things seemed to become lighter.

"Well my friend, here you are…back in your world," the Kahuna said.

CHAPTER SIX

Everything was hard, requiring unusual effort. Just walking away from the rock and to his spot where he had left his things, proved laborious. His legs felt clumsy, like walking on stilts. The air going in and out his lungs felt as though he were breathing through a bellows.

Back at the condo Martin found himself distracted by the demands of his body. He became aware of the many times he went to the bathroom and how often he had to drink water. One moment he was hot, the next he felt an itch, then he had to cough, or wipe sweat off his face. He was conscious of how hard his feet came down on the ground, of the jarring it caused his body, and of how stiff and heavy his body seemed.

Martin found it odd that it was only eleven of that same Sunday morning. He had left the condo a little before eight. Now he was back after three very full days, yet only three hours had passed.

He had agreed with the Kahuna that they would meet again the following afternoon, right around sunset, at the same place.

He felt a mishmash of emotions. He was relieved to be back. He also felt that he was about to cure his depression. The Kahuna was right about its cause, the deep seated sense of brutality and uncertainty. But also, Martin was excited about his past life, and he wanted to know more about Joannes.

He kept seeing in his mind the violent scenes from the battle, especially the mercy killings. He remembered watching as a young man held an older man's head in his lap, probably a son comforting his father dying from a deep stomach wound, his entrails spilling over on the ground beside him. A man then came over, and stood silently for a moment in front of the father, sword in hand. The son and the man exchanged glances, and the son kissed his father's forehead as the man stabbed quickly in the heart without saying a word. The son had then remained by the corpse for some time. *How can people endure such things?*

Martin walked back into the living room and stared at the phone for a moment. He felt anxious about Adam; he wanted reassurance that he was fine, that nothing bad was happening, and he wanted to hear his son's voice. It was time to call home. Then he remembered that he had called the day before.... It felt like a lifetime ago. He looked at his watch. It was eleven-thirty; in California it would be two-thirty. His wife and son would still be at Jenny's mother's house. Martin made the call.

When he hung up he was glad he had called, the sound of Adam's voice had filled a gap in his heart. Jenny on the other hand, had sounded matter-of-fact. Obviously she was glad he was gone.

Years ago, when Adam had been around three, Jenny had made green eggs and ham. They had read Adam the Doctor Seuss story and the following morning she had gone through all the trouble to make them the colored eggs and ham. The boy had been amused and Martin deeply touched. They all laughed as they ate the colorful breakfast. Martin remembered her face as she laughed.

That had been around the time they had gotten the kittens. One day Jenny told Martin how much she missed the cat she had as a child. That same afternoon they went to the pound and got two small kittens. "Two, so they'll keep each other company," she had said. Actually, Martin knew it was because she couldn't stand to separate them, as they were brother and sister.

Martin sighed. He decided to go out and get lunch. He walked out of the building and down the street alongside the ocean. As he sat at a table waiting for his order, he thought again about the battle. Now it felt remote. It belonged to another era, more than fifteen hundred years ago. *Did it really happen?* What if the Kahuna had hypnotized him? The whole experience entirely made up by the Kahuna? *Interesting.*

Then Martin decided it didn't make much difference, because he would still want the experience and what it was doing for him. If at some point he could lead a happy life, if that was to be the end result, then nothing else mattered.

The waitress brought his food, a fish burger with home fries, and a milkshake. Simple food, but at that moment it seemed like the best meal in the world, he was so hungry. Maybe his mind was telling him he hadn't eaten for three days.

That night Martin dreamt about the battle. He woke up in the middle of the night, his heart throbbing, with vivid images from the dream still wedged in his mind. Again he could see people dying, being crushed by the rocks over and over again, screaming. *That battle happened just a few hours ago.* Time would take the edge off; he knew that.

He tried to think of something else. He reviewed in his mind some of the fun times he had spent with Adam. They used to go for long hikes on Saturdays with the dogs. It was a challenge to see how tired they could get, so they would sometimes hike for eight hours, all at a brisk pace, then come home and plop down to huge amounts of liquid refreshments, snacks, and a couple of video movies. That was a lot of fun. He wondered when was the last time they did that. Maybe a year? Then there were all the times they had gone to Japanese restaurants and they would bet who could eat the most horseradish. Adam would end up stuffing his mouth with the stuff, tears rolling down his cheeks. *What a sight.* He'd have to do that again with the kid, when he got back.

That afternoon as he left for the beach, Martin thought to pack something. Then he laughed. He would probably be back in three hours, but there was no telling, in actuality, how long he would be gone. Anyway, there was nothing to pack; he didn't need anything where he was going.

Martin drove up to the resort entrance. The man with the red hair was gone, and instead a young kid looked at him from inside the booth. *What if the Kahuna isn't there?* Martin had expected for everything to be the same for the thing to work, the magic. He hurried down the road and sprinted the whole way to the beach, anxiety pressing his chest.

He was relieved when he saw the familiar figure on the rock. The moment he stepped on the sand from the trail, he noticed him: his gaze, a smile and a small wave of the hand.

Martin looked around. This time the beach was deserted, except for a large dog at the very end who appeared to be staring at the horizon. It was a malamute, and it reminded Martin of Nicolaus' wolf. Its owner didn't seem to be around. Maybe it was lost. Martin decided that afterward he would investigate whom the animal belonged to. He then heard the Kahuna and his voice pulled his attention.

"You seem rested, Martin. I'm glad you made good use of your time." The Kahuna wore the same clothes, a loose white shirt and beige pants. His long black hair flowed freely in the breeze.

"I am rested and well, thank you." He seated himself in front of the man. He was going to learn how to look; then, off to Britain.

The Kahuna asked him how much he knew about meditation. Martin told him he had practiced on and off for about five years. Both he and Jenny had studied yoga meditation, and it seemed to be helpful for relaxing, and relieving stress.

The Kahuna asked Martin to close his eyes, and proceeded to guide him. His words carried an energy that made things happen; it was as though everything he said became so. First, he told him to relax, and Martin felt tension he didn't even know he had leave him, and his body felt limp. The Kahuna then told him to take three deep breaths and expel them, and with each exhalation to let go of all tensions and thoughts; and that's how it was— his mind became a sea of calm. Then Martin was instructed to sit with his spine straight, with his hands comfortably on his lap, and to be still; and Martin felt as though he were carved out of stone.

"The you who thinks, the you who uses that body and experiences life, is the you who has always been and always will be. You don't die, you were never born." The Kahuna's voice seemed like his own, as though it was his own voice coming from inside his head. "When you take on the physical consciousness you are deluded into seeing yourself as the mortal self. This is part of the process of self-creation. This process started when you decided to become like God and this is the painful route you took, a physical entity separated from your divine self. Now we are going to make that physical consciousness disappear." Martin felt the Kahuna's finger at the point between his eyebrows. He saw a golden light, but not with his eyes; it was rather that he could sense it. He felt drawn to it; it gave him the impression of deep serenity. A blue ring surrounded the golden glow.

He heard the sound of bees that shortly became more like bells, crystal bells, and it was music; it had a melodic quality. Then he felt an energy that was like fire coming up his spine, until it stopped at the point between his eyebrows and the bells became a roar. Martin felt the Kahuna's touch still at the point between his eyebrows. His voice told him this was his spiritual eye, and to concentrate all his attention there, and the point became the center of his being. The roar became louder, and as it increased his body seemed to melt with it, to flow with the sound and the light. Then he became aware of the most extraordinary peace in his heart that began to spread over his body. Martin's breath slowed down as the peace increased until it reached a point of no breath and total peace. His body was happy to expel the breath, and the peace was all over, no longer localized in his body but everywhere and in everything, and he was everywhere and everything. Then he noticed in this place, this state, there was another being who was as much a part of him as his own self, and he felt an overwhelming sense of completeness and belonging. At this his heart was filled...and he was totally and utterly complete and whole, in a joy that seemed ever to increase, filling everything. He was in the presence of the Other, part of the Other. There were no words, no thoughts...only presence...and he wanted to dive in completely, to become one.

Martin didn't know how long had passed, but he felt the Kahuna touch his hand. He opened his eyes, still feeling the deep joy. *This is love, real love, real being, real life, reality.*

For a time they were both silent, Martin wanting to keep the feeling he had in his heart, reveling in it for as long as he could, knowing it would eventually dissipate.

"You just got a taste of who you really are...and of your new looking skill."

Oh, yes, if that was the true self, then he really wanted to become that. It was definitely worthwhile going to hell and back for.

"But it's not only me, is it? I felt something that was not me, but where I belonged."

"Yes, there is more than you in the physical sense. What you call it doesn't matter, but it is there."

What should he call it? Martin knew it was way beyond anything he could possibly verbalize. He perceived it with his heart, still throbbing with overwhelming joy…with his whole being that at that moment was transfixed, transformed.

The Kahuna had been following his thoughts. "You don't need to call it anything, as long as you know that it is there for you to be with; and you know how to go there, to be with it, her or him, the total."

Martin knew he had touched an indescribable being or state of being, a part of himself, but also beyond anything he had ever experienced.

"Martin, you now know what it is that you are seeking. You know it exists."

"I assume there was a reason you gave me this training here and not in my astral body."

"You needed your physical body for this phase of your learning."

Yes, now he realized the whole point was to transcend his physical self. *Like an obstacle course.*

"I am very grateful for this experience, for all you have done for me. What can I ever do to repay you?"

The Kahuna smiled and Martin thought he saw his eyes become a bit moist. "Get to your destination."

"My destination. I imagine that will require a lot of meditation."

"Yes, meditation will become the mainstay of your practice, but it alone won't do it. To be one with Spirit, you need to let go of demons you acquired through many lives."

"Demons?"

"Yes, the fears, attachments and misperceptions that keep you bound to this world. Everything that makes up your physical consciousness."

"And how exactly do I let go?"

"As you practice meditation you will start seeing right through your misperceptions, to a deeper reality, to the one moment of total understanding. Then you can start letting go of your demons."

Martin knew what the Kahuna meant. Everything was now clear…so clear. He could feel the attachments, the demons, and he could sense that he would come to a moment of completeness...of understanding...of acceptance.

"I will do whatever is required. Just tell me."

"When you go back to Britain you will face some very crucial moments."

"Crucial...for me or for others?" Martin had the feeling he was supposed to do something important for someone; it was a hunch he felt very powerfully at that moment.

"For yourself there is one moment, what you will identify as the dance of life and death. That will be your moment of total understanding, when you will embrace creation."

The dance of life and death is the key. Somehow the Kahuna's words were imparted with some special meaning, and Martin realized that the moment he was talking about was a magic catalyst of some sort for him.

"Then you can be of great service to someone," the Kahuna said.

Martin understood that he was being prepared for a mission. The thought made him happy, as though he had been waiting a long time to come to that very point, that awareness.

It was time to go. That was enough instruction for one day. The Kahuna told him to practice what he had been taught and to meet him the next day at noon.

As he got up, Martin looked at the end of the beach. The large dog was gone. In semi-darkness he made his way back to his car.

That night he sat on a chair to meditate. He felt his body relax, and peace start in his heart, but then after some time it seemed to go away. As the minutes passed, he found himself daydreaming. He tried again, but it was the same. Then he got tired of trying. Frustrated, he decided to go for a walk before his next attempt.

Martin sat again to meditate, but almost the same thing happened. Obviously he had been able to attain the higher state because of the Kahuna. By himself it seemed hopeless. *So much for my new self.* If he couldn't meditate he knew his depression would return. He went to bed.

As morning broke, he decided to meditate no matter what. There was no way he would live his life the old way. Maybe, like the Buddha, he would not get up until he felt the presence of Spirit, as he did at the beach. Maybe that kind of determination would do it.

Martin skipped breakfast and instead drank some juice. Then he showered, put on a comfortable jogging outfit, pulled up the chair and tried again. He sat for over three hours, with just a little tinge of peace flowing into his heart, but no other sign, nothing. He stopped when he felt as though his head was full of cotton. At times he caught himself nodding off to sleep. It became an exercise in frustration, and he wondered why the Kahuna put him through it.

This time he went to the beach crestfallen.

The Kahuna told him how crucial the breath was, to observe it and not try and control it. The breath would take him deeper and deeper into a state of peace, and then he could go into a state of wholeness. He also told Martin that intention was key; he needed to know what he wanted, and to make the effort, but not to expect anything, as expectation was rooted in physical consciousness, and was a burden. With that he instructed him to go back and try again. They agreed to meet the following day at two in the afternoon.

Martin went back to the condo, and as soon as he closed the door behind him, he went to his chair. He sat down with his spine erect, his hands resting on his lap. Then he lifted his gaze and his attention to his spiritual eye. He wanted so much to experience the Spirit he had met, a sweetness that seemed so far away. He tried not to have any expectations, but he wanted that state desperately.

To his relief, the sounds started again: this time the bells preceded the roaring, and led him in a short time into a state of well-being. Then there was that feeling of completeness and Martin relaxed into it; with each breath he took off a layer of…the world. Martin saw the light, the beautiful light, and it seemed to carry him off. He opened his awareness to what was there and then the miracle happened. Again he felt the presence of the Other.

He went out to breakfast, still feeling the afterglow of his meditation. Martin had thought that after finding such joy he would stay in meditation for many hours, but he found his mind pulled away and then started to wander. *It must be like any other skill; one needs practice.* However, now he knew he could meditate anytime he wanted, and he could do it without the Kahuna. *Alleluia.*

He picked a restaurant facing the road that fronted the ocean on that part of Kona. As he sat waiting for his order he noticed a young girl walking a puppy without a leash. The small dog was way too playful, exploring and sniffing, meeting strangers who bent over to pet him. Martin got a sick feeling in his stomach that something bad was going to happen. In a matter of seconds the puppy noticed a leaf on the road being blown by passing cars. He bounded into the middle of traffic and was immediately run over. Martin sat transfixed, with the blood drained out of his face. The dog lay on the road, as the girl stood gasping at the curb. The car that hit the puppy never stopped.

Martin went over and gently picked up the dog. Its eyes were still open, and save for the trickle of blood coming out of its mouth, it might still be alive. But it was dead; there was no heartbeat, no breath. Martin laid the dog by the girl's feet. He avoided looking at her. Anger had overtaken him—anger at her, at the driver of the car, at the world. He went back to his table, halfway noticing the people staring at him. He left a twenty-dollar bill and left without touching his food.

He walked along the sidewalk looking out to sea, with sorrow and anger flooding through him. In his mind he could see the dead puppy's face, sweet, innocent. With a jolt he then remembered his dog. At the age of three he had watched as Jake was hit by a car in front of their house. He had been watching him play in the front lawn through the living room window. Martin could now recall the room, the feel of the glass on his face, the chair to his side…and that it was a red car that had hit his dog as it ran out into the street.

He then thought of his cat Gimpy. *Sorrow comes in many different packages.*

Martin stopped by the short wall that separated the sidewalk from the ocean. He stood absentmindedly looking at the waves. His heart felt heavy.

In rapid succession the images of the puppy, of Jake and Gimpy vanished, and to Martin's mind now came the memory of his grandmother Marina. A sweet pang filled his chest. He could see her as she read a book to him as a child; he could hear her voice, and the smell of her breath, and her hand caressing his head as she read. How did he forget her? At what point had he stopped missing her, and how? Had he put the thought of her out of his mind because it was too painful…or too scary?

Below him the waves were crashing. They had cremated her body, and spread her ashes in this same ocean, the Pacific Ocean, out there in California just beyond the Golden Gate. Maybe small particles of her were still in those waves.

Martin remembered going to the hospital to see her, and how his mother clutched his hand, and the face of the nurse who had intercepted them with the news. Grandma had died. They walked into her room, and there she was, with a big tube sticking out of her mouth. Things became fuzzy after that. But he remembered staring at her leg, her hand, and he knew that she was gone. Then came the boat and the spreading of the ashes…and emptiness.

At the condo he sat looking out the window, breathing deeply, wanting to erase the image of the dead puppy, and Jake, and Grandma's body lying with a tube sticking out of her mouth.

At one o'clock he picked up the car keys and headed out the door to meet the Kahuna.

The beach had some people on it now; there was a group of young men, probably in their early twenties, carrying on at the entrance to the beach. No matter—sitting on his rock was the Kahuna.

As Martin started toward the Kahuna, he had to walk through the middle of the young men. On his way by he accidentally knocked over a beer can that had been propped up on the sand. He looked over for the owner, intending to apologize, and was met by a drunken face. The young man looked him over and uttered a string of profanities with an anger that surprised Martin. He stood still, smelling trouble. Now the six or seven young men had him surrounded. One, a wiry blond, stood in front of him in a karate pose, one leg slightly off the ground, apparently ready to strike. Martin felt fear at first, a paralyzing fear, but then intense anger flowed through him. He felt his body flow with adrenaline, and the anger surge to the point where he didn't care whether he lived or died. He wanted to fight, and above all he wanted to hit, to destroy. As the young man raised his leg, another grabbed Martin's arm, and he felt his hair being pulled from behind. Then something—a sound, a force, coming from the ocean—enveloped the group, himself included, all froze, almost suspended in midair, while the word "stop" resonated, vibrated. Martin knew there was no alternative but to obey. He felt the force in his gut and all around. Then he heard the Kahuna say, "Go," and he knew it was directed at the men around him. After a pause, they left without a word. Angry and shaken, Martin stood motionless for some time, then turned and went over to the Kahuna, who was serenely looking at him, as though nothing of great consequence had happened.

Martin realized the Kahuna had done something to get rid of the gang. He sat down at his usual place in front of him. He started calming himself, watching his breath, focusing on the spiritual eye. Breath by breath, the sense of himself started to return.

After some time the Kahuna spoke. "Feeling better..." It was more a statement than a question.

"Yes. And thank you for helping with the gang. Without you here, I'm sure they would have beaten me up. I just wonder, what exactly did you do to get rid of them?"

"Eventually you too will learn how to project your energy, your chi. Sometimes the knowledge just comes to you, if you want it."

"How exactly do things come to me, just like that?"

"The more you are your true self, the more you will realize all knowledge, all power is yours."

"Can't wait for some of that knowledge to come my way." Martin was completely calm, maybe even calmer than before.

"Now, about the gang." The Kahuna spoke slowly and deliberately. "Why do you think that episode happened?"

Happened? Why did it happen? *Chance…no, of course not.* Now he understood; the Kahuna had orchestrated the whole thing to teach him something. But what? To keep calm, to stay centered, no matter what. It had been a test to see if he would lose himself in anger.

"You set the whole thing up, didn't you? Somehow you can bring people and events around for a desired effect. Can't you?"

"No, my friend, not me. It was you who brought the young men to the beach."

"Me? And how exactly did I do that?"

He saw the Kahuna smile—a subtle smile with his eyes.

"You attracted the young men directly and forcefully. You wanted them here."

"But I never made that decision; I never conceptualized a scenario where a gang would attack me…"

"No, your conscious mind is not capable of such a thing, at least not yet."

"Maybe you could tell me the mechanics of how, without my knowing, I decided to get attacked by a gang, then made them appear."

"There's a part of you which is tremendously powerful, infinitely so. But this element is dormant, and it will someday be awakened. Until you learn who you are, and how to master yourself, this part of you responds to certain triggers and sets events in motion."

"Almost like being pre-programmed?"

"No, not pre-programmed, more like a chemical reaction. There is a difference. The world around you responds to who you are at that very moment. When you change, it changes. Change can come about by a powerful emotion, a new perspective, sometimes by sheer will power, and best of all, through a change in consciousness."

"So how did I call on the gang?"

"You reached a point where several things needed to come to the surface, so that element in you called on the gang."

"And the young men, did they agree to participate?"

"Yes, they also needed you, so you can say at some level they agreed."

"And what was the purpose of the event? As far as I can tell it was just a nasty incident."

The Kahuna raised a hand with four fingers outstretched. With the other hand he started counting off one finger at a time.

"Number one," he indicated with his forefinger, "the incident showed you the role you play in your own destiny, how you manifest events in your life. You manifested the gang; and maybe this will also help you understand how you bring about everything else in your life, including the death and drama that has caused so much havoc. Number two, you learned how powerful delusion is, how it works through your emotions to keep you bound. When I asked you not to get involved when you were in Britain, you didn't quite understand why. Now perhaps you will. Number three, this incident was triggered by your anger. You need to come to terms with this demon. And number four, you felt capable of violence. You now realize we all have the same potential for anger and violence, as well as for peace. This is a very complex issue for us all, but as we evolve we have a choice."

Martin took a deep breath. If he could only see things that clearly! He then recalled how Mojo had told him he had manufactured his crises.

"Do you know Mojo?"

The Kahuna smiled. "Yes, I know him."

"Do the two of you work together?"

"In a way you could say that. Destiny has brought us together in a number of lives, some involving you."

I knew it. Mojo is somehow connected to me…and the Kahuna too?

"You are telling me both you and Mojo are a part of my past? A past life?"

The Kahuna looked solemn. "Martin, please focus on what's important. Don't get sidetracked and start looking for people from your present life, in Britain. That's a diversion!"

"Love is not a diversion. The connection we have with people in our lives is important."

The Kahuna stared at Martin, perhaps a bit sad, or concerned.

"I heard what you said before," Martin said, "to keep in mind what's important, and I am! You gave me a taste of my true self, and I will go towards attaining that consciousness with relentless effort. But what's the harm in finding that sacred connection of the heart?"

The Kahuna still looked rather sullen, but he shook his head and his eyes smiled. "You are correct. If you maintain a healthy approach in your spiritual pursuit, this will translate to how you deal with issues like this one. Very well. Yes, both Mojo and I are connected to you in that life in Britain."

"So I will find you there as well?"

"Yes."

That's incredible…and wonderful. Like looking for family.

"Martin, be careful, dear friend. This can become a trap that can distract you from your true goal."

Martin told him he would be careful, nothing would distract him, and he would use his time in Britain well. The Kahuna seemed reassured. At that moment Martin felt tired, worn down by all that had happened. He was thinking of postponing his departure for Britain once again, although once there, he could always make it over to the cave to meditate and sleep. It would be nice to be free of the body once again, to be light.

He noticed the Kahuna's gaze. It seemed his thoughts were being read like an open book.

"So Martin, what will it be?"

"Well, I think I am ready to go back to Britain. At least I don't have to deal with rowdy gangs there."

"No my friend, no physical confrontations there. But you have to be very careful to stay centered, and if you do, you will receive all the guidance you will ever need. Please remember."

Martin nodded.

"Whenever something happens," the Kahuna said, "something that can take you off center, you always have the choice, you have a window of opportunity where you can veer toward Spirit or toward the lower consciousness. The choice is always yours."

"But I may not be strong enough. I may not have the discipline."

"Spirit is always there to help—it's 'the Other' you met in deep meditation. That is part of your choice, the window of opportunity."

"What about you—can't you protect me?" Martin said. "You seem to be able to do supernatural things. Could you watch over me?

"I could. But you need to exercise your new abilities. That is part of your growth."

Like a baby bird learning to fly.

Martin told the Kahuna he was ready. He was tired and he wanted the cave.

The Kahuna obliged with a warm smile. This time he simply looked at Martin, straight into his eyes. Martin felt himself go. First there was the sense of intense motion, again like an explosion that was happening all around him, and then he was in the dark tunnel with the light at the end. He spiraled rapidly, with a force capable of tearing him apart. He closed his eyes until he felt everything stop.

Martin found himself again in the glen. This time he was sitting on the grass, and he wondered why…why sitting? Then it occurred to him that's what he had pictured when he had asked the Kahuna to take him back to Britain. He had pictured the meadow and himself sitting in the middle, on the cool grass.

He knew the Kahuna hadn't come. He knew this time he was alone, and that was fine. He looked at the sky and by the sun he guessed it was late afternoon.

He got up with a gentle, sweeping motion that took him above the treetops. There he looked around and carried himself quickly to where the cave was. He descended in front of the entrance. Carefully, he went inside. The place was quiet, still, and inviting. He went to the middle and laid down, let himself go and relaxed. He felt he could sleep for a long time.

When he woke up, all was dark, and he had the sense it was around three in the morning. The feeling of the cave was as he remembered, soft and homey, welcoming. He sat up to meditate, and without the physical body it was much easier. The mind was still an issue, but he seemed to go right into a state of meditation. As he sat he felt his consciousness rise, with a sweet swelling in his chest. Whatever feelings he had at that moment about the gang, his wife, Adam…all seemed to melt away and he was again in total peace, and then joy, joy that was the Other.

Time passed, he didn't know how long; but when he opened his eyes, he knew he wasn't alone. In front of him was a young woman. She too had been in deep meditation, and now she opened her eyes. Martin realized she was the same person he had sensed those previous nights in the cave; he recognized a certain feel about her. She was human, and she was not afraid of him. Obviously she could see him, as she was staring right at him, making eye contact.

CHAPTER SEVEN

Martin sat in silence. He looked down at his body, and he knew he was invisible to human eyes; he could only see the faint shimmering blue light. He wondered how it was that the woman in the cave could see him. He looked up and saw she was still looking into his eyes, smiling.

"And who might you be, spirit?" The young woman said. Her speech was in a high cultured Latin. Her voice was soft and gentle, without a trace of fear.

"I am...not really a spirit being."

"But you are a spirit, dear one. I have seen some like you before, and I know you are not of this world."

He noticed gold in her aura. She was young, in her early twenties, with thick rich gold hair braided into two long tresses. She had a long, well proportioned body, which she covered with a white simple tunic, not unlike the one worn by Joannes and his son, except in her case it came down to her ankles. To Martin, she looked Scandinavian: the golden hair, blue eyes, long face, strong chin, and generous lips. All and all she was a very beautiful woman, and one he felt he recognized. Something about her was familiar. At first he had felt like bolting out of the cave, but now he was excited and delighted by her presence.

"This time you are not afraid of me?" Martin asked.

"No," she said with a smile. "I can see and feel you are one who communes. Nothing bad can possibly come from someone who gets so close to God. But, please do tell me, who are you?"

"I come from far away. My teacher helped me to travel with my body of light, for otherwise it would be impossible for me to come. My physical body is still alive, so you see, I am not really a spirit being." *This was meant to be. Meeting her...it feels so...natural.*

The woman seemed to ponder his answer for a while, and apparently accepted his explanation. She acted as though anything was possible, as though she had seen even stranger things.

"I have heard of people who can travel like you. I was told one came to this cave, to join us in our gathering."

Martin was caught off guard. *Other people come here.*

"What kind of gathering?"

"Oh, not to worry; it is we, the Seekers, who gather here to commune. For many years, perhaps centuries, wonderful souls in search of a life dedicated to spiritual search have gathered around these parts, and have used this cave for communion."

"What is communion?" Martin asked.

The woman laughed. "Dear one, what you were doing but a moment ago, is communion; when you become one with God."

As she talked, a reassuring feeling of déjà vu enveloped him, and Martin felt as though he had known her for a long time and they had sat together like this many times before.

The beautiful woman seemed to be getting used to him. She had studied him carefully, scanning his body, and seemed to be in awe of him, but as they talked she appeared increasingly more natural, at ease.

Maybe she also remembers me.

"But tell me, dear one, what do you call yourself?" she asked.

"Martin. And you?"

She mouthed his name for a while. "Strange name, but then again, everything is odd about you. I am called Maria Lerna and I am from a town not far from here."

"Have you lived here long?"

"I have lived among the Seekers for three years. My father had committed me to wed a man who was to be a king, but he was evil and I ran away. My teacher had told me about this cave in the forest where people gathered to commune, a powerful and magical place, and instructed that if I was ever in need of refuge from the world, to come here." Martin thought she had become a bit sad, and was silent for a moment, staring down at her hand. "So I took my slave, a strong man who was my guard, and together we made our way into the forest. It took us several weeks to get here, but we were guided, because we found the Seeker Colony and this cave."

As if recovering from an unpleasant thought, she again looked at Martin, and her eyes seemed to envelop him. "The last time I saw you, I ran away because I became scared, but only momentarily, because spirit beings are not common. Then I realized if you were here, you must be a good spirit. And I was right, because this time I saw you were in communion, saw your gold light and felt the goodness coming from you."

Martin was pleasantly surprised he too had a gold light. "But how is it you can see me, when others can't?"

A shy smile played on her lips. "It is just one of those things I was born with."

She asked him to materialize so she could take a good look at him.

Martin obliged, and was relieved his clothes had come with him. He wondered how that was, then realized that he was projecting his concept of himself, and that included the clothes he wore.

Maria Lerna seemed amused by his physical body. She commented he was taller than most, almost as tall as her guard, and that with his clothes and his hair, he looked very different. She asked him about his past and how he came to be in that very cave.

Martin told her the story of how he had been told to go on a pilgrimage, had gone to an island and there had met his teacher. Then he told her of his first trip to Britain, his meeting Joannes and Philippus, the battle, what it had brought up for him, and how his teacher had helped him by teaching him communion, the "looking skills" that would allow him to make sense of the world. Now he was back, ready to learn. He told her about Jenny and Adam, and how difficult his life had been back home.

"I know life can be hard and brutal, and I understand your pain, Martin. But you are endowed with good fortune, because it is obvious you have a teacher who is one with God."

"Yes, I know what you mean. Thank you." Martin said.

"I must return to my house," she said suddenly as she stood up. "Is there anything I can obtain for you next time we meet?"

"No, thank you. Having someone like you to talk to is all I need. But I do ask that you keep my existence a secret."

"I understand. But in that case it would be best if you visit me at home. My guard is like an extension of myself, so it's not like telling someone else, not really." She paused briefly to glance at his eyes, looking for his reaction. "People use this cave to commune, so my house would be best all around. We seldom have visitors."

Martin was touched by her invitation, and also very glad. He now realized how much he had yearned for human contact in this world. The situation was perfect. He wondered what the Kahuna would say about it, and then remembered that he had told him about meeting someone special, and Martin knew it was Maria Lerna whom the Kahuna had in mind. He thanked her, and assented. He would come to her house in the evenings. Martin asked how to find her house.

In response she signaled for him to follow her.

They left the cave and walked for what seemed an hour along a trail only she could see. To him it all looked the same, as they passed through the forest and the occasional clearing; but he did notice she was leading him through obviously well-trod places, because the forest had a different feel. It seemed many feet had made subtle paths only a practiced eye could follow.

They came to a clearing, and before him appeared a small house built of logs and mud. They went inside. The floor was made of stones, but unlike the Roman road, these were rough. Tables and chairs had also been made of logs. Against one wall was a stone stove built with the opening for the fire on the outside and the back protruding into the house. Apparently the cooking was all done outdoors, but some heat made it into the structure. A door led to a separate room, evidently her bedroom. All around was her essence, a pleasant feminine presence he could now identify.

Through a window he saw another small hut, and outside it, working on some leather, sat a huge man, with head bent, concentrated on his task. Maria Lerna led Martin outside and they approached the big man.

She called him by name, Eldyn. He stood up and bowed to her.

On close inspection the man was even more impressive—a giant for the times, a good six-foot-six. He had dark brown hair and beard, thick eyebrows that topped deep-set eyes, a prominent forehead, a square jaw that seemed more like a rock, and a wide, flat nose.

He sat down again and continued his task as they talked. His voice was deep. They spoke in the local brogue, a combination of Latin and a local language, and Martin noticed how deftly and efficiently he worked, cutting the leather with heavy scissors.

"Is there anything I can do for you, my lady?" Eldyn asked.

"No, Eldyn," she said. "I brought a new friend I want you to meet."

At this, the man rose. He stood and looked around, apparently trying to see whom she was talking about. Martin noticed a slight tension in his manner, how his arms hung at his sides, motionless, but apparently ready for anything.

Maria Lerna turned to Martin, and although he knew he was invisible, she looked right into his eyes.

"Could you make yourself into a body, Martin?"

Martin obliged her, and slowly materialized in front of both of them.

There was just the smallest hint of surprise in Eldyn's eyes, or at least as much surprise as he allowed Martin to notice. The rest of him remained still and guarded. He looked Martin up and down, as though double-checking that what he was seeing was real. Then his gaze rested on Martin's eyes, carefully studying his expression, his probing eyes surveying him with great concentration. Martin was sure no detail and no evil intent could possibly escape such scrutiny.

Maria Lerna then told Eldyn how she had met Martin, and that he had been in communion in the cave. At this Eldyn seemed to relax; his manner changed and he smiled. His head bowed slightly in Martin's direction.

Martin noticed there was more to Eldyn than he thought. Surely this was no common slave or servant. His manner was very protective of Maria Lerna, so obviously he was a guard of sorts; but Martin could also sense a deep peace and calm about him. There was also his aura, a bluish light with a golden tint, just like Maria Lerna's. *Could it be Mojo?* The two were very much alike. Martin studied the big man. He was not black like Mojo, but they resembled each other in other ways. It was as though nature had made them from the same mold: the big, strong bodies, thick square faces with strong features…and again, Martin could see wisdom and kindness etched on an otherwise brutish face.

Maria Lerna told Eldyn Martin would be coming to her house as a visitor, and to keep his existence secret.

Eldyn nodded, smiled, and went back to his task. As he continued to work, Martin noticed the man's attention flowed towards him, still probing, perhaps unsure of what he was seeing and hearing, or perhaps simply more in awe of Martin than he would ever show or say.

Martin turned toward Maria Lerna. It was time to go. He would be back that evening, they agreed.

"How should I come…that is, should I knock, or just show up in your house?" Martin asked.

She hesitated a moment. "Please announce your presence, and only come into the front room, because I want privacy in my chamber."

Martin bowed at her, the same way he saw Eldyn do it.

He left the pair and absent-mindedly ambled through the forest, feeling a peace that emanated from the entire area as though it had been soaked in Spirit.

She has never befriended a ghost before, so everything is new, for both of us. Of course she has to define her boundaries, and she did it in such a natural way.

In retrospect, Martin knew he wouldn't have lasted very long without some sort of human contact. He was mystified by the Kahuna and his admonition not to get involved in this world, while at the same time letting him know that meeting her was fine. *Strange contradiction.*

He found it interesting that she meditated, calling it "communion." Martin could still feel her essence, so pleasant. Maybe she was a princess? And Eldyn…he had to be Mojo.

But it was time to rejoin Joannes and the others.

As he came to the battle scene, Martin felt the horror of the place rush in. His first reaction was to go somewhere else, but realized he needed to be there. As he came down onto the Roman road, he pulled himself inside, and tried to look at the surroundings with detachment.

He took stock of the situation. First, the time. He knew he had returned to Britain immediately after his departure. *The battle happened yesterday, and this is the morning after.* Martin slowly walked through what had been the battle scene. He observed the still-unburied men and the activities taking place.

So far, it all seemed unreal. Not shocking, nor gruesome. Martin had expected to react as he did before, but now he felt calm.

There was a lot of activity. Martin saw some men gathering weapons, while another group was busy burying the dead. Some of the latter were Caledonians, closely watched by soldiers. Wounded men from both sides were all in one group, being treated by Caledonian women and men from Isca. A large group was saddling horses, while a small number of leaders were gathered under a tent, eating the morning meal.

Martin came up close to listen and see who was present. They all seemed attentive, as Joannes and Arcadius reviewed the battle and made plans for the day. It appeared they were primarily concerned about the treating of their wounded and transporting them safely. Then someone asked about the party going to hunt down stray Caledonians. Martin gathered that one group, led by Arcadius, was to go scout the road up ahead to find any of the enemy who might have escaped, and to look for their casualties at the site of the first clash. A second group was to gather the prisoners and the wounded and start marching toward Isca.

Martin heard that Philippus had already left the previous evening for Isca with a few select men, to tell people of the victory, and to make sure all was well at home. Mateus and his men had already left, as well.

Martin had thought it odd that they were only now going to look for wounded comrades at the site of the ambush, and he heard one man ask the same question. Arcadius answered that the risks had been judged too great the night before, since a group of riders in the dark could be subject to an ambush from surviving Caledonians, so they had decided to move a large force in the daytime instead.

The men talked about the battle. Maybe the threat from the barbarians was over, someone said. Maybe word will spread among the Caledonians that they were too strong to attack. Some other voice mentioned that the Picts, and Martin understood this to be another term for the Caledonians, had always been a troublesome bunch, the Romans and then the Big Council had had a lot of trouble with them. After some thought, Joannes said that yes, the Caledonians would surely come back. The group agreed, yes they would be back. Heaviness hung in the air for a while, but then it subsided. For now they were victorious. Now they could go home and enjoy their peace.

Joannes bid Arcadius farewell, telling him he would start out toward Isca the moment they finished clearing the battlefield. The general would catch up with the troops later.

Arcadius walked over to mount his horse.

Martin decided to follow the general that morning, having decided that he liked him. There was something about Arcadius that spoke of loyalty and strength. Maybe it was the way he related to his men—always looking out for them, his calm gaze reviewing the ranks, assessing each one, making sure they were properly saddled and had their weapons, that all was well. Martin looked closely at Arcadius. He was of average height for the time, maybe five-three; a heavy-set man full of scars, that Martin guessed were from many battles. He was of obvious Mediterranean stock, with dark skin, black hair and brown eyes. Arcadius carried himself with the air of someone who is used to authority. He appeared sure of himself, and his eyes seemed to always be taking the measure of any man he had not met before, and once satisfied, he moved on to someone else. Martin saw him fight during the battle. Arcadius had come down from one of the hills when Joannes arrived with his men, and immediately took a front-line position, moving up and down the formation, plugging a hole with his shield and sword, then moving down again to another weak spot, defending it until a soldier took over, and moving again. Following the battle, he had gone around inspecting his men, counting the dead and the wounded, all with cold efficiency.

As the group started up the road, Martin stayed by Arcadius' side. Then he rose above the men, and took in the sight of the vast forest, and the mountains they were passing through. Down the road he saw Joannes and his men clearing the battleground, and up the road he could already see the place where Joannes had ambushed the Caledonians, still bearing evidence of the violent clash, with bodies strewn about. He went over to the site and descended onto the middle of the road.

Most of the people had been long dead, he could tell by scanning for auras. There were a handful of Isca men, but the rest were obviously Caledonians, with their tattoos and dirty, unkempt appearance. As Martin walked around, he heard one man groan. It was a Caledonian with a deep stomach wound. There was another with a badly wounded leg. Martin saw a couple of men that were apparently mobile, and wondered why they had not escaped, or tried to help the wounded. The rest were dead, and none of the wounded appeared to be from Isca.

All and all, about ten men seemed to be still alive, but maybe there were more hiding in the forest. Martin scanned the area beyond the tree line, and in fact could detect human auras here and there. He walked toward the back of the group but saw no survivors. As he continued surveying the place, he knew he was rather calm and detached and thought maybe this time around he had prepared himself. Maybe by now he knew what to expect…or perhaps it had been the Kahuna's intervention that had steeled him.

Martin circled the main group of dead Caledonians and came to a group of women and children. The sight of them tore at his insides, and he had to make a special effort. *It's okay, it's okay…they are already dead, there is nothing you can do about it…it's life.* As he stood studying the scene, he heard a cry— it was a child, a young child somewhere. Quickly Martin tried to find the source. He walked among the corpses, listening, looking for movement, for auras, for anything. There it was again—the cry wasn't strong, it was tired, a whimper. Underneath a woman he saw a little hand moving. A small face was poking out from beneath her long hair. Both mother and child had auras. Maybe both were on the throes of death. *What to do, what to do?* He had been told not to interfere.

He brushed the hair away, and saw the baby's mouth gasping for air. Martin pushed the woman's shoulder away. She groaned. *Lord, she is very much alive!* He saw that her leg had been crushed, and an arrow protruded from a shoulder blade. Not a deep wound, judging from the length of the shaft that was visible.

Behind him, Martin heard the sound of hooves and voices. Arcadius and his men were arriving, and in another five minutes they would be here. *What to do?* Surely they would have to kill the woman, for she couldn't walk. That was apparently one of the rules about prisoners; if they were too much trouble, kill them. Martin was certain they would also kill the baby. What was he to do, stand by? If he let it happen, wouldn't he be just as guilty of killing by doing nothing? But what about destiny? He didn't belong in this world, so his meddling was not part of the equation…and interfering meant he was disrupting what was supposed to happen. Maybe this was a test to see if he could stay detached. *Well, to hell with the whole thing.* He didn't care much for this test; he didn't care much for letting this happen, for doing nothing.

Martin looked to where the sound of horses and men came from. They were approaching, but the woman and child were hidden from view by a dead horse. He looked at the woman and grabbed her good arm, then with the other hand he picked up the baby. Crouching down, still hidden by the horse, he dragged the woman slowly away from the road and toward the trees.

He was careful not to draw attention, hoping no one would see the movement or see him, because now he was visible.

With relief he came to the edge of the forest, and then he was inside it with the woman and the baby. He stopped at the point where the growth became too thick, about fifty feet inside the line of trees. Martin propped the woman against a tree, careful to avoid contact with the arrow. He placed the child on her lap and instinctively the woman cradled her baby, bringing it up to her chest. Martin took a couple of deep breaths. Her leg had stopped bleeding, but the shoulder wound was still oozing. The calf showed a compound fracture, with a piece of bone sticking out. Hopefully that was all; the horse that must have stepped on her fortunately had not crushed the bone.

Obviously both mother and child were very weak. Martin studied the woman's face. The eyes were half open, but she was unconscious, her eyes not registering anything. Her face sported two tattoos, designs of some sort, one on her left cheek and another on her forehead. The baby was now suckling at his mother's breast. He was probably three months old. The mother looked to be around sixteen years old, with fresh skin, a thin frame, but strong hands that were already used to hard work.

Martin looked at the wound on her shoulder. The arrow had not penetrated her lung, he was certain; otherwise he knew it would have collapsed, and she would not be breathing normally. He ran his fingers around the entry wound, feeling the shaft of the arrow. It had a metal point, but he knew the Isca arrows were not barbed, so he could probably pull it back without having to cut the flesh around it. But then the wound would bleed. *She might die in the process; she's weak...and then, what about the baby?* If only he had help. Could he bring Maria Lerna over to this spot? He could hide the woman and child and then bring Maria Lerna and Eldyn over. No, walking through the dense forest would take them at least two weeks.

The woman and child were now temporarily safe, but now what? Left alone, wounded as she was, the woman would surely die, and her child shortly after. He couldn't transport them a long distance; there was no way to carry them both. He needed help, human help.

Martin went up above the trees to look around the surrounding area, but found only burned out farms and what looked like a big fancy house, also burned. In the forest he saw wild animals, but no humans. Maybe if he looked for auras, he could find a human, maybe a Caledonian hidden somewhere. Then he stopped himself. Supposing he found someone, what would he do? Go up to him, materialize, and in his strange speech ask the person to risk his life to save a woman and baby? How would he explain that he himself could not save the woman and child, but was asking for the other man to risk his life by braving an army from Isca. *Yeah, that would be a tough sell.* And what could someone else do that he couldn't? Transport them. Where? To Caledonia? No...what they needed was medical care and he probably knew more medicine than any Caledonian. *I have to do it; it's all up to me.*

Martin went back to where he had left the woman and child. She was resting and the child was still feeding. He looked around. There were branches he could use to make a splint. He could use strips of her clothing for bandages. He noticed she had a scarf of sorts tied around her waist. That was the cleanest piece of clothing. Her dress, or tunic, was otherwise a dirty, bloody mess. Or he could go to the road and find something. He would have to wait until Arcadius and his men were gone, though. A moan or cry from the woman or child would attract their attention. Martin decided to wait.

He wondered about his reaction to the current situation. He was a lot calmer; he seemed to be dealing with the cruelty, the death, and the barbarism of the place with detachment. Detachment, yes, but he was doing something. He was doing what he could; he was saving two lives. That would have to be enough. If it meant breaking his promise to the Kahuna, so be it.

What if she dies?...Damn.

After some time Martin heard men scouring the edge of the forest on both sides of the road. Martin heard one group approaching. They seemed to be some two hundred feet away. He looked at the mother and child. They were hardly visible, but would definitely be found when the men came this way.

Martin went to look at the men and what they were doing. There were two of them and they were thorough, scouring each foot of space between the road and the thick growth. Occasionally they found animal trails leading into the growth, veritable tunnels through the brush which were the size of a large pig or small deer, and these the men looked at and sometimes followed for a distance, before coming back to the road.

Slowly they approached the place where the woman and child were.

Think of something! But what? What to do?

When they were but twenty feet away, Martin went into the forest and rustled against the bushes, as a person would do trying to crawl away. As he thought they would, both men came into the thicket, hacking their way in. Martin continued for some time until they were a hundred feet inside. At this point he rushed back to the woman and baby, and carried them to the area the soldiers had already checked, more than two hundred feet back. He laid them down carefully on the ground, and to make sure, covered them with brush hacked by the men from Isca. He then went back to where the soldiers had gone in. Shortly they emerged, sweaty, out of breath, and obviously disappointed. Without a word they resumed their search where they had left off, poking and hacking at bushes.

Relieved, Martin went back to his charges. Fortunately, they were sleeping quietly. He pulled away some of the branches from their faces, and studied the mother. She looked like many teenage girls he had met, except for the tattoos. Reddish brown hair, oval face, thin lips. Rather pretty, he thought. He brushed a bug away from her forehead and smoothed her hair.

He sat next to them, and after some time, he decided to go to the road and see what was happening. The men had gone meticulously through the dead and wounded. Martin saw that they had mercy-killed some Caledonians, had gathered weapons, and had collected the wounded they were to take back. These they had on horses. He was surprised they had kept many more alive than he thought they would. Perhaps after the bloody battle they could afford to be compassionate...or they had horses to spare. The wounded Caledonians had their hands tied behind their backs, and their feet tied with ropes that reached under the horses' bellies. However, they all wore bandages, so some care had been exercised by their captors.

The captives who could walk were tied together. They apparently were to walk behind the horses. There was a party of Isca soldiers digging a mass grave, and bodies were being moved to the edge. The men were anxious to get back home, and their work seemed hurried. At this point, another group of horses came down the road, with about twenty Isca men escorting another group of captives.

Several hours passed. Arcadius prepared his men to move out. The men from Isca split into a group in front of the prisoners and another in back, and a single line of horsemen on either side.

Martin watched them go with relief. He went back to the mother and child. First things first. He would look after the woman's wounds, then he would figure out what to do next.

He realized that he had to take the arrow out and set her broken leg, but for that she needed her strength. Martin gathered scattered provisions and water jugs from the road. He fed her by putting small pieces of food in her mouth, but she seemed to relish the water most of all. She ate and drank without waking up, but she was conscious enough to grab the water jug when he put it to her lips and poured water into her mouth. After the feeding, he decided they needed shelter. He had found clothing, which he tore into makeshift blankets. With branches and grass he built a lean-to against a tree, and it was a good structure, about four feet high and five feet wide and long enough for her to fit under, lying down. He placed the two in the shelter, built a fire, and proceeded to tend to her wounds.

She screamed awake when he worked on her leg, pulling at her foot to bring the broken bone into place, and then she fainted. Martin took the opportunity to pull the arrow out and cauterize the wound with a burning ember. While setting the splint on her leg, she opened her eyes and looked around momentarily. Then she went back to sleep.

Martin decided to spend the night with his charges. But first he paid a brief visit to Maria Lerna and Eldyn, to tell them what was happening. Back with the mother and child, Martin kept thinking of Maria Lerna. Being with her, even for a few minutes, left him feeling…happy. She was like no other woman he had ever met: generous, soft and nurturing, with a beauty that went well beyond physical appearances.

Martin meditated, but his meditation was punctuated with concern. What in the world was he going to do with these two? So far, he had no great ideas. But at least the woman would heal and her son was fine. He guessed she had bled a lot before he found them, so water and nourishment were mostly what she needed. He could only hope that somehow they would be safe.

He lay down next to the lean-to and prepared to sleep. After an hour or so he again heard sounds coming from the east, along the forest's edge. Martin stood still at first, but then decided to investigate. He approached the source of the noise, wishing he had put out the fire earlier, for he could smell the smoldering embers that far away. He saw a horse, with no rider, slowly meandering along the trees, and coming his way. He was relieved at first to realize it was only a horse. Then he was glad, as he realized that maybe that was all the help he needed. He didn't know exactly how, but certainly having a horse opened up options.

Martin approached the animal and grabbed the reins, then stroked its neck, talking soothingly. The horse seemed tired, but it was young and strong, and his well-toned muscles glistened in the moonlight. Martin ran his hand over the shoulders and rump. He had seen most horses get the brunt of the arrows in those parts. He didn't feel any wounds. He walked the animal over near the lean-to where he had seen some grass growing. He took the bridle off so he could graze. Then he loosened the saddle strap. He brought a jug over and gave him water from his cupped hands. He knew that the horse was a miracle, providing him the one means of helping the mother and child. Maybe he could mount them on it and lead the animal by the reins, along the forest edge until they reached other Caledonians. Well, that was a possibility.

He went back to the road to look for rope. Instead, he found some more clothing, which he ripped into strips. These he tied together and made a rope about twenty feet long. Once the animal was tied securely to a tree, he went back to the lean-to and quickly fell asleep.

When Martin woke up it was early morning. The woman was sitting up, examining her splint. She looked around, apparently trying to figure out who else was in the camp, who had helped her. Then she noticed the horse. She tried getting up, but at first she found it too painful. After some time, and with a great deal of effort, she managed to stand up, painfully favoring the one leg, but standing nevertheless. She carefully touched her leg, and brought her hand over to her shoulder blade where the arrow had been. Martin watched as she went about relieving herself, then washed her face with water from a jug. Her furtive glances each time she heard a noise suggested she was scared of whoever she thought had helped her. She was certainly a very strong and brave girl, for he knew she had to be in great pain every time she moved around. After she took care of herself, she went over to the baby.

She was moving a little easier now. Her shoulder was obviously painful, judging by the way she favored it and winced when she picked up her son. Martin watched as she cleaned him, using some rags and water. She now sat to feed him, all the time looking around, expecting or dreading that someone would come back. Martin could tell she had made a decision, for she kept looking at the horse, at the provisions and the clothes strewn about. As soon as her baby had been taken care of, she set up to bundle the provisions. Then she made slings with the clothes. She brought the horse over and loaded the animal with the makeshift saddlebags. One of them contained her son, whom she slung by the horse's neck, with a counterweight of a water jug hung at the other side of the horse.

Martin realized she was making her getaway, that she was concerned whoever had helped her would soon return. Basically she was stealing the horse, or so she thought, and the provisions. With great effort she clambered on the animal, looked around and headed in the opposite direction from Isca and towards home.

Martin followed her for some time, thinking she might faint again, fall off the horse, or maybe encounter refugees on the road who would take her horse and kill her. But the girl seemed to know what she was doing; she set out carefully skirting the forest, staying out of view. And she obviously knew how to ride. No, Martin decided, he had to let her go, he had done as much as he could, if not as much as he wanted for her and her baby. The rest was up to her destiny. Still, all and all, he was disappointed she never once seemed well disposed to meet whoever she thought had helped her. Surely, after someone had set her broken bone, and pulled the arrow out, saving her and her son from the Isca troops...why would she think he would want to harm her? And the horse…she had no trouble taking the horse, not caring how the person who helped her would get around and whether he would survive. At least she could have left some water, some food.

Martin watched her ride on, looking back over her shoulder a couple of times, as if still concerned the person would come running after her.

Heaviness was now in his heart. *Let her go.* But still, he felt bad, betrayed. This was life, and a person in his own world, under similar circumstances, would probably act the same way. The girl had seen much death, had seen how easily it came to people around her, so certainly he couldn't blame her for being afraid. Anyway, she was gone, and he no longer had to think how to get her to safety. *Funny about the horse.* Someone else had figured out how to best help the girl.

Martin turned around toward Isca. He felt like walking a bit; no need to hurry. He knew Joannes and his men were marching back slowly, because of the wounded and the prisoners on foot. As he walked he felt the heaviness and wondered what would lift it. He remembered the Kahuna had said to stay centered, so he decided to meditate.

Martin went to the spot next to the lean-to where he had sat the night before. He could see where the mother and baby had lain; the grass mat was crushed where her body had been. He felt the heaviness inside him growing. His thoughts revolved around the woman, and he recalled the scene of the gang attacking him. *Why, why them?* Martin tried to push the thoughts away, but they persisted; it was as though this was a knot that needed untying before he could do anything else.

Martin stood up and started walking. He was aware of anger that stood in the background and was trying to surface; it was gnawing at his insides. Maybe he would think about the woman first. The first image that came to mind was of her leaving with the horse. Didn't she care the least bit about his welfare? Couldn't she have left at least one jug of water? The little bitch! For all she knew he too could have been wounded and in need of the horse. He again saw the young men around him, felt his hair being held back, his arm trapped and the scrawny punk getting ready to strike him with his foot. He realized, at that very instant, all he wanted in this life was to do harm to the skinny jerk.

The image of violence was satisfying, and also disturbing.

The Kahuna said to veer toward Spirit, to stay centered.

With an act of will Martin moved away from his anger with what felt like a great deal of effort, until he felt the violence leave his being. He brought his attention to his spiritual eye again, and imagined his breath flowing in and out of his body. With this cycle he felt better, the anger subsided, although there was still a knot inside his chest, an ugly blotch left over.

He was left mystified by what he had discovered; how anger took over as a result of an otherwise unimportant event, bringing to the surface what he was really angry about. *But where does it come from?* Was that something he learned? Martin recalled his father's violent fits, the yelling. Is that where he had acquired his temper? No, that wasn't the whole truth. *We manifest in this life what we need to learn.* That was a lesson he learned from the Kahuna. He had manifested a violent father, to learn about anger all over again.

Then what had been the consequences in his life? He knew he had attracted the gang at the beach. And what else? Is that why he had married an angry woman, one who could mirror his own temper? He felt a sudden pang of realization. Martin recalled the scene when he had come home with the pizza. Now he realized his role. He had a wife he knew well enough that he could incite various emotions, and manipulate situations so she would erupt. And she did the same for him. *That's one of the reasons why we are together.*

Jenny, too, had started life with an angry father. He saw her eyes full of tears as she described the slaps in the face at the dinner table, the time he hit her with a broom, and how he threw her out of the car on the side of a highway because he didn't like her wearing makeup.

Then she had married an angry man.

He knew their marriage was over. Anger had left too much damage behind, had created a mountain between them.

Martin went up to float. Up where white clouds lazily hung in a blue sky. To float and not be, not feeling. Sadness engulfed him, but it was a good sadness, purifying and cleansing.

CHAPTER EIGHT

Martin followed the Roman road past the mountain pass, and past the glen. Then he saw the throng making their way down the road. Arcadius' party had caught up with Joannes, and was now integrated into the larger group.

Martin walked alongside the prisoners, looking at their tattooed faces, trying to figure out what made those people behave the way they did. He recalled the burned out farms and houses, the bodies of farmers lying about, cattle slaughtered for no reason; it was destruction for its own sake. The prisoners' appearance didn't tell him much. Seemingly they could be anything in their daily lives back home. But they were rough and for some reason violence was natural to them, a part of their lives. That was baffling and repulsive. Maybe they were somewhere at the bottom of the evolutionary scale the Kahuna had mentioned. Their spirits behaved like animals, because perhaps they were still at that stage, incapable of empathy.

But presently they were quiet and sullen, engulfed in defeat. The men from Isca had allowed some of the prisoners to mingle with their wives and children. They walked together, talking little, their body language and their shuffle speaking of a humiliating loss and an uncertain future.

Martin noticed a man walking in the middle of the column of prisoners. His gait was subdued but dignified. The rest of the Caledonians acted with deference towards him, keeping a respectful distance. He even seemed to have other prisoners in attendance, although with difficulty, for they all had their hands tied. Arcadius was watching the Caledonian as well, seemingly riding casually on the edge of the road, outside the line of riders guarding the prisoners. The man walked calmly and very erect, perhaps conscious that he had to be an example to the others. His aura was blue with the gold fringe. *That's no animal.* Perplexed, Martin drew near, and realized it was the young man he had seen praying at the Caledonian camp before any of the fighting had started. He was alive! Martin was glad; he assumed he had been killed. The last time he saw him, he had been riding in hot pursuit of Joannes and his men. Martin realized that as he walked he seemed to be mumbling a prayer, silently, but with his lips moving ever so slightly. He didn't have any visible tattoos, and his clothes were finely made, as good as Joannes' and actually very similar. One man came over from behind to offer him a jug of water, slightly tapping his arm as he did so, but then lowering his gaze when the young man turned his head. The young man thanked the other and drank two polite mouthfuls, then gave back the jug.

The line had stopped moving. It was Arcadius who had made everyone stop. He dismounted and then walked over to the young man and directed a guard to untie him. Once free, Arcadius motioned for him to step outside the ranks of the prisoners. There, he offered him a horse that a soldier had brought over. He was to ride beside the prisoners with one guard on each side. The young man looked at the general, the horse and the guards, apparently weighing the new circumstances offered him. He looked back at his men. They were smiling at him. The young man climbed on the mount, with no word of thanks, but continuing his silent prayer all the while. Arcadius watched him, and apparently also noted the reaction from the other prisoners. Martin thought that this was a clever move by the general; he had found a popular leader of the Caledonians, given him the special treatment that befitted his rank, and now he had won a measure of gratitude, or maybe even respect from those wild people. Or perhaps Arcadius was just as curious about the young man as Martin was.

Five miles or so from the hills, the landscape changed. The forest gave way to farmland, beautiful undulating land with a variety of crops and cattle. There were also big impressive houses that seemed to be on the choicest part of the land, and always with a group of farms around them. It was then that Martin understood why the Caledonians had to be stopped at the hills; they would have wreaked havoc with places like this that obviously fed a lot of people.

They were still in Mateus' kingdom, but in a short time, some two miles or so, they crossed into Joannes' kingdom. Now at intervals they would stop and Joannes would allow some of the men to return to the houses and farms they were passing.

The men from Isca were still reveling in their victory. Martin learned theirs was a particularly well-trained army, for the King and the general shared a passion for soldiering, and that had been the bond that brought them together many years before. In later years the Legions of the Big Council had grown lax in training and discipline, so while other soldiers got drunk in the ranks, stole from civilians and deserted, Arcadius' Legion had a reputation for discipline and fighting skills. Joannes and Arcadius had met as young men while serving in the same Big Council Legion, which Arcadius eventually led, with the prince from Isca as one of his top lieutenants.

Martin also heard talk about the captives, now considered slaves. They had been tallied and Martin understood they had well over five hundred. Normally they would have been exchanged or sold in Iberia, but now things were too uncertain. The news they kept getting from abroad was dismal; the barbarians who had begun their attacks some fifty years before throughout the Empire had destroyed and disrupted things to the point there was no telling if any given city was still standing, or if a ship would make it back. Large groups of barbarians from far-off lands were reaching places deemed indestructible, like Hippo. Rome herself had been sacked several times. They would have to wait for a ship from Cartagena, in Iberia, to see how things were. That city was still a vital port, well-fortified, en route to Africa, Italia and Constantinople, so news and goods flowed from there.

The talk then gravitated to how things had been before, in the old days of their grandparents, before the Romans left. They had been safe and well cared for; everything a man had wanted was there. A person could travel unarmed anywhere; women and children were safe; they had no need for walls; only Isca and other port cities had walls to protect against pirates. Surely, the Empire would recover; it was just a matter of time. Constantinople was still very strong; eventually they would send the Legions out and bring back order.

Martin went on to the head of the formation, and there he found Joannes riding with two other men. These were like Arcadius, also Mediterranean in appearance, darker than the rest, who tended to have reddish blond or brown hair and lighter skin. Joannes, he noted, seemed of mixed lineage, with sandy hair but darker skin, and his features were what Martin now recognized as Roman.

They had been talking about their families, but then the conversation switched to the subject of the prisoners. They had five hundred seventy-two men, two hundred twelve women and thirty-seven children. They discussed taking some of the prisoners to Londinium and selling them there. No, Joannes said, they would be too scared to have Caledonian slaves. That would invite another invasion to free them. He thought maybe he would send word to the Saxon chief he knew, a man called Erouf. Perhaps he would buy the slaves, or exchange them. Certainly they couldn't keep them in Isca or Lindinus.

Martin gathered Erouf and his men had made landfall one time some years back not far from Isca. When confronted by Joannes and his troops, he had walked on ahead of his hundred men, and without weapons had asked to talk. He spoke Latin and apparently wanted to trade. Erouf ended up spending a month in Isca as Joannes' guest, and since then had shown up two more times, each time bringing furs and slaves in exchange for wine and grain. Joannes had high hopes for working an alliance with this man who seemed to want peace. Martin noticed the reaction the mention of Erouf by Joannes brought on his men; they glanced at each other and shook their heads in disbelief.

At noon they stopped. The prisoners were fed and given water, and the wounded were tended to. The young Caledonian leader, now dismounted, went around talking to his men, still accompanied by the two guards, who behaved at times more like an escort, keeping a respectful distance from their charge.

Joannes came over to where the young chief was, accompanied by Arcadius. Joannes addressed the Caledonian in Latin, and to no one's surprise, he responded with ease in that language, sounding well cultured.

"What do call yourself, Caledonian?" asked Joannes.

"I am Mowan."

"You look and sound as though you were brought up Roman. Where are you from?"

"My clan is known as a kingdom, one of several in Caledonia that have adopted Roman ways. I was raised by my teacher Mirio, in Ninian's abbey."

"Were you to be a monk?" Joannes sounded incredulous.

"I was a monk until my father called me to take my place in the clan. He became ill of late, so it fell on me to lead the clan on this raid." Ten clans, totaling nine thousand fighting men and some women and children had comprised the invading force. Yes, the total number had been around twelve thousand. His was a particularly strong and important clan, so he was viewed as one of the main chiefs. He was twenty-eight years old.

It was obvious that both Joannes and Arcadius were rather taken by Mowan; he was so different from any of his fellow Caledonians. They continued questioning him, apparently curious about him, but maybe also trying to engage him. But Mowan continued formal and distant, and curt in his answers. In response to Joannes' query about what and who instigated the current invasion, he answered that they had heard the southern kingdoms were still steeped in the Roman ways, rich and soft, leaving them ready for the taking. They had been making forays into the northern kingdoms for many years now, ever since the Romans had left, and each year they had gone farther and farther south. Three years ago, he told them, they had undertaken their most ambitious invasion yet, and had been so successful, so rich and easy had been the haul, the clans had immediately started preparations for this invasion.

Joannes asked no further information, but stated that if there was anything he needed, to let him know through one of the guards.

Mowan bowed in his direction.

Joannes and Arcadius walked away, trailing their horses behind. Martin followed them rather absent-mindedly, still thinking about Mowan. He heard

Joannes mention that he noticed the difference between the Caledonians and his own men. They stood to one side comparing the two groups. Beyond the issue of tattoos and physical cleanliness, it was apparent the Caledonians were in better physical shape; they seemed harder, stronger than their captors. Arcadius commented on how hard they had charged at the wall formation. In his mind they could have gone through had it not been for the boulders and the arrows. Joannes mentioned that in future encounters with these people they could not rely solely on tactics and training, all things being equal, he was afraid they might lose. If there were people like Mowan across the border, it also meant some barbarians knew how to fight like Romans, so it would be a matter of time before they encountered a force of well-disciplined Caledonians. Arcadius agreed. It appeared to them both that in the many years of relying on the peace brought about by the Empire, and then the Big Council, they had become soft in the ways of war.

They concluded that their reliance on slaves for physical labor was now working against them. Apparently some of their own soldiers had been slaves who had recently bought or been granted their freedom. Arcadius pointed out several to Joannes, who concurred. Martin also noticed how these men stood out from the others; they seemed stronger than the rest. Some were Saxons and Angles; others were Scots from Hibernia. Most had been captured in battle. The tougher looking lot seemed to be the ones who had more recently bought their freedom, with some notable exceptions—men that in Martin's opinion appeared to favor physical activity regardless of their occupation or social status. Another thing that stood out for Martin, but was taken for granted by Joannes and Arcadius, was that freed slaves almost never returned to their original country, apparently because they found their new lives so much better than anything else they had known before.

After the noon break, they marched on until sunset. They passed several more farming enclaves. Most of them had the big fancy house, the villa, surrounded by the farms with their functional buildings and fields. The farmers stood on the side of the road, some with gifts for the soldiers, relieved and jubilant. It was touching to see women, children and older people look for a husband, father or son; and when a loved one was found, their elation was palpable. Others went through the ranks mentioning a name and asking for news.

Martin watched the men set up camp, and then he decided it was time for him to go for the evening. His heart skipped a beat at the thought of Maria Lerna, and was surprised by his reaction. She was certainly very appealing, and a very special girl, but how could he possibly envision, or think of her in terms other than...even friendship was a questionable concept. Martin tried to remember back to when he had just met Jenny, and whether this was the same way he had felt about her. *Maybe so.*

When he came to her cottage, Martin made himself visible and called Maria Lerna's name. By now he knew Eldyn couldn't hear him unless he made his body solid first, and he assumed that would be the case with everyone except Maria Lerna.

Eldyn opened the door and politely stood to one side. Inside there were wonderful smells, some of freshly cooked herbs and spices, of flowers that stood on a vase on the table, and her scent. She was sitting on a chair, sewing, and was now smiling at him in welcome.

They were about to eat dinner, and Eldyn set a place for him.

"Thank you Eldyn, but I don't eat."

"It's the intention that counts," answered Maria Lerna.

Yes, It's the thought that counts, and they are both kind. Martin felt mostly glad to talk to someone. He told them about the girl he had saved with her baby, how she departed, and his reaction.

"The girl saw you as a ghost," Eldyn said. "She felt your hands but saw no one, and was scared."

This took Martin aback; it felt a bit like a shock wave going through his body. *Of course.* She had been terrified, and who wouldn't?

They sat in silence for a moment while Martin collected his thoughts.

"The deed you performed for that mother and child was commendable," she told him, "but did you do it for her sake, or yours?"

That's silly. "For her sake. I was trying to help her."

"Yes, dear. But when she did not act the way you expected, you were upset."

Martin understood. He had become involved in the situation. It dawned on him that the Kahuna's warning to not get involved perhaps meant more than he thought.

"The horse was manifested by your energy, which at that point was clear because your intent to help was also clear," she said. "You did perform well at many levels, Martin, and your spirit's prayers for the girl were answered. The girl's spirit returned the favor by showing you a load you want to shed. Your anger."

He thought of her words, and decided she was right.

"Soldiers and gladiators get themselves into a state of agitation before fighting," Eldyn said. "That's how they get over their fear and feel strong. That's a good use of anger, and in life it's what makes people go forward."

Martin remembered Mojo telling him about the same thing.

"You know that in this place and time you have powers," Eldyn said.

He knows I came from another time? Good lord! "Yes, I know that, Eldyn. I have a body that can do things others can't, but I wouldn't do anything wrong, nothing evil."

"Powers always mean a heavy burden," Eldyn said. "The burden is what brings wisdom, but it depends on how you handle it, whether it brings wisdom or harm."

"Harm to myself or to others?"

"To yourself, dear," Maria Lerna said. "The things you may do to others are not as consequential as what you may do to yourself. There you can do long-lasting harm."

The advice was unexpected, and Martin recognized there was truth in what they were saying, a very deep truth. In fact it was something he would have expected from the Kahuna, not from them. So far that evening, his hosts had shown a depth of…wisdom…that's what it was, wisdom, which surprised him.

Harm to myself, that's the real danger. So there has to be a…detachment. "You say powers are a burden. How so?"

"Anything we are given," Maria Lerna said, "whether great intelligence, a talent, powers over nature, or powers over people—these are all the same. They are tools one has at the moment, like an ax, or a hammer, or a saw. Do you see any advantage of one tool over another?"

"Well, it depends on the job at hand."

"Yes, it depends on what needs to be done," Eldyn said. "Wisdom comes when you realize what the tools are about and how to use them. A man becomes a fool if he pursues the tools for their own sake, and begins seeing them as his own achievements."

"There are many dangers you are not aware of, and powers you haven't counted," Maria Lerna said. "Please be cautious, and stay in your heart, dear Martin."

"My heart?"

"Yes, dear. The heart that feels for others, the heart that is part of God."

This admonition seemed to be the same as the Kahuna's; the one about staying centered. Martin smiled at them realizing he had found the two for a reason, a very good reason.

The following morning he bid his hosts goodbye. It had been a wonderful and restful night. Martin had slept in a corner of Eldyn's small hut. As he departed he took one last look at Eldyn, marveling at his various personas. One moment he was Maria Lerna's guard, physically attentive to details, concerned about her well-being and safety. Then he would change, and become soft and wise, definitely a highly evolved spiritual being, and Martin wondered at those times if he was even the same person.

CHAPTER NINE

Martin caught up with the group making their way toward Isca. The morning was overcast and drizzly, and it looked like this weather would continue for a long time. He went to see Mowan first, and found him sitting quietly astride his horse. He was not praying this time, and his aura lacked the gold hue, appearing weak and pale. He seemed to be withdrawn, introspective, as though realizing his fate for the first time, and trying to make peace with his lot in life. But then again, Martin saw him looking at his people, and his gaze went from one wounded man to the next, taking stock of their wounds, studying their faces, observing how they walked. Then he appeared to observe the whole lot, downcast and miserable, making their way in the drizzle.

So it's the fate of his people that makes him sad.

Martin stood right behind him. In his heart, Martin carried a deep peace from that morning's meditation, and he tried to send it to the Caledonian, the way he imagined the Kahuna would.

As he extended his being to Mowan, he felt the man's essence, the clarity of his soul, and the current weight on it. Martin embraced him with his own essence and, to his surprise, felt love in his heart; and he knew it reached Mowan. The Caledonian turned around slowly, his aura changing, his air lifting, and then, with a smile, he scanned the area right behind him where Martin was. Surprised, Martin stood still as he felt Mowan's probing gaze searching the air. After a few moments the monk turned away, looking a bit puzzled, but apparently relieved of the mood that had afflicted him.

Having touched the Caledonian's spirit left Martin uplifted, as though this too was a form of meditation. It also left him with a clear perception of the man, and he thought that was a wonderful way to get to know someone, touching a stranger the way the Kahuna had touched him. Of course he couldn't do it quite as well, not as strongly, but it had worked. Something inside had guided him, and he had known exactly what to do. Was that one of the powers Maria Lerna and Eldyn had talked about? A knowledge "that just comes to you," as the Kahuna had said? Was that how healing worked?

It was mid-afternoon when they came within sight of Isca. The city sat on the east bank of a wide and placid river and it appeared that it was a seaport. There were a variety of vessels presently going toward it, so the ocean could not be far. Effectively, after a look around, Martin noticed the sea was but ten miles or so downriver. A bridge crossed the river in front of the city.

Isca lay on top of a flat hilltop, surrounded by valleys, which in turn were ringed by more impressive mountains in the distance, all looking vibrant with life and color. Two roads came into the city, one from the southeast and one from the northeast, and converged into one.

Isca covered an area Martin thought would equal about fifty blocks of a city in his own time. It was surrounded by a wall several miles long, made of a lavender-colored rock, about twenty feet tall and ten feet thick, which had been built on an earth mound that rose some sixty feet. On the west side, the wall fronted the river and here the tabletop was the highest, rising about two hundred feet. On the other three sides it was much lower, and a ditch had been dug at the bottom of the slope. An approaching enemy would have to go down to the bottom of the ditch before climbing the now-imposing hundred-plus feet before reaching the bottom of the fortification. There were wooden platforms all around with catapults and what appeared to be vats of hot oil.

Anyone approaching the city would be easy to spot from one of the towers on the wall, where guards could see up and down the river for several miles and clear across the valleys. There were two gates on the wall, each consisting of a massive metal door, with guard towers on either side. The gate on the west side faced the river; and the other, on the east side, was the one the soldiers were presently about to go through. Inside, the streets were clean and orderly, all cobbled, flanked by structures of various sizes and styles. Some were ornate buildings and others were constructed simply and looked like square blocks. Most had been built using the same lavender rock; others, of white sandstone. He noticed water and sewage pipes, and what looked like public bathhouses and toilets.

The whole city seemed to be out on the streets to welcome their troops back, and by then, the drizzle had stopped. People were lined up along a big main street that led to what looked like a citadel. Martin watched as the soldiers and prisoners passed under the gate to the city. From up on top, flowers were dropped on the soldiers and people were chanting some kind of singsong. Soon the soldiers were also singing, their pace noticeably lighter.

The soldiers marched all the way to the front of the citadel. What appeared to be an official welcoming committee awaited them. Martin recognized Philippus standing next to a handsome woman, whom he assumed to be Queen Martigena. By her side stood a child of about twelve. These two were in the middle of the group, obviously the most important. Next to the royal group stood Nicolaus. All around them were dignitaries in fancy robes.

Martin drew close to the woman, curious to see if she would elicit some sort of recognition on his part. She was good-looking, with fine features, unusually bright red hair, and green eyes; she was big boned, tall, and slender, and carried herself with a regal bearing. Her face showed character and strength, and a will that Martin guessed challenged Joannes often. Her eyes were now fighting back tears as she smiled at her husband. Clearly the couple loved each other, for Joannes had met her gaze, and apparently was seeing hardly anyone else but her.

Martin felt no pang of recognition, but maybe that would come later, as he got to know her better.

He watched the proceedings for some time, and decided his time was better spent with Maria Lerna and Eldyn.

On his way, he meandered through Isca. Here was something he had only read about, a Roman city complete with temples, statues, bathhouses, and private homes. Martin wondered how old the place was, and what it looked like in his own time. Was anything left?

He found Maria Lerna sitting alone in her house. The door was open, and he peeked inside. She was lost in thought. He knocked gently, and watched her look over. She saw him and he felt enveloped in…her essence.

"Ah, sweet Martin. Come in. Eldyn is visiting someone who is ill."

He came in and sat in front of her on the floor. The house seemed quiet and still as though everything around needed a rest. It turned out that Eldyn was trying to help some woman with an ailment in her chest, but they both already knew she was to die that night.

"Half way between midnight and sunrise, she will pass," Maria Lerna said.

"How do you know?"

"There are forces involved, dear Martin. Mostly her spirit's. She wants to go, and her husband is hanging on to her, but this is a lesson for him to learn, letting go of her. With these things combined, there is no other way." Maria Lerna was visibly sad by the prospect.

"If it makes you sad to see her go, can you do something to keep her?"

"We could, but then it wouldn't be healing. Healing is harmony, and in this case harmony is dying."

"So, what's Eldyn doing for her?"

"Helping her pass with ease, with little pain and no more sorrow than necessary."

Martin understood that the pain was the woman's and the sorrow the husband's. Maria Lerna sat in silence for some time, and he waited until she looked at him and smiled to ask his question.

"Can you heal people?"

"Yes, both Eldyn and I can."

"Can you explain to me how you do it?"

She spoke softly and carefully. "You start with a clear intent to help, then embrace the other person with your spirit. You will feel God coming through, and you let the feeling flow, let it express freely." She raised one hand for emphasis. "To extend your spirit, to embrace the other person, is the critical part. You feel love, which is God working through you. Sometimes it's a challenge because we all have our likes and dislikes and our own desires for the person, and it's important not to let that get in the way of your embrace." She thought for a moment, then added: "When God is present, then nothing but the best can happen, and dark spirits are no more."

He then told her what he had done for Mowan.

She smiled at him, perhaps in encouragement.

They talked about the need for healing. She saw the world under the grip of dark forces and spirits, much like a human body that needed healing, and Martin understood that by forces and spirits she meant what the Kahuna called consciousness. The destruction of the Empire and all its knowledge and institutions by fierce and ruthless barbarians, the invasion of their own lands by the Caledonians, these were manifestations of the ailment that was overtaking the world. Maria Lerna told him the dark forces had come because it was necessary. The progress of mankind required the dark to do its part, so that in turn the light- in the process of countering it, could become stronger.

"Eldyn and I are able to feel the dark forces at work, and we know when something is about to happen as a result, such as the recent invasion by the Caledonians," Maria Lerna explained, her expression calm, matter-of-fact.

"Our role as healers is to fight the dark with our own spirit energy," she said. "This is how the universe works, Martin; this is our challenge and opportunity."

Martin asked her how long the battle would last.

"The battle is an ongoing struggle in creation, dear one. What is different now is that the dark is growing very strong, and mankind will be overtaken by it for many centuries to come. Fear-based beliefs are destroying spirit-based knowledge." She paused and then spoke forcefully. "It's urgent to establish an ongoing force strong enough to survive the onslaught of the dark. That force in the case of Britannia will be manifested in the life of a good and great man with divine qualities who will act as an anchor, keeping the power of light alive and saving mankind much misery."

"Eldyn and I, and two other healers who will come soon, are charged with creating enough positive energy so the life and events of this great man can take place."

"Is this great man already born?" asked Martin, aware that what he was hearing sounded far-fetched.

"Yes. He is presently a child, a second son. Eldyn and I became aware of his existence some time back. We know he is physically near, within a day's flight of the crow," she told him.

Her gaze was now far away, as though she was seeing something. "Soon a reunion will take place, and we will meet the other two healers, and the child. Of that I'm certain." She paused as though deciphering images. "The two healers have a specific role to help us start the child's journey. They both will help with their strong presence. On a practical level, one will help with his vast knowledge of machines and such things. The other...will bring a new perspective." She then let out a sigh. "Then one day, their jobs done, the two will go on their way, leaving Eldyn and me with the task of guiding the child throughout his life, until he dies in battle at age sixty."

Martin sat transfixed, listening. He somehow knew that she was not making things up, but was telling him what she saw.

"His life will create a healing force to be felt for years to come. All the way to your time, Martin."

She told him that in the case of the recent invasion, they felt the Caledonians coming. So some time before the battle in the mountain pass was to take place, Maria Lerna and Eldyn projected their healing energy over the land so a victory over the invaders became likely.

"Maria Lerna, what you are saying is that by virtue of channeling energy you can change the course of a battle, and even have a specific child born?" Martin heard his own voice, and he sounded incredulous.

"Dear Martin, nothing ever happens without the power and will of God. But it is our role on this earth to come in contact with that will, and be a channel. This is also God's will, for us to be his instruments by our own choice and to exercise our true nature so we can become like him. That is, in its purest sense, the meaning of life. And that is also why there is evil in this world, Martin...for us to be challenged and grow."

Martin knew the words were true, and they resonated in his mind like an echo. But there was one nagging element; the God she spoke about bothered him.

"God imposes his will, then, and we have to follow it?" He was amazed by the sound of his words, as though someone else had said them, and he realized that he knew the answer even as she began to speak.

"Oh, dear one, that's a simplistic and painful way of thinking." Maria Lerna said. "God is not a person, nor an entity that your mind could know, so it's not 'will' as we know it. Realize that you can never know God with your mind, because at that level God is indefinable. But he is, or perhaps more precisely, God is true reality itself. And you can only know him with your heart. Then you will understand that his will is likewise indefinable...I personally think of it as harmony manifested."

Martin understood what she had described, and to his heart there came the enormously sweet presence he felt in meditation. He knew then that she was right, his mind could not grasp the concept and he would have to let his heart be the knower.

Maria Lerna had been studying him intently. She then let her eyes smile, and resumed her topic. "Our mission is a legacy passed down from other healers," she said. "They were the ones who made the life of the great man possible. We are following on their work."

"But let's suppose you do nothing; would that mean the world would be doomed?"

She thought for a minute, apparently searching for the right way to explain. "No, that is not so. But let me explain by giving you an example. Let's assume you are walking along and see a child about to drown in a river. What happens to the child if you do nothing? He would drown but he would be born again, and in short order no great difference would be felt in the world or the child's soul. But you could have prevented a mother's intense grief. By your actions you could have made the world easier for someone to live in. And then, tell me, why were you there at that moment?"

"Fate. Destiny."

"Yes, destiny made your life intersect with the child's. It is your free will to act, to do something, or do nothing. This is the free will God gave us, and by using your abilities properly at the precise time, the tools we talked about, you can promote light, and make the world just a little better. That is your choice."

It occurred to Martin that she didn't seem like the sweet girl he had first met, but rather a formidable woman of great power and presence.

"I choose to do everything I possibly can to make the world a better place." Maria lerna said.

"But then, how do we know that by saving the child, we are not interfering with the mother's destiny?" Martin asked.

"The one thing you can go by, is that if you are present, then you were supposed to be there. If it requires your decision, then that moment was brought along for your benefit as well. Maybe you are the result of a mother's prayers that moved enough energy to bring you along."

"So when you move energy around, when you do your healing, does it make things happen, or does it just make things possible?"

"It makes things possible; it changes the balance so the outcome may change."

Martin wondered what the Kahuna would say about all this. At that moment Martin felt the gentle man standing in front of him; his presence was strong, tangible. Martin guessed he had come without materializing. He sensed the Kahuna telling him through his heart that what he was hearing was right.

Then he was gone.

Maria Lerna had apparently felt him as well, but she didn't say anything. However, her eyes had moistened and she closed them for a moment, perhaps to better absorb the great soul's presence. Then she looked at Martin with keen interest.

CHAPTER TEN

In front of the city and paralleling the river was a canal with locks at either end. Martin understood the use of the canal, as ships maintained their place on the quay while the river level went down with the receding tide. A few ships were now docked and were being loaded with sacks of grain from nearby warehouses. On another ship furs and leather were being unloaded by sailors who looked Scandinavian and spoke in broken Latin to local men.

Isca's streets were wide and well laid out in a grid pattern. Chariots were everywhere, inside the city and in its periphery. It seemed that for longer distances people went on horseback. In the center of the city lay the army barracks and next to it the forum and the main public baths which were shared by most of the population. Next to the baths was the market place. That morning many of the citizens had already made it to the baths. He caught conversations here and there. The languages he heard included, classical Latin; common Latin, the combination of Latin and the local tongue;, and then he heard some people speaking the local language exclusively, people from the countryside by the looks of them. Martin also heard what he surmised were Germanic languages. There seemed to be quite a number of these individuals, and he could tell the recent arrivals from the ones who appeared to be second generation; the former were bilingual and at ease in their surroundings, while the latter struggled with the new language and seemed out of place.

Martin caught the festive, jubilant mood of the city. He overhead people talking about the recent events. A group of five men stood talking in front of a house next to the baths. They wore expensive robes fastened with jewelry, and smelled of perfume. They stood in studied postures, and judging by their soft bodies, had seldom or ever done anything physically taxing. Martin guessed they were noblemen, and after listening to them for a while, his guess was confirmed.

They too were excited by the battle's outcome. The victory had been a major surprise, considering the number of cities that had fallen. They had been getting refugees from just about all places north and east of the city. Isca was one of the few fortified cities, so they knew they had a chance behind her walls. They had thought at the time that Joannes had been foolish to leave and engage the enemy in the open just to protect the farms. They had expected him and most of the soldiers to get killed, and then perhaps a siege. After that, they had hoped for the enemy to eventually get tired and go elsewhere, perhaps fan out through the countryside picking at easier targets.

That day there was going to be a Mass at the church to offer thanks for the victory. Then a day of celebration with food, music, dances and performances at the forum. That was exciting. About time Joannes spent some of his money on something fun.

They wondered if Joannes was going to punish those who had not joined him. They were certain that soon they would find out, and questioned whether it wouldn't be prudent to go on a trip to the countryside and stay there for some time, now that it was safe.

Their talk switched to the prisoners and the rumor that they were going to be shipped to Saxony. They hoped they would get good slaves in exchange, for they could always use strong slaves, there being so much work to be done.

Curious, Martin looked around to see who was doing the work, and sure enough, even the farmers who brought the goods seemed to be slaves; they looked foreign, and carried themselves with a different air. At any rate, it was easy to spot slaves, and they were all over the place.

He visited the Citadel, which had been built near the east portion of the wall. He couldn't call it a palace, for it wasn't luxurious or grand; it was practical, a self-contained enclosure with tall strong walls.

The royal quarters consisted of a villa surrounded by various buildings. One of those was obviously a kitchen, the only place with sounds of people working at that time of morning. Martin went to the villa, and all was quiet except for the central courtyard. There he found Nicolaus and the youngest prince he had seen the day before. The monk was teaching the child math and Martin followed the instruction with interest. *How odd, they made him the prince's teacher.* He understood the monk to be a spiritual teacher, not this kind.

The child's name was Ambrosius, and he seemed bright. He listened to everything Nicolaus said with eagerness, as though hungry for knowledge. Martin studied the young man and found something very distinctive about him, a maturity way beyond his years, as though a grown man was hiding inside a child's body. There was something else about the child that made him special, and Martin couldn't quite figure out what it was, just a feeling every time he laid eyes on him or heard his voice. It was odd.

He remembered Maria Lerna's description of a second son, and the young man certainly filled the bill. Maybe he was making more of the boy than was warranted, prompted by her description, but there was no harm in speculating. Martin noticed the gentle air about him, the way he talked and carried himself. He appeared self-assured, as befitted a pampered prince, but then again, he talked with simplicity if not humility.

Martin decided he would have to tell Maria Lerna about Ambrosius.

Some time later the King and Queen came out. They were holding hands, and had a rested, loving glow about them. It was time for Ambrosius to take a break, and the morning meal was served. Philippus came out to join them.

It turned out the monk had talked Martigena into letting him take over teaching the prince, which until then had been the responsibility of his mother and the local priest. Martin heard her say that she had long realized her son needed a more learned individual to teach him, and now spoke to her husband in glowing terms about Nicolaus and how he had opened a new world of knowledge for Ambrosius.

Nicolaus responded that he wanted to be useful, but Martin suspected that he had taken a keen interest in the prince. He talked with enthusiasm about the youth to his parents, and there appeared to be a bond already growing between the two in the seven days Nicolaus had been around. The ease, or even affection, with which they interacted was apparent.

Martin learned Ambrosius was about to have a birthday; he was turning thirteen in two months and Nicolaus and the royal couple talked of preparing a feast in his honor. Nicolaus told them the young prince had a special destiny, and stressed how important it was to prepare him properly.

I was right! This is the child Maria Lerna talked about. Nicolaus saw it as well. The monk was also very special, Martin thought as he contemplated his aura and felt his serenity. *One of the healers she saw coming?* Why not? He had not seen anyone else like him save for the Kahuna, Maria Lerna and Eldyn. If it was true, Maria Lerna would be very excited with the news.

At one point Arcadius came in. He seemed angry. "Noble King, I have bad news. Three days ago, while we were busy defending the land, two farm enclaves and a village were raided by bandits from Julius' kingdom. Mostly they stole cattle. Some women were violated and they killed two old men and three young boys."

Joannes' face turned somber. He sighed deeply. "Those two are at it again. The cowards, attacking while the able-bodied men are away."

"The men are back, they won't dare attack anymore," Arcadius said.

They talked about Julius and his general, a man named Cassius. So far the two had been a nuisance, but now were becoming a threat. King Mateus had told them of incursions into his land. They heard the same was happening with other kingdoms nearby.

There was not much they could do. Julius had fortified his city with tall wooden walls. Maybe one day they would catch him out in the open.

"Cassius is the one I am after," Arcadius said, "He's evil."

"They both are, my friend," Joannes replied.

Talk then centered on the immediate future, the issues at hand. Joannes was to travel with the slaves to Saxony. All except for the young chief, Mowan, whom Joannes thought they should try and win over. He could be a powerful ally, but Joannes wasn't quite sure how to treat him or what to do with him.

Nicolaus suggested they could make him a teacher. Incredibly enough, the royal couple seemed to consider the idea, and Martin gathered that teaching was not an uncommon occupation for slaves. They didn't seem concerned that he was an enemy, that just a few days before he would have tried to kill Joannes, Arcadius and Philippus. Nicolaus was making a very persuasive argument on behalf of the Caledonian, he commented that from what he had heard, Mowan was quite cultured, had been a monk and as such had probably been trained as a teacher. He said that with one look he would be able to tell if the Caledonian was a sincere man of God, and if that were the case, they would be able to trust him implicitly, provided he gave his word to serve them. He and Mowan could take turns instructing the child, and this would give Nicolaus a chance to keep an eye on the man, and perhaps befriend him.

Joannes and Martigena appeared to like the idea, and gave Nicolaus tentative approval. It was interesting how quickly Nicolaus seemed to have become a member of the family, but he appeared to belong somehow. It was also curious how persuasive he was...and how passionate about the Caledonian.

The family went to Mass and Martin followed them. The rest of the day was taken over with the festivities, which Martin observed with curiosity. Wine and food were served in large quantities, all provided by Joannes. There was dancing, and Martin was reminded of the typical Greek dances he had seen, where people gather in circles and dance together. Then there were games, and he saw people playing what appeared to be soccer, games of chance played with dice, games of skill involving archers and javelin throwers, and wrestling. In the early afternoon they all gathered at the forum, a large building like a coliseum, where comedies were shown.

After some time, Martin decided he had enough, and wanted some solitude. He found himself constantly thinking of Maria Lerna, and wanted some time to meditate alone. He had to find another cave, a place to be alone and call his own. That would be ideal.

He decided to look close to the ocean, so he went west until he came to the coast, and then followed the rough shoreline north. Near a small island he came to a sheer cliff. Martin was sure there had to be a cave in there somewhere. After some time, he found what he was looking for, a small out-of the way cave just big enough for him. Inside there was no evidence of human habitation, only signs that birds had used the place at some point. He went inside. Not the same cozy feeling as the other cave, but it would do. He figured that after he had spent some time meditating in his new hide-away, it would feel just fine.

He let his mind take him into meditation, allowing the images of the world to peel away. He felt the welcome sense of grace bathe him, fill him. After some time he opened his eyes but consciously stayed in a meditative state as he allowed his mind to review the image of Maria Lerna. This was definitely one of those situations the Kahuna had warned him about, when he told him to stay detached. He knew if he could just bring his feelings under control she could be an immense help, support and guidance...and wonderful company. He had already learned much from her. She was definitely a highly evolved soul, perhaps as evolved as the Kahuna. But if he became attached he knew he could spoil it all, that the relationship could not possibly go on.

Why? Why the strong feelings for her, so sudden, so fast? Maybe he knew her from his previous life, maybe he was the man she had been supposed to marry and he had carried a flame for her through lifetimes. Maybe just because she was an extraordinary woman, incredibly beautiful, and one most men would feel drawn to...so in that regard the attraction was natural. But could he still find her very attractive, recognize she was wonderful and let it be at that? Celebrate her beauty and all of her qualities without wanting to possess her? Love her as a sister, as a friend? Even if he had loved her before, he could transmute that feeling into something...practical under the circumstances. Still, the yearning was very strong, a desire to touch her, to feel her skin against his, to hold her in his arms. That, he knew would be heaven, right at that very moment.

He realized that for some time now he had been carrying a hunger for affection, for a soft caress, a gentle touch, all the loving he once had received freely from Jenny. Well, it was hard, but he understood perfectly what he had to do, and it required discipline. He didn't want to stop seeing Maria Lerna. He certainly would never express or demonstrate in any way to her how he felt; that was obvious, it couldn't be clearer; he was only concerned she would detect his feelings, read his mind. That would be embarrassing and possibly create a distance between them. So he would have to control not only his feelings, but his thoughts as well. *So be it.*

At that moment he felt her presence. Instinctively he turned to look to his left, and there she was, sitting beside him, bright and beautiful, holding her knees inside her arms, calm and natural. But how? *How did she get here?* His mind racing, he felt his chest about to explode.

He looked at her, and her eyes held a most tender and loving look.

"I am proud of you, Martin. That was very difficult for you, but you went through it all and now you are stronger for your effort."

"But...how in the world did you get here?"

"Ah, dear Martin, you think perhaps you are the only one who can travel with your body of light?"

She had felt his turmoil and had decided to help, she told him. She had assisted with her energy first, which had probably led him to find the cave. Then she had decided to watch his process, and now had one last bit of information to offer.

"Which is?"

"That there is another way to express love."

His heart, or that part of him that felt like his heart, was now calmer, the feelings in his chest had subsided...she had helped, he was sure.

"Love? Is the attraction I feel for you...love?"

"It is the love of Spirit, not the human love you are used to. Only, because of your long standing habits, when you feel love for a woman, you channel it in the only way you know how, through physical yearning."

"How do I express my love for you, in a spiritual way?"

"The same way you did for Mowan. Extend yourself, your spirit, and embrace me."

He did as he was told, and felt a floodgate open where his being came and met hers. They merged and he felt the full flavor of her being and deep love. She had enveloped him, or he her, and their two selves became entwined and joined. He held her heart in his; her mind was inside his own. And now he knew her: loving and calm, bliss and beauty, bright as the sun.

Gently, slowly, they separated, and now he could see her, still sitting, just a few feet away. The imprint of her essence remained inside him.

She told him it was natural to feel greater kinship for some people than others, but eventually he would feel the same for all people, for animals, for all of creation; and the means to do that was to practice with others what he had just done with her. In their mutual intention they had beheld God in one another, and that was the beauty of it all.

"You don't need to be embarrassed you love me, dear one. But stay with Spirit, and you will be doing right, and gain the most." She paused. "Know I too love you deeply, always have and always will." She said with a softness Martin had not heard before.

Always have? Her words and manner had just confirmed what he suspected all along; they had known each other from a past life. So that's why his feelings for her were so strong. "Maria Lerna, have we known each other before?"

He watched her hesitate. "Oh dear Martin, let us not go into that." He gathered that the topic was best not discussed.

So be it, some other time. He agreed the "embrace" was more meaningful than any physical contact. He was happy, very happy now. He loved her, and it was alright…as with everything else he had learned of late, there was always a spiritual side to things, even physical yearning, and she had shown him.

"Have you always been able to travel with your body of light?" Martin asked.

"Only since meeting you, dear one. After hearing your story I realized I too could do it at will." She smiled shyly. "I only waited for the need to arise. And here I am."

She had been concerned about him, worried he might leave because of his feelings, and she didn't want to lose him, so she had decided to intervene before he had a chance to make a decision.

They agreed to go to her house. He followed her and when he entered her small hut she was in her physical body, sitting in a chair. When he arrived she was opening her eyes and smiling at Eldyn, who was sitting at the table busy with something.

"That was easier than I thought," she told Eldyn, who smiled back at her.

As she made a move to stand up, Martin decided to tell them about the child Ambrosius, and his belief that the two monks were the healers she had talked about.

Maria Lerna and Eldyn were both silent for a few minutes and Martin could tell they were checking with each other, and also checking the images of the people he had talked about. He felt them physically reviewing his thoughts: it felt as though they were actually reaching into his mind, turning his mental images around and inside out until they were both satisfied.

It was Maria Lerna who spoke. "Martin, you have turned out to be quite the most wonderful scout for us. Yes, you are right; those are the ones, the child and the two men. Brothers." She stood up, circled the table then stopped behind Eldyn's chair. "Eldyn, they are here!"

There was immense relief in those words and now Martin realized the importance of the child and the monks in the scheme of things. They had prayed for them to come, had felt their presence from afar and now they were real. And somehow they were able to communicate all of this to him, not with words but with what he could now tell was energy, a forceful, tangible projection of their selves; and by just sitting quietly, he was able to get the full meaning of what they felt.

"Yes," said Eldyn, with no apparent emotion.

"How do we meet them, Eldyn? What do we do now?" she asked excitedly.

Eldyn's face registered a faint smile. "I trust you will figure that out, my lady."

She looked at him, then thought for a minute. "I will go with Martin in the morning," she said as though they were going to walk, "and show myself to the one monk, the Roman one."

"Nicolaus," Martin said.

"Yes, Nicolaus. I almost think he's expecting me. The other one, he still doesn't know why he's here. We need Nicolaus to tell him."

Then she told Eldyn he would have to wait to meet the child and two monks, it wouldn't be prudent for them both to leave the colony.

Martin understood it was a matter of maintaining the energy in the place, like a dynamo that keeps an engine running, and that one of the two had to be present, or on site, and whatever else that meant.

"That will be fine, my lady," Eldyn said. "One day the three will come to me, will come to visit the colony."

"Yes, that will come to pass," she said, lost in thought.

Eldyn nodded. He looked at Martin.

"You may have to prepare yourself to be seen."

Good lord. "Why would you want me to be seen?"

"It's not that we want you to be seen, Martin," Maria Lerna said, " but at some point it will become necessary for you to intercede, and you must prepare yourself for that, because it will happen."

They sounded as though they were looking into the future, and seeing him involved in events. *Why me? No need to be actually out there.* "I'm just here to watch, Maria Lerna, there is no need for me to get involved."

"Dear Martin, remember the drowning child."

He remembered the drowning child, all right. *There are times when helping someone is unavoidable…that was the case with the Caledonian woman and her baby.*…But the thought of being seen filled him with dread, and he couldn't quite figure out why.

Sounds came from outside. Steps. Maria Lerna looked at Martin. He quickly bid them good-night, saying he would be back at dawn. With that he vanished into his light body, and seconds later a man and a child stepped up to the open door and looked inside. The man had brought the child for some healing, he said, he was sorry for the intrusion, but she was complaining of a pain in her stomach, and perhaps Maria Lerna and Eldyn wouldn't mind the late visit.

With a smile they welcomed them, sat them down, and Martin watched as Maria Lerna approached the child, as Eldyn talked to the father.

Martin left the house and headed for the little cave on the bluff.

He watched early light come through the cave's opening. He had woken up while it was still dark, four in the morning he guessed. He needed less sleep, now he could make do with four hours or so. He had meditated. *Just a sweet moment of feeling whole.* He came out of his cave and for a moment stood watching the ocean, and then went to meet Maria Lerna.

As soon as he announced himself she stood up eagerly, eyes flashing excitement.

"Come, Martin. Let's go." She extended her hand for him to hold. He did, and they both left. Touching her hand felt like an electric charge, and it was her will that took them away.

Martin guided her to the Citadel, and to the royal chambers, for he supposed Nicolaus would have his bedroom next to the boy's. But that was not the case, so they searched through the house, going in and out of chambers. He felt a tug of her hand and she asked to see the boy, she wanted to see him that very instant, the monk could wait.

They stopped at the prince's chamber and she went over and stood by the sleeping boy, carefully studying his face, and Martin could tell she was crying. There were no tears, but the emotion was palpable. She looked at the golden hair and soft face of a pre-adolescent. He was a good-looking child, and resembled Martigena with his high cheekbones, straight nose, and long face.

They were off again on their search. Interestingly, they found a tunnel that led away from the royal chamber. He wanted to follow it, but felt her urgent touch on his hand. *Fine. Let's find the monk.* Their pace quickened, she was certainly in a hurry. Finally, in one of the outer buildings, what appeared to be guest quarters, they found Nicolaus in one of the rooms. He had apparently been awake for some time, for he looked as though he had bathed, his hair was wet; and at present he was sitting upright on the floor, legs crossed, engrossed in meditation. The wolf lay sleeping at the foot of his bed.

They both stood for a minute, feeling the sweet vibrations that filled the room, and Martin could tell that like him, Maria Lerna was taking in the full essence of the man.

Maybe he felt their presence, for he opened his eyes and looked about the room. Maria Lerna let go of Martin's hand and he felt her materializing beside him.

The monk's face registered surprise, but he remained sitting cross-legged, his eyes fixed on the apparition before him. Then he took a deep breath, and there was an audible exclamation as he saw her face.

"Oh, I know you!" With this he quickly stood, and bowed in her direction. "You are the one who has come to me in dreams so many times…who are you?'

Maria Lerna had made her body solid, so she could talk. Martin noticed the wolf was now sitting up, looking at Maria Lerna but not making a sound.

"I am Maria Lerna, and I have been waiting for you to come, Nicolaus." She explained she had summoned divine intervention to help with the darkness that had befallen the land. She told him Spirit had shown her the boy in a vision, and she knew he was the answer to her prayers. She then had seen both him and the other monk, Mowan; and she knew they would come, for she needed them both.

Nicolaus appeared to listen intently to every word she said. His eyes discreetly scanned her figure, studied her face. He tentatively reached out and touched her arm, then stood back, clasping his hands together in front of his chest. He seemed to collect himself, then spoke.

"Most venerable lady, I saw you several times in dreams. Each time you were summoning me. So I came. I let Spirit guide me, take me to you, then when I saw this city I knew this was the right place…I knew in my heart I would meet you here. I also saw the boy in dreams, and when I first lay eyes on him I recognized him. I knew it all fit together, you and the boy. I know the boy is special; he has a mission. But I have yet to meet the Caledonian, I don't know what he's like. I am to meet him this very morning, after my session with the boy. I had planned to meet Mowan and talk to him, feel his spirit." Nicolaus' voice was tentative. "Then, if I am reassured that he's a man of God, I meant to bring him here to become a second teacher for the Prince Ambrosius." He looked at Maria Lerna. "That's as far as I have thought things out, and I hope I'm doing the right thing, most revered lady."

"Spirit guides your every action, dear Nicolaus," she said softly. "I trust you. It's of great importance to befriend Mowan. He's a good man, and destiny has brought all of us together."

Maria Lerna placed her hand on his arm. "For now, only you will know of my existence, but when the time is right, I will meet Mowan, and then the boy. I too will impart knowledge to the prince, special skills."

Nicolaus assented. "I will do your bidding without question, my lady." Then tentatively he asked, "Are you an angel, Maria Lerna?"

"No, I am human. I am using my body of light to come to you, for otherwise it would be almost impossible to do so."

She took two paces back and he bowed to her. "I will show myself again very soon," she said, and then vanished from his sight.

Martin saw her approach him and then felt her hand once again, but instead of leaving like he expected, she wanted to follow the monk that morning.

They watched Nicolaus as he met with the child in the royal villa's courtyard, and then moved indoors to a room with a blackboard where he taught him geometry. Maria Lerna followed every one of Ambrosius' comments and responses and wouldn't stop exclaiming how smart he was. She was only distracted by the wolf. Apparently she was taken by the animal as well, and said it was an extraordinary being. All in all, she seemed to be enjoying herself and couldn't figure out why she hadn't done this type of travel before.

When it came time for Nicolaus to leave, she became visibly excited at the prospect of meeting the other monk; her eyes shone bright and her whole countenance seemed to smile at Martin.

They followed Nicolaus and a royal guard out of the Citadel and through the streets to the prison. There they met Arcadius, who had been waiting by the gate. Maria Lerna studied the general closely and said something to the effect that he was a "good soldier." Martin couldn't tell whether she meant it as a compliment; there was no energy behind her statement, and maybe it was just her observation that he was good at what he did.

Nicolaus and Arcadius, with Martin and Maria Lerna behind them, followed two prison guards and the royal guard through dank corridors, and Martin felt himself shudder at the smell and feel of the place that spoke of fear, anger and desperation. Maria Lerna appeared calm but sad, and her lips kept moving, Martin guessed in silent prayer for the prisoners. What they could see of the cells—through small openings in the doors—appeared to be crammed with human flesh…and human waste. They stopped by a door, and one of the guards opened it.

The feel inside that cell stood in stark contrast to the rest of the prison, for Spirit filled the small room. They were all visibly moved by it: the guards, the general and Nicolaus , and there in a corner sitting on his cot was the source of the vibrations, a man stripped completely naked. He was alone in the cell.

CHAPTER ELEVEN

Nicolaus looked at the naked man and their eyes met. A recognition took place in that silent moment, and Martin felt it as tangibly as he could feel the floor beneath his feet. Apparently Nicolaus didn't need any further proof or talk. He bowed to the Caledonian and then motioned for him to follow.

Mowan stood up slowly and fell in step beside Nicolaus, in his dignified way. Now there were additional guards following them, and the Roman monk strictly forbade anyone to touch Mowan, much less put chains on him. It seemed Nicolaus had been shocked by the state in which he had found the Caledonian. In spite of the vibrations in the cell, it had been an appalling place, dark and wet, a layer of grime covering the walls and a pool of putrid water over most of the floor.

The general took off his cape and put it around Mowan's naked shoulders as he explained that the prisoners were stripped naked because they sometimes hanged themselves with their clothes. Mowan felt the military garment with his hands, a heavy cloth of deep red, and turned to Arcadius and quietly thanked him. It was obvious there had been a softening of the veteran soldier, for the air about him, his manner, was now changed.

As they walked behind the Caledonian, Martin saw Maria Lerna crying, moved by what she had just seen and felt.

They all walked out of the prison and towards the Citadel, passersby looking long and hard at the strange group being led by a royal guard: the young Caledonian chief they had heard so much about, wearing the general's cape, escorted by the Roman monk, with the general himself walking meekly behind.

The group proceeded to the guesthouse where Nicolaus was staying, and where a room adjacent to his had been made available for Mowan. Nicolaus took care of his fellow monk; he took him to the baths and procured him clean clothes, a white robe like his own, and then left him in his room to rest and meditate before they were to meet the boy, his parents and Arcadius in the courtyard. Nicolaus then went to his own room to meditate as well.

Maria Lerna decided to appear to him once again. She waited until he had closed the door, and slowly made her appearance.

"Nicolaus, it is I, Maria Lerna."

Although surprised by her unexpected appearance, he smiled broadly. "Yes, my lady. I am at your service."

"I won't come to you unexpected like this anymore, unless it's urgent, and I think this is urgent. I want to meet with you and Mowan tomorrow in the morning before your session with the boy. Without question, the Caledonian is a very special soul; you can trust him…except when it comes to his people. Advocate in his favor so he may help them, then you will have his undying loyalty."

"Yes, my lady, I have gathered as much myself, but the King may be of a different mind."

"That is the reason for my visit now, before you meet with the King. If you see an opportunity to help Mowan help his people, do take it."

"As you tell me, so I will act, and may God be with us."

The statement, Martin realized, was an affirmation. The monk was bringing the divine presence to bear on his actions.

Maria Lerna took Martin along to a remote corner of the courtyard where there were two benches and a small fountain enclosed by shrubs. There they sat to meditate, and she asked him to join her in directing their healing energy in the direction of the King and the monks when they met.

The monks came into the courtyard, both calm and peaceful, their auras shining a bright gold light. Soon after, the royal couple made their entrance, with Ambrosius and the general trailing behind.

Martin did as he had been asked, and opened his heart to those present, and soon he felt them, and he embraced them, and he opened more and he felt them closer. He sensed the monks, resonating with Spirit, and the child, a soft, peaceful presence, and then the parents, both restless, but strong and resolute. Martin felt Maria Lerna's and the monks' prayers. It seemed to him everything had changed as a result, and all around him all things, the stones, the flowers and shrubs, everything was for the time being a part of another world, a gentler, softer place, where anything was possible.

The monks rose and bowed when the father, mother and child approached them. The general remained a polite distance behind.

"Your August Majesties, greetings," Nicolaus said.

Whatever statement the King had prepared apparently vanished. His gaze became soft and his manner calm.

"Thank you, Nicolaus. Mowan, you are welcome in my home." Then signaling toward his younger son, he went on, "And this is Ambrosius, your young charge. You are to teach him together with Nicolaus. Teach him well so he may be instrumental in bringing safety and peace to our lands."

The group discussed the manner of instruction they expected for the boy, and as the conversation went on, the distance between them diminished, the

King and Queen making an effort to bridge the gap, relaxing the difference in their status.

Nicolaus suggested they be given a small house adjacent to the villa, which had been built for the daughter of some long-forgotten Roman general. There the monks could live with Ambrosius and instruct the child without interruption. "Maintaining a sound environment of peace and devotion will help the prince," Nicolaus said.

Joannes consented, and was apparently pleased by the request and the reason.

It was Mowan's turn, and he spoke softly, with eyes downcast. "August King, I would be honored to teach the Prince, and if necessary lay down my life for him. But, if I could be so bold, please in return, show compassion for my people, the prisoners who are now at your mercy. Sending them to lives of slavery in a far-off land would mean a great hardship, the dissolution of families, and the death of many of them. I would rather have them executed. On the other hand, if what you want is peace, and for my people never to attack this land, I Mowan, can help ensure that."

"Tell me how, Mowan." Joannes seemed interested

"My people," said Mowan, "are awed by the manner in which they were defeated. They have never seen anything like that, so swift and deadly. They now respect and fear you and your men. That can be parlayed into a lasting peace. They would all be glad never to set foot on this land again, but they have to make it appear as though they are doing it for a reason other than fear. I propose that the men be sent back home, each under oath never to set foot again on this side of the hills where the battle took place, and to take word back with them that this kingdom is not to be touched. I, in turn, will stay for the rest of my life to serve this kingdom and take a vow to kill myself the moment I see one of them cross the mountains to attack this kingdom. For my people a vow is sacred. I am a prince held in high esteem and all Caledonians will respect my vow."

Joannes appeared impressed by what he heard. "Are you willing to give me your oath of loyalty? As a man of God?"

"I am." His words resonated with conviction. "I give you my word before God that I will vouch my life to you, your family, your people and this kingdom."

Joannes was deep in thought, staring at the Caledonian. "So be it," he said, "I accept. In return your people can go back to their homes, each one under oath."

Mowan was silent, his lips moving in prayer. Then he extended his open hand, which the King took in his. The oath was sealed.

Arcadius appeared perplexed, as did Martigena. Maria Lerna and Martin looked at each other, smiling. Martin realized magic had taken place. His only concern was that Mowan would never set foot in his homeland again, and that this must weigh heavily on him. He told Maria Lerna as much.

"Yes, that is in his heart. But the happiness he feels for saving his people is far greater than the pain. Also, by now he knows his destiny is here."

The following morning Maria Lerna met with both monks. They were sitting in Nicolaus' room meditating when Maria Lerna materialized in front of them. She silently came, sat and joined them. Martin sat as well, but at a distance. They remained like that for a long time, apparently caught up in the grace each one held in their heart and that embraced the room. Then they all opened their eyes at once and beheld one another; Mowan looking at the apparition in front of him, first seemingly in awe…then with love, as his heart and not his eyes beheld Maria Lerna.

"You are everything my good brother told me, and more, revered lady," he said while bowing.

"Thank you, Mowan. I am very pleased you are here with us." Martin gathered she meant more than his physical presence and was referring to the oath he had given the King.

She told them Ambrosius would be King, not Philippus, and he would be a great ruler with consequences far beyond the kingdom, so their lives would be well spent given to that service. Eventually, she too would start instructing the boy. She told them about Eldyn, and how he supported their efforts from afar.

"Now," she told them, "will the two of you vouch to devote yourselves to the boy, for as long as it takes?"

The two monks signaled their agreement.

Perhaps as a way to seal their intent, they stood up and faced each other. Martin could feel scenes play out, and he realized they were events from the future the three were seeing and trying to influence. There was war and violence, but also wisdom and learning, justice and honor…and ultimately, peace. This was a form of prayer, he gathered, a way to make a living affirmation.

That afternoon the Caledonians were let out of the prison. As they walked out they were met by Mowan, who explained that he had pledged to give his life in bondage to the kingdom in exchange for their freedom. He also told them he had vowed to take his life should any one present ever come to make war on Isca.

The Caledonians mumbled and whispered among themselves, then some stared at the ground or at the sky, apparently angry or sad.

One man, perhaps one of their chiefs, spoke up. First he bowed to Mowan and said his heart was grateful for what the "noble prince" had done, but he would rather be a slave than have Mowan held hostage. Then another, an older man, said Mowan was more than just a prince, he was their future.

Martin was astounded. None of them seemed happy at the prospect of freedom.

Mowan spoke again. His voice was soft but it carried throughout the gathering as everyone fell silent so they could hear him. "I already made the vow. It was my decision alone. I am more than willing to spend the rest of my days in this land so you can return home." The gathering was now still, as if frozen. "What I need from you is your vow that you will never come to this kingdom bearing arms and with the intent to do harm, or I will take my own life." There was muted silence after that. Then he asked for a show of hands if they agreed to take the oath. At that point some stepped forward offering to stay as well, but Mowan told them he had already pledged his word to Joannes, and that was enough. They all took the oath, apparently grudgingly.

That was amazing. They were barbarians, but had a lot of principle, and Martin wondered if the men from Isca who were present were just as impressed as he was. The prisoners then had their chains taken off, and were led to some barns where they would be housed until their departure, still under guard, but more comfortable. They would be allowed to come out, but only in small groups, and escorted by soldiers.

Martin heard Joannes say to Arcadius that now he had a new problem: how to transport the Caledonians back to their land. If they went back the way they came the people they had savaged would surely attack them; and now, as a much smaller group, they would be vulnerable even if armed. The answer was to send them back by sea, but there were not enough boats. Only five big ships were available and at least five more would be needed for that many people…and time was running out. This was the middle of spring, and they had until the middle of fall at the latest to set sail before the seas would turn too rough for travel.

To Martin it seemed a contradiction that Joannes was now concerned about the welfare of people he had been busy killing only recently; but somehow now he viewed them differently.

In the next few days Martin heard a lot of excited talk around the Citadel concerning Nicolaus. The man had traveled quite a bit, for he was from a wealthy Roman family with the means to do so. He had an interest in rare devices and had been to Alexandria where he had learned about exotic machines. Martin then heard Martigena telling one of her lady friends that Nicolaus had brought with him the designs of the great Archimedes, and was now helping Joannes' builders redesign the war machines protecting Isca. He had also shown Philippus a drawing of a device to be used by horse riders, which was quite revolutionary. Arcadius, in turn, had been most excited about a liquid called "Greek fire," that produced flames impossible to put out.

A month later the city was all excited about a test firing of one of the new war machines. Martin had missed the test but by the talk he heard around town he surmised the new catapults were a big improvement over the old ones.

About a month later, the alarm sounded on the wall, trumpets ringing out with a shrill sound. Martin watched as soldiers rushed to the wall, busily removing leather tarps from their new war machines. He now noticed these were contraptions that shot out many arrows at once, and some that shot one big arrow, more like a harpoon; and yet others that were big cantilevered things with a basket on one end. He saw these could shoot either one big missile or several smaller ones at once, depending on the basket attached. The machines could go back and forth in grooves on a pivoting platform. Nearby there were round amphorae already filled, and some empty ones. Martin understood the filled ones contained Greek fire; the empty ones were for oil. He also noticed oil vats kept warm with fires. He watched as soldiers got busy stoking the fires to make the oil boil, while archers manned the walls.

The alarm was over a ship flying the Londinium flag, being pursued by five ships. The canal gate opened to let in the friendly ship, while the soldiers at the machines prepared to fire on the other five. The distance from the city wall to the river was quite substantial, about three hundred yards, Martin thought. The wall rested on top of a slope that ran down some two-thirds of the distance; then came the docks, then the canal which was separated from the river by a towpath. That was a considerable distance, but then again, the machines were all told a good three hundred feet higher than the river, lending the advantage of shooting down, rather than on a flat plane.

With their prey out of reach, the five ships were turning around, preparing to leave. Joannes stood at the wall watching, when Arcadius approached asking if they should let out their ramming boats. Joannes said no, he wanted those pirate boats whole, he needed them. Instead he decided to try out the new machines, and directed the catapults to load up with oil amphorae. The boiling oil was poured into big round clay containers, which were then tightly corked. The catapults were lined up with their targets using a crank to pivot the heavy machines. One of the soldiers in charge carefully gauged the distance, sighting the boats with what looked like a sextant, and told the crews to adjust weights on the catapults, which had already been winched back to firing position. The oil containers were then fired. Martin watched as the baskets sprang up and forward, rocking the machines back and forth in their grooves. The missiles whistled as they flew through their arched trajectory and hit their targets with amazing accuracy. The effect was devastating: the balls shattered on impact, sending boiling oil all over the boats. Even the ones that were near misses caused a lot of damage; they shattered on the water and spilled oil on the boats. Martin saw men jumping overboard screaming. The ships, however, remained intact.

Then Joannes let out his boats to capture men and ships.

The pirates were Saxons. Most of them were brought back alive, some badly burned. Wounded and able-bodied alike were put in chains and taken to the prison, with no attempt made to help those who had been burned and were writhing in pain.

Instead, Joannes and his men concentrated on the crew and passengers from the Londinium ship. It turned out they had been heading to Cartagena, and had encountered the pirates on their second day. Their only hope of escape had been to seek refuge in Isca, a full days' sail downwind. The captain had only hoped the ship would outrun the pirates, and that the wind would hold. As luck would have it they could scarcely keep ahead of the five ships, and had to fight them off three times, each time barely escaping being rammed and boarded. He feared being surrounded, and had ditched their cargo of dried meat, and the passengers' belongings. There were a total of six passengers and eight crewmen, and three of them had been wounded in the attacks. The passengers consisted of two couples and two children.

One woman sat crying and rocking forcefully back and forth as her husband tried to console her.

The Caledonians were the ones in greatest awe after the victory. A group of them had watched the defeat of the pirates from the walls and kept talking about it excitedly.

Arcadius was now training a good many new soldiers, and Martin noticed there was always a group of Caledonians taking it all in, not missing a single day of training, even when it involved nothing but constant marching. They watched the infantry go through several of their formations, and watched the horse troops train endlessly on their mounts. Martin wondered whether some of those techniques would be well learned and then used by the Caledonians the next time they invaded.

Right around this same time Martin witnessed a marked change in the royal family. After the initial talk in the garden something had come over the Queen, and she had insisted they "converse" with the monks every day. Martin now saw them each morning, the entire family, Joannes, Martigena, Philippus and Ambrosius; all gathered, being taught meditation by Nicolaus and Mowan. Also there, unseen was Maria Lerna, watching them. And the change was rapid. He could see the way it affected each of them; Joannes was visibly becoming…wise. There was that air about him, and his aura reflected it. For Philippus, it was introspection; he became enclosed within himself. Ambrosius appeared to be blossoming. Martigena seemed enveloped in serenity.

The peace in the Citadel stood in sharp contrast to the rest of the city, which was restless, nervous with uncertainty. Martin overhead many conversations on the subject: the world around them was collapsing. The two couples from the Londinium ship had told of the chaos that ruled in Londinium, where "every man for himself" was the new rule, and gangs roamed the streets robbing at will. They told how the forts along the coast all the way to Londinium were fighting off pirates every day, how some were being breached, and how everyone knew Londinium would be next. They told of Saxon settlements to the north of the city and how their area of control was slowly expanding.

The times when the country had been under the Romans was the stuff of legend; a world far removed from their present scope of vision. People talked about what was lost from the era: peace, knowledge, refinement, culture, and the technical attainments in science and technology. In their more recent past they had experienced the safety brought about by the Big Council and its legions. Then had come Vortigern, the king who took over the Council and eventually caused its dissolution. One man, talking to a group in the baths, said that the decline started in the year four hundred forty-six, when Vortigern died, the same year the plague struck. His listeners agreed. Over the next few years, the Big Council lost its power, then some years later it disbanded. No one really knew why. The Big Council legions eroded when the soldiers were no longer paid. There had been no one to pay them, no one in charge.

Even the monks talked about the violence. One morning Martin went with Maria Lerna when she paid a visit to them. Following their morning meditation together in Nicolaus' room, the three talked about the recent pirate raid. That led them to talk about war and the Caledonian invasion. It was odd, for Mowan stood talking about the topic with Nicolaus and Maria Lerna, as though he had been not one of the attackers, but an observer.

"Mowan, you are a man of God, but you found yourself forced into war;, that must have been hard," commented Nicolaus.

"Yes, I killed in battle, and acted against my spirit," Mowan said. Martin thought he seemed anxious to tell his story, to explain himself. "From early years I had a premonition my life could go in either direction, war or God." He took two steps to stand near Maria Lerna. "One day, I must have been around six, I told my mother I didn't want to be a warrior, I wanted to become a monk. I asked her to help me, for I feared my father had plans for me to follow in his footsteps and join him in battle as soon as possible."

"She gathered me in her arms and she cried. I understood there was no way out for me."

"So you ended up a warrior...and a monk?" Maria Lerna sounded baffled.

"No, one went against the other. The path that brought me here is a convoluted one. The year after I asked my mother for help, she became ill and was dying. The day before she passed, father and I gathered around her bed and she requested a dying promise from him; to send me to Ninian's abbey, now run by a saintly man called Mirio. She wanted me to become a monk. Father swore to grant her wish, and by that I could tell how much he loved her." Mowan looked at Maria Lerna. "I believe she died for me, that dying was the only way she knew how to help me."

"A month after my mother died, my father sent me to the abbey. At first I only mourned my mother with all my heart, and I wanted to die. But Mirio took me in and became my teacher, my mother, my father and my friend. I soon found I was the happiest I had ever been."

"I studied with six other children of varied ages. There were no other monks around. Once trained and initiated, Mirio's disciples were sent all across the land, wherever they were needed. The seven of us were to become monks together, on a day of his choosing."

"We were taught how to live a well-rounded life, how to see God in everything and everybody. We spent our hours in communion and prayer, and long talks with Mirio. He also taught us martial skills, and at the time I didn't know why. The years went by without notice, and I found myself becoming a man."

"One day, Mirio announced we were all close to taking our vows. He told us that on the following full moon we would all be initiated. I was seventeen years old."

"But that was not to be," Mowan raised his head and looked through a window at the courtyard. "He died within a week, the second time in my life I suffered a great loss. He had boarded a boat for one of the islands, when a gigantic wave swallowed the craft. We were all standing on a cliff waving goodbye and saw the entire thing. Everyone drowned."

"This time I had the advantage of having Mirio's gentle teachings, and I looked at his death with sorrow, but also as the conclusion of a successful and wonderful life, so my heart was also glad for him."

"There was no other man of God around to initiate us, so we all had to go back to our homes. Father welcomed me with open arms. He felt his vow to my mother had been fulfilled, and now I could become a warrior."

"I decided that on my first raid I would allow myself to be killed. It was then I suffered an accident; a horse threw me and I landed wrong. I spent months healing, but it wasn't until a full year had passed that I could ride again. In the meantime I started instructing others in the martial skills my teacher had taught me. Warriors I trained spoke highly of me, and other clans brought their young men to me. My father had no choice but to keep me at my post. This way I managed to avoid going on raids for eight years."

"Then the clans planned the biggest raid ever, and they needed every man. I couldn't avoid it." Mowan looked at Maria Lerna again, his manner subdued, perhaps apologetic. "That was the raid of three years ago."

"I decided to go with my original plan and let someone slay me, but a voice inside told me I had a destiny to fulfill, and to trust God."

"I prayed to God, Mirio and my mother to deliver me, as I rode into my first battle. I knew once my hands had been bloodied, it would be hard to cleanse my soul." Mowan kept his gaze fixed on Maria Lerna's eyes. "As we approached the enemy, an arrow struck me on the shoulder of my fighting arm. I looked up at the sky and thanked my saviors with all my heart. By the time the shoulder healed, the raid was long over and we were back home."

"Six months ago, while the clans prepared to invade again, my father fell ill and I had to take his place and lead our clan into battle. That same night in my dreams I saw Mirio. He took me by the hand, as was his custom, and told me my life as a warrior would be brief, that soon I would meet a monk who would initiate me." Now Mowan's gaze was fixed on a point somewhere on the wall in front of him. "We rode into battle and I killed."

Maria Lerna looked solemn. "I am sorry, dear Mowan. Killing must have been a heavy burden."

Mowan's eyes were moist. "Yes, it was. Although I never killed anyone who was not armed, and I never stole, or destroyed. Not with these hands. Although I did witness my men kill wantonly, rape and lay towns to waste…I could only be responsible for my own actions, that's the best I could do." With this he bent over, deep sobs convulsing through his body.

Nicolaus put an arm around Mowan's shoulders.

"The day Joannes defeated us," Mowan said, "was the day I was saved. That evening, after our defeat, I recited a prayer of gratitude that my warrior days were over."

"But, dear soul, you have not been initiated yet?" Maria Lerna's voice was gentle.

Mowan straightened up and looked at her. "I found a monk to initiate me." And he turned his gaze toward Nicolaus.

During the next few weeks life in the city appeared to quiet down and people started to talk about other topics beside war: business ventures, the latest comedy from overseas. Then, a month after the Londinium ship arrived, a rider came from one of the farms, announcing they were under attack by barbarians.

Joannes, Arcadius and Philippus assembled their cavalry and headed toward the farm cluster. They had decided to take two hundred riders, leaving two hundred to defend the city. The rest of the troops had been given leave. Martin followed them, watching the soldiers ride at full gallop.

After running for about an hour, they came to the farm cluster. Some of the buildings were already in flames, and there were many bodies about, most of them farmers who had apparently tried to defend themselves with poles and sickles. The attackers were presently concentrating on two structures, one a barn, and a good distance away, the villa, which was the only building surrounded by a protective wall.

The Isca men divided into two forces. Joannes and Philippus took on the barn attackers, while Arcadius went for the villa.

When the riders first arrived, the attackers had turned around to face them. Some shot arrows in their direction, but most stood at the ready with axes and swords, expecting the riders to dismount and fight. However, the soldiers just kept coming at them at full gallop. They rode in tight formations of ten horsemen per group, each group acting in unison. Martin watched as each rider took out about five of the enemy with each swoop of his long lance, made a quick turn, and then came around again for another deadly swoop.

In a matter of minutes all was silent, the horses still, foam coming out of their mouths, their bodies covered in sweat.

They stood for a moment surveying the scene. No enemy was left standing. The destruction had been so devastating and so fast, Martin stood in wonder, not quite understanding how the Iscans had managed to do so much damage so quickly.

The riders sat on their horses, both animals and men breathing heavily. Martin could feel a raw energy in the air, and it came from both men and beasts. At the height of the battle, it had been as though there was no separation between human and horse; they fought as one, they moved as one, and he understood by looking at them that they relished the fight. Now it appeared as though they all needed time to savor their victory.

Eleven of the horses and two riders had been wounded.

The riders dismounted and split up into four groups. One was to take care of the enemy who were still alive, another went to assist the wounded and dying farmers, the third went to put out the fires. The fourth group went around looking for additional enemy who could have escaped.

A few hours later their work had been done. Eighteen of the raiders were still alive out of a total of two hundred and ten. Well over a hundred had been mercy-killed. The soldiers had to put down three of their wounded horses.

They questioned the prisoners and found they were Saxons who had landed undetected a short distance up the coast. Then they had marched along the road until they found their first farm cluster and attacked. Joannes had been sure all possible landing sites were under surveillance; but somehow someone had been lax.

That following day Arcadius, accompanied by about fifty riders, went to investigate how and where the invaders had landed.

Three days later Martin heard Arcadius had returned to Isca and reported to Joannes that all landing sites were secure, so he had no idea where the Saxons had come from, unless they had traveled by land all the way from the east coast.

Martin found Joannes, Philippus, Arcadius and other officers, talking in the barracks. The conversation had started some time before, but Martin got the gist of what they had discussed.

The Saxons had lied. Following interrogation, the story finally came out. They were part of a large force under Erouf. They had come at the request of Cassius, King Julius' general, and had been staying in Dunum for the past month.

"That's a threat I had not imagined," Joannes said.

"Cassius knows the lay of the land, and the Saxons are brutal fighters. Yes, I think we have a problem. We need to do something," Arcadius said.

"And fast," said Joannes. He turned around and walked toward the Citadel.

Afterward Martin heard a group of officers talking for some time about Julius and his kingdom. Apparently the place had been a source of trouble ever since the Big Council collapsed.

Julius was described as an evil man, someone who enjoyed violence. "He is simply a barbarian who welcomes bandits to his land," declared a senior officer. "He then lets them act with impunity and shares the spoils with them. He's profiting while his people suffer. Word has it that in Dunum no one is safe and those who could leave have already done so."

"This Cassius, did he serve with our general and King?" asked a young man of one of the older officers, a man with a barrel chest and gray beard.

"No, Cassius was but a foot soldier in one of the southern legions. But the officer he killed was well known by both."

"How did he become a general? asked the young man.

"Ah, noble friend, that's the kind of man who suits Julius best." It turned out Cassius had been a legionnaire who had been caught stealing from a farm, and when punished by his superior officer, had sneaked into his tent in the middle of the night and killed him. A tribunal had sentenced him to life at hard labor, but in the years of chaos that followed the break-up of the Big Council, a lot of prisoners had escaped or had bribed their way out. At any rate, Cassius had escaped prison and was now in Dunum, in a position of power.

A few days later they heard of another raid.

Again the soldiers rode off, but this time Martin stayed behind.

That afternoon the riders came back with news that they had been too late. The raiders had struck fast. They had managed to kill six peasants on one farm, and then left. They were definitely Julius' men, according to the farmers.

Joannes sat with Arcadius and Philippus in what looked like a sitting room at the Citadel.

"This is a new strategy. They are striking and leaving before we can act." Joannes was clearly upset, his voice harsh.

"Why would they do that?" Philippus said. "They didn't steal anything."

Arcadius shook his head. "Terror. They want to terrorize the farmers."

"But why," Philippus sounded incredulous, "what do they gain?"

"They want to weaken us," Joannes said. "Before long the farmers will want to leave, and without them we have no food."

"Then let's attack them, and wipe out Dunum."

"Lay siege to a fortified city?" Arcadius said. "It takes a lot of men. Many casualties. They have the advantage of sitting behind walls shooting arrows and pouring oil."

"But one day we'll have to do it. Get rid of those two bastards, Julius and Cassius." Joannes' jaw was clenched, his face red. "Let's figure out how to protect ourselves, then we'll come up with a way to wipe out Dunum."

CHAPTER TWELVE

The following morning Martin found Joannes, Arcadius, Philippus, Martigena and another noble named Horatius in the royal villa's courtyard, discussing ways to defend the kingdom. They had to link the outlying areas and Isca into one unified kingdom, like the Romans and the Big Council had done with whole areas of Britannia.

It was decided that cavalry units would be posted at strategic points. But the cavalry needed modifications. Philippus had tested the loop Nicolaus had talked about, and had the metal smith produce several hundred of the devices. Their first test had come during the recent Saxon raid, and they had all seen how devastating the newly equipped riders were. The device facilitated the holding of a sword in one hand, or a lance for charging, because the rider had something to stand on. It also made mounting and dismounting much easier. Martin realized they were talking about stirrups, a deceptively simple device. From then on, their cavalry would all use the loops.

They drew a plan to protect the front of the horses with armor, for that was the most vulnerable part of the animal when charging against foot soldiers. Arcadius said they were still working on a longer and heavier sword, one a man could wield from a horse, for that had been a problem they discovered while fighting on horseback: their swords were not long enough. The shields, on the other hand, were too cumbersome, too big.

It was determined they also needed a system of scouts to keep an eye on the kingdom. Arcadius told them he had some soldiers already being trained for that purpose.

There were forts from the old days, before the Romans, scattered throughout the kingdom. These hilltop fortifications would be refurbished and used again. A cavalry unit of thirty riders and scouts would be located in the fort closest to each farm cluster and village. The riders would patrol the farms, and if they needed help, they could dispatch riders to neighboring forts or to Isca. The city would thus become a center for the administration of defense. Somehow they needed to maintain on-going communication with the farm clusters and villages, not only during emergencies but also on an ongoing basis, to find out how things were going.

Arcadius had already instituted a program of rigorous physical training for the troops, and he reported they actually seemed to enjoy it and take pride in what they could do. He saw the need to somehow bring the entire kingdom into better physical shape; that would translate into stronger recruits to begin with, and better citizen soldiers when they were needed.

The cavalry units they had already trained were dispatched to forts around the farm enclaves and villages in the north-east, where raiders from Dunum had struck. They just had to train more soldiers to cover the rest.

In the following weeks news came of cavalry units fighting off two bands of raiders. Then the attacks stopped. Two full months went by without incident and people started to relax and go about their business; the nervous talk disappeared from around town. People forgot about war for the time being.

In the Citadel, they continued making plans for the kingdom, and the group met several times over the following few weeks. Martin made sure to be present. It was interesting for him to see how healing energy translated itself into practical steps.

During those meetings Joannes and the group decided that other aspects of the kingdom also needed change, that changes in defense needed to go hand in hand with other, far-reaching, changes. It appeared all of their ideas were tied together. They needed to abolish slavery, first because it felt right, but also because slavery made citizens lazy and physically weak. Everyone should work.

To institute the new reforms they needed public support, and they also needed communication with the villages and farm clusters, so Joannes proposed to bring back a council form of government. It was apparent to Martin that Joannes was a great admirer of the ancient Greeks, perhaps as a result of Nicolaus' influence, who had talked with him at length of the statesman Pericles. They decided to form something along the lines of the old Athenian assembly, but on a small, manageable scale. For this they consulted with Nicolaus and as a result they came up with an entity they called the Circular Table Council, to distinguish it from the table where the Big Council had met, with Vortigern at the head and all decisions eventually deferred to him. Before Vortigern, various kings had headed the Big Council. Before that, the Roman Governor had headed the Ordo. Now things had to be different. They decided that for the new council to be effective it had to operate with all members having an equal voice.

They set out to invite a core group of citizens to be members of the Circle Council, as they now called it, and then they would ask those people to nominate additional members, until they reached thirteen. That was a good number, and should include members of villages and farm clusters as well as city dwellers. This was a sure way of having a cohesive kingdom, rather than a city surrounded by villages and farms. The Circle Council members would, by the simple fact that they came from various communities, share their experiences and seek counsel from their neighbors. All decisions were to be voted on, and that is why they had settled on thirteen, an uneven number, so there would never be a tie. Joannes' function would be to implement the council's decisions.

Once formed, the Circle Council would order the abolition of slavery.

"What if they don't go along?" asked Arcadius.

"Let's make sure we select good people, then; those with good hearts and sound minds, and let's see where it goes," said Joannes.

They decided to also adopt the old Athenians' process of "ostra," the voting out of Circle Council members who proved quarrelsome or non-effective.

Nicolaus was an enigma in Martin's eyes. It was curious for him to observe the man helping with a noble concept such as the Circle Council, but then see him another time design machines for killing. But apparently he saw no conflict. His manner was calm and apparently one with Spirit at all times. He also had deep knowledge in astronomy, botany and medicine, what he called "Natural Philosophy," and he shared his know- how with those who were interested, such as the two medical men in the city.

Both he and Mowan were well steeped in Greek philosophy and were now engaging Joannes, Philippus, Arcadius, Martigena and other nobles in open discussions. Mowan was the more introspective of the two, and the one who seemed to most embody an artistic, or perhaps sensitive bent. He spent many hours entertaining the nobles by reciting entire passages of the classics, including Homer's Iliad. They in turn, book in hand, would try and catch him in an error, but his recall was flawless.

Mowan was also teaching Ambrosius how to paint. One time Martin found the entire royal family and the two monks collecting wild flowers outside the city, just so Mowan and Ambrosius could then paint them. As they picked the flowers they sang songs, most of which Mowan taught them. He would recite one line at the time, until they knew the entire song, then he would sing it for them so they could learn the tune.

The monks seemed to have found a new passion, physical exercise. Some afternoons would find them with Ambrosius, at the army barracks, drilling with the soldiers and sparring. Mowan was very good with a sword. Sometimes he was used by Arcadius as an assistant, and the two men would spar in front of the troops.

Walking back home from the barracks one afternoon, Nicolaus asked Mowan about his teacher. It had been Mirio who instructed Mowan in martial skills, and Nicolaus wanted to know more about the man. Mowan talked about him for some time, saying Mirio believed that a well-rounded life included martial knowledge. Then Mowan asked Nicolaus about his teacher.

"His name was Aramas, a wise and wonderful man," said Nicolaus. He went on to say that he had spent many happy years in his school in Greece.

The next morning when the teachers met with Maria Lerna, Mowan casually asked Nicolaus to repeat his teacher's name.

Upon hearing the name Maria Lerna turned and exclaimed, "Aramas!…That can't be!" as her eyes filled with tears.

She asked him if he was Greek, and the town he came from.

She told them that Aramas had been her teacher, her brother's and Eldyn's. In a way it was like having a common father.

"And how did you meet Aramas?" asked Maria Lerna.

Nicolaus told them that he had been but a small boy of ten when he accidentally met the great man.

"Prior to my birth, my father moved our family to Milan, the new seat of power after Rome was sacked in the year four hundred and ten. All of Italia was in chaos and there were many poor refugees wanting to escape the violence."

"There were baths in a major thoroughfare well known in the city, and each time I went by with my parents or a servant, I would see the men and women, sometimes entire families, gathered around because they had no other place to stay."

"One day I asked my father if I could take these people some food, and he consented. So accompanied by a servant, for the streets of Milan had become dangerous in later years, I went with a basket full of leftovers."

"I distributed the food as best I could so everyone got at least something to eat, and they were grateful. One of them was an old man, a gentle man, who caught my attention. Unlike the others, he took a polite amount, a piece of bread and some fish, and even of this he gave part to a child sitting nearby. 'A growing child needs more nourishment than an old man,' he said. Then he asked me for my name, and my favorite pastimes. I told him I liked to read and learn about nature. We talked for a while, and then I had to leave, but all through the night and the following day the image of the old man kept coming back. Perhaps it was his gentle manner, or the light in his eyes or the peace I felt around him. I just remember that he had made quite an impression."

"In following days when I came back with food, we would talk at length, about learning and books, and the old man told me about the wonderful library at Alexandria that contained all the knowledge in the world. He seemed to have read the entire library, for his knowledge was impressive. He told me about Archimedes and his wondrous inventions, and Pythagoras and the beauty of mathematics. And each day I came to hear more, and ask him questions, and I figured he was the most knowledgeable and wisest man alive."

"One day, though, he was gone. I anxiously inquired around but no one knew where he was. Sad and disappointed, I guessed he had been a traveler who had continued on his way, and I would not see him again."

"Weeks later, a famous strong man came to town. He was known as the Lion Man and he was from Africa. It was rumored he could lift and carry a horse on his shoulders, bend iron bars with his hands and bite through a sword. All my friends were going, so I asked my father to let me go see him."

"My mother took me, accompanied by a strong servant. That day it seemed half of Milan had come to the Coliseum to see the Lion Man. As my mother and I and the servant went past a building, three men came out and tried to grab me. In those days the city had become depraved and boys were stolen and sold as sex slaves, and highborn boys were in great demand. Two of the men knocked down the slave, and one threw my mother on the ground. Then the men grabbed me and were about to put me astride a waiting horse, when I saw the old man come seemingly out of nowhere. As a child I didn't understand what Aramas did next to get rid of the bandits, but later on I realized fully well. He used the energy of his spirit embodied as a physical force. I saw the old man gesture with his hand, and the three men thrown around as though a powerful gust of wind blew them away. With the three bandits lying unconscious, the old man helped my mother up. He then helped the badly beaten servant. He introduced himself as Aramas, a Greek monk."

"My father, grateful to Aramas, invited him to stay in our home for as long as he liked, but the monk replied that he was on his way back to Greece where he had disciples waiting anxiously for his return. But my father insisted, and he graciously agreed to spend a month with us. During that period Aramas became a second teacher to both my sister and me, for we already had a family teacher. He impressed my parents with his knowledge and his skills. In no time at all my sister and I became very attached to the wonderful man, and learned like never before. It was as though doors of understanding opened up when he talked, and everything became clear."

"One day, at the eating table, Aramas told us that it was one my father's closest friends who had been behind the failed abduction. Shocked and highly offended, my father at first refused to even consider the notion, but the monk asked him to confront the man, and gave my father the names of the friend's associates and the secret society he belonged to that was responsible for the abduction of children around the city. Asked how he knew, Aramas told him that was unimportant, what mattered was my safety and that of many other children like me."

"My father's friend, who usually came on Sundays after church to visit, had decided to come a day early. My father had his friend sit down, made him comfortable and calmly offered him some wine. Then, with Aramas and my mother present, told him he knew who had tried to abduct me, and sadly, it was a close and trusted friend. He mentioned the names of members of the secret society. At these words his friend dropped the wine, turned very pale and tried to flee, but servants had been summoned to block all the doors. Then my father had soldiers come and take his former friend away."

"The following day my father asked Aramas to take me with him to his school in Greece, to teach me, and keep me until I was a grown and learned man. I was sad at the prospect of leaving my family, but also tremendously happy to go with Aramas."

Maria Lerna stared at Nicolaus, but her gaze was lost, and she was looking right through him. "Aramas was my family's teacher for five years," she said. "I don't know what became of him…or my family."

Nicolaus pensively looked at her. "Aramas was already old when he taught me, he would be well over a hundred by now."

"I never knew his age." Maria Lerna seemed to have become uncharacteristically upset and was making an effort to control her emotions.

"Can't you visit your family?" said Mowan. "You could bring them all here."

But Maria Lerna was dismissive; she shook her head and changed the subject. It was obvious there was more to her tale, and that it was a painful subject.

"How did you manage to come to Britannia, Nicolaus?" she asked.

"At the age of twenty, Aramas initiated me," he told them. "He bid me to first go to Alexandria, 'and do not waste time getting there, for soon the library as we know it will be no more,' he said. Then he told me I was to travel to Britannia, and to look around until I found the city where I had an appointment with destiny."

"I could have stayed in that library for the rest of my life. There were books on everything, and men of great learning to converse with. I spent several years studying, until one night, I had the first of several dreams where I saw you, dear lady, and I knew I had to find you. So I obeyed my teacher and headed for Britannia. A year later I heard that a month after I left, the library had been ransacked and a great many of its books destroyed. That's the Empire's greatest loss so far," Nicolaus said.

A sad smile crossed Maria Lerna's face. "He was such a great man. You are fortunate to have had him as a teacher for all those years."

That evening, as usual, Martin went to visit Maria Lerna and Eldyn.

After a few pleasantries, Maria Lerna started telling Eldyn of the day's activities at Isca. She told him that Aramas had been Nicolaus' teacher, and then proceeded to tell him the monk's story. When she finished, Eldyn sat staring at a pot on the table.

After a silence he stood up. "I loved Aramas," he said with his back to them. "I first met him nine years ago when both he and I were gladiators."

Maria Lerna looked surprised. "Oh, so you were a gladiator! And Aramas too? How did that happen?"

"It's a long story, my lady."

"Eldyn, you already began, you can't just stop now!"

Eldyn glanced at her, and he appeared grave, as though facing a long forgotten memory. "Spectators liked me because I could fight two men at once. At the beginning, I felt excited each time I fought, it was man against man and only the best survived. I lived not knowing if that day would be my last. But things changed, or I changed and anyway, at some point I was becoming tired of the killing, the violence, but mostly of the spectators. I started to hate those people who enjoyed the violence and cheered when one of us got seriously hurt or killed."

"But I thought gladiators had been outlawed many years ago," said Maria Lerna.

"Yes," replied Eldyn, "Emperor Honorius stopped the games when a monk was killed by spectators after he tried to stop a match. But that was before my time. After the barbarian invasions, many cities brought back 'the games,' and this time without rules."

"How did you become a gladiator, Eldyn?" Maria Lerna asked.

Eldyn glanced back at her. "I had been a crewmember aboard a boat that carried cargo and sometimes passengers. One time we carried gladiators, that's when the man who owned them bought me from the boatman." His manner indicated that those details were unimportant, and he went on with his story.

"I knew some gladiators could buy back their freedom, but my master would not let me go because I was very popular with the crowds. I thought of escaping, but that was not possible, I was too well known, and knew I would be captured and punished. Refusal to fight or fighting poorly meant torture. My only other alternative was death, or letting myself be wounded to the point of being useless as a fighter. I was thinking all of these things, when one day I met an older gladiator, a Greek named Aramas. The same man my lady later knew as her teacher."

"He had been a monk, but at that moment he was a gladiator, and a good one. It was said he was a magician because he never got hurt, and sometimes he moved so fast the eye could not see him. One moment he was in one spot and about to be hurt, and then he appeared unhurt some distance away. He was the wonder of all the other gladiators, but the audience never noticed how great he was."

"One day, as we waited for our turn to fight, Aramas told me his secret; he said inside him, his spirit was very still and what happened outside, to his body, did not matter. And that was why he had no fear of death, and in fact had no fear of anything, for nothing could ever happen to him to change his interior world. He said in that state he could muster a force that took over his being and made him fast and strong. He then showed me; I saw he moved like a panther, and I could tell what he was talking about, a change had taken place, a change hard to see, but to me it was plain as day. Aramas glided around without effort, and his movements were graceful but extremely powerful. I could feel the raw strength in his gestures, strong enough to cut through rock."

"In the arena Aramas was in total control, and he said as long as he was still inside and kept his force, he could extend his spirit and be everywhere at once. I was curious about the man's secret, and asked him to teach me. He did, over many days and nights, even in the pits before and after our matches."

"I can't see Aramas killing anyone," Maria Lerna said. "Did he ever talk to you about it?"

"Yes, one day before entering the arena I asked Aramas about killing, whether it was a sin. He responded I should do well everything destiny required of me at the moment."

Maria Lerna seemed to think about the answer.

"What does killing well mean to you, Eldyn?" Her tone was inquisitive.

"For me it was awareness, knowing that when I killed I was killing a part of myself, for we are all one; and the grief I was causing, I would feel one day."

"But then, understanding that, you still killed."

"Yes."

Maria Lerna appeared to be thinking about Eldyn's answer and it seemed it would take some time for her to come to terms with the concept, but she was anxious to know more of Eldyn's story, so she asked him to continue.

"One day, Aramas started talking," Eldyn said, "and his words took hold of me and I don't remember going out and fighting, all I remember that day was Aramas. And the following day I felt the magic for the first time. I felt compassion for my adversaries, even love, and saw through the brutality as nothing more than a make-believe dance. No one ever died, I understood; and I knew the killing and the dying were necessary for all of us to learn how to live, how to love. With fear and revulsion gone, I too was able to extend my spirit over the arena, and was at once untouchable and unconcerned. And I felt the force course through my body. At that moment, I found I was detached from life but at the same time very much a part of it; I was one with everything."

Martin felt the same, he could feel what Eldyn had described and he wondered whether that was 'the dance of life and death' the Kahuna had told him about. *If so, this is my moment of understanding.*

Martin then heard Aramas talk to him; he was certain it was he, it was so vivid he was almost sure it was Aramas' actual voice, and in his mind his own voice repeated the words he heard: *Being present…is applying meditation to life. It means being one with Spirit in every action, every breath…and it is the same whether you are saving a drowning child, killing or dying, or picking up a leaf from the ground…it is the dance of life and death, of Spirit and nature.* With those words Martin felt a force that surrounded him and was him; it was how he felt during deep meditation. He was aware of every cell in his body and every leaf on every tree, every speck of dirt on the ground…He was in everything…and everything was a part of him.

Now he knew what understanding meant. And it was all in his heart.

Martin became aware that time had stood still for him. Eldyn and Maria Lerna were still there, and Eldyn was still talking, but nothing had taken place. He accepted what he had experienced, noted it as a moment for him alone, and he listened to Eldyn once again.

Eldyn was saying that after that Aramas had taught him communion. "Aramas told me that communion was the ultimate battle every man must win, and it changed my life. What happened outside of my being became unimportant and I concentrated my efforts on keeping this inner peace, and that gave meaning to what I was doing, to everything on the outside. The world became harmonious. After that I knew I could escape the violence, that it was a matter of time before my outer world would reflect my new interior peace. "

Martin found himself not just agreeing with Eldyn, but also living what he had just described.

"We spent a few more months together, maybe two or three, it was hard to tell, but one day we were to go different ways; Aramas to Alexandria and I to Rome. When we said goodbye, Aramas told me we would meet again, and when that happened I was to face the greatest challenge of my life."

"He let me know the reason he had become a gladiator was so he could meet me and train me to become an interior warrior. Now that his job was done, he could resume his life as a monk. By this time I was not surprised by anything Aramas told me or did; so I thanked him, because I realized the extent of the effort he had gone through to reach me, and I asked him why, why did he go through all that trouble for a simple man, a gladiator, a slave?"

"Aramas answered that he loved me, and would have gone to the ends of the earth to find me."

"We parted with an embrace. This was the first time anyone embraced me, or loved me. And that is how we parted."

"A month later I heard the ship carrying Aramas on his way to Alexandria had sunk with no survivors. My heart ached and I knew I would never see him again."

"That was, until six months later when I was being sold as a slave in Dunum. I was there because of a dream I had. Just a few days after Aramas left my life, my old owner died and his son took over. I had befriended my new owner when he was but a child, and we had spent many hours sparring, and of late, talking about communion. The moment he took over, he offered to free me, and it so happened I had the dream the night before. In the dream I saw I was being sold as a slave in Dunum and I knew that was my destiny. So I asked my owner that instead of freeing me, to send me to be auctioned off in far-away Dunum."

"Surprised, my owner agreed, although it took a bit of doing, the town being such an out- of -the-way place. But he guessed I wanted to go home, because that's where I was born."

"As I climbed up on the auction block so everyone could see me, I looked at the audience, and saw a familiar face: it was Aramas, an older Aramas, and next to him a young man, who as it turned out, was Marius, my lady's brother. At first I thought the old man must be Aramas' father, but then I recognized his essence, and was sure it was him. My heart was as happy as I had ever been. Later I learned it was Aramas who had convinced Marius to bid for me."

"In the five years we lived together in my lady's home, Aramas continued teaching me, picking up where he left off a few months before, as though no time had passed, and offering no explanation for how old he looked, or how he survived the shipwreck, or how he got to Dunum. But one day he mentioned in passing, that when he needed anything, things just came to him. I guessed he had made his body young for the time he needed to become a gladiator, but when he went back to being a monk he became his regular self."

His tale finished, Eldyn resumed staring at the pot, lost in thought.

Maria Lerna sat, as if in a trance. "Dear Eldyn, there are so many things about you I never knew." She looked at Eldyn as though seeing him for the first time.

Martin ended up meditating for several days. He found no obstacles, nothing pulled him back; it was as though something inside of him had finally been resolved. When he came out of his cave he found it was late afternoon of a bright sunny day. He looked at the ocean in front, and the forest to one side. He wondered if he was now ready to go back home and resume his life. The moment of understanding the Kahuna had told him about had happened, of that he was certain. He felt calm and realized he had changed. *Should I go now?*

"No," he heard the Kahuna's voice. "You are not ready yet."

That was fine. He would know when it was time. He went in search of Maria Lerna, and found her with Eldyn outside her cottage. They were in the process of cooking the evening meal.

"Greetings, Maria Lerna and Eldyn," he called out.

"Dear Martin, it's so nice to see you,." she answered. Then looking at his face and probing into his eyes, "you have been in deep communion, friend, and you made the transition."

"Transition?"

Eldyn turned his head in Martin's direction. He also seemed to probe and look him over.

"Yes, sweet one," she said, "the big step when you are willing to let go of who you are."

He told them he had been meditating all this while and he did feel different, and he thanked them for their role in helping him reach his new state.

"That understanding you experienced happens to all of us," she told him, "and sometimes it is a sight, sometimes a word someone says that precipitates it."

From that day on, Martin fell into a nice routine where he would meditate long hours, and then he would go and see what was happening at the Citadel...then he would go back to his cave. In the evenings he visited with Maria Lerna and Eldyn. He let the days go by, one after another.

One evening, Maria Lerna sat with needle in hand and looking solemn. "Dear Martin, tell me about your time. What are people like? What about Christians? What do they practice?"

"Well, let's see, what can I tell you?"

"Oh, I know. Don't tell me anything. Instead, think of your world with your heart, and let me look inside. Words are a bother sometimes."

He did as indicated, and felt her probing, like a sponge picking everything up, all at once.

She was disappointed by what she saw. She found most Christians far removed from Christ's teachings. "The darkness will cover everything." She did see the presence of saints, and was elated. She was particularly intrigued by some of them and asked about Saint Francis. When he told her and she smiled, it was as though she was personally meeting him. She commented on Thomas Becket and Peter Abelard. She was also drawn to Father Damian, Saint Teresa of Avila, Saint John of the Cross and Brother Lawrence.

Martin was left with the impression that for her time was not a barrier, that once she was aware of a person or an event, as she had just become through him, she was able to transport herself to that time and place, for she talked about events, people and places as though they were happening right in front of her eyes...and gave details well beyond Martin's knowledge. She talked about Saint Francis as though he was a contemporary. "He is doing such wonderful work, my sweet monk."

"It will take time, but people will begin communing again." she said. "You know it was the Greek thinkers who led the way to Master Yesu and communion."

"I didn't know that."

"Yes, dear. When the mind is expansive, it leads invariably to questioning what is real. That's what Socrates, Plato and Pythagoras did for us. They paved the way for communion, for looking inside to become one with God. They made the soil fertile for Yesu and his teachings. In fact, when we heal someone, when we commune with one another, that was called 'agape' in ancient Greece."

"Agape? What does the word mean?"

"It means divine love, dear. That's what we spread through our spirits, the divine essence."

Martin paused for a moment. *That's a beautiful concept.*

"You said that the Christians of my time are far removed from Yesu's teachings," he asked. "Is that because they don't commune?"

Maria Lerna looked at him. "Oh, Martin. Christians today are no better. What you see in this colony are the vestiges of what once was. Yesu became one with God, and his life and his teachings were meant to show us how we can become like him. We all have the same potential. Do you see what I mean?"

"Yes, Maria Lerna, I think I do."

"Sadly," she added, "we don't seem to learn. The same teachings and message have been borne time and again by many great souls. And it will be repeated many more times."

Whenever he went to the Citadel at first light he would invariably meet

Maria Lerna who usually was already sitting at her appointed place. Then the monks would show up, then the royal family, and they would all meditate, Martin and Maria Lerna together, the others gathered around in a circle a few paces away. Then the monks would talk with individual family members, and sometimes as a group. Afterward Ambrosius and the monks would go to their small house where the monks would teach the prince the day's lessons.

Maria Lerna would usually appear to the monks after the child was gone to play with his friends, right before the noon meal. She now planned to appear to the entire family, to make her presence known, before she started teaching the boy.

The following day she asked the monks to prepare the family for the appearance she was planning to make the following day. She felt they were ready, their auras were very beautiful to behold, all clear blue with tinges of gold.

Both Martin and Maria Lerna listened carefully the following morning as Nicolaus approached the subject with the family, saying someone very special wanted to meet them.

The royals appeared intrigued, but Joannes spoke of his concern that an outsider was coming to their private quarters.

Nicolaus surprised him even more by telling him it was not a human who was coming. "Maria Lerna is a special being, not of this earth; in my mind she is an angel, who has come in bodily form for a special mission. She's the one who brought brother Mowan and me to this kingdom. She has been protecting young Ambrosius for some time because he has a special role in coming years."

Martin looked at Maria Lerna while the monk spoke, and she was staring at Nicolaus wide-eyed, with a surprised look on her face.

Martigena's face beamed with happiness. "I knew, it! For some time, I could tell of a heavenly presence about. At first I thought it was because of you brothers. I know you two are saintly. But tell, when is this angel going to appear?"

"Tomorrow at our usual meeting is when she promised to come," said Nicolaus.

Joannes and Philippus looked at each other incredulously, while Martigena embraced Ambrosius and happily danced about with him all over the courtyard.

The following morning when Martin came, earlier than usual for he didn't want to miss anything, there was a tangible feeling of excitement in the air. Freshly cut flowers had been placed all around the courtyard in vases. In each corner now burned some type of incense, filling the place with a wonderful aroma.

Maria Lerna was there with him shortly. She was serene, prepared for her appearance, very quiet. He noticed she sat to meditate, and he decided to do the same, and send her his support, whatever he could muster.

The monks came next, as usual, and then the royal family appeared. Martigena looked dazzling. She was dressed in her finest, a light blue gown with gold borders. The rest of the family had also dressed up, and gathered in the usual place, sitting in front of the monks. The group sat for some time on their benches facing each other, the monks in deep meditation, and the royals visibly excited.

Maria Lerna walked over to stand in-between the monks and the royal family, and then very slowly she appeared.

CHAPTER THIRTEEN

To Martin she was the most beautiful apparition he had ever seen, and perhaps he was looking at her through their eyes, but her hair was very gold, and her eyes very blue, and she radiated calm, a soft serenity that came from beyond her own self: a manifestation of Spirit.

They were all silent, in fact the world seemed to have come to a standstill...and Martin now got a measure of the full magnitude of her being when she was one with Spirit. He felt the impact of her essence, powerful and present, Spirit as profound, magnificent love.

"Greetings, noble ones, from your servant, Maria Lerna." She spoke softly, and to Martin she sounded indeed very much like an angel.

They looked at her in awe, and silence remained for some time.

"Greetings, revered spirit...it is we who are your servants," Martigena said, her voice heavy with excitement.

Maria Lerna took Martigena's hand, perhaps as a gesture that she was more human than appearances showed, or perhaps as a way to communicate her unconditional love; and whatever the reason, Martigena broke into a radiant smile, tears of joy rolling down her cheeks, looking all the while into Maria Lerna's eyes.

"I am here to help you through the crisis you are going through," Maria Lerna said as she held the Queen's hand. "The Empire will soon be no more; it is best if you forge ahead on your own. Everything you need is within you. It's possible to not only survive, but thrive, materially as well as spiritually. In difficult times, souls are born with great potential, and such is the case with your family and your kingdom, and each one of you has a particular role to play. Do it well."

"I will help each of you individually." She looked at the young child. "Ambrosius I will teach special skills, but all of you will be the focus of my attention." She turned her gaze to Joannes. "You are a good king, honorable sir. See you instill high spiritual values in your people. Teach them about altruism, honor, courage, justice and truth. One reason why the Roman Empire is falling before your eyes is because they abandoned those values. Master Yesu came and they were unable to understand and much less adopt his teachings, otherwise they would have changed their ways."

She congratulated him for starting the Circle Council. She then took Joannes' hand as well, and kissed it.

With that she vanished.

Martin was as mesmerized as her audience was. The monks had not spoken nor moved a muscle the whole time.

She walked over to where he was and again sat next to him.

She too seemed quiet, and he asked her how she felt.

"Spirit came and filled my being."

The next day Maria Lerna showed up at the teachers' house after the morning meal, and before the formal instruction were to start. She made herself visible and approached the monks and child. She told them she would be visible to them from now on in this house, and she would be in a body like theirs.

From that day on she showed up in the early morning and was waiting for the trio in the courtyard of the smaller house. She then followed the instruction the monks gave, joining in at appropriate moments, and it was apparent to Martin that her role was to teach the young man, and indirectly perhaps the monks, in the healing she practiced so well. But her intent was also to bond with the child, to have him accept her the way she presented herself, for theirs would be a life-long relationship. Her strategy worked, and in no time her presence was taken for granted, and it was no longer odd, she was simply Maria Lerna, or as the child now called her, "Marli."

Two weeks later, Martin was outside the Citadel when he saw Arcadius, accompanied by an officer and a young boy, walking hurriedly towards him. They went into the Citadel and inside the royal villa.

They found Joannes sitting alone studying a parchment, spread out on a table in front of him.

"August King, this boy insists in talking with you," Arcadius sounded matter-of fact. "Try as we may, he won't talk to anyone else, and insists he has very important information."

The officer informed Joannes he and his men had been out on patrol at one of the farm clusters close to the eastern border, when the boy approached them. "Stubborn little rascal won't say much to us, except that he's from Dunum, and says he will only talk to you, Majesty." The fact he was from Dunum told them it was important, so they had brought him.

Joannes looked at the boy, and Martin studied him as well. He was short and wiry, fourteen or so. His clothes were rough and dirty, a peasant boy. His eyes shone with a glitter of intelligence, and he was biting his lower lip, looking at the King, and the room around him.

"What do you have, boy?" asked Joannes.

"A man in Dunum gave me two coins, then made me memorize a message for you, and told me I would get five more coins when I returned with a lock of the Queen's hair." He spoke the same brogue language Martin heard Eldyn speak.

"Who is this man?" Joannes had stood up and was facing the boy.

"I don't know. He pulled me into an alley, it was dark, and he wore a cloth over his face."

"So what's the message, boy?"

Philippus had come into the room and was standing next to Arcadius, a quizzical look on his face.

The boy looked straight at Joannes and sucked in air. "I need the bit of hair first."

"Do you know who you're talking to?" Arcadius said as he took a step toward the boy.

Joannes raised his hand in his direction. "Philippus, please ask the Queen for a lock of her hair. Tell her it's important."

As his son walked away, Joannes faced Arcadius. "The boy has no way of knowing the color of my wife's hair, and that it's unusual. But the man does. This is a way of making sure he delivered the message."

Martin had not thought about Martigena's hair before, but now he realized how different it was, *like flames*.

"Clever," said Arcadius.

Martigena walked in followed by Philippus. She had a lock of her bright red hair in her hands, with a ribbon tied around it. She appeared amused. "I hear I have an admirer in Dunum."

She handed the hair to Joannes, who in turn gave it to the boy.

"Saxons in large numbers are about to land at the next full moon." The boy had his eyes closed, and the words he uttered were in Latin, obviously a language he barely knew, so he had no idea what he was saying, and obviously had memorized the whole thing. "Two thousand will land by Bird Rock, and two thousand at the White River Mouth."

The room was silent. Joannes looked at the boy and asked him to repeat the message. He did so, several times. Then Joannes dismissed the boy, who hurriedly left.

They tried to figure out who in Dunum had sent the boy. It had to be some one close to Julius and Cassius, and a nobleman who knew Martigena. They listed several, and realized there was no way of knowing for sure.

Joannes nervously paced the room. "Let's concentrate on the news: Erouf is getting reinforcements, and that probably means they plan an attack. A big one."

"Four thousand men, we can beat them. But we need to call the citizen soldiers," said Philippus.

"That's in addition to the men they already have," said Arcadius.

Joannes looked at his son. "Erouf probably arrived with a thousand, and we slayed two hundred; and the bandits number maybe…"

"Less than a thousand," said Arcadius, "all told, about eight hundred."

"Right. And Julius' army ranged around five hundred."

"So we are facing roughly six thousand men," said Philippus.

Martin could sense the dread in the room. Martigena stood motionless, her gaze fixed on her husband. Arcadius was looking down at the floor.

They realized Cassius, Julius, and Erouf had a plan. Probably to draw out the Isca troops with a massive raid on several of the farm clusters, and ambush them.

Joannes had been standing near a window looking out toward the north. "The man who sent us the news knows all this. He also knows our only option is to attack them shortly after they land, and defeat them before they unite."

They guessed the Saxons were landing in separate locations to minimize the time it would take to disembark that many men.

"The next full moon is in less than two weeks," said Philippus.

"They will probably send a force to kill the scouts we have on those sites, make landfall quickly before being detected, and link their forces in Dunum," said Arcadius.

Both landing sites were in neighboring kingdoms, places with no organized army. Joannes had posted scouts in that no-man's land.

"I think we can do it," said Joannes, "let's call in the citizen soldiers, every single one."

During the following week, foot soldiers arrived in Isca. Most of them appeared relaxed, even happy. Joannes had instructed Arcadius not to tell his officers about the threat. Rather, they told the men they were going to be trained for the following two weeks out in the country. "The fewer people who know the better. We don't need word getting back to Dunum, somehow," Joannes had said.

Martin saw them practice with the Greek fire Nicolaus had taught them how to make. They attached small containers to arrows and shot them at woodpiles, followed by flaming arrows. The woodpiles seemed to explode. The fire was impossible to put out; it kept burning no matter what.

A few days later, the soldiers filed out of the city. There were two thousand foot soldiers and thirteen hundred cavalry. A hundred horse soldiers had stayed in Isca and a hundred more in the countryside.

Martin stayed near Joannes, Philippus and Arcadius. He noticed Joannes turning to look at the city. Up on the wall, stood Martigena, with Ambrosius and the teachers. Martin realized Martigena was the only one who knew the soldiers' real mission.

Once they reached the coast, the soldiers split into two groups. Joannes and Philippus took the cavalry and Arcadius stayed with the foot soldiers.

"I will see you at White River in three day's time," said Joannes to Arcadius.

"I'll be there. Victorious."

Martin followed Arcadius, who was heading a few miles down the coast. Joannes and his son took off with their troops at a trot. They had until sunset to reach Bird Rock.

After six hours of hard marching, the two thousand foot soldiers under Arcadius reached White River Mouth. The sun was still high up in the sky. Martin guessed it was four in the afternoon. Two scouts came out of the bushes to meet them.

After a rest, Arcadius assembled his officers and told them of the coming invasion. He instructed them to set up positions along the forest, by the river, out of sight. He posted scouts in four directions, about half a mile away. If everything went as planned, he expected troops from Dunum to show up the following day. That following night was to be a full moon.

No fires were lit, and the troops were silent. The site was peaceful. Martin could hear only the sound of the ocean.

By midmorning two scouts ran back, announcing they had spotted a large troop of Saxon warriors on horseback coming their way. There were about five hundred of them.

About an hour later, Martin saw ten Saxon men, with axes and swords at the ready, silently making their way along the river.

They all seemed to disappear, once they made past a bend in the river. Martin knew where Arcadius' men where, and surmised that they had been ambushed.

The rest of the Saxons came on horseback, down the trail the scouts had been on. Martin watched as arrows, fired from both sides of the trail killed most of them. There was some hand-to-hand combat, but that was at the end of the confrontation, when the Saxons tried to flee. It happened fast. About an hour later, the place was once more quiet and serene.

In the afternoon, five ships came into the mouth of the river. Arcadius went out to meet them. Surprised, Martin realized those were the five pirate ships Joannes had captured some time back. After a short conversation, the boats put out again. Martin followed them and observed them follow the coast to a small cove.

The rest of the day went without incident. Mostly the troops rested and looked around the river, no longer trying to hide from view.

Then night came. Martin watched the moon rise to his right. There were few clouds, and if ships came, they would be plainly visible. The men built fires on several spots along the river mouth.

Then they saw the boats, many of them approaching. They could hear the sound of the oars, and voices calling out.

The men from Isca started shooting. Arrows rained on the boats, first the Greek fire, Martin guessed. Then he saw the flaming arrows, making their arc in the sky. Surprisingly the boats kept coming in a straight line. Then a good number of the boats exploded with fire and men started screaming and jumping overboard, most of them flaming torches themselves.

Behind them, Martin saw the five ships from Isca standing in the back, waiting.

Some of the burning boats made it to the shore, and men, some on fire, came rushing off. A solid wall of soldiers met them. Other boats turned around to leave, and met the five ships. When they were within range, Martin saw arrows coming from the Isca ships. Now Martin saw that the five ships looked the same as the Saxon ships, and the invaders approached them thinking they were their own. Soon, the remaining Saxon ships were on fire.

As far as Martin was concerned, the fight was over. He left White River and decided to look for Joannes and Philippus.

He followed the coast due east. Soon he came to a bay where there were many boats at anchor, and not far away, the sound of men shouting and horses whinnying.

He found the Isca men already busy clearing a battlefield. Joannes was shouting orders. Martin noticed that Philippus had a nasty cut on his right arm, and Joannes was clearly upset, feverishly trying to stop the bleeding. There were other wounded, and some dead Isca men. The rest of the place was covered with Saxon bodies.

A short time later, all was quiet. They were all lying down, resting, including Philippus.

The return of the troops to Isca was as noisy as on the previous occasion. Now everybody knew what had happened. Joannes had sent riders out that same night. One troop had gone in to check on Arcadius, and when they determined all was well, four riders had gone on to Isca, and two back to Joannes. All was well.

The following day, Martin caught sight of Joannes and Martigena in their private quarters. They were sitting across from each other on low chairs.

"I know you are going to attack him, the question is when," Martigena was saying.

Joannes let out a sigh. "Not right away. Erouf was slain, we found him among the dead. He came out with all the men he had to meet the boats, so now Julius is back to what he had before; a bunch of bandits and thugs, not much of a threat."

"But he'll still be a nuisance…and maybe invite more Saxons."

"Yes, but for now, I want to get rid of the Caledonians. I don't trust them."

A week later Martin heard that Joannes had decided the Caledonians would have to go home by land. Arcadius had convinced him the trip by sea was impractical; even if the boats left right away they would not be able to make it back before the waters got too rough for travel.

Martin found soldiers in the barracks making preparations for the long trip. He found out Joannes had decided to send five hundred of his troops to escort the Caledonians to the border. It was for their protection, because he knew the chances that they would be set upon by some of the kingdoms they had savaged were very high. Philippus volunteered to lead the troops, and it was agreed they would escort them all the way to Hadrian's Wall. Word was the Caledonians would be effective ambassadors of their kingdom, for they were convinced Joannes was a magician, and that his kingdom was invincible, so the trip was seen by Joannes and Arcadius as a sound investment.

In four days they were ready to march, and started early in the morning with the rising sun of a long late summer day when the days were still long and warm. Mowan rode with them for some distance, ambling among the line of Caledonians on a horse, chatting with some, giving advice to others, and sending word about his vow to his father with those from his own clan, and that he was here to stay.

Martin had decided to accompany Philippus; somehow he had trepidations about the expedition, a sick feeling he couldn't shake. He went to talk with Maria Lerna about it, and she listened to him intently.

"Beware for yourself and Philippus, dear one. This won't be an easy journey."

Philippus rode in front with a hundred of his riders, then came the Caledonians on foot, escorted by a double line of riders on each side, and finally the rest of the troops, about another two hundred or so, trailing pack animals, with more provisions than the entire Caledonian army had originally taken, according to the Caledonians.

Philippus was constantly on the lookout for soldiers, especially in the afternoon of the second day after they had passed the mountains and were in Julius' kingdom. From then on he had scouts riding ahead of the troop. On the third day, a scout came to tell him there were some two hundred soldiers from Dunum, waiting for them up ahead.

He told his officers to be on guard and proceeded forward. As he approached the soldiers, their commander, with a small group, came to talk to him. One of their men had spotted them and had brought the news of a large group of Picts and soldiers from Isca going north. What was Isca doing with the primitives? Why had they not killed them outright? When Philippus told him they were being escorted back to Caledonia, the commander called him crazy.

After the encounter, Philippus told one of his lieutenants to hurry. He wanted to put some distance between himself and Dunum as soon as possible. He was concerned Cassius might come after them, and they would have to fight him. With relief they passed the road that led to the city.

Martin understood from listening to the Caledonians that the Dunum soldiers had put up weak resistance before most of them went to hide inside city walls, leaving their farms and villages at the mercy of the invaders. Apparently that happened quite a few times with the places they had attacked, and they still seemed to relish the memory, judging by their laughter. Now their comments about Joannes and how he defeated them made sense, because up to that point they had found the local armies met their expectations of a soft and spoiled people. It was apparent they could not reconcile themselves to having been defeated by mere mortals, and the only way they rationalized their defeat was to attribute it to magic, a magic that became more surreal and terrifying the more they talked about it.

By the afternoon of the sixth day the soldiers from Julius' kingdom caught up with them. Now there were close to a thousand of them, and they came up from behind just as the column was ready to stop for the day. They arrived on horses, most of them riding two to a horse. They dismounted some distance away, and were getting ready to charge on foot.

At least Cassius was not their commander, Philippus told his men after studying the enemy.

Philippus ordered a "wall" to be formed at the rear of the column. These were the biggest and strongest soldiers who put up their shields from one side of the road to the other, from tree line to tree line. Behind them he ordered a unit of archers to stand at the ready and shoot "at a cadence of five."

Philippus mounted his horse along with some two hundred other riders.

They were going to charge the foot soldiers. At a signal from him, the archers and the wall would break ranks to let him and his riders go through.

Martin noticed a group of older soldiers, who were of higher rank and acted as Philippus' lieutenants, and who at this point seemed nervous, anxiously milling about waiting for his orders,; glancing at one another, talking in low voices.

The soldiers from Julius' kingdom attacked. They were now yelling at the top of their lungs, while running wildly toward the wall formation. At this point Martin saw a group of Caledonians come up from behind and attack the last line of the Isca horsemen. They started pulling soldiers off their horses; some grabbed sticks and rocks as weapons, but then they wielded captured swords. Philippus saw the skirmish and rushed with some twenty of his riders to save his men. As Philippus charged on ahead, he was immediately surrounded by Caledonians, and two of them pulled him off his horse, as two more rushed over with rocks held high over their heads, ready to strike.

Martin moved fast; he made his body solid and grabbed a sword from a soldier's scabbard, then reached Philippus and the Caledonians. He saw them moving very slowly, and realized it was he who was moving very fast. He hoped no one could see him.

He hit one of the men wielding a rock with the flat side of the sword on top of the head as hard as he could, then the other. He saw the impact of the sword on the heads and knew they were going to fall…and they started doing so, but slowly. He got out of the way of flailing arms and swords with ease. A third man seemed to have seen him and charged at him. Martin easily dodged and stabbed one leg then the other until the man faltered and was on his way down. He was surprised he could move that fast, much faster than any man possibly could, and in his case skill was not necessary; he moved faster than the eye can see. His sword now slashed an arm with a rock…then another arm and another.

At this point riders charged into the Caledonians, dispersing them.

Martin turned around to look for Philippus. He met the gaze of the man, who had stood up and was now almost beside him, a mere three feet away, still dazed, but looking at Martin long and hard, possibly trying to place him. Martin moved away from Philippus and as he dissipated his body, the sword fell away from his hand.

He then surveyed the situation. The Caledonians had given up, by falling to their knees. Mounted soldiers were now going around looking for trouble spots. When they found none they turned their attention to the rear, where the fighting with Julius' soldiers was still going on.

Philippus ordered a group of archers to guard the Caledonians. The rest went to stand behind the wall formation and fell in line with the other archers, apparently shooting in some sort of pattern at the enemy. Martin marveled at the precision and discipline of the troops. With unseen signals, wall formation soldiers would duck quickly at random intervals and long enough for the archers to shoot. After some time the tactic seemed to be having its desired effect, for the enemy stopped attacking, and were busy trying to shield themselves from the arrows. Then they turned around and ran back to their horses.

The battle was over. Martin realized the veteran soldiers were very likely old hands whom Arcadius had asked to keep an eye on Philippus. He remembered it was they who were at the scene first after Philippus hit the ground.

The older soldiers had now congregated and Martin overheard the manner and tone of the conversation. They were going to do their best to make it seem as though Philippus was in total command, while at the same time making sure that from then on he made the right decisions. They discussed the battle, and the Caledonian uprising. They blamed themselves for not having made sure the Caledonian males were in chains and at half-rations to keep them weak. They wanted to find the leaders of the revolt. On the other hand they were glad the Caledonians attacked when they did, as Philippus was about to charge a thousand foot soldiers with two hundred riders, head on! Sure suicide, one commented, as another shook his head. They had almost lost him, the crazy kid…and twice.

They talked about the two soldiers who saved Philippus. They were of the Royal Guard, said one. No, responded another, he saw them clearly; new cavalrymen, big men. They had never seen anyone move like that with a sword, those two were cutting and slashing so fast and fiercely it was all like a blur. Maybe they were special soldiers Joannes had trained to protect his son. "Let's look for them and find out," muttered one with a gray beard. And they did, they went through the ranks looking for the "two big men," but to no avail. After some time, they stood to one side of the troops, still looking.

Martin decided to leave them for a while and go to his cave. He felt the need to meditate, clear his mind and heart and then introspect. There was something about the whole incident that didn't sit right, something amiss.

He meditated, but it was a struggle, his mind was busy the whole time, pulling him back. He guessed his heart was full of emotions, and he had a hard time prying himself away.

He did the best he could, and then decided it was time to figure out what was bothering him. His heart felt a bit more peaceful, his mind had cleared up. It was time.

He reviewed the incident, from the beginning, from the time they left Isca, the reason for the trip, how carefree and...possibly happy the whole group seemed. There had been no distance to speak of between soldiers and Caledonians. It had been like a journey they were taking together, and the soldiers were there to protect, not to guard. Yes, so that was one piece that bothered him. Clearly the Caledonians had betrayed the trust placed on them. He had seen them playing together, a game of catch. Their laughter and light-hearted competition had been genuine. So what happened? How could they then all of a sudden throw that away and decide it was time to kill those same people they had been playing with?

Was there anything else to it? Philippus taking crazy chances? Trying to prove himself? Well, he did almost get killed. If it hadn't been for the hunch that prompted Martin to come along, Philippus certainly would have died at the hands of the Caledonians. So he had a premonition and then acted on it, successfully. What was wrong with that? What was wrong was...he was afraid Philippus and maybe Joannes believed themselves under "divine protection." He remembered their words: "an angel had been sent to protect them." But the "angel" was fallible...and human...and so was he. One day one of them would not be able to protect the royals and someone would get killed. And if they somehow did manage to protect them, then they would become soft, pathetic beings that could not defend or think for themselves. Yes, that was wrong. Talk about interfering, good lord! That was it! The misuse of his powers. Well, for now, apparently people believed there had been two soldiers responsible for saving Philippus. That was fine.

He wanted to talk with Maria Lerna. He visualized her and opened his heart to her, and when he was able to feel her essence, he embraced her. He felt her answer back. He visualized her next to him in his cave. Slowly he felt her presence become more tangible, and he felt her next to him, so he opened his eyes, and there she was, sitting in front of him, a quizzical look on her face.

"Well Martin, you have summoned me. And I suppose it has saved you much time in finding me and traveling to where I was."

He laughed. That was the first time he had ever known her to be sarcastic. The statement was now accompanied by an impish glimmer in her eyes.

He told her about the incident with the Caledonians, and what he had done to save Philippus, and that he might have fueled the concept that the royal family were now under divine protection, and that he was concerned.

She listened intently. Then thought about it.

"Martin, you acted as your heart told you to, but I do see cause for concern. Because of who you are, and your abilities, you may eventually find yourself doing more harm than good. This is perhaps where you need to exercise your wisdom."

"I agree, Maria Lerna, but I am not talking just about me, but also about you. I think the entire royal family might now live and act differently, thinking no harm may come to them because you are protecting them. I overheard them say as much."

Maria Lerna became unsettled…and perhaps angry.

"I act and say exactly as Spirit tells me to. I can't possibly make any mistakes. It's not me who talks and acts. It is God! There is no Maria Lerna anymore. Now there is only Spirit in her place."

Her reaction was surprising to Martin. His heart sank. *God does speak through her lips, but there is always a mind, in this world there is always the human mind…and the resulting ego.* Her mindset was wrong, very wrong, he could feel it deep down. In his mind and heart he prayed for guidance, for he felt this was a crucial moment and what he did or said would tip the balance one way or another.

He embraced her with his essence, dearly, desperately, with all his might.

"Maria Lerna, open your heart to me, and then look at mine." His words were soft and pleading, his manner reflecting what was in his heart. Grief.

She paused…looked at him for a minute, but then did as he asked. She sat upright and closed her eyes. He then felt her essence, and it felt harsh, he felt her will, her strength, now directed against him, and in response he kept embracing her, pouring out everything he had…and then…to his relief she began to soften, and he felt her going through the thoughts in his mind and the feelings in his heart. After some time he knew she was very still, having gone completely into Spirit. He joined her in meditation, and they sat together transfixed for some time. He could sense the intensity of her prayers, her intent to do right.

"You are right, my beloved Martin." She sounded contrite. "I was convinced I always stepped out of the way when Spirit was manifest, but now I realize the dark forces are very subtle and can get in the way, and is perhaps the way it was intended by God, so we question everything. I fell into the ultimate trap; where the mind assumes the identity of Spirit and its attributes."

Martin was glad it was over, and at that moment he felt they had escaped a great evil, for it seemed that a dark cloud lifted, a cloud they had not seen except for its absence that made everything now seem clear and pristine.

She decided she was going to talk to the royal family at first opportunity. She then looked at Martin for a long time, with a loving look in her eyes, and he felt her essence enveloping him, and she held him. Then she was gone.

Martin slept that night longer than usual. He assumed it was perhaps due to all of the issues he had dealt with the day before. He also dreamt about Adam and in the morning realized he missed him a lot. Even though no time was passing out there in California, the days were piling up in his present time, and his heart felt his absence. With morning light he meditated and then went over to where he had left Philippus and his party.

He was now debating whether he should let them go on without him. He knew the danger for Philippus was over…or was it? Was he also beginning to think of his inner voice as infallible? He laughed at himself. He would follow Philippus for some time and see how things went.

The group was already underway when he joined them. The Caledonians were now prisoners once again, and marched along in silence. The wounded soldiers had been sent back to Isca with a small escort. Fortunately they had suffered no fatalities, but had twenty wounded, six seriously enough to be sent home. They were the bearers of the news of the attack, and Philippus made them promise to put a positive slant on things and to reassure his mother he was well.

Martin noticed the veteran soldiers now surrounded Philippus. There were about ten of them, and it was obvious who they were, it wasn't just that they were older than the rest, but there was an air about them, a confidence with which they carried themselves. It was touching how protective they were of Philippus, rather like mother hens, he thought.

Philippus seemed as sullen as the prisoners, as though he too had been punished.

That day Martin ambled among the prisoners from time to time, as he did among the soldiers, but it was from the prisoners he gathered the most valuable information. By this time he understood their language with no difficulty.

Martin gathered the attack on the soldiers had been engineered and carried out by a rather small group, but once underway, loyalties were such that the rest of the men joined in to back up the ones involved. After listening in a for a while Martin realized the main motivation for the attack, what had been on everyone's mind all along since leaving Isca: for them to return home without weapons was seen as a terrible humiliation, a situation they would want to remedy at any cost. In fact, they were trying to figure out how to jump the soldiers again, and then run away with the weapons; or even to steal them in the night.

Most of the instigators of the attack had been killed, except for two. Martin went over to look at the two men the prisoners talked about. They were both wounded, one on one arm, the other one on both legs. The last man was being carried, and prisoners took turns with him. Martin recognized him as the one he had wounded, and he realized he was the one Joannes and Philippus had made prisoner, the sole survivor of the group who had attacked the women and Nicolaus.

That was quite a coincidence, he thought, it was as though fate was saving this man, or maybe it was his intense anger that made him carry on and survive. Matters were made worse by the nature of his new wounds. Martin understood the Caledonians recognized his wounds as disabling, and in their minds someone had deliberately chosen to wound the man rather than kill him, and that was an indignity he would have to suffer. It was obvious this person, whom the prisoners called Gren, would spell trouble. He was of higher rank, so to his face the Caledonians appeared subservient, but behind his back they held him in contempt. They said he had been captured in a fair fight but kept making up stories of how he had been overwhelmed by a large group of soldiers.

Martin decided to keep an eye on Gren. He also wondered if there was anything he could do to let the prisoners return with weapons. He realized they were willing to go to great extremes for this cause, and it worried him.

The following day they came to a village. The places they had passed up till then, farm enclaves or villages, had been completely destroyed and were presently deserted. This place was different:, there were about fifty people all told, men, women and children, all busy rebuilding. Martin could see that the fields had not been ravaged; there were orchards and a few head of cattle grazing.

A middle-aged man and four men in their twenties came to greet them. It seemed that this was the self-appointed "governor" of the place and his sons.

He respectfully answered Philippus' questions about the village. This had been one of four villages within half a day's walk of each other. He had gathered the survivors from the other three places and had decided to concentrate their efforts on rebuilding this one. His name was Dogan and he had been the innkeeper in one of the other villages.

Philippus decided to spend the night in the outskirts and welcomed the offer of fresh meat from Dogan. Shortly afterwards he had made other offers, including women to entertain the officers and a virgin for Philippus. Philippus declined, and so did the veterans, but later on Martin saw one of them with a woman in his tent.

As Philippus was about to retire, the veteran with the woman came to his tent. He brought her along to talk to Philippus.

Her tale was that they were captives. Dogan had gone around the other villages after the occupants had returned to rebuild, and taken people by force.

The woman had been a farmer's wife, the Picts had killed her husband, and now she was being forced into prostitution. She was an attractive woman in her early twenties with red-brown hair, round face and a generous figure. She spoke angrily, with tears in her eyes.

Philippus listened to the woman, then, together with an entourage of five veterans he went to talk to other villagers. The story proved correct, Dogan and his sons had made them all slaves. Philippus was about to go see Dogan, when two of the veterans asked to talk to him.

They told him this same story was being repeated all over Britannia, ever since the Romans had left and long before the Picts attacked. In situations like these, someone had to take over, and often that person was not scrupulous, but what could they do? If they did away with Dogan and his sons the place would fall apart. At least he brought some sort of order and protection to the villagers. The same was happening in farms and villages within a day's ride from Isca.

Philippus was astounded at the news. In their own kingdom? Yes, they told him, Joannes' authority could only extend so far, and where there was no central authority, things fell where they might, and often things were not pretty. Was his father aware of this, he wanted to know, red in the face. Yes, they told him, he had his hands full with Isca, and there was no physical way to extend his power all over the kingdom. You needed Rome for that.

No, he told them, that was being fixed. He told them about the Circle Council, and about how the kingdom was going to be defended.

They stood listening silently, exchanging glances. By the end, it was obvious they were duly impressed.

"God be with King Joannes," said one of them.

That night Philippus retired early, conceivably to think about Dogan, the village and the woman. Martin did the same; he felt very sorry for the woman, and had decided to help her. It was the same situation as with the Caledonian girl and baby, he couldn't save all the villagers, but he could help the woman escape.

He went to his cave and after meditating he had the strong feeling he should leave the woman alone, and that was strange, but the feeling was very strong. He decided to pray for her. He could always go back and help her. He would just sit with his feeling and see what happened.

The following day when Martin came to the group, they were about to get underway. Philippus had gone to see Dogan, but it had been only to thank him for his hospitality.

The next few days went on without further incident, but no incident was necessary to make everyone miserable. The weather as they progressed north became a never-ending rain. Dark and gray clung everywhere, impregnated the sky, the forest, and clearly, the moods of all.

As they approached Hadrian's Wall, it became clear to Martin that the prisoners had no intention of arriving home without weapons. They had decided to attack the moment they were let off their chains. If they all died they were certain their women and children would make it back with the tale.

During a break, Gren stood with other leaders, to all appearances, sharing a water jug. "I have another plan. We can pretend we are going home," he said, "then we double back and attack the soldiers. We attack while they are marching, starting with the rear guard, as we tried before, and this way allow enough men to gather weapons before the main body of soldiers realizes what is happening. This time, if we are fast, it could work."

"The problem," said a short balding man, "is that the soldiers are protected and no matter what we do, Joannes' magic will win out."

"Well, no matter," said Gren, "in that case, let's make sure we all die and not be made prisoners again."

Martin felt at a loss. What could he do? He knew that interference was dangerous…but only if it was seen as divine intervention. Maybe he could somehow alert Philippus what was about to happen without any apparent supernatural evidence. They were now just a few days' march from the Wall and he didn't have much time left.

That night he slept fitfully knowing something dreadful was about to happen and he still had no clue what to do.

At first light he meditated and at the end he prayed for guidance. Finally, he intoned a silent prayer for them all, including himself. An answer came to him, that all was in the hands of Spirit, to let go. He got up and made his way to the camp. His heart was now lighter and he realized what people meant when they said "may thy will be done." Whatever the outcome, he knew it would be for the greater harmony.

He found the camp deceptively peaceful. People were still eating the morning meal and soldiers and prisoners milled around their respective fires, shaking off the night's cold. A gentle mist was falling and fog surrounded the trees, the sun barely visible through the heavy gray layer.

Martin felt compelled to find Philippus; it was as though a voice inside him told him it was important to be with him that very minute.

He found him in his tent talking with one of the veterans. They were discussing some visitors, a group of soldiers from one of the kingdoms they had passed some two days before, who had shown up at nightfall the day before. They had wanted to have a go at the prisoners and Philippus had stood his ground; he told them he was to deliver the prisoners to the other side of the Wall and after that his responsibility would be discharged.

The visitors had left, but both Philippus and the older soldier were sure they were amassing a troop to attack the prisoners once they were released.

"I have a moral duty to protect the prisoners," Philippus said, his voice unsure.

"Your duty is to stay alive, for your family's and the kingdom's sake. Those primitives are not worth dying for. Let's cut them loose, turn around and go back right now."

Philippus listened intently, a grave look in his eyes, apparently trying to decide what was right. "No, that's not an option. I promised my father to deliver the prisoners all the way to the Wall, and that's what I will do."

Both men stood silent for a moment, looking at each other.

"I will not allow armed men to butcher unarmed Caledonians," said Philippus. "Upon release I will give them weapons so they can defend themselves. Go order the soldiers to assemble the prisoners, I will address them."

The veteran soldier stood looking at Philippus, apparently not believing what he had been told. He argued his point, but Philippus told him his decision was final.

Martin felt elated. He would never have thought of coming up with a new threat to solve the problem of the Caledonians and their weapons. He felt like dancing…but for the moment he sat around and watched Philippus ready himself. Martin realized the "crazy kid" had grown up as a result of recent events. The decision about the Caledonians was made by the new Philippus. There was a sense of honor, and fairness, also respect for the word he had given his father. And lastly, he had stood up to the veteran, in a good way. Martin watched him put on his armor, the chest plate, groin guard, then the helmet and arm guards. He secured a sword to his side and walked outside.

The prisoners had been assembled, the men in front in chains, and the women and children behind them. Two prisoners stood in front of the group. When Philippus came out, the soldiers saluted by bringing their right fists over their hearts. Then they listened.

Philippus told the prisoners that a group of soldiers from a kingdom they had ransacked wanted to kill them; that he had told the soldiers that Isca's responsibility toward them would be over as soon as they reached the Wall and were released. The two prisoners in front translated, and Philippus waited until they were finished.

The prisoners stood silent as they absorbed the news, and the translators seemed to repeat the words, apparently for emphasis. The tension among the

Caledonians was tangible, and anger appeared to rise by the minute.

Then Philippus told them he would not stand by and let them get massacred, no matter how deserving he thought they were of that fate; he would give them their weapons back when released so they could defend themselves.

The prisoners' anger gave way to wild joy. They happily jumped in place and slapped each others' backs in spite of the heavy chains.

The soldiers, including Philippus, looked at each other perplexed. Martin heard them mumble that the Picts were crazy; they were going to be attacked and were happy at the prospect. Yes, they were definitely barbarians.

After the talk, they broke camp and started out.

Martin ambled among the Caledonians for some time. He approached Gren and found him riding a horse, morose as usual, but apparently calm. The rest of the prisoners were infused with a wild energy, like small children at the prospect of Christmas, and were pushing forward almost at a jog, with the soldiers apparently glad to let them go as fast as they could. To make their travel faster Philippus ordered that wounded prisoners be given horses to ride, and full meal rations resumed for the male prisoners so they could get their strength back.

Martin decided to go back to his cave for the rest of the day and meditate. He felt like giving thanks to Spirit for the miracle that had taken place, and he also felt the need to immerse himself fully in her essence.

Next day he meditated until noon, and then decided to join Philippus and the rest. He came on the troop as they were breaking camp after the noon rest, eager to make the last few miles to the Wall. A large body of soldiers with assorted weapons, some on foot, some on horseback, were now trailing the Isca troops.

Now Martin understood the scenario: the group that had gone to talk with Philippus and request that he hand over the prisoners had been a detachment from a fairly large contingent of about eight hundred soldiers. When Philippus and his group had caught up with them, they again tried to reason with him to hand over the Picts, but again Philippus refused. Now they were trailing not far behind.

They arrived at the Wall at mid-afternoon. The tired Caledonians requested a break before being released, knowing they would have a fight on their hands shortly thereafter.

The soldiers complied, feeding them, then apportioning some provisions for the rest of their journey. After two hours or so, the Caledonians stood up, signaling they were ready.

Philippus assembled half his troops as archers. The rest, save for twenty or so, stood mounted with lances in hand. The twenty soldiers went around taking the chains off the Caledonians and then distributing their weapons:; the long- handled axes, swords, bows and arrows.

Martin realized they had meant to give them back their weapons at the Wall all along before the attack. *How ironic.*

They allowed Gren and a few more men to keep their horses. He and two other leaders fell in at the head of the group, ready to lead them. Martin studied his face, and detected that the man's anger had now been overtaken by anticipation.

The men ushered the women and children ahead of them. The soldiers watched as the group went through an open gate, which stood beside what had been a fort built right on the wall.

Hadrian's Wall stretched as far as the eye could see in either direction and was not as formidable as Martin had imagined, certainly not as tall nor as thick as the fortifications around Isca. It was about ten feet thick and about fifteen tall, without question easy to breach, so it seemed it had been intended as a border demarcation more than a fortification. There were no signs the wall and its fort had been used for quite a while. There were weeds growing on a crumbling catwalk that would have been used by soldiers to defend the place.

The area in front of the wall had been cleared of trees and rocks;, it was an open plain for about a mile.

Once the women and children were a safe distance away, the Caledonian men broke away from the soldiers and rushed on ahead. It was telling of the nature of these fighters that even the seriously wounded remained with the group, ax or sword held up with a good arm.

A small group of the pursuing soldiers had mounted the wall and were now looking at the Caledonians, heatedly arguing among themselves.

Then two went over to talk to Philippus.

They bitterly complained at his foolishness of giving the barbarians their weapons. What was he doing? Didn't he know they would not hesitate to attack all of them again? It was just a matter of time for those Picts to come across the Wall again, in another invasion. They demanded the Isca men join them in attacking the Picts. They certainly deserved it.

"I didn't go through all the trouble of escorting them all this way, just to kill them," Philippus told them. "Besides, they are afraid of Isca, and will spread that message around their country. They are our best assurance no Caledonian would ever dare attack our kingdom again."

The two leaders stared at him for a moment, then turned around and walked back to their group. They talked among themselves for some time, then assembled their men and started back the way they had come.

Philippus and the veterans climbed the wall and looked over at the Caledonians. With some apparent satisfaction they noted they had made a formation resembling one of their own; a protective square enclosure with their shields.

One of the veterans, the barrel-chested one, laughed. "The only problem is their shields; they are round instead of rectangular. That's no turtle formation. Those fools would've gotten killed."

Philippus and his men stood studying them for some time. They debated whether to send a rider to tell them their attackers had changed their minds. But Philippus decided they would figure that one out eventually. "Let them fret for a while; it will do them good." In the meantime they could get under way themselves and start for home.

They surveyed the Wall one last time. Apparently only a handful of them had seen the famous structure before. Philippus commented that the Wall had not been manned in some time. They agreed. If the Caledonians decided to mount another offensive, they would have a free run all the way to Isca.

They mounted and headed back home at a brisk pace.

CHAPTER FOURTEEN

On their way back they passed the village with Dogan and his clan. Martin wondered about the woman they had forced into prostitution. He had thought about her a lot, but the feeling inside kept telling him to do nothing.

He went into the village and looked everywhere, but couldn't find her. When they had been underway for over three hours she came out of the forest, went straight to Philippus and asked for his help. She had escaped and had been hiding in the forest for over a week, subsisting on whatever she could find, waiting for the troop to make their way back. She looked bedraggled and desperate. Philippus took her with them.

A day away from the mountains they endured the worst weather of the entire trip. A cold wind blew and ice covered everything. It got so bad that when the sun went down they decided to keep going, rather than set up camp. They walked beside their horses all night to keep warm, and with first light mounted to sleep fitfully astride them.

Once they crossed the mountains the weather subsided, and they hurried on home. A day later, in late afternoon, they could see the gates of Isca opening up for them.

The soldiers hurried up the pace of their tired horses, and even the animals seemed uplifted by the sight of the city. Martin watched as their tails twitched and noses flared. A number of men took off their helmets and some laughed out loud, apparently at nothing at all.

The troop disbanded at the barracks and Philippus made his way on foot back to the Citadel. Martin watched as he met his parents in the dining hall. After a quick embrace, he bathed, changed clothes and returned for wine and conversation. He learned the wounded had made it safely back, and they had reported the attack by Julius' soldiers. Joannes had already decided to attack Dunum and had been waiting for Philippus to get back; they needed the extra troops. They would use Greek fire on the wooden fortifications to burn down a portion of it, and then march right in.

Julius' men had laid low these past few months. The last raid attributed to the gang was three months earlier, in Mateus' kingdom.

"Maybe they are running low on men," said Joannes.

"No such luck," said Arcadius, "I've been getting reports that bandits keep drifting in. I would guess they have upwards of two thousand by now."

"Wish we knew who the noble was who warned us about the Saxons," said

Philippus. "Maybe he would tell us the exact number."

Joannes patted his son's shoulder. "Glad you are back safe. Rest up, and we'll take on Julius and Cassius. It doesn't matter how many they have, you are witness to their fighting skills."

Philippus laughed. "Yes, even with Cassius commanding them, I could have beaten them back with half as many men." Then he went over the trip in detail, and his most riveting account concerned the Caledonians. He told them about the woman he had given sanctuary, and described Dogan and the village.

"You did well taking the woman with you," said Martigena. Joannes looked at his wife and there was understanding in his gaze. He told Philippus they would personally take care of the woman.

Philippus turned to his father. "Is it true places like that village exist in our land?"

Joannes nodded. "At present there are still some localities where power has gone into the hands of rather nasty people, and I let them be because they keep order. But the Circle Council is taking over, and now we have three- quarters of the kingdom covered. Be patient, son."

Martin decided to leave Philippus and his family, and find Maria Lerna. His heart yearned to see her again. He now thought it strange he hadn't contacted her in the intervening time. He knew if he had wanted to, he could have seen her every day and still kept up with Philippus very nicely, but maybe it was that he had to concentrate all his attention and energy on Philippus and the journey, and had known that at some level.

He found her by the side of her house busy with her garden. She was preparing the soil for spring planting, and was making furrows for a vegetable patch. Eldyn had been gone for two days on an errand concerning another neighbor. Again he was to heal someone, this time a child who seemed a bit disturbed.

He told her of all the events after he had last seen her, how he had feared a final uprising by the Caledonians had become inevitable…how he had prayed for a better outcome and how his prayers had been answered.

He spoke of his intuition that Gren was destined a violent death, and she sadly agreed. Then they talked about evil and anger, and he mentioned that Joannes was going to attack Julius.

He saw a wave of shock and grief course over her countenance; it erupted and took over her being. Then she appeared to regain control of herself.

"What's wrong, Marli?"

She seemed to make an effort to control her emotions. "Four years ago I was to marry Julius." She watched the shock in his face. "No, the reason why

I am upset by the upcoming attack on Dunum is not because I'm fearful for his life. It's something else. My family lives there and I have not seen nor heard from them in four years. I have good reason to fear for them."

Tears ran down her cheeks and tension and fear were now written all over her face. Martin recalled the time when she had talked about her teacher and her family with the monks, and how upset she had been.

"Is there anything I can do?" asked Martin.

Maria Lerna hesitated. "I don't know what to do…I was forced to flee Dunum with Eldyn." She then broke down in sobs.

Martin took her hand and led her to a nearby bench. It was clear to Martin she needed to talk; he sat next to her, held her hand and waited for her to tell him what had happened.

Maria Lerna gave him a sideways glance, took a few deep breaths and was calm. "I was born to a well-to-do family in Dunum," she told him, "which had been a quiet town under the Romans. In the years after the Big Council disintegrated, there was chaos, until Julius emerged as king. I had known him for many years and our families knew each other well. My father was a wealthy merchant and we lived in town, a happy family, my mother, brother, father, our teacher and me."

"Our teacher was Aramas, the man you heard Nicolaus and Eldyn talk about. I wish you had met him, Martin. The holy man taught us all communion, and also the nobler teachings: philosophy, mathematics, art, natural philosophy, and how to live a balanced and healthy life based on service to others; for the latter are the tenets of the Christian faith. Oh, he was such a beautiful soul, my dear beloved Aramas."

"Is he dead?" asked Martin.

"I think so…yes, I am sure," she said.

"Well, my brother Marius and I really took to the old monk's spiritual teachings," she said. "He was a very wise and wonderful man, one whose presence brought out the best in people. We both knew he was truly a man of God and one who had mastered his own life. At times, when communing together we would open our eyes to find him in total ecstasy, and the room saturated with Spirit. What joy! His teachings seemed to touch a chord in both of us, and in time we decided that was what we wanted to do with our own lives, to become like Aramas. Our parents didn't seem to have taken much interest in his teachings; to them it was perhaps something to do because it was in fashion. Poor souls."

She absent-mindedly brushed some dirt from her hands. "Now about Julius. What a tragic man! He was neither a good nor a bad man. Do you know what I mean? He was simply a weak person with no apparent principles whose actions were driven by whatever got him what he wanted, or to appease whoever made the strongest demand of him. Although for the first few years he was an efficient king, in short order he attracted nasty people around him, and their goals became his."

"The bandits, for that's what they were, began raiding local farms and then those in nearby kingdoms. Chaos became the rule of the land, with people afraid to be noticed or do business. You could hardly step out of your own front courtyard for fear of being attacked. Farmers still came to market, for there was no other choice, but they had to pay off the bandits, and so did the merchants, and still they got attacked. The rule of law had vanished, there was no order, no one to complain to, no Big Council soldiers to restore order and take the culprits to prison. And there was no place to go. It was terrible!"

"At the beginning people could come and go as they pleased, and some rich families wisely left, but then Julius decreed no one could leave without his consent, and when someone asked, they would be brutally beaten. So there was nothing else to do but to put up with the bandits and Julius, and hope things would eventually return to normal. People started praying for the Romans to return; that had become the wish on everyone's lips, and by then their corrupt ways were totally forgotten."

"I had known for some time Julius wanted me for his own, and shortly after he became king, he decided to let his feelings be known."

"My father felt the union had a lot of merit and that I would learn to be happy. I pleaded with him not to commit me to Julius, but it seemed he didn't want to acknowledge who our King was becoming, arguing that during upheavals drastic measures were required by rulers; that, bandits would always take advantage of such times, and Julius in due time would bring about order. My father agreed with Julius to set the wedding for the following summer."

"But didn't you have a voice in the matter?"

Maria Lerna looked at him quizzically. "I think your times are very different. Here, the head of the family has complete control over your life."

"As winter drew near, I dreaded the passage of time, trying desperately to find a way out." Her eyes reflected fear and confusion as she relived those days. "All this while Julius would come over to my house, his manner deteriorating with each passing day, apparently assuming I was for all practical purposes already his wife, and judging by his attitude, this meant something between a whore and a slave. He tried to take liberties with me, and when I resisted, he would become physically rough. My only hope was to always remain around other people, but it was impossible. I tried to reason with him, appealing to the friend I once knew, asking him for a return to respect and civility,; but he didn't care about my feelings or my welfare. His visits became more and more dreadful until I was living in a state of constant semi-terror. I don't know how I managed to get through those horrible days!"

"The greatest influence in Julius' life at the time was his new friend Cassius, whom he had placed in charge of his army, and I could tell when they had spent a lot of time together, because his manner changed. He would become more irascible, even violent, sarcastic and cruel. He spoke with Cassius' words: 'you take what you can in life,' and referred to my views as 'simple-minded mumblings' and 'justifications of the weak.' At this time the brutality of Julius' associates escalated. My father kept turning a blind eye to the entire goings-on, but not my mother and brother Marius. They became very concerned about what was to become of our lives under Julius, and what would become of me as his wife."

"One day, while walking in the garden with Mother and my brother Marius, we talked wistfully about moving away, perhaps even to Constantinople, where life was orderly and safe. We had secretly inquired about ships, and talked about what to pack. We imagined living in the city, learning their foreign ways. Mainly it was a fantasy, for we knew there was no practical way to go. Not with Julius around."

"I told them that maybe after I became his wife, I could ask him to let them go, but neither Mother nor Marius would agree to leave me completely at his mercy. As we talked, Julius arrived with Cassius, and another man, a self-proclaimed poet who had made himself a nasty reputation for violence in a very short time and was now Cassius' top lieutenant and friend. Encouraged by his friends, Julius made boastful and rude demands of me, while humiliating Marius and degrading Mother."

"It was awful, Martin. I suffered mostly for Mother and my brother, and I would have acquiesced to his horrible demands if I knew he would leave them be. But experience told me that would be like giving a morsel to a hungry tiger. We stood silent hoping Julius and his two friends would eventually leave. We dared not even make eye contact. I could feel my brother's anger rise and was afraid he might do something to be regretted, but he controlled himself."

"Eventually they left with no incident. But a short time later, Julius came back alone, this time a changed man, and apologized profusely to Mother, Marius and me, explaining that he had to keep up appearances and that we had no idea how nasty those people were. He seemed genuinely distraught, and we finally understood he was a mere puppet among the circle of characters he had attracted."

"Two days later he came again, this time in the late evening, half-drunk, and in a state of near -hysteria. He told us, and this time Father was present, that he could not help things, his friends were urging him to take me by force, and 'prove he was a real man.' He told us Cassius had designs on me. At that moment he appeared a pitiful man, a wretch."

"We thanked Julius, and I embraced him, feeling very sorry for him and fully understanding the position he was in, the horrible world he had constructed for himself."

"There was no escape; any attempt to leave would be detected by Cassius. Julius then asked, and even begged to make me safe. If somehow they could remove me so no one knew where I had gone, then I would be out of Cassius' reach, and my family would no longer be in harm's way. With this, Julius left, and we all realized it was so as not to hear our plans, and thus avoid divulging them to his friends. When he was gone, we sat around trying to decide what to do."

"Marius proposed the only option available. He had a slave, who turned out to be Eldyn, whom up to then I had not met, only seen occasionally with my brother. Marius had bought Eldyn some five years before because he had wanted a sparring partner, and Eldyn was a truly spectacular fighter. My brother suspected he had been a top gladiator, for he possessed unparalleled fighting skills. My brother told us that while sparring he had noticed the ease with which Eldyn avoided being hurt, while giving the appearance of losing. In the five years he had known him, the two had become very good friends, and Marius could vouch for his honor and loyalty. He would command Eldyn to take me away to the Seeker Colony Aramas had told us so much about. We could get directions from Aramas how to reach the place, which sounded like it was deep in the forest. He was sure the two of us could slip away unnoticed, and Eldyn would protect me from any stray bandits we might run across. He was certain to be a fair match against at least five men. One man and a woman would hardly attract much attention, while a bigger party without a doubt would be stopped. It was the best chance I had of escaping."

"It was a desperate plan, but we had no other options. I begged them all to go, that it was worth the risk to get away and we could all hide in the forest with the colony of seekers.'"

"No, Father said, once I was gone he could go on with his business, and they would all be fine. It was apparent to me Father was not about to let go of what he had worked so hard to obtain all his life, and I knew Mother would never leave his side. Marius would stay on to protect them. It was his duty."

"I understood our choices were limited, and it made sense that once I was gone my family would cease to be the center of so much unwanted attention. Yes, I had to go, and that very night, for there was no telling what Julius and his friends might do. They could come at any time."

"Marius called for Eldyn, told him of our plan, and asked if he would do that for him, not as a slave, but as a friend. Without hesitation the giant man agreed. Then Marius made him take an oath to take care of me. I was a bit apprehensive, but trusted my brother's judgment, and Eldyn seemed very loyal and had an air about him I immediately liked."

"When we consulted with Aramas, he agreed with the plan, and told us it was destiny."

"Marius then instructed Eldyn to take weapons and provisions. Eldyn chose two swords, two blankets, some water, and dry biscuits. He told Marius the forest would provide the rest.""

"I bid Aramas goodbye. The gentle teacher blessed me, and told me he would always be with me."

Maria Lerna was silent for a moment. "Our departure was sad but quiet, and it all happened so quickly we had little time for sorrow. That would come later, in the middle of many nights when I would lie wondering about their fate, as they must also have, of mine."

"Eldyn took me by the hand and we climbed over the courtyard wall and then down a quiet street. After a short walk we came within sight of the wooden fortification Cassius was building around the city. It was at that point things became blurry for me. I saw two soldiers approach us. Eldyn and I had stopped as commanded, and I trembled with fear. But when the soldiers were but two paces away, Eldyn fell them both with a quick flash of the swords he kept hidden, one under each arm. It happened so fast and it was so unexpected that at first I didn't realize what had come to pass. Eldyn stood with one sword in each hand and the soldiers were on the ground, blood pouring from their severed throats. He pulled me away by the hand and politely suggested that from then on, when soldiers approached, I close my eyes."

"We continued on past the palisade, and it seemed to me that the same thing was repeated several times; I saw soldiers approach us, then some who looked like bandits, and each time I closed my eyes, and each time when I opened them the soldiers had been slain by Eldyn, who seemed to proceed calmly, as though it was all pretend, a game, in which he was reluctantly involved. I was terrified, and not sure of what; of getting killed, or watching Eldyn kill again, so easily...I didn't quite know what to think of him; he was a brutal killer, but also my savior."

"Finally we were out of sight of Dunum and had walked for two more hours through wooded thickets until we came to the top of a hill from which we could see the city, and even my house. Eldyn stopped to let me rest. He took out a leather water bag for me to drink. I looked over at the quiet place, and could see a faint light coming from my house, what I imagined would be Mother's chambers. I saw her in my mind's eye, lying in bed crying, while Father and Marius tried to comfort her."

"It was then I realized there was more to Eldyn than I had imagined. While grief and fear had me in their grip, I felt a gentle wave of love envelop me. In that miraculous moment I knew all was fine, for the presence of Spirit was everywhere, just as Aramas had told me so many times, but now I felt it. And I knew it was Eldyn who was embracing me with his spirit, lending me his essence, the depth of the divine he knew. I turned around to look at him. He had put down his swords in front of him and was sitting cross-legged on the ground facing me with eyes closed. He didn't look anything like the terrifying killer, but had changed and was now one of the most beautiful and awe inspiring sights I had ever seen."

"In the four years since then, I have grown a lot, and I feel it's mainly due to Eldyn and his gentle presence in my life. I now recognize he is an extension of Aramas, and at times he even looks like him. He speaks as little as possible, but when he does, he says things that come from Spirit, full of wisdom and love. But mostly, he has taught me through his essence, lending me his being to the point that at times we seem as one. He has never veered from his vow to take care of me, and has put all of his energy into the task."

"If only my brother knew to what extent Eldyn would fulfill his request!"

Martin watched tears of gratitude flow freely down Maria Lerna's cheeks. *Without him she wouldn't be in this place, and wouldn't be the Maria Lerna I know.*

Then she was quiet. The tears had subsided and she was thoughtful.

"That is quite a story, Maria Lerna. But tell me, have you visited your family in your body of light?"

She hesitated; bit her lip and appeared tense. "No, something has stopped me from going. The moment I learned I could travel freely was when I met you, when I saw it was possible. Then I immediately thought about it, but something has kept me from doing it...I think it's fear."

"Fear?"

"Yes, I am afraid of what I might find. When I try to look with my spirit's eyes, I find my vision is clouded and I can't see. I know God's will is being done, all will be best, but I don't know what that means in worldly terms, whether they are imprisoned or dead. And I am so afraid."

Her voice trailed off and new tears formed in her eyes. Martin knew he would have to help her, they would have to go see, and then if necessary they would do something. In his heart there was a feeling of urgency, that something was about to happen, and he hesitated to tell her; he didn't want to make her apprehension any worse. Nevertheless, it was time.

"Maria Lerna, let's go see. I will come with you."

"Thanks, dear Martin. Yes, that's a good plan. We'll go first thing in the morning."

"No, Maria Lerna. We'll go now. If they are in danger we could help them. If they are dead, we'll find out, and if they are fine you will then rest easy. Either way it's best to find out right away."

She acquiesced with a nod of her head, and silently walked over to her house. Martin followed. Inside she sat down on her chair. Once she felt that her body was comfortable, she extended her hand for him to take so they could begin their journey.

They found themselves outside a large house, what Martin guessed was her family home. It was a well-kept big villa with large gardens. It looked peaceful.

She stood outside, listening, looking around, tension and concern on her face. Martin led the way into the house.

The house seemed orderly, furnishings and everyday items neatly kept, but there was a tension in the place, and a feeling of sadness. Maria Lerna led the way to her mother's chamber, which was on one corner of the central courtyard.

There on a sofa lay a middle-aged woman who, without doubt, looked like an older version of Maria Lerna. She seemed to be asleep. Maria Lerna crept closer and, making herself visible, bent down and took hold of one of her mother's hands. The woman slowly awakened, as from a deep stupor. Martin now noticed a cup nearby that contained some sort of liquid, and judging from her appearance and Maria Lerna's reaction, a drug of some sort.

Maria Lerna's mother didn't seem surprised, but looked slowly at her daughter with teary eyes and deep sobs that shook her chest. Maria Lerna too was crying, at the joy of seeing her mother again.

Her voice was gentle and soothing. "Mother of mine, I am fine, don't cry for me, sweet one."

"Oh, Maria Lerna, sweet, dear heart. I'm grateful you came to me, if just in a dream."

"Mother, how are Father and Marius? Please tell me."

Her mother seemed to be convinced she was talking to a figment of her drugged mind, but she was fixated on her daughter's eyes, happy to see her, a broad smile across her face.

At her daughter's question a cloud of sadness came back to her eyes. "Shortly after your escape Julius and Cassius came here with many soldiers. They tore the house apart looking for you, growing angry as they realized you had escaped."

"They had heard reports of a big man who escorted a girl out of the town, killing many men in the process. Now they knew for sure that it was you. One of the servants provided the information that Eldyn was Marius' slave."

"They sent soldiers in all directions with instructions to kill Eldyn and bring you back at any cost. They set themselves up in the house and remained for several days. On the third day the soldiers returned empty-handed, telling them Eldyn had killed six more of their comrades.'"

"Mad with anger, Cassius and Julius took Marius into the courtyard, and in front of your father and me beat him merciless, all the time demanding to know where you had gone." Maria Lerna's mother cried, wiping her face with a cloth. "It was your father who caved in, and at the time I believed it was to protect Marius, but later on, I learned it was because he had grown fearful Julius and Cassius would take our house and even his other properties and investments."

"Your father told them you had gone to a place deep inside the forest, a place Aramas knew about."

"They dragged Aramas out, and proceeded to question him, and then torture him for your whereabouts. The dear old man remained silent, his lips uttering a prayer the whole time, his eyes not seeing them, but somehow fixed on someplace or something very far away."

"They beat him until he was still, his old crumpled body a bloody mess; but the holy old man never talked. I could swear he smiled at me right before he died."

"Frustrated, they left with Marius, promising to kill him if you did not return soon. That was four years ago, and I have not seen Marius since. It's rumored he is in one of the prison cells being tortured every day."

"In the meantime, I have not spoken to your father, but we are not being bothered, maybe because I was a friend of Julius' mother. I don't really know."

"Your father is fine, however. He's busy with his business deals, and is presently on a long journey, and is not expected to return for another year or so."

Maria Lerna stroked her mother's head, and gently ran her hand along the older woman's face, wiping away tears. She then kissed both cheeks, and with teary eyes stood up and faced Martin.

"We must find my brother, wherever he is, dead or alive." This was a different Maria Lerna who now spoke, her manner hard and forceful.

She took a hold of his hand and he noticed her touch; it was now cold but it didn't feel angry; a force seemed to had taken over, but this was still very much Maria Lerna. She then led him to what he supposed was the prison, a place very similar to the one they had visited in Isca, except smaller.

They entered the building, and she seemed to be following her intuition, for they went straight to a small cell on the bottom floor. Inside the windowless room and tied to the wall stood what barely resembled a man, but was rather a skeleton with skin and hair, badly bruised. Two men stood in front of him, and one held a whip.

"He is no longer responding. Let's bring out the hot poker again." This was said by the older of the two, a solidly built man with a clean-shaved face. He then leaned over and yelled in the ear of the man they were torturing.

Martin felt a strong aversion to the older man; he never remembered being so repulsed by someone before. It was as though the man was pure evil, and Martin thought this was probably what being in the presence of the devil felt like.

"You will ride with us,"—here he shouted some insults Martin couldn't make out—"and you will kill, and you will rape, or you will die. And then I will find your sister and rape her and kill her."

Martin was struck by the sheer anger behind the words.

He noticed Maria Lerna's reaction: this was clearly her brother being tortured, and judging by the weak aura emanating from his body, very near death. She was calm, however, very calm and calculating. She pointed her hand at the torturer's chest, and Martin felt a bolt of energy go from her hand and into the man. The man grabbed his chest in agony, and doubled over. The other man, who appeared to be a jailer, bent over the fallen man, calling him "General."

Martin realized he was looking at the famous Cassius.

The jailer, anxious about what was happening to the general, went outside to look for help.

Maria Lerna wasted no time and went over to her brother's side. There she stood, pouring energy into his weakened body. Martin could see the immediate result in Marius' aura. He opened his eyes and looked around, but Maria Lerna was not visible. He softly whispered her name several times.

Cassius lay groaning, and he held his chest with both hands, apparently semi-conscious.

At that moment came the sound of footsteps outside, then the door flung open and four men came in, looked at Cassius, and anxiously took him away.

Marius had lost consciousness, and Maria Lerna went over to loosen his ties. He again opened his eyes and this time was face to face with her, her body having acquired substance to untie his ropes. His eyes immediately brightened and a smile creased his bloodied lips.

"Sweet Maria, you have come to me…"

"Hush, brother, save your strength," she said as tears ran down her cheeks.

He continued staring at her, his own eyes moist. She loosened all of his ropes, and motioned for Martin to help her carry him. Martin made his body solid and as he was about to walk over, the jailer swung the door open and burst in. Martin hit him hard with his fist on the side of the head, knocking him unconscious. The man slumped limply to the floor. Martin then went to help Maria Lerna carry her brother to a cot on the opposite side of the small cell.

"We can't possibly leave him here," she said, her voice tinged with apprehension.

Martin understood she was trying to think what to do next. It occurred to him to disguise himself as the jailer, then take Marius' limp form and walk out.

She agreed. They would walk out and do what they could. The alternative was to let Marius die in that cell when Cassius recovered and came back to torture him again.

Martin donned the jailer's outfit: a dirty tunic and a belt that held a variety of implements, whose use he could not figure out on first sight. He then took Marius in his arms and walked outside with Maria Lerna leading the way, her body visible to his eyes only.

They walked down the long corridor without incident. The jailers they met would at first give them a cursory glance, and those who recognized the man Martin was carrying stood to one side with a look of shock or disbelief in their eyes, but no one tried to stop him.

And so they made it to the front yard. Beyond was the front gate of the prison. In the yard they found a number of horses tied up. Maria Lerna went to two horses that were close together. She undid the ropes. Martin, taking his cue from her, positioned Marius on one horse and climbed on the second.

They walked toward the gate and the two soldiers standing guard before it. As they approached, the soldiers asked Martin for something or other he couldn't make out, possibly a pass of some sort. He watched as Maria Lerna again extended her hand and made them double over in pain, each man clutching his chest. She then opened the gate and they walked outside the prison, to all eyes, a jailer taking an unconscious prisoner somewhere. On impulse, Martin got down to close the prison gate; it just seemed that's what a real jailer would do. Having done that, he jumped back on his horse, leading Marius' horse with one hand.

That way they went on down the streets, Maria Lerna's invisible figure in front. Martin was immensely relieved when they were out of sight of the prison, and all the while thinking: *We did it, somehow we got away.*

They made it to her house and into the front courtyard. A servant came out to inquire, and on seeing the prostrate figure, rushed over to the horse, calling Marius' name and alternatively calling for someone from the inside. Two servants took hold of Marius and carried him inside.

Without a word, Martin took the reins of the second horse and headed back toward the prison. As he got closer, he decided to shed the tunic and belt and let them slip to the ground, as he dissipated his body and dismounted. He watched as the horses continued on towards the prison.

He marveled at how easy it had been to sneak Marius out, and how conveniently the jailer had come back into the cell at the right moment.

Then he wondered how they would manage to keep Julius and the others from finding Marius. But so far everything had worked out fine, and he was sure it was due to Maria Lerna's energy, so calm and serene but nonetheless very forceful, so it made all the right things happen. Martin recognized her presence was like a prayer in action, a dynamic force that shaped events around them.

It took him a while to find the house, for as he meandered through the streets it seemed all the houses looked the same, but eventually he found the right place.

There he found Maria Lerna in the central courtyard, sitting on a bench, apparently lost in thought, but when she saw him, she burst into tears and hugged him.

Feeling a bit puzzled, he held her; she now seemed to him a confused and hurt girl. Perhaps it was her reaction to seeing her brother in that sorry state, and now it was a safe time to let go, he thought. Maybe also the news of how Aramas had been killed.

She remained in his arms, and then he felt like she was somehow feeling bad for him, she had the feel of a mother holding a long-lost small boy…maybe transferring her emotions, he thought. *Probably this is what she feels for her brother.* She clung to him for a moment longer, and then he felt her slowly return to her serene self, her emotions apparently spent.

"Oh, dear Martin," was all she could say. Her eyes were moist with tears and she looked at his face with deep concern and feeling.

They discussed what to do next. She felt her brother was dying, had felt his spirit tell her this was his chosen destiny, and to please let him go. She had no choice but to comply with his wishes.

As they talked they saw a man walk past them accompanied by a servant and a woman.

"The medical man," Maria Lerna said.

They followed the group into Marius' room. He was lying in bed, with his mother keeping a silent vigil by his side. The doctor started by feeling his pulse, then looked at his nails, lips and eyes, and smelled his breath. The woman, possibly the doctor's assistant, was busy ministering to the many wounds and sores on his body. A servant was carefully pouring a liquid into a spoon and into the mouth of the half-conscious Marius.

Maria Lerna stood silently at the foot of the bed looking at her brother, her lips uttering a prayer. She had asked Martin to stay by her side, and he had agreed. They would stay together.

If soldiers came, they agreed they would do what was necessary, for it was clear they couldn't move Marius without causing him further suffering. Martin guessed there were internal organs damaged by the extended beatings and starvation. So at any cost, they would defend the man and the house, even if it meant taking solid form and the resulting consternation their actions would cause.

Two days went by without incident. The doctor and his assistant came by twice a day to minister and give instructions. Servants took turns providing liquid sustenance to the prostrate figure, who would occasionally moan, but was mostly silent, and peaceful. Martin thought he seemed almost like a saint, someone who was no longer of this world. Occasionally he would open his eyes and look at his mother and smile. Several times he looked straight at Maria Lerna, as though making eye contact, whispered her name, smiled, and then fell back into his semi-conscious sleep.

On the afternoon of the third day, while standing at the foot of the bed, both Martin and Maria Lerna suddenly became aware of a silent figure that had made its way into the house unnoticed. It was eerie, as through the figure had floated in and not walked. They turned their heads at the same time. To their surprise they found it was Julius. Martin recognized him by her description, there was no mistaking him: the blond hair, thin gaunt face and small-boy blue eyes that gave the appearance of innocence and cunning at the same time.

Both he and Maria Lerna reacted in shock and panic, looking over Julius' shoulder for the soldiers they knew must be there, and worst of all, Cassius.

Martin felt Maria Lerna change, she had summoned that force back to her, and he felt getting ready for anything. But Julius was alone, subdued, and they realized this was a different man. Judging by his energy, there was no doubt something had changed in him, and he meant no harm. On the contrary, he appeared concerned for Marius, and there were tears in his eyes as he looked at the thin and battered form.

He stared at Marius' mother by his side, and perhaps mostly for her benefit he started talking, alternatively shifting his gaze between mother and son. Martin now noticed the dark circles under his eyes and the weariness of a person who has spent many sleepless nights. He stood there, penitent at the foot of the bed, unaware he was standing not two feet away from Maria Lerna, who at first had examined him carefully, but was now resting her eyes on her brother.

"My heart aches with sorrow for what I have done," he told them, his voice a low monotone. "I can only blame myself, no one else. You gave me a treasure, your love and trust. As a child, when I used to come to this house to play and I received the affection I lacked at home, I remember fantasizing this was my home as well. Over time I loved you all, better than my own family; especially the beautiful and gentle Maria. I think at some point she loved me too. And I threw that away. I allowed Cassius to mold my thinking, and to guide my hand."

"You know I never married, always dreaming of the day she would come back to me."

"When we first took Marius away, I insisted he be kept in a nice cell. And he was fed well." He said the words looking at Maria Lerna's mother. "Then Cassius started to visit him and talk, and I would come along. The conversations at first were probing and almost friendly, Cassius wanting to know if Marius knew exactly where his sister was. Then he wanted to know about the place where she was hiding, and about the teacher we had beaten to death. Who was he and what did he teach? He seemed genuinely curious about the whole thing, even excited, as though for a change he had found something that caught his interest. As the days passed, everything else—the raids, women, plotting against other kingdoms—all of that seemed to fade by comparison; this was a new game for him, a new thing to captivate him, and whatever it was it was embodied in Marius."

Julius' recount was met with mostly silence. Marius lay almost motionless, with an occasional moan, and when he did look he would either turn his head to look at his mother, or stare right where Maria Lerna was standing, beside Julius. His mother kept looking down at the ground, her face impassive, except for a sob now and then.

"Marius told us about his and Maria's beliefs, and their practice, that under their teacher's tutelage they had learned to look inside. I remember he told us how they both wanted to live lives of high principles to reflect their inner selves, lives of service, of honesty, loyalty, simplicity and purity and that those principles were worth living and dying for. But those things were only outward manifestations of what was inside, a journey into the higher realm, a state of being that made life worth while, a place where true joy existed." Julius' recounting had the eerie sound of someone who was able to recall word for word what he had heard, and Martin got the impression he had repeated the words to himself many times.

After a deep sigh, he continued. "At first Cassius laughed at Marius, and then he seemed to want to challenge him, and they would engage in discussions that turned into arguments, but one-sided arguments. Cassius angrily told him the world was set up so the strong always triumphed over the weak, and the strong could and should take whatever they wanted, and that's how things were and always would be. That's how it was in nature, how animals behaved, and that's how man was supposed to be. He was one of the strong, that's why he was a general, and Marius his prisoner."

"As time went by, Cassius seemed to become increasingly angry. That's when the beatings started, but at first they weren't that bad, not as punishing and terrible as later on. Then one day he decided Marius should come and ride with us. That was just a year or so ago. We were going to raid a farm, and he wanted Marius to kill and rape, or he would feel the full brunt of his anger. Cassius was convinced once Marius felt what it was like to impose his will on the weak, to kill and take things by force, his true nature would take over."

"Marius went along, but when it came to raping and killing, he instead defended the peasants they were attacking, furiously and expertly fighting off the raiders, until Cassius and four others overcame him."

"This time we took him to a dark cell on the first floor of the prison, the place reserved for torture." Julius' voice trailed off as he stared at Marius.

"It was amazing how strong Marius was, how he resisted the most awful torture and seemed impervious to pain, his face impassive as Cassius did horrible things to him. It was as though it was happening to someone else, his gaze always serene and his lips seldom uttering a single sound unless he lost consciousness. Then he would moan and cry out."

At this point Maria Lerna's mother started sobbing. Julius waited until she had regained composure, a sorrowful look in his eyes.

"At first," he continued, "Cassius would constantly ridicule the teachings he heard Marius describe, but eventually he sounded less and less convincing, as though the words he was hearing had a power over him and were showing him something."

"It then occurred to me it was Marius who was torturing Cassius, for although his body showed the signs of the cruel mistreatment, his spirit was calm, while Cassius was losing his mind. In his chambers, he would walk around in circles, around and around all through the night, cursing at Marius and Maria and at their teacher, muttering something about trickery."

"I also suffered. Oh, yes. I would lay awake at night, especially after one of our raids. I would see the faces of the people we killed, the women we took. But I was powerless. The following morning, in Cassius' presence, I would change. I could feel myself becoming like him, and wanted to please him, make him happy. I was also very much afraid of him…terrified."

"Around this time, Cassius met the Saxon chief, Erouf. I became very concerned about my kingdom, but there was nothing I could do! I just knew Erouf would end up taking over. His men were fierce and powerful; but Cassius just laughed at my concerns, told me he was using Erouf and would get rid of him in due course. Erouf had taken over planning the raids, and decided to bring all of his men from Saxony to defeat Joannes once and for all. I decided to take action. I made a plan to recruit a young ruffian they called 'The Fox' to carry a message to Joannes. I knew the boy came and went wherever he pleased. One day I looked at Marius' beaten body, and could feel his courage, and it was as though I was able to borrow a part of him. That same night, I recruited The Fox. I can't tell you how relieved I was when I found out five days later the message had been delivered. I also felt stronger…perhaps."

"The defeat of Erouf and his men didn't seem to concern Cassius. I had expected a violent reaction, but he didn't even seem to notice. His entire attention was now on Marius. He insisted on taking him on two more raids, the most recent only three months ago. But even with his body almost crumbling, Marius did his best to protect their victims." Julius' gaze was fixated on the unconscious man. "Dear courageous Marius. He's a holy man, you know."

"Cassius beat him, and brought him back to the prison. There the torture continued, Cassius now spending most of his time in Marius' cell, alternatively torturing and yelling, and sometimes just sitting there, staring at Marius, his sunken eyes bloodshot."

"Then three days ago they brought him from the prison after he collapsed with a bad chest. That day I saw a new Cassius, I saw a defeated man. In his delirium he kept murmuring Marius' name, over and over. Once he stared up at me, his eyes bulging out, grabbed me by the tunic and muttered: 'the trickery, it's all trickery.' Then he closed his eyes and resumed reciting Marius' name."

"When he regained consciousness and learned Marius had escaped, he sent a trusted lieutenant to inquire how Marius had gotten away; for it was rumored one of the jailers had physically carried him out of the prison, and he wanted desperately to find out who it was. But all of the jailers had taken responsibility, and no one would identify the single culprit, for they apparently had all rejoiced in Marius' get away, and took pride it had been one of their own who had finally done it."

"The lieutenant returned with the news and his appraisal of the situation. He was awaiting orders outside the general's room to round up all the jailers, when a servant came out with word that Cassius had taken his own life. We rushed in and found him hanging from one of the rafters, his face contorted into what looked like a grotesque mask."

"As I stood looking at the dangling body I heard Cassius' lieutenant shouting orders outside, and it dawned on me the man was filling in for his dead boss. That's when I decided to take over, and not let the same thing happen again. I had the man imprisoned, and then began to take back my kingdom...and my battered honor."

"I also came to tell you both, that although I will never measure up to Marius, I will do what I can with what I have. As I speak, I have taken direct control of my army and am rounding up the bandits, one group at the time. I am going to bring back order; it's the least I can do to correct in some measure the wrong I have done."

"After that, I don't have any plans, but to ask the people I have wronged for forgiveness." Julius' eyes were now full of tears. "I started with you."

His tale finished, he turned around and left as silently as he had come.

Martin looked over the hushed room. Marius' eyes were now open, his gaze on the departing Julius. He had heard it all, apparently. His mother sat looking at her son, tears running down her cheeks, her face reflecting an effort to keep from breaking down altogether. Maria Lerna stood serenely looking at her brother.

Marius died two days later. Maria Lerna was standing in the courtyard with Martin, when she looked at him and said, "He's gone, my brother is gone."

They rushed to his room. He lay with a smile on his face. The room itself was bathed in a glorious peace, what Martin guessed was Marius' spirit saying goodbye to them all. His mother was asleep on the chair beside him. Maria Lerna leaned over and kissed her brother's forehead, then she kissed her mother, who woke up, and realizing her son was dead, broke into sobs. Maria Lerna stood by her, giving her loving energy, invisibly consoling her. After some time she turned around, took Martin's hand and led him away, away from the house, the town, and back to her home.

They found Eldyn by his hut, peeling some vegetables, a pot on the fire already boiling. He looked up when he felt their presence. In his brogue he talked to Maria Lerna. He seemed to know she had been back in Dunum and that she had seen her family. He also knew her brother had passed away, but he wanted details.

She announced that first she had to take care of her physical body.

About half an hour later she emerged, her face freshly washed. She was eating some fruit and said she had found herself very hungry and thirsty. She continued eating items she had in a sack as she stood in front of them, and told Eldyn about her brother's death.

"He was so beautiful, Eldyn, you should have seen him, a radiant face, and his spirit shone through his bruised and wounded body, victorious. It was such a wonderful death, and successful life." Her words sounded cheerful but Martin could sense they had a quiet pain behind them and he guessed she had done a bit of crying.

She talked first about Aramas and how he died, but they had known long before that he had passed. Somehow they both had known. Now Maria Lerna was providing graphic detail. Eldyn nodded his head looking down at the ground. Then she related her brother's suffering at Cassius' hands and how he never gave in, but maintained his internal peace and resolve and was able to leave an energetic legacy of tremendous power whose immediate effect would be to change Julius' kingdom, and set the stage for when Ambrosius' time came.

The tale of how he persevered was already circulating, according to her, and would probably reach Isca in a few days. As time went by, Marius' story would give people renewed hope for the future. Soon they would start looking for a person to fit the same mold; someone with mystical stature to show them a way to live and prosper. In fact, they would be creating Ambrosius. As painful as it was for Maria Lerna and Eldyn to contemplate Marius' and Aramas' deaths, it was all part of a magical sequence.

She provided the details from Julius' own account, and Martin saw how moved she was, and the impact it was having on Eldyn, who although dry-eyed, obviously felt deeply the passing of his friend and master, and was proud of him.

Maria Lerna stood silent for a moment, perhaps feeling her brother's spirit; and then she talked to him directly.

"At first, dear brother, I was sorry I hadn't gone earlier, I could have stopped the torture and you would be alive this very moment. But then, I realized the way things happened was for the best. It was crucial you died at home, and Martin and I were the only ones able to do that for you." She walked slowly a few paces away, staring into the distance.

"On the surface, Aramas was dying so as to not reveal our whereabouts. On the other hand, his death and torture was an example to you, showing how inconsequential death and physical suffering are...and how important it is to live for the right cause."

Maria Lerna became silent and stood very still.

CHAPTER FIFTEEN

Four days later in Isca, Martin heard that an army headed by Arcadius had gone to Dunum to settle things. In bits and pieces from conversations he got most of the story.

Arcadius and his men had come within sight of the city and were getting ready to attack, when Julius came out alone on his horse to meet them. He surrendered to Arcadius and told him how sorry he was for all the bad things people from his kingdom had done, himself included.

Arcadius simply took over the city. He then returned to Isca to meet with Joannes; and they discussed what to do with the place, whether to make it part of their own kingdom, or find a capable man in its midst to rule. For the time being they decided to put Julius in his own prison and institute order. They were mystified, but grateful for the turn of events. Arcadius—and shortly after, all of Isca it seemed, speculated that perhaps the mysterious nobleman who had risked his life to tell them about the Saxon invasion was behind Cassius' death. No one believed that he had committed suicide. A few days later, a nobleman in Dunum died when he accidentally fell down a well. His wife told her neighbors that it had been he who had sent the message to Joannes that led to the defeat of the Saxons, and that he had told her of his plan to kill Cassius. He was soon celebrated as a hero, and it became obvious to everyone that his death had been no accident.

Martin was listening to a group speculating about the events, when he felt Maria Lerna summoning him. When he fixed his mind on her, he knew she was at the Citadel with the royal family, and that something important was about to happen.

He found her with Martigena, Joannes and Ambrosius in the room that served as the library. They were looking out through the window down into the street that led to the entrance to the Citadel.

They watched as Philippus came through the gate on a horse. As he approached, a dog ran right in front of him. The horse reared just as Philippus was getting ready to dismount. He was thrown violently on the pavement, and landed on his head. They all rushed outside to find him unconscious. Miraculously he was not badly hurt, and after a short time he got up, a bit shaken.

After the scare, Martigena turned to Maria Lerna. "You could have prevented that," she said to her, and it sounded like an angry accusation, but

Martin realized she wasn't angry, but scared.

Maria Lerna in turn remained silent, quietly observing her. After some time, she placed a hand on Martigena's shoulder.

Joannes, Ambrosius and Philippus now came to stand by their side, Joannes bringing Philippus along with an arm around his shoulders.

Martigena now had tears running down her cheeks. Then she looked at her friend. "Forgive me, Marli, I don't know what came over me."

In response, Maria Lerna took Martigena's hands in her own.

Martigena looked at her family as she spoke to Maria Lerna. "I know what you are telling me; your function in our lives is not to keep us from physical harm…it's to keep us from spiritual ignorance." She looked into Maria Lerna's eyes. "Forgive me, dear soul, for my ungrateful words. Never will I ever say anything like that to you again…never."

Later, Martin asked Maria Lerna whether she knew the horse would throw Philippus but not hurt him seriously.

"Yes" she said, "I could feel something was going to happen, I just didn't know exactly what."

A week later, he felt she was summoning him again.

He found her chatting with Nicolaus and Ambrosius at the teachers' house, waiting for Mowan to show up.

At that moment Mowan walked in and without a word to anyone went directly to Maria Lerna, his manner grave and tension on his otherwise calm features. "I received a friend of mine from Caledonia yesterday evening. He came to tell me of a group sent to kill Joannes and Philippus. I will have to find them before they reach Isca, and kill myself in front of them. I came to say goodbye."

They were all very quiet, a sullen quiet that spoke of doom.

The prince went up to Mowan and embraced him. "But the Caledonians took an oath not to return with arms. They are breaking their word."

Mowan affectionately patted Ambrosius' back, then walked over to look out a nearby window. "Honor is paramount in my culture; once a vow is made it can't be broken, and I made a vow. They sent men who were not part of the war party and therefore are not bound by the oath they took. I'm afraid they sent men to kill Joannes and Philippus, not only as revenge, but also to demonstrate they are not the magicians people make them out to be."

"But if you kill yourself in front of them," Maria Lerna said, "that wouldn't stop them from proceeding with their mission."

"I have to keep my vow. I have no choice."

Nicolaus approached and placed a hand on Mowan's shoulder. "I for one can't let you do it, brother, not while the men can be stopped. I'm sure if we tell Joannes, he will send soldiers to capture them."

"These are hunters very skilled at stalking silently and killing," Mowan said. "They are hard to detect, that's why they were sent. In my land, whenever a chief becomes a threat to his people or to other clans, he is dispatched this way, without war. Just the hunters who come in and do their job. I'm sure they sent the best hunters they could find. If I live and they succeed, Joannes' and Philippus' blood will be in my hands."

"But your father," said Maria Lerna, "whoever sent them, aren't they afraid of what your father might do?"

Mowan was staring down at the floor. "Obviously those who sent them don't care much if after they have killed Joannes and Philippus I kill myself, and whether the hunters are slain as well. My father will vow revenge, but he won't know who sent them. And then the other chiefs will convince him it had to be done. That is their plan, I am certain."

"Mowan, I can't let you do it either," Maria Lerna said. "You are too valuable for Ambrosius' training, and dear to our hearts. I will take care of it. I will keep them from crossing the mountains and therefore you won't have to kill yourself."

Nicolaus, Mowan and Ambrosius were now looking at her.

"Let us take part, dear Marli," said Nicolaus. "I am certain you can stop the men, for we have seen your powers. But it is our moral obligation to take part. Mowan, because they are challenging his vow. Me, because I have become Mowan's brother."

"And me because he's my teacher,." Ambrosius said.

They all looked at him.

"No, dear one," Maria Lerna said. "We can't put you in harm's way."

"If you won't let me take part, you are going against the principles you taught me: honor and loyalty. How do you expect me to give up on those high values when my teacher's life is at stake?"

Martin knew his words had an effect on those around the room for they had certainly impacted him. The young prince was right, and on the sheer merit of his argument, they would have to include him. He was young in age, but Martin had noticed how easily people forgot when talking with him. It was very clear Ambrosius meant to come along, and would do everything in his power to do so.

Maria Lerna became adamant. She would take care of the hunters; there was no other way. Otherwise she was placing all of them at risk, and she could never allow that.

"I am being trained for a life that will require special skills, traits and abilities," said Ambrosius. His manner was forceful, his voice calm. "Is it possible this task is meant for me? Maybe Spirit has devised a special challenge for me to overcome, and you are to be my witnesses. Would you consider that?"

Maria Lerna stood silent for some time. So did the teachers, and Martin knew they were probing with their intuition, asking whether the child was right...and they decided he was. This was a challenge for all of them, but especially for Ambrosius.

They talked at length about what to do. It was a hard choice, but they couldn't tell Joannes;, he would never allow it, and in all likelihood would insist on hunting down the Caledonians, with the possible result that he would be killed.

They decided to tell Joannes and Martigena instead that they wanted to visit the Seeker Colony. They had talked many times before of making the journey, and it was one of those things they kept postponing, looking for the best time, the right opportunity. So now when they brought it up, it would not be a surprise for Joannes and Martigena. This was a trip that would take several months but they would be reassured their son would be under Maria Lerna's care.

They talked with Ambrosius about the fact that they would be lying, and concluded they would have to actually go to the Seeker Colony. They would deal with the hunters first, and then go on.

Ambrosius convinced them that it would be wise to approach his mother first.

Martigena gave her consent, albeit with some misgivings at letting go of her son for such a long time. This was to be Ambrosius' first lengthy departure from home. Previously he had done no more than go on overnight journeys with his teachers or his parents.

Joannes gave his approval, and it was obvious he was glad Martigena had agreed first; this was not one of those decisions he would want to impose on his wife.

They left the following day on horseback. The two teachers flanking Ambrosius, with Achilles the wolf trailing behind. They had taken some supplies and weapons for the journey but traveled light, following the monks' habit of relying on the universe to provide along the way.

They traveled all day at a brisk pace, and made camp as the sun set over the tree line. That night, with Achilles on guard, they meditated. Maria Lerna had forged on ahead with Martin and spotted the hunters a bit more than a day's ride beyond the mountains. The men had just stolen some food from a farm. Martin and Maria Lerna followed them until they made camp. They were being cautious not to be noticed, carefully avoiding travelers on the road. There were four of them, all on horseback, and they carried impressive bows, large weapons about as tall as a man.

When Maria Lerna reported back to the group, Ambrosius asked her not to interfere from then on. He thanked her for spotting the hunters, and said that for him to be tested and grow as a result of the challenge, he would have to rely on his own abilities. What Maria Lerna could do was to pray for him.

After Ambrosius spoke, it was apparent he was now in charge of the expedition; somehow it had happened and they had accepted it without so many words.

That night they sat around the fire. Ambrosius talked about their pilgrimage to the Seeker Colony. He wanted to meet Eldyn...and he wanted to see Maria Lerna in the flesh.

"But you already see me, almost every day, dear one."

"I know, Marli, but I want to know you are also like us. I want to know you have a body just like mine, one that doesn't appear and disappear when you least expect it."

The monks smiled, and Maria Lerna seemed to understand.

Nicolaus and Mowan commented that they too looked forward to meeting Eldyn. In their quiet way, they also seemed excited at the prospect of visiting the Seeker Colony.

Achilles approached Nicolaus, and lay down next to him, placing a paw on his leg.

"Nicolaus, how did you acquire Achilles?" asked Ambrosius. "It's unusual to have a wolf as a companion."

Nicolaus looked at Achilles, then he looked at the prince. "Two years ago I was wandering through the northern territories and ran across a mother wolf and her pup. The adult wolf was badly wounded, it seemed as the result of a fierce fight. I felt the energy waning from her body, and as she stood in front of me trembling, I had the feeling she had been looking for a way to protect her pup after her passing."

"I walked closer to the mother and pup and sat in communion, sending loving energy to both. Soon the mother lay down a pace in front of me and quietly passed away."

"The pup clung to the mother, and at her passing begun to whine softly. I felt her spirit come and lead the pup over to where I was sitting. I bent over, picked him up and cuddled him against my chest. From then on we have become inseparable, and we know what the other is feeling, even when separated."

He told them about the time when Achilles had defended him during the attack by the four Caledonians, and how that was just one of the many times the wolf had protected him.

"The same happened many times before when we encountered bandits," Nicolaus said. "It appears that he knows when someone with bad intentions is coming near and he hides. At first I thought he was fearful, but soon I learned it was all part of Achilles' strategy. He would hide and when whoever approached tried to rob or harm me, then he would dash out growling fiercely with bared fangs. Invariably that was enough to scare people away."

Achilles lay by his master, enjoying the nearby fire.

The following day as they made their way north and could already see the mountains, Maria Lerna asked Ambrosius if he had formulated a plan of what to do once they found the hunters.

"Yes, Marli. I was just going to discuss it with all of you."

It was apparent Ambrosius had thought long and hard about his plan. He wanted to collect a medicinal root Maria Lerna had told him about, a compound the Seekers used to put people to sleep when they had to do something physically painful, like cutting off a leg.

"I have seen it growing on the side of the road. We have passed several bushes," she said.

They were to collect the root and make bread with the extract, then place the bread somewhere where the hunters would see it and steal it. Then when the hunters were asleep, they were going to cut off a hand from each one of them.

"Cut off their hands?" asked Mowan. "What would that accomplish?'

"They won't be able to use their bows," Ambrosius said.

It was true. It was impossible for a man to use a bow and arrow without the use of both hands. Ambrosius went on to say he wanted the men to live, not only because he respected life, but also because it was the most practical.

"Without a hand they won't be able to carry out their mission, they will have to turn back. They won't know who cut off their hands; to them it will appear the act of a magician. Then they will return to their land, helping to spread awe and fear of our kingdom."

The teachers and Maria Lerna were impressed by the simplicity and wisdom apparent in the plan. It involved a crude element, the cutting off of hands, but this too was appreciated, because it told them Ambrosius was prepared to take drastic action when necessary, based on practicality rather than emotion.

The crucial element was to make sure the hunters ate the bread.

They rose before dawn and started out at a trot. They reached the mountains where the battle had taken place before noon, and by early afternoon they approached a cluster of a villa and surrounding farms.

It was a small enclave still in the process of recovering from the invasion, for although more than a year had already gone by, the level of destruction had been devastating. The place still bore scars: some buildings had not been rebuilt and some were in the process. However, the fields looked green and plentiful, and that was the most important factor.

One of the farms sat next to the road, it's main house close to the line of trees. That, they decided, would be their trap. Both Maria Lerna and the teachers felt the Caledonians were now but a short ride up the road.

The two teachers and boy approached the villa to introduce themselves to the lord of the place and ask for his assistance. The owner was a rotund man who seemed apprehensive at the sight of strangers. He looked them over, paying attention to the boy's fine clothes. When he learned of their identities, he became solicitous, calling for servants to bring food and drink for his honored guests.

Nicolaus inquired about any other farms up the road.

The nearest one was a good two days' ride, the man told them.

The setting was perfect, the hunters had to stop by to get food, there was no other place. From what Maria Lerna had seen, they were relying on stealing for their food.

They asked the lord to lend them the use of the one farmhouse nearest the road and by the tree line, for the next two days. They told him they were weary of traveling and had the need to prepare medicinal bread the Prince required for his sustenance.

The lord quickly agreed. They were most welcome, and he was honored to house the son of King Joannes of Isca, may he and his family be healthy and forever prosper.

The group followed the man to the farmhouse that sat near the road. There he brusquely ordered its occupants to vacate the premises for the next two days.

Ambrosius, the teachers and Maria Lerna grimaced at the man's manner and looked on sadly at the family they were displacing, but there wasn't much they could do about it, except to embrace them with their energy. They watched as the man, woman and two children grabbed some meager possessions and went over to a neighboring farm.

The group made their way to the forest where Mara Lerna found the plant she had talked about, and showed them how to harvest the root.

Back at the farm they pulped the roots and extracted a juice. They searched the house for other ingredients, and soon Maria Lerna was satisfied she had everything she needed.

They fired up the brick oven in the kitchen house, a structure adjacent to the farmhouse. Martin watched as they all worked excitedly, all wanting to do more than their share, getting in each other's way.

"What if the hunters don't steal the bread?" asked Nicolaus. "What then?"

Ambrosius had thought about it. "We will then need to ambush them," he said, "but let's see what happens."

How the three would ambush four experienced hunters was beyond Martin. *Maybe that's when I will need to intervene again...or Maria Lerna.*

That evening they had five loaves of bread spread out on the kitchen window sill, apparently left overnight to cool down.

They tried a portion of one of the loaves on a dog. Martin noticed that after about five minutes the animal started to act groggy and then he simply fell down, almost in mid-stride. They tried another piece on a pig, a huge beast twice the size of a normal man. It too collapsed after a few minutes. It seemed whatever drug was in the bread was very potent. They observed the unconscious dog and pig for about an hour. They poked them and pricked them with little reaction. It was obvious the root extract worked well.

They took care to leave a light in the room, so the window could be seen at night. Then they waited.

Maria Lerna went out with Martin and they spotted the hunters two miles up the road, making their way toward the farm cluster. When they came within sight of the farms, they dismounted, left one man to care for the horses, and three of them made their way to the lights they could see in the distance.

As they approached the farms the men spread out. One went for a chicken coop, another for the house where the breads were, and the third toward another house. Martin watched with awe how they walked and moved. They made absolutely no noise, walking with great care not to step on branches or even leaves, and with awareness of the direction of the wind so neither horses nor dogs could pick up their scent. Martin observed how a dog continued sleeping even as one man stepped almost over it. A young couple walked but a few feet from one of the hunters without so much as a hint of suspicion that there was anyone there. The man had stood perfectly still, not breathing, and had appeared to be another silent shadow.

The trap worked. The hunter noticed the loaves and took two, apparently just enough for one meal.

Martin went inside the farmhouse. In short order Ambrosius saw the window sill, noticed the stolen loaves, and notified the monks. They decided to wait until past dinnertime to start searching for the hunters. They figured that was enough time for them to set up camp and consume their stolen goods, and so they waited until near midnight before setting out.

They left the house and started their search, aware they had limited time to do their work. Martin noticed Maria Lerna's discreet assistance, directing the group to the right spot, while appearing to keep her word not to interfere. She kept sending energy to Ambrosius, who led the group. When he walked in the right direction she sent positive energy to his heart; when he veered away, she cut it off. It worked well, and Ambrosius led them straight to the camp. First they found the horses in a clearing, and further into the forest they found the campsite.

It appeared to Martin the hunters were all under the influence of a powerful soporific, unaware of the two adults, the young man and the wolf who gingerly walked up to their camp.

They watched the men to see if they stirred, then proceeded closer. Ambrosius picked up a rock and struck one of the sleeping hunters on the chest. The rock made a loud thump against the man, and he grunted but did not wake.

Satisfied, they approached.

First they set things up. They tied the men just in case, with heavy ropes. Then they threw more wood into the fire, fanning the flames. The hunters had built a subdued fire for fear of attracting attention, although they had gone deep into the forest. The monks and Ambrosius drew out three swords and clean strips of clothing and placed them carefully on rocks so as not to soil them.

The three worked as a team, and they performed their dreadful task with dexterity, cutting off hands, stopping the flow of blood with tourniquets and then rapidly cauterizing the open wounds with hot embers.

The men thrashed, moaned and even screamed in their stupor, but did not wake up.

Ambrosius seemed pale and shaken by the act they were performing, but he did his part, applying a tourniquet and bringing a hot ember to a fresh wound.

Nicolaus and Mowan seemed unperturbed, perhaps having seen or done similar things before.

The stench of burning flesh hung in the air, and blood had splattered all over the place. It was a very messy affair. Martin looked at Maria Lerna, but she seemed focused on Ambrosius, and appeared to be only aware of his actions and reactions. Martin knew she was appraising not only what she saw, but also the emotions and energy behind the actions. She appeared satisfied. Ambrosius had acted calmly most of the time, and on the occasions when he had been overcome with revulsion he seemed able to bring himself back to centeredness.

They decided to leave the severed hands forming a crossed pattern on the ground, plainly visible for the men when they woke up. They broke the big bows and then placed them in the same pattern on the ground.

Their gruesome task done, the men left the camp, relief written on their faces. Silently they made their way back to the farmhouse.

The following morning the remaining loaves were buried in the forest by Mowan, buried deep so not even animals would be able to smell them and dig them up.

Nicolaus went over to thank the lord of the farms and tell him they were leaving early, while Mowan and Ambrosius went looking for the house occupants, to thank them, and Martin noticed, make a gift of one of the swords and some silver coins, both greatly appreciated.

They left the horses behind, to be picked up at some later time.

The group now seemed caught up in the excitement of their trek to the Seeker Colony, Ambrosius asking Maria Lerna a myriad of questions, the monks quiet but listening intently, and Achilles perhaps expressing everyone's mood best by playing like a puppy; jumping and frolicking around, occasionally picking up sticks and dropping them in front of Nicolaus.

CHAPTER SIXTEEN

The group made their way up the road for about two hours, according to Martin's estimate; then, apparently reading a sign only she could see, Maria Lerna guided them into the forest.

At first they had to skirt trees and push their way through the underbrush, but then the forest became virtually impossible to traverse and she took them through some sort of secret maze. Whenever they appeared to have met a solid wall of trees or impassable brush, she veered just a few feet in one direction or another, and there somehow they would find a space wide enough for a person to get through.

More than once she led them through a hole in a tree, and they would have to get on all fours and crawl, only to find another obstacle, and another hidden passage, often an animal-made path.

Trying to hack their way through, they all agreed, would have been very hard.

It was apparent to them all how the energy of the place changed the deeper they went into the forest and left the civilized world behind.

At first they had been bothered by thorns and insects and were apprehensive of the strange surroundings and noises, but after the seventh day their reaction changed; they didn't seem to be bothered much by anything, and the same sounds now seemed to be welcoming.

Martin noticed they didn't seem to get tired and seldom stopped for water or nourishment; it was as though the forest was now providing their sustenance, and it was tangible, a soft and gentle energy that came from all around.

He wasn't the only one to notice.

"Marli," asked Mowan, "we seem to be sustained by some external force, and it doesn't seem to come from you. Is it the forest?"

"It is," she said. "This is a holy place made so by many souls who have come here in search of a life with Spirit. The power of their spiritual essence has changed the place, and because your intent harmonizes, the result is a new state of being in which your bodies draw sustenance from the force that is always around you."

"Once in the colony people have found they no longer need to be so concerned about their bodies; just minimal attention is sufficient, so they end up eating very little and sleeping but a few hours each night, yet remain very healthy."

They walked for twenty days. On the morning of the twenty-first day when they reached the top of a hill, Maria Lerna showed them where her house was, pointing out a valley nestled in between two mountains. Then she left them.

As the group approached her house they saw her standing next to Eldyn, smiling at them.

They both held a basket full of flowers. The group came over and reverently bowed before the two, and each was showered with the colorful wild flowers.

The first evening together they talked about the hunters and what they had done. Ambrosius was still concerned about deceiving his parents, and this apparently weighed heavily on his heart, more so than the hacking off of the hunters' hands.

Eldyn listened to Ambrosius' account and told him he had done well.

"Man's actions cannot be judged by a single measure," he said. "In your case lying was the best course of action. Erase the guilt you feel in your heart, and remember your intent."

Eldyn seemed impressed with the way they had dealt with the hunters. "You have acted in worldly ways with the wisdom of Spirit," he told the Prince.

Ambrosius and his two teachers slept with Eldyn in his hut, on a layer of leaves, all four side by side with Achilles by his master.

Each morning they got up and meditated together. Then they would visit a different resident of the colony, spending most of the day in that person's house or small farm, getting to know them, helping with chores. In all, there were forty-seven different houses for the seventy-four members.

The colony was spread out over a large area, probably several square miles, most covered with thick forest, interspersed with cultivated fields, orchards and vegetable gardens. Roughly in the middle of the whole thing was a lake with a dome-shaped island. One day they rowed to it and found that a maze had been outlined with rocks. This was the "walk of life," explained Maria Lerna, and she instructed them to walk the maze while in a meditative state. The experience, she told them, was always different, and if done properly, would give them a new insight each time. They found the walks very rewarding, and would to do it several times during their stay.

In the evenings the entire colony gathered in the communion cave, and meditated together for several hours. Martin came to realize the power of those gatherings. He felt each person come to a place of peace or joy, and then he felt the embrace of the entire group by each individual. It was truly a communion, a union of each person with Spirit and of each person with the group, all made possible by their common intent.

In their group they seemed to have a cross-section of skills and talents. Maria Lerna and Eldyn were the healers; they cared for people's ailments, which included the entire spectrum: physical, spiritual, mental and emotional. Other members brought different talents. There were carpenters and builders, farmers, tailors, teachers, writers and even actors and comedians.

No hunting was necessary, for the group didn't need meat for sustenance. They did use leather, and gathered the skins after the animals died naturally. It was as though the small colony was a few degrees removed from the reality of the world so some of the unpleasantness could be done without, such as the killing of animals, and that perhaps contributed to the harmony felt everywhere.

This distance from "the real world" was also evident in the way people related. Martin noticed there was no bartering of goods and services, things were just done and given to those who needed it.

He wondered how transgressors were handled, and one morning he, and the rest of the group, had a chance to see.

It happened with a man, an older man, perhaps already in his seventies, who angrily complained he was doing more than his share. He was a tailor, and several people had asked him for clothes at the same time.

Eldyn was called to help, and he walked into the man's house accompanied by the two teachers and Ambrosius, who sat quietly in a corner, watching Eldyn heal the man.

Eldyn sat by the eating table and asked the man to join him. The older man was still upset, the anger etched on his face, and it appeared to Martin that being upset was something that happened to him often, judging by his energy.

The man did as directed, and sat facing Eldyn. For some time nobody spoke, and the man fidgeted in his chair. Eldyn sat motionless meditating, and apparently sending him energy, embracing him and trying to penetrate through the defensive wall of anger the man had put up.

"Detrius, people are saying you are acting angry, why is that?" asked Eldyn.

In response Detrius went into a lengthy and angry discourse on how he was tired of some members not pulling their weight, and how some like him had to do the job of many. Why weren't these people going to the other tailors? A neighboring tailor, Aldus, wasn't doing much of anything, but he had a good way of turning people down, so it was for him, Detrius, to do the work Aldus refused to do.

"Have you asked Aldus why he is not working more?"

"No. I know if I ask him he'll give some sort of excuse, so what's the use?"

Eldyn didn't respond; instead he meditated, and after some time Detrius seemed to be meditating as well. That went on for what Martin thought was an hour or so.

"If Aldus is not doing what he is supposed to and you end up doing his work, you have my gratitude." Eldyn said. "Also know if you do his work and then pray for him, and if he is not ill, soon he will see what he is causing, and will change his ways."

Martin could feel Eldyn was not just speaking, his words matched the energy he projected, and each sentence seemed to punctuate the energetic communication.

Detrius was paying close attention, and his face had softened somewhat.

"We are but one Spirit, we are all part of each other." Eldyn's words were more like an affirmation than an argument, and they seemed to have a profound effect on the older man. Eldyn repeated the words again.

They meditated in silence for another short time.

"Tomorrow," Detrius said, this time without any anger, "I will go see Aldus and I will ask him if all is right with him, and if he hasn't been able to work because of an injury or illness, I will offer my help. I will also go around the neighbors I have offended with my anger and ask for their forgiveness."

Eldyn smiled at the man, and Detrius smiled back, a shy, apologetic look in his eyes. After some time Eldyn stood up and left. The two monks and Ambrosius followed him, all affected by the healing that had taken place.

That night around the fire, they discussed Detrius.

"I didn't expect anyone could get angry in this place," Ambrosius said.

"We are still part of the world," Maria Lerna said, "and must bear the burden of the dark that is part of our existence. But unlike out in the world, the light here is dominant, that's the difference." She told them that on the outside, Detrius would have ended up killing.

"Why does God allow for darkness?" asked Ambrosius.

"Because we need conflict to move us forward," Nicolaus said. "Humans need contrast to see. Peace is recognized only because of war, just as we need sadness to know when we are happy."

"But what's the function of war, besides making us appreciate peace?"

"Humans create war to learn many valuable lessons." Mowan said.

"Like what?"

"Ultimately," he said, "to learn the value of life. They also learn to live in the moment. Most learn to love for the first time...once in the battlefield only your survival and the lives of your friends is real."

"But is it possible one day we won't have any wars, we will have permanent peace?" asked Ambrosius.

All eyes turned toward Eldyn. Somehow they figured he had to answer Ambrosius.

Eldyn took a deep breath and it became a sigh. He was now looking intently at the young prince, perhaps seeing his future of warfare, the endless wars stretching into the future, seemingly without end.

"Yesu told us to love our neighbors as we love ourselves," he said. "When we all evolve to that point there won't be any more wars. In the meantime, remember our spirits all want peace. When fighting you can also strive for peace."

"We can't escape our surroundings," Nicolaus said. "I for one passed on the knowledge of war machines I had studied to Joannes, knowing it was my duty. Given the circumstances, that's what was required of me. I knew eventually those machines would lead to the making of peace."

"You had righteousness on your side when you did that, Nicolaus," Ambrosius said. "My father only wants to defend Isca from invaders. Righteousness is everything. If a person kills and he's justified, surely he can draw on the power of Spirit."

Eldyn's gaze was now lost in the fire. "The attacker can feel righteousness as much as the defender. Humans are capable of making sense of any situation."

"I don't understand, Eldyn; you are saying there is no right and wrong?"

Eldyn sighed again. "I am certain the Caledonians, Angles and Saxons are just like us, except they view the world differently. Imagine that they are wolves and we are sheep. Neither one is good nor bad, just different; and just as with the animals, our differences cause us conflict."

"Some of us kill because we have to," Eldyn sounded sad. "Brother Mowan at one point felt he had no other choice but to let himself be killed. That was also my only other choice for a long time. We both chose to kill rather than be killed." Eldyn was silent for a long moment. "We construct our lives moment by moment, and the circumstances I found myself in were of my own making, that I learned from my teacher," he said. "I also learned my real option was to construct a different life, inside; then the outside would reflect it. But until I reached that ability, I knew I would continue to find myself in situations I didn't like. In that case, I decided to do the best with what I had in front of me."

Heaviness lingered for some time, until Maria Lerna talked about Aramas. She pointed out he too had to deal with the same issue; he became a gladiator to reach Eldyn.

Then Mowan told them about Mirio, and how he taught him how to fight. His teacher knew what his future had in store, and made sure he was prepared.

The group compared the two teachers and found many similarities, even in their appearance. They told stories, things the teachers had said and done, and again the similarities were striking.

"I wish I could have met them, "Ambrosius said.

With those words Martin felt a sweet feeling that started as a wonderful aroma, something akin to flowers, but this smell was much more fragrant.

It seemed the others felt it as well, because no one spoke, instead they extended their beings all around, in loving welcome of whoever was trying to reach them.

The attention of them all, including Martin, was drawn to a place to the left of where he was standing, in front of the fire, and across from the group. It was then that slowly a blue shimmering light materialized, accompanied by a loving feeling. As they looked the feeling grew stronger, and then it seemed to concentrate and the light did as well, revealing two figures, both clad in white robes.

"Marius!...Aramas!" Maria Lerna shouted as she rushed toward the figures, who by now had taken solid form.

"Mirio!" exclaimed Mowan, staring at Aramas.

Maria Lerna embraced her brother and teacher at once, deep sobs alternating with wild, happy laughter. Then Eldyn stood up, and perhaps surprising even himself, went over and embraced the two figures as well. Shortly Nicolaus and Mowan, smiling broadly, did the same, and took Ambrosius with them.

Martin was awestruck by the sight. Marius appeared strong and able bodied. He looked a lot like Maria Lerna; he was tall and gave the appearance of a very strong man. Martin immediately thought of a Greek god, one of those perfect specimens of man. His eyes shone with love for his sister. He looked at her, and then at Eldyn, Nicolaus and Mowan. Then he rested his eyes on Martin and held him in his gaze. *He remembers when I carried him out of the prison.*

Aramas was a shining and loving figure with his white hair and short white beard framing his gentle face . . . gentleness that held immense strength and wisdom...and love, great love. He seemed strangely familiar to Martin, a face he almost knew.

The teachers, Maria Lerna, Ambrosius, all seemed to be lost in their own individual rapture, absorbing the presence of the two apparitions.

Aramas turned and looked at Martin. "Come, dear Ashar, come join us."

Martin was surprised by the name and by being addressed directly as though Aramas knew him. Then he figured he was confusing him for someone else, but decided to comply and join in the embrace, wondering what the teachers and Ambrosius thought now that they knew about him.

As he walked over, Aramas addressed them all. "It has been too long, dear ones, since we have been all together."

Martin willed his body to take form and joined them. To his left he felt Maria Lerna's shoulder, and on his right Aramas' arm. He looked at the teachers and the young prince, but they had their eyes closed.

They stood in a circle, their arms entwined around each other's shoulders. Martin felt the energy moving around and through him, and it was the energy of all of them, including his own, mixed in; and curiously he knew the energy, he knew them all…it was old, from long ago…an essence that was so familiar.

He felt confused, but decided to ignore the feeling and fully enjoy the experience.

Martin didn't know for how long they stood like that, communing silently with each other, but at some point he knew Marius and Aramas were gone, he felt their absence. He then opened his eyes.

The group remained silent, and after some time they each walked away.

The following day, Martin joined the group at their morning meal. He had decided to appear only if they asked him to. Obviously now they all knew he existed. As he approached he heard them talking about Aramas and Marius.

They realized Aramas and Mirio were the same person. But how had he managed to be both in Greece and Caledonia at the same time? Nicolaus and Mowan did some calculations and figured that in the space of seven years when they both knew the same man by different names, he was in two places at once.

That wasn't the only mystery. Nicolaus recalled that Aramas was an old man when he knew him, perhaps close to eighty, yet he became a strong and able gladiator some years later for Eldyn's sake.

Eldyn laughed, and it was the only time Martin ever heard him do so.

"Wouldn't be surprised if he shows up again, as a young man," Mowan said. "Odd how he included martial knowledge with my instruction but not with yours," he told Nicolaus.

"In Greece every disciple's instruction varied," Nicolaus said. "Aramas told us it had to do with the destiny he saw for each one of us."

"It was a rare gift to see them again," murmured Maria Lerna. She told them that for each of them the visit would mean something slightly different;

but overall, their common lesson was that they had learned how they were connected.

They agreed. It was obvious they had spent past lives together, and with Aramas and Marius as well. They all felt a close kinship with Maria Lerna's brother, and surmised that's why he had come with Aramas, not just for her sake.

But no one mentioned Martin...or Ashar.

During those care-free days, Martin was touched to see how the two monks and Ambrosius reacted to Maria Lerna. They acted visibly thrilled to see her in her body, eating, drinking, and walking just like them. Ambrosius particularly enjoyed hugging her, and grabbing hold of her hand when they walked alongside each other.

But it wasn't Maria Lerna's physical presence alone that made their stay special. The place had a certain appeal for all of them, and it was reflected in their comments.

One evening, coming from group meditation, Nicolaus told them this was the most comfortable he had been anywhere.

Eldyn, who had been walking a few feet ahead, turned his head. "Once you come to this place you never leave. Your body might, but your spirit will always remain."

"I wish I could live here, Eldyn"

"Your destiny lies elsewhere. You will live in a place much like this one, one you will create. On an island, with brother Mowan."

"Yes, Eldyn," Mowan said, "I see the same."

Ambrosius seemed concerned. "But you can't leave me behind. I will come with you."

Maria Lerna went over and took a hold of his hand. "Dear Ambrosius, we all must follow our destinies. You are needed in Isca and I will stay by your side always. But our beloved monks will be needed elsewhere."

"Yes, Marli, I think I know that. But I am sad at the thought of us not being together, having to part."

Nicolaus approached the prince and put an arm around his shoulders. "Look inside, Ambrosius, and you will see that in reality we will never part. Once you are united at the heart with someone, there is no separation."

"It is so with Marius," Maria Lerna said, " even though he has died, I feel his presence every time I think of him. The same with Aramas."

Days passed by without effort in the colony, and Martin realized how easy it would be for them all to just let days pile up one after the other and one day realize years had gone by. He approached Maria Lerna when she was alone and told her as much.

After looking inside for a moment, she decided Martin was right; they had to move on.

That evening after the evening meal, she broached the subject. "Dear ones, you have been with us for four months now. It is perhaps time to return to Isca."

They were all surprised four months had gone by. Yes, it was time to return.

Two days later, in the morning, Ambrosius and the two monks assisted by Eldyn were busy preparing their provisions for the long walk back to the farm where they had left the horses. They sat around the fire outside Eldyn's hut, each busy with a backpack of sorts, stuffing dry goods, water jugs and articles of clothing.

Achilles sat nearby, his body language speaking of anticipation for another trek; his ears twitched and he raised his head to smell the wind.

The morning was crisp and cool with fog still clinging to the trees. They alternated packing with eating what Martin thought might be a porridge of some sort, a concoction of grains and herbs.

They noticed Maria Lerna when she came out of her house, a disturbed air around her normally placid ways. She approached the group, slowly taking in the task at hand.

"Is there something wrong, my lady? asked Eldyn.

She paused for a minute, seeming to hesitate. "I just visited Dunum, and heard a disturbing tale about Julius. They are going to let his people try him. I am certain they are going to execute him, because of all the people who hate him."

They fell quiet, looking intently at Maria Lerna. This was after all the man who was responsible for so much of her grief. But Martin sensed they also understood she still saw Julius as a friend from childhood and as the man who stood by her brother's deathbed, changed and repentant.

"To execute him now would be simply to satisfy peoples' thirst for revenge, it would not be justice." Maria Lerna's voice was sad.

"I wish there was something we could do for Julius, but I think his fate has been sealed," Ambrosius said. "He will be punished according to the law, in all likelihood decapitated in the central square."

They explored having Maria Lerna free him just like she did her brother, but even as they spoke the words, they realized that it was not to be. Marius had wanted out and his righteousness had given power to his wish, which had made the entire thing possible. Julius felt himself guilty and in need of punishment.

Other options were as improbable, such as asking Joannes for clemency and having Julius sent somewhere far away. That was an alternative for lesser crimes. The law circumscribed Joannes' options.

"I will go see him and do what I can for him," Maria Lerna said.

They stood up to begin their journey and as they did so, she suggested they go back by way of the ancient temple. "It's a bit out of the way, but will lengthen our trip by no more than ten days. That will make the pilgrimage complete. The temple is a place of great energy, an ancient gathering place much like the cave is for us here."

No one knew what Maria Lerna was talking about, but they decided to follow her advice.

She went into her house to "lay down my body." Minutes later she came out in her light self.

Eldyn was saying goodbye to them all. When it came Ambrosius' turn, he stood in silence for a minute in front of the young man. "Whenever you need my skills you need only to think of me. My arms will become your arms."

Martin understood Eldyn was bestowing his essence on Ambrosius, his fighting essence.

"Thank you, Eldyn." Ambrosius apparently understood the significance of the words for he appeared deeply touched. "I hope I can also reflect your spiritual essence, holy man."

Martin observed the group walk on ahead of him, first Ambrosius and Nicolaus, the wolf, then Mowan. Maria Lerna was now right beside him and had taken his hand in hers.

Neither one was now visible so their words were not heard by anyone else. He wanted to talk about Aramas' and Marius' visit, but she had other pressing things on her mind.

"Dear one, I know you will need to leave us soon, and perhaps you already postponed your departure, but a little more time would be well spent," Maria Lerna said.

She then talked about Julius and her brother. She mourned her brother but didn't blame Julius or Cassius for his death; that was about three souls who had played their roles in life, it was over. "But Julius, is in pain and needs to see me. That's what I kept hearing. Would you come along with me, dear Martin?"

"Will they know their way to the ancient temple?"

"Yes, I am well connected with Ambrosius, and will be guiding his steps through his heart...besides, we won't be long."

She then pressed his hand, and he let her guide him.

They found themselves in Marius' old cell. Martin recognized it immediately; the feeling in the place still reverberated of Marius' essence, his physical suffering. Now the occupant was Julius, who sat on the cot, his legs propped up in front of him, his arms hanging limp by his sides. His face bore the signs of the conflict inside him.

Martin wondered if someone had decided on that particular cell as part of his punishment, or was it a coincidence? But there again, he knew there were no coincidences in life, not really.

Maria Lerna slowly materialized in front of Julius.

His reaction was one of utter stupefaction. He continued sitting, but now his mouth hung open, and his eyes reflected awe and shock.

"Who...who...are you?"

He had not yet recognized Maria Lerna.

She stood before him in silence, and it seemed he slowly realized who it was who stood before him.

"Is that you, Maria?" The voice was tentative, almost pleading for it to be her.

By contrast her voice was calm and soothing. "Yes, Julius, it's me."

"But...are you real?"

"Yes, I'm real."

To reassure him she went over and placed a hand on his shoulder. The touch, Martin knew, was gentle and loving, the energy healing.

Julius started to weep, slowly at first, but then with what became a big release of emotions. He cried for some time with her hand on his shoulder.

Martin felt sorry for him, for his suffering was intense.

"I prayed for you to come, to see you once more before I die, dear Maria."

"I know."

"You seem real, and maybe you are a ghost, but you are here. Can you please forgive me for all I did to you and your family? Your brother, dear wonderful and holy man—I killed him."

Julius then went on to tell her the story she already knew. About Cassius, how he had taken over his very soul, but it was his fault, he had let him do it. He went over it in great detail, and it seemed that with each word he was clearing his heart, giving it all to her.

He ended with Marius' death, and how he had gone to his house and asked for his forgiveness...and now he realized Marius had forgiven him.

"But there is more, so much more. Marius woke me up. In those last months of torture when Cassius insisted I come along, I saw Marius in sharp contrast to Cassius, and to myself...and that made me want to change, to change so I could become like Marius."

"The day Cassius killed himself, it was like the devil had left me, and I could see for the first time what all I had done. And I found myself a different person. But too late to change things, to undo all the torture, to undo all the robbing, the killing…too late."

"But not too late to grow and change, dear Julius," Maria Lerna told him, "and that's what counts, and that is why my brother died…for your sake as well as Cassius'."

There was silence in the cell. Julius kept looking absently into Maria Lerna's eyes, tears rolling down his cheeks.

"When they execute me…I will think of your brother…I want to die thinking of him."

"You will do him honor, if instead, you spend the last days going inside your spirit, and when you die, think of God."

Julius turned his gaze down at the floor. "I seem to have spent my life without God in it, dear Maria. When I look inside me I see ugliness. I'm so ashamed of the life I spent. I don't know God, and I don't know how to think of him like you do."

"Then dear friend, by all means think of my brother. Bring him into your life and ask him to help you. He will serve you well; he will help you reach God."

Julius' stare returned to Maria Lerna's eyes. It was as though in there his spirit was gaining strength, and as he kept looking a new light came into his teary eyes. Martin thought it was hope.

"I will, Maria, I will do as you say."

Maria Lerna sat next to Julius and closed her eyes. She took hold of his hand. Martin felt her becoming one with Spirit, so he too sat next to her and meditated. It was hard at first, there was that hard and sullen energy from Julius, but then he felt another presence in the cell, and Martin could tell Marius was now with them.

Maria Lerna stood up and faced Julius. "I am leaving now, Julius. God be with you."

"Thank you dear Maria, thank you." The words were now much calmer.

She vanished from his sight, took hold of Martin's hand and they left.

They rejoined the small party silently making their way through the forest. Maria Lerna was now visible to them and walked near Nicolaus. She bent down to stroke Achilles, who in response raised his head in her direction and met her gaze.

"How did you find Julius?" asked Nicolaus.

"He is a sorry man, but is making his peace and will die well."

Summer was almost over, but the days were still long and warm, which made traversing the forest this time harder than on their way in, but fortunately water was plentiful; streams and springs were everywhere they went.

That evening they approached a bubbly spring as a pair of wolves heard them coming and made a dash for the safety of the trees. The group watched Achilles as he looked at the spot where the wolves had hidden. All through their walk Martin had marveled at the extent of wild life; it seemed they were running across animals which had never seen the likes of humans. Some would run at their approach, like the wolves, but others, especially bears, would curiously peek from in-between trees.

Maria Lerna told them the problem the colony had had with bears eating all of their apples when the trees fruited, and some times even the entire tree would disappear. They had decided to communicate with the animals and ask them to eat some of the apples, but to leave enough for the colony and not to destroy the trees. The strategy had proved successful.

"From time to time they need reminding, though," she said.

They made camp next to the spring, and as they built a fire, Nicolaus asked Maria Lerna about the temple they were going to visit.

"It's from ancient times," she said. "The present temple is some four thousand years old—that is, what remains of it, but there had been a temple on that site many, many thousands of years before, when an extremely advanced civilization lived on this land. Those people knew complete peace and harmony and it was a time of great purity. The world has been in a steady decline since then."

"What happened to them?" asked Ambrosius.

"It is what happens every time. There are cycles to creation and when the majority of people on earth have reached liberation, then it is time to start anew. They disappear and a new cycle starts with barbarians taking over."

Nicolaus and Mowan said Aramas-Mirio had talked about the cycles of creation and the high civilizations that came before, but they didn't know the particulars of the actual people who had lived in these parts so long ago.

"When a people evolve to that point," Maria Lerna said, "the world around them reflects their spiritual attainment. The ancients who built the original temple were such people. The feeling of the world at large was much like at the Seeker Colony except even more evolved... wellness and wholeness were the norm."

"So this temple was built by these very evolved people?" asked Ambrosius.

"That is not so. The temple we are going to see was built on the same site as the temple built by the ancients. This one took its place and it became a place for worshiping nature by primitive people; they built with large stones in alignment with the stars they worshipped. They felt the sacredness of the site and decided to build a holy place as well."

"Over the years the temple has been used by many different people, some for sacrifices, some for prayer. You can tell by feeling the different energies that remain," she said.

Ambrosius seemed interested. "And why are we going to this temple?"

"So you can feel the ancients and know what's possible."

Four days later they arrived at the site.

They walked around the big circular structure, inspecting the huge stones, the big arches. Then they walked inside, led by Maria Lerna, to the middle of the place. They sat forming a circle themselves, and meditated.

Martin joined them, next to Maria Lerna. He noticed Mowan had moved to one side at the last minute, to leave enough room for him to sit next to her.

The group meditated for some time, and then stood with hearts open.

Martin felt the layers from many peoples and many years. Recent ones were crass and wild, speaking of fear and superstition...even some human sacrifices...then there was the feeling of prayer...and underneath it all, a great peace and joy, the unmistakable presence of Spirit. Figures and faces came before his eyes. They were tall, lean figures that glided by with sunny features. They communicated a quiet, harmonious state of being, reaching out from across millennia.

At that moment Martin knew peace was possible in creation, he could feel it, taste it, know it. He looked around the group and knew they were experiencing the same. He concentrated on Ambrosius, and felt him absorbing the energy left by the ancients—a magic seed that would germinate when it reached the right heart.

The group stood in reverent silence.

Ambrosius looked at the rough giant stones that had obviously required great effort to bring from somewhere, and then to place.

"This took so much work . . . and you say, Marli, this place as we see it now was built by primitive people, barbarians?"

"Yes. They brought stones and propped them up..."

"They felt the sacredness of the place, at least their priests did," Nicolaus continued, as though he too was watching the same scenes played out before his eyes, "and they felt the urge to preserve it, so they built something solid they thought would last a long time. Later civilizations did not understand what had been built or why, but they saw the place as grand and used it as such."

"But what was the original place like? The one the ancients built," asked Ambrosius.

"It was a big building with a dome," Maria Lerna said, "made with beautifully polished stones...."

"And it glistened in the sunlight," this time it was Mowan who spoke, "with openings to all sides. Inside, the floor was very smooth and shiny. And people sat cross-legged in concentric circles in deep communion, sending their holy energy throughout the world, in circles."

"The first went around this temple," Nicolaus said, "but these were ever-expanding circles, like ripples on still water...that spread throughout the entire earth...and are still here."

Martin could see it all as well. People so concerned about the impending misery of the world they decided to help the only way they knew would be of any consequence; leaving an energy behind to help rekindle light and the memory of what is possible on this earth...in this life.

The group slowly left the place and looked all around, trying to see other signs left over by the ancients, but there was nothing else.

The rough rocks now stood like ghosts of a greatness gone by. As they walked, they came on a puddle. It was a beautiful sight, an oval-shaped small pond with a green leaf, perhaps blown off some tree by the wind, now placidly floating almost right in the middle.

Ambrosius threw a pebble at one end of the water, and they all watched as the ripples spread, rocking the leaf, and propelling it forward.

"Look Marli," Ambrosius said, "we are like the leaf on still water..."

"Being propelled by the ripples from the ancients," concluded Maria Lerna. "And very appropriately, Ambrosius, the ripples can only be seen if the water is still."

She then looked at Martin, straight into his eyes, a look he knew he would never forget. It was a powerful stare connoting a deep sense of urgency.

"Will you help me?"

He didn't know what she was asking of him, but he knew he would do anything for her and he responded, "I will do anything . . .dear Marli." So saying, he had a profound sense of deja vu, as though he had said it before to her. He also felt a great sense of doom, as though she were in great danger. Shaken, he stood for some time looking at her, but then the feeling abated and all was fine, he could again feel the wonder of the place.

They stayed around the site for another day meditating and taking slow, long walks, absorbing the energies, the vestiges from long ago.

As they picked up to leave Mowan looked around. "Marli, was the Seeker Colony located where it is so it could be near this temple?"

"I think so, brother. The colony was started many years ago, and people have always made pilgrimages to this site. Without doubt the light from this place helped create the colony; so one way or another, yes."

CHAPTER SEVENTEEN

They started on their way back to Isca, with Ambrosius leading as usual, this time walking beside Maria Lerna, then Mowan, Nicolaus and Achilles, and Martin behind.

Martin had to know what Marli needed from him, and he knew he would have to wait to ask her. What could possibly threaten her? And what could he do that she couldn't?

For the moment he pushed all thoughts aside and decided that for now walking felt fine, and it was very pleasing to his spirit, an effortless motion. And the dear souls he was walking with…he felt their essence and tried to imprint it in his heart so he would never forget the moment, the experience they all shared, the joy that seemed to float in the very air. Achilles' tail slowly wagged as he walked, his lean body slightly swaying from side to side. Nicolaus appeared fully conscious of his surroundings, seeing Spirit in everything; and like the wolf, at ease, taking in the sights of the forest, smiling whenever he saw an animal, and extending his spirit all around him. Mowan marked his steps with a staff, and he seemed withdrawn. His was a constant communion with Spirit and he gave the impression of someone living out of this world in a realm far away. He was always surprised when someone addressed him, as though he had to be reminded that he indeed was still in the flesh, still of this world. Ambrosius walked with sureness of gait, one who knows where he is going and perhaps already fully aware of his destiny.

That night when they slept Martin approached Maria Lerna.

"Marli, back at the temple…you asked for my help. What can I do?"

She hesitated before speaking. "Martin, my dear friend, beloved soul. You are about to find out much more about yourself; but I am not the one to tell you. That will come soon enough."

Martin closed his eyes and took her hand. He then embraced her with his essence, and felt hers.

"I will…do anything for you."

He knew she could feel the full force of his words, and that he meant it. He would do anything for her, no matter what.

She looked at him with great tenderness.

They caught sight of Isca late morning on a crisp, bright day that already felt like fall. As they approached they saw a chariot coming their way with two figures riding, and an escort of soldiers behind. Scouts from Isca had spotted them the day before, so they assumed news of their arrival had reached the city the previous evening. They dismounted to wait for the riders.

As the chariot drew near they recognized Martigena and Philippus, the horses at a trot, coming their way.

Martigena got off and rushed to embrace her Ambrosius.

After a joyful dance where the young man was literally swept off his feet, Martigena wanted to hear all about their journey.

Maria Lerna embraced her lovingly, and as they all talked in turns, the two women walked, holding hands. Philippus also dismounted and walked beside them, listening intently.

Ambrosius told his mother about the temple, and the ancients, and how he knew they were still imparting their blessings, helping them. He then talked about the colony and Eldyn, Aramas, Mirio and Marius.

And so it was the tale was told backwards, with interjections by the monks. Interestingly enough, when they came to the beginning of their tale, it was Martigena who interrupted them.

"And you went and took care of the Caledonian hunters who were sent to kill your father and brother."

Ambrosius froze in place. Then he looked around to see which one in his group had told his parents, but they all appeared just as surprised as he was, including Maria Lerna.

"You knew all along?" asked Maria Lerna looking into her eyes.

"Yes. Joannes has scouts very adept at spotting outsiders. The moment the Caledonian messenger entered the kingdom in search of Mowan, we knew about him. After he delivered his message, Joannes had him brought before him, and he told us everything." She turned towards Mowan and added, "and he was let go unharmed."

"We had talked to the messenger the night before you came to ask permission to go on your journey. Joannes thought of going after the hunters, but we both had a strong feeling this task belonged to all of you. We imagined Mowan would take the lead, and that perhaps he would ask Arcadius for some soldiers to come along. We were confident no ill could come to you because of Marli. I don't know exactly how you dealt with the hunters, but I know you did somehow, for the scouts did not spot them crossing the mountains, and when they investigated, caught up with the sorry lot on their way back; one-handed, terrified and in great pain."

Nicolaus told her the entire story, and how it was Ambrosius who had devised the plan and carried it out with their assistance.

Martigena seemed pleased with what she heard. She turned and looked at

Ambrosius, and there was pride in her eyes, but also it appeared she was trying to take his measure, seeing him in a new light.

Philippus in turn kept shaking his head in disbelief. "That's ridiculous, all that trouble. I would have met them face to face with three of my best archers; let the arrows fly and see who's best." Martin was surprised by the uncharacteristic response. He expected better from Philippus.

Two days later there was a dinner celebration at the Citadel. Ambrosius sat in the place of honor, the one reserved for important guests, at the center of the large table. The monks were at either side of him. The entire membership of the Circle Council was present, and they sat across from Ambrosius, flanking the royal couple, Arcadius occupying a prominent seat in their midst. Important nobles lined the rest of the table along with three neighboring kings, including Mateus.

The jealousy coming from Philippus was tangible. He morosely looked down at his plate and answered in monosyllables. Ambrosius seemed well aware of the situation, and he cast sideways glances at Philippus, apparently concerned with what was happening to his brother.

Martin observed how both Ambrosius and Nicolaus diverted the conversation at their end of the table toward archery and horsemanship, and eventually managed to engage Philippus, who spoke up to clarify various technical details.

"My brother is the best archer in the kingdom," Ambrosius said aloud, "and I will be honored to serve under him when he becomes King."

Philippus appeared relieved of his mood and began talking, joking, and at one point playfully threw a bread ball at his brother.

That episode was, in Martin's mind, more significant than the recent test with the hunters. The young prince was a man, and a wise man at that.

Throughout the evening Martin heard the news of the land...how the cavalry units were now in place all over the kingdom, and how the scouts were successful in intercepting outsiders, or following them silently when required. Arcadius detailed the number of interceptions, whom they had tracked and how. The scouts heard all kinds of tales and reported back to Isca. This way word had come of further Caledonian incursions across the wall, but these were now limited to the northern territories.

Word had now spread about Isca and the powerful magician who protected it. They hoped this fable would also work on the Angles, the Saxons and the Scots.

Some of the changes brought about by the Circle Council had been hard to implement, and sometimes had required a cavalry unit to enforce. The hardest one had been the abolition of slavery. This had caused riots in some localities, including the market place in Isca.

A number of noblemen had left, some for Byzantium, some to Iberia, but that had been only a handful. The general consensus was that the changes brought about were good, the people felt well protected, and if they had to give up their slaves in return, it was worth it.

Most of the slaves had stayed put, some biding their time, some having worked out new arrangements with their former owners.

The cavalry units had already faced numerous tests, rounding up the bandit groups at nearby Dunum and fighting off three more Saxon raids. King Mateus had also requested assistance with some roving bands. Now he was interested in forming a permanent arrangement with Isca for mutual defense, as were the other two kings who sat next to him.

Joannes formally thanked Nicolaus for all his help, the knowledge which he had so readily made available to Isca. He said he had seldom been so happy to rescue anyone, and he had to thank the Picts for indirectly leading Nicolaus to his kingdom. Then he acknowledged Mowan as well, describing him as "my Caledonian brother."

Martin looked around the table at the happy faces. They were weathering monumental changes in their lives, and they seemed to be doing it well. Overall, they felt their kingdom was now invincible, and the mood around the table was one of cheerful optimism, perhaps even boastful, he thought.

He looked at Maria Lerna, who stood beside him, invisible to all eyes except his.

"This is perhaps the only place in all Britannia that feels safe," he told her.

"Yes, Martin. This will be a safe haven for years to come…they will have to fight for it, but they will be safe."

During the next few days he found himself saying goodbye.

Martin watched some of the cavalry units patrolling a quiet countryside, and a Circle Council member officiating a meeting of village elders, listening to their concerns.

He observed Joannes and Martigena walk hand in hand in the courtyard, talking. They discussed how best to expand the Circle Council to encompass neighboring kingdoms. She told him of her reservations regarding one of the kings.

Martin visited all of the familiar sites: the mountain pass where the battle had taken place, the spot where he had built the lean- to for the Caledonian mother and child, the ancient temple and the Seeker Colony with its cave. He relived the experiences in each location, and remembered the person he used to be.

One afternoon he found Maria Lerna and Ambrosius by themselves in the courtyard of the teachers' house. They were practicing how to move the energies inside the body, and the force Martin thought of as chi.

They had been sparring with staffs, and now the young man was sitting on a bench next to Maria Lerna. He turned around to face her. "Marli, how will I know when I am ready to fulfill my destiny?"

Maria Lerna walked over a few paces and took a sword from a nearby scabbard. She stood looking at a stone that was part of a low wall around the courtyard. She raised the sword with both hands and held it very still with the point aimed at the stone, then with a fluid motion she brought it down. The sword sunk into the rock all the way to the hilt, with a swishing sound, and a ringing of metal.

She smiled at him. "Dear child, the day you pull that sword out of the rock, then you will be ready."

Ambrosius sat transfixed looking at the hilt protruding from the rock. "That was truly amazing, Marli." He then went and ran his fingers over the rock, and grabbing hold of the sword, tested it. "This is very solid. I don't think a team of horses could pull it out."

"But you will, dear one. You will know when you are ready, you will feel the force within you and your heart will let you know it is time."

She turned to look at Martin with a sad look. "My sweet child. He doesn't know the day his father and brother die he will be asked to become king, and that's the day he will pull the sword out. Joannes and Philippus will defeat a Saxon army, and pay with their lives. A seventeen- year- old Ambrosius will take over."

"The sword in the stone will become a legend," Martin said, "of a King…"

"Ah, Martin, I'm aware how people change things around;" she said, "made-up stories are not important."

Martin understood what she meant, legends take a life of their own. But still he realized that he had witnessed a monumental event, something that obviously awed and inspired people. He himself felt awed. "Little is known of the actual events," said Martin.

"I sank the sword in the stone to let Ambrosius know how the energies are when they feel right…physical prowess is very much secondary."

Maria Lerna then seemed to go into a trance. "The day before he pulls the sword out, he asks to join his father and brother heading out to battle. They are leading a large army from four kingdoms, to confront a number of Saxon chiefs who had joined forces to invade Dunum, Lindinus, Velium and Isca, seeing the four places as key to their conquest of this part of Britannia." Her voice had gotten very soft, and she spoke slowly; Martin guessed the scenes were evolving before her eyes, and that she was mesmerized by them.

"Joannes, perhaps knowing what is about to happen, orders his youngest son to stay behind. The King tells him that should anything happen to him and Philippus, 'then it would be a good time to pull that sword out of the rock.' That following day, a scout comes into the city with the news: the enemy has been defeated, but both King and Prince are dead. The Saxons are gathering again, and the British armies are in disarray with no strong leader to command them. Arcadius has summoned Ambrosius in the hope he can bring the armies back together. At the news, Ambrosius rushes out of his classroom with tears running down his face. He goes to the stone, and in front of his mother, the monks and the scout, pulls the sword out. He then rides out to the battlefield and takes command of the troops who welcome him with wild cheers. In two days he defeats and captures the remaining Saxons."

Maria Lerna sighed and shook her head, as if waking up from a dream.

That was going to happen in a short time. Martin stood looking at Ambrosius and could see him doing those things, could see him becoming a king while still mourning his father and brother.

"What about the two monks, what will happen to them?"

"They will both leave shortly after Ambrosius becomes King, both understanding their role in his life has ended. Ambrosius will release Mowan from his vow to stay as a safeguard against his people attacking again, seeing that threat completely vanished. One day will find both monks going up the road, both visibly sad, but understanding that their destinies lie elsewhere. Ambrosius and Martigena will stand watching them walk up the road with Achilles, on their way to the land they both saw in a dream."

"Together they will start a monastery on one of the islands in between Hibernia and Caledonia; it will become a well-known place for learning, and a refuge for many who want a life immersed in Spirit."

Martin then recalled the time when Aramas and Marius appeared.

"Ah, yes, what a blessing that was!" she said.

"I noticed Aramas called me 'Ashar.' Who was he?"

Maria Lerna smiled. "You will soon find out everything you want to know. But not from me."

Martin looked at her. *Another mystery.* Then he felt the Kahuna's presence, and he understood. *For some reason he's the one who will tell me.*

He mentioned how the monks and Ambrosius had heard Aramas address him as Ashar, and had seemed to know about him, but never acknowledged him.

"So, why didn't they…say something?"

"Out of respect for you. They felt you wanted it that way."

"Did they ever speak about me?"

"Yes they did. About a year ago, Ambrosius came to me and asked who my friend was. Nicolaus then interceded and told him it was not polite to inquire about 'Marli's friend.' It seems they already had talked about you, dear Martin. They had decided there was a reason why you chose not to show yourself."

"At what point did Nicolaus know about me?"

"He told me from the very beginning. The day he and the women were attacked and Joannes and Philippus saved them. At first he thought you were a lost soul, one who doesn't know he is dead."

"You mean a ghost?"

"Yes, dear. That's what I thought about you as well the first time I saw you in the cave. Then he realized you were with me, so he and Mowan assumed you were an advanced soul sent to help me."

"What did you tell them?"

"I told them they were correct."

Martin smiled. "Does anyone else know of my existence'?

"No, no one else."

"What about Martigena, what will become of her?" asked Martin. *Poor woman, she will lose her husband and eldest son at the same time.*

"Martigena will receive the news of her husband and son's death with her heart already full of the knowledge, and resigned that this is the way Spirit has arranged their destinies. A week after Ambrosius' coronation, she will bid her son goodbye and start her own pilgrimage to the Seeker Colony, saying goodbye to the world as well, ready for a life dedicated to her soul. I will keep her company on the way and welcome her along with Eldyn and the other residents. She will live in the Colony until her death, at age eighty, a saintly woman."

"Ambrosius will learn how to visit in due time, and the place will become his refuge, where he will replenish himself. He will always refer to the colony as 'my home,' a code word few around him will understand."

That evening Martin decided to say goodbye. He met Maria Lerna and Eldyn inside her house.

Martin joined them for a few hours of deep communion.

"I am saying goodbye to you, dear friends. It's time for me to go back."

For sometime they remained silent, Eldyn's gaze meeting his. He saw Maria Lerna's eyes grow moist.

"Goodbye, dear Martin." She was staring at him with sadness in her eyes. Martin thought she looked the same as the day he met her, but also, so different; she had changed in his eyes and in his heart.

He knew in some way or another she would always remain with him.

"You will be with me always, sweet Martin," she said.

He went over to Eldyn and embraced him, and felt the big man embrace him back. Then Maria Lerna joined in.

He left her house and made it over to the glen. He found the spot were he had first materialized. He visualized the Kahuna and the rock.... and he felt the Kahuna touch his hand.

CHAPTER EIGHTEEN

Martin opened his eyes and saw the Kahuna's gentle face.

He drew in a breath, and felt the air course through his lungs. He had braced himself for getting back into his physical body, and it was a shock, but not as terrible as he thought. Mainly, he felt terribly heavy, as though he were made of lead.

He needed to lie down, and the Kahuna helped him get up and move over to the sand, where he lay face up, then the Kahuna sat beside him gently stroking his arm.

No wonder babies cry when they are born.

"That was quite a journey, Martin. This time you were gone for well over a year."

Yes, actually a year and a half. It seemed longer, and so much had happened.

Martin sensed the energy of who he had been back then, his essence when he left. He felt it in his heart and in his mind, it was all about missing without knowing, a life full of fear and anger. Now he was whole, at peace, and the absence of fear and pain was tangible. The negative sensations left a void—an emptiness he was glad to feel.

The sky above him was blue, and the air felt warm. The sand felt moist under him. That felt fine; everything was fine now. He tried to sit up and managed to do it. He looked at the Kahuna.

"It was time to come back; it felt right. I think I learned what I had to learn." He looked at the Kahuna for confirmation.

"Yes, my friend. You've changed. I'm very happy for you."

Martin smiled. "Does that mean my life is over? Am I done?"

The Kahuna laughed. "Don't you like it here? I was going to suggest a few more lives." Then on a serious note: "Look at the realization of the self as a process. You know who you are. Now the real work begins."

"Yes, I think I know that, inside. It's time for me to go back and fix my life. I'll be going back home as soon as possible."

The Kahuna gave him a long, meaningful look. "You are home, Martin. At this moment you are home asleep in your bed. You never left."

It took some time for the information to sink in. Then Martin realized what the Kahuna had said. "Everything...all of this is a dream? Nothing ...nothing really ever happened? That's impossible...no Maria Lerna...and then…I'm still my old self? What about Mojo? Was he part of the dream as well?"

The Kahuna gently interrupted him. "Look at what I have told you with your spirit, not your human mind, Martin. You might as well start that practice now. You entered another dimension, except that within the framework of your reality you call it a dream. Your life in Britain was perhaps more real than anything else in your so-called 'real life.' Measure reality by the effect experiences have on you."

Yes, of course…what is real and what isn't…everything is relative…of all people, I should know that. "Yes, I agree, everything was very real…I learned…and I loved. So, what happened…how did it happen?" Martin asked.

"What you went through happens to everyone at some point. We come in, one of us, a teacher, and we take you away during sleep, which is a state of suspended reality, a state where your mind can accept anything. This is the only time when we can put people's lives on hold and provide them with a radical intervention to awaken their spirit."

"We do it during a crisis, when they have reached a climax and can't take it anymore; that's when their psyche is ready and eagerly accepts our intervention. They also have to be willing to change…"

"Willing to change—who wouldn't be willing to change?"

"Sadly, some are attached to their suffering…and they want more of it. Some others are attached to their lives, what they see as real and meaningful, and are afraid to let go."

"So how do you know they are willing to change?"

"We leave it up to them. There is a step they must take, a catalyst for change. In your case you had to actually go to Hawaii…"

"I see; so in this other dimension, this dream state, I actually traveled to Hawaii."

The Kahuna nodded. "You came to Hawaii, knowing it would change your life. That previous night you went to bed telling yourself you couldn't take it anymore, that something had to give, or else."

Martin remembered going to bed that night in the darkest despair he could remember, tired of everything; to the point he had stopped caring. He had wished for his life to end…he remembered that.

"Yes," Martin said, "I remember my despair that previous evening. I wanted out of my life."

"And I took you out of your life, my friend. Tell me, as the person you have become, do you think you could go back to your life and deal effectively with the challenges?"

Martin placed himself, the new self, in his old shoes, and he relived all the misery. The scenes came back with vivid weight. The loss of the contract, of the cat. Martin saw his wife's face and could feel her anger and what had been his emotions at the time. It was almost laughable…if it wasn't so sad. He watched himself as an adult would watch the silly antics of a child, and he felt compassion for himself, and for Jenny…and it was funny how serious everything seemed at the time, when now he could see through the self-created imagery…a game.

"Yes, of course. Now all of those things that bothered me are like child's play. Nothing really matters, except my interior life."

"And your depression?"

Martin remembered the old emptiness, the gray. Like a long forgotten nightmare, the feeling was gone. He felt the peace inside and knew it was there to stay.

"No more," he said with a broad smile.

The Kahuna looked at him and returned his smile. "Yes. You are ready to re-enter your life."

Is that it? Is this the goodbye? "Will I see you again?"

"Yes, Martin…we are not done, you and I."

"What about everything that happened…will I remember?"

"No, at least not right away. You will wake up as the new you. It will appear to be a magical moment of enlightenment. You will feel the urge to meditate, and you will be endowed with the intuitive abilities you learned and the wisdom you acquired. You will feel and act very differently, and people around you will be amazed. But your human memory will not remember."

Martin smiled. That was a wonderful thought. His old self gone, a new calm and serene Martin in his place, dealing effectively with life.

The images from his marriage came back to him. He still loved Jenny; he knew that now. But he also knew how sick it all was, dysfunctional…beyond repair. *Oh well. She could marry whoever she was having an affair with….*He would have to love her from a distance. The important thing was that everything he did from then on would be done well.

He was sad, however, that he would not remember Maria Lerna. Her image would have been a wonderful balm for the rest of his life.

"Don't worry, eventually you will remember," the Kahuna said, still smiling.

"When and how?"

"You will start taking control of your self, your life. And as you go along getting closer to your goal, memories will start surfacing, until one day you will come to this place."

"This very beach?"

"Yes dear friend," the Kahuna laughed. "You will be drawn to this beach when you are ready, and you will love it, and start coming time and gain, and the place will start triggering a remembrance."

It was gratifying to know that at some point he would remember what happened and have once again the memory of all those dear people.

Martin looked around. It was truly a wonderful place.

"Tell me one thing: why Hawaii, why this particular beach? You could have constructed any reality, so why this place?"

"Martin, it wasn't me who constructed your dream. You are the dream maker. I just helped you. But the reason for Hawaii is that this island is one of those places on earth that can be called an energetic vortex, a place where what you experienced is more likely to happen. And that part of Britain where you landed is also one of those places."

"What's an energetic vortex?"

"Let's say it's a place where the laws of physics can be circumvented."

"What makes a vortex?"

"The energies left by people who lived there. Both here and in that part of Britain, ancient people who became highly evolved left their imprint."

"Yes, I remember the feeling at the ancient temple. That was amazing."

"Both places are amazing, and they served you well. And they will continue to serve many people. That was the intention of those beings of so long ago."

In his chest Martin felt gratitude, and he felt the presence of the ancients, as though they were gathered around him and the Kahuna, their smiling faces beaming at them.

Images of his journey came rushing into Martin's mind. He saw Joannes and Martigena, Eldyn and Maria Lerna, the monks…and Ambrosius.

"And Britain at that particular time…why?"

"In part, because your past was calling you."

"So now we can talk about it…my past life."

"Yes, that was a previous life of yours. But I didn't want your focus to be on that. If you knew who you were from the beginning, you would have lost your perspective. It was hard enough for you to remain detached."

He remembered how much he wanted to be Joannes. *Yes, I wasn't ready then.*

"But now that it's over, would you tell me who I was?"

The Kahuna smiled at him, a broad smile. Then Martin saw his face change and it kept on changing until he saw the face he had seen that one time at the Seeker Colony and had found somewhat familiar: Aramas.

Martin stared at the face of the teacher. A quiet smile lay on his lips, and the eyes spoke of wisdom and love. It was someone he definitely recognized, with his heart.

"You are Aramas!" he called out to both the Kahuna and to the form in front of him.

"Yes, dear Martin...or may I call you Ashar?"

At the mention of the name Martin was transformed. He remembered, or rather he became once again a consciousness steeped in Spirit, and the memory of a life spent in deep peace came back to him.

"You may call me by that name, beloved Master." He felt a pang of love for the teacher he had not seen for so long. To his mind came the images of his fellow disciples. He recognized Maria Lerna who was then Jamani...and Nandaji who had become Eldyn...and Mowan, and Nicolaus, then Ambrosius. How funny, he had been an old man, or at least had been much older than the rest of them. And he saw Julius...he had been a quiet monk named Matuk.

His heart reviewed them all...and he saw them change through incarnations, as his heart beheld them in different lives. He saw Mojo...who then changed into his old self Julius...Julius became Mojo! And he recognized Percy as Maria Lerna's mother. He felt his heart sing with joy as he took them all in, and rejoiced again at the knowledge that he never lost them, but recognized them again and again.

"So now, Ashar, you realize who we were is not that important, is it? It's who we are at the moment, that counts."

"Yes. But what was the trajectory that made me Martin? A person depressed, fearful, anxious, at rope's end. So different from Ashar." Martin realized that the deep peace, the joy had been buried under all the depression, but was ready to come out, to awaken. He looked at his beloved teacher's face.

"Ashar, remember when I gathered all of you and then we bid each other farewell?"

Martin remembered. The Kahuna, that is Aramas, was then a Yogi master named Najdal. He was then short and bald, with a white moustache and crinkly eyes.

However the essence was the same.

It had been a beautiful day and they all sat by the entrance to the main cave. Najdal had asked them to gather, and by now they were all near the end of that incarnation. Some were old, some still young, but the time was drawing near. In their hearts they understood that in the next year they would all pass on, and the first to go would be their teacher, that same night.

Ashar remembered how Najdal had told them they were now ready for the lives ahead; their training was now complete, and they would embark on different voyages, but always together, playing different roles for the sake of their souls.

At times one would become an evildoer, steeped in delusion, and it was fine, for that was necessary, and the others would then help reawaken the sleeping soul.

They would change gender, nationalities, and looks, but underneath it all they would remain the same...the same essence, the same beloved souls.

They had embraced, all together, in a circle. They were all absorbing their combined essences, vowing never to forget each other.

Then they were gone, and new images came to Martin's mind. He saw himself now as a husband and father. Maria Lerna was now his wife and her name was Ura, and Nicolaus was a neighbor, a rich and powerful lord.

He remembered how he and Ura loved their daughter, a precious, beautiful little girl with golden curls and a laughter that could fill a house. But one day their daughter died of a fever, and they were both heartbroken, especially Ura, who would not stop crying. Nicolaus started coming to console her, then his visits became more frequent, and he had some magic touch that made Ura's pain go away. Martin let them be, for he loved her. Nicolaus was a friend; Martin trusted them both.

And one day he came home after a journey and his wife, his beloved wife was gone. Then came the search, and the realization she had run away with his neighbor. In fury and agony he went after both of them. The shame, the dishonor! The betrayal! There was no more life, nothing to live for anymore, only anger. He killed them both...then the remorse, the grief, and the hatred. Hatred so intense...he hated everything and everyone, but especially God who had made a life so perverse.

He remembered killing himself, and it had been an attempt to obliterate an ugly world, and to reach God, so he could obliterate him as well.

Then he saw his next life. Anger was the predominant feeling—anger, desperation and a deep sense of betrayal. He remembered the rigorous discipline that made life orderly, that was the highlight of his life...order. But corrupt idiots were in charge, and they, not he, got richer, and they, not he, accumulated power.

The farm, owned by that low-life, slow-witted man who thought he could be his friend. Got him drunk, and got him to gamble. First for money, then for his favorite slave, then for his farm, all won; but he reneged on the bet.

He would teach him a lesson. The dog.

Sneaking inside in the night. *Will take his wife's jewels, the coins, the rings* he owns....*Scum...idiot scum...if he comes out I'll just kill him...snap his neck. They'll never find me. Stupid bastards, I'm smarter than them. The slave...she saw me...I'll just kill her...damn her! She ran away and is hiding...maybe sounding the alarm. Have to get away.*

Images of his tent being searched. *The idiot centurion...twenty lashes for stealing...they'll never hear me scream...I know he has it in for me, always has...he's afraid of me, jealous. I am the better soldier...I am better...ten more lashes to go...idiot...you owe me. Ah, killing him...the satisfaction...the fire in my gut...kill him...kill...him...strangle him with my bare hands. I want to see the life snuffed out of him...his eyes looking at me as I kill him...I will kill him, I will...I must.*

Martin stopped the images; the anger was so ugly, the memories terrifyingly vivid. And he knew in his heart who he was; he could feel it in every cell of his body: Cassius.

His body trembling, he looked at the Kahuna.

The face in front of him was of the old Greek man, Aramas...Aramas! It was so confusing...he remembered him now.

Cassius could see a weak old man, a despicable weakling he had to crush, but he wouldn't crush. The stubborn old man was still alive. *Kill him...crush him...wait! There is another memory...something older...anger and love mixed in...what is it? Kill the old bastard...he's laughing at me!* Memories of the old man dying, but he could see it in his eyes, and could sense there was something in him that was untouchable. *He's laughing at me...wait...I remember now...I remember him, something in his eyes.*

Something in his eyes had awakened a memory, and for a moment, as the old man lay dying, he felt a twinge, an ancient memory. The father he never had, the mother who never loved him. And he had just killed him. *No...no...that's just trickery...the old man is a magician and doing his trickery.*

His guts burning with anger, he kicked the prostrate form, and kicked him and stomped him until there was nothing but a bloody heap.

For days afterwards, the image of the old man haunted him, and the face changed from the old Greek man to someone else, and there were scenes, very different scenes, of a time long before. Happiness, then great sadness. *So glad the old man died...I won't have to deal with that trickery any more.*

The images stopped and a shaken Martin looked at his teacher. Cassius' anger was still inside him, eating his insides. He focused all of his effort on his spiritual eye and sent the energy soaring through his spine, upward and then downward, cleansing, cleansing, up and down until he felt relief, clean and whole, but the impression was still there, like an imprint in his heart. He never knew that much anger was even possible, so dark and evil. And dear lord, that had been him!

The Kahuna, or rather, Aramas was looking at him, his eyes fixed on his, and there was nothing but love staring right at him.

"I am so terribly sorry for what I did to you, dear Master. Please, please, forgive me!" he told his beloved teacher, Najdal. He felt a part of him devastated with shame, regret and sorrow, while another part of him remained detached, the recounter of the memories, the witness.

Aramas spoke calmly and lovingly.

"Don't fret over those old memories, dear one, for we all did what we were supposed to do; we fulfilled our destinies, and we learned, and we changed."

Martin remembered Marius. *Oh, Marius.* He saw the battered form, unbending. *He thinks he is better than me...that he is holy.* And then the face changed, and he saw his friend, dear friend, he hadn't seen for so long. *Trickery, damn trickery again.* Then they told him Marius had escaped. *All of them, traitors...they love him and they are willing to die for him. Why? What does he have? Find out, must find out... Why?* Then the face came back again, the friend from long ago, and he loved him too...but he had tortured him. And he was glad he escaped.

Martin inhaled deeply and exhaled, getting rid of the consciousness, and with that the memories stopped. That was enough. Then he remembered how Marius had looked at him when he appeared with Aramas at the colony. *He knew who I was!*

"I know it's painful, my friend," Aramas said, "but necessary. You need to know the entire story. Every soul at some points needs to review everything, and understand. But that requires strength, wisdom and detachment."

There was truth in what he said, and Martin felt immense relief, as though an old weight had been finally lifted from his soul.

"Did Maria Lerna know I was Cassius?"

"Yes," responded Aramas. "But she also knew you were Ashar."

"Did she know I was Cassius and Ashar from the very beginning, when we first met?"

"Shortly thereafter, the day I came to visit you, when you summoned me."

Martin remembered that day. He had asked the Kahuna in his mind if what Maria Lerna said about healing was true. He had felt his presence and he remembered she did as well, and then she had given him that quizzical look. *At that moment she knew who I was.*

He wondered how she felt knowing he was Cassius.

Then he remembered, at Dunum in her family's home, with her brother dying, she held him and it had felt as though she was sorry for him. At the thought he felt his eyes moisten. *That is quite a woman.* And he knew he loved her with all his heart, and would miss her terribly. For the rest of his life he would feel her absence. How could he not?

In the following life he was a woman.

She saw herself and her sister Beatrice as small children living a comfortable life in what seemed like medieval times. There was a big house with servants, and Mama and Papa who loved them dearly.

There she was on her father's back as they played horsy, her father laughingly making whinnying noises and stomping his feet. Then the four of them out for a walk, her mother singing in her beautiful voice. And it was French, the songs were in French.

Then it was a time of fear. A siege...hunger...then soldiers everywhere...killing, brutalizing. They came to her house, and her father made them hide, but her mother would not leave his side and he tried to protect her with a sword...and she watched in horror as the soldiers killed her parents. Together with her sister hiding in an attic crawl space, watching as the soldiers brutalized and then butchered their parents. She had to cover her sister's mouth so she wouldn't cry out, hot tears streaming down her own face.

Afterwards the two sisters had lived with an uncle. And the uncle had abused her sexually, many times...in the night...with the promise he would leave her sister alone.

Then there had been an early marriage while Beatrice was sent to become a nun.

Later, her husband, who had tired of her, had their marriage annulled by the bishop, and had her banished to the Abbey where her sister was.

Her only happiness in life, her beloved little sister. And now looking at that life, Martin could tell that Beatrice had been Julius not so long ago. The same soul, the same essence, but now stronger, and at peace.

And then alongside her sister, she also became a nun, Sister Marie. And he still felt her intense anger, anger at the world, but mostly anger at men; men who had controlled her life, men who had all the power and abused it by raping and brutalizing, men whom she hated with all her might.

But Beatrice, she was now so devout, a sweet soul who made her life bearable.

Then she remembered a crusade, and how excited the nuns became, because they could all take up the cross and go to the Holy Land with the soldiers to nurse the wounded.

But she, sister Marie, came up with another plan. She left the Abbey, disguised herself as a man and took up the cross as a foot soldier.

This was her chance to kill men, which she did. Martin saw scenes of tremendous savagery, much of it her own doing. He saw her kill Turks and he saw her kill her own men when no one was looking, because those were the ones who savaged women. On their way to Constantinople and Jerusalem she had seen them rampage through Greek towns. She remembered the faces of those who had done the raping and killing, and systematically killed them, one by one...some as they lay wounded on the battlefield, some whom she caught alone in the night.

Then she simply killed, any man, anywhere she could get away with.

There was a big battle. The Turks attacked them, and they were overrun, pushed back. She fought until exhausted, then fought some more.

Finally the enemy retreated. The battle over, she went looking for Beatrice, desperately looking. She knew where she had been last, by a big rock. She walked through what remained of the camp and found her little sister badly wounded, and dying. She had been savagely raped, then mutilated, and left for dead.

Marie took off her helmet and chest armor, and not caring anymore whether someone found her to be a woman, crying, lifted her sister's head. "Beatrice, please don't leave me," she begged her, over and over, realizing how much she meant to her.

She anxiously held the dying Beatrice, who recited a prayer. She could barely make out the words as she heard her mention her name.

Beatrice stopped to look into her eyes, and said, "Please forgive the men, as you forgive yourself, dear Marie." Then she made her swear on the Sacred Heart of Jesus and the peace of her soul that she would no longer kill, but devote her life to penance, and said her soul would not rest unless Marie kept her vow.

Marie held her dying sister next to her chest, with the blood flowing, spurting, covering her completely, and she held her close, feeling the life pulsating out of her.

As Beatrice died in her arms, she was filled with intense grief, and she cried bitterly for the loss of a beloved and dear soul who had been her companion for so many hard years.

She shed her soldier's garb and put on a habit, and for the rest of her life did penance for her sins and prayed for the soul of her beloved sister. And she grieved...oh, how she grieved for those long, painful years. Martin could feel the weight of her sorrow, a heavy, inexorably ever-present pain that haunted her even during sleep.

Then came another life. The anger was there, but even stronger was a heavy feeling of impending loss. He saw himself as a soldier. It seemed they were in World War One, as he recognized the helmets, and he was sitting with other soldiers in a trench, waiting.

There was intense grief in his heart and the desire to die. He had been married and he missed his wife very much, and their little daughter. He no longer had a family; he had nothing.

They were still waiting. The waiting…the hours were very long that day, long and painful. The Germans were on the other side, and now they were waiting for orders to attach bayonets and charge.

All morning they had numbly watched in disbelief as wave after wave of their regiment was machine-gunned by the Germans. One battalion was called at a time…and when they were mowed down, the next battalion would be called.

The day before, they had watched as another Regiment had been completely annihilated. The brave lads would come out of their trenches yelling, running and shooting toward the German lines, only to fall, never reaching the enemy, without even a chance.

No one could believe this was happening, but it was.

Today it was their turn.

There was a feeling in his stomach; it felt like ice, as though he had eaten something very cold.

As they awaited orders to charge, he hoped to go first, so he wouldn't have to watch John getting killed. He would try his best to protect him, maybe by shielding him. Maybe if he knocked him out with his rifle butt, then he would be spared. What If he shot his foot? Yes, something like that might work. Poor John, he was but a young lad, too young.

But they were all young, children almost. How could he save them all?

He watched John pray. And it was fine; the lad needed his comfort. He wished he had a bit of scotch, that would be his comfort. He hated to die with the feeling in his stomach.

Then John looked at him; they were some four feet apart. His eyes were very peaceful, so peaceful.

"Mark."

"Yes."

"Are we going to die today?"

"Yes we are, my lad."

They had been together since training. A good chap, sad to see him die, but the good ones always died first.

"I'm glad we get to die together, then."

So the lad had made his peace. With God, he assumed.

All was quiet for a moment, so he peeked over the top of the trench. Maybe the bloody thing was over. No, he could see the German lines.

They called the battalion next in line before theirs.

He watched the men spring from their trenches and charge. They were now jumping over the other dead; some made it some twenty feet, others thirty, a handful some fifty feet...and now they were all gone...so fast, so fast...they were all gone...none left standing.

Now we get to step over them.

He looked around the trench, and most of the men were like him, already dead. Some, like John, were praying; others were crying, some with pictures of their girls.

He for one was glad to go; this life was nothing to cry about.

His Martha and young Elise dead.

He remembered how his daughter had embraced him before she died, her weak little arms encircling his neck. "Daddy, I'm going to see Mommy soon."

Did she know? But she was so young, who taught her how to die?

Then they charged.

John, poor lad, didn't quite make it out of the trench. He tried to go to him, but they were all charging, he was caught by the wave behind him. So he charged and ran, and yelled and shot his rifle. Then he felt the burning in his leg, then the other, then something slammed his chest...he fell and all was dark...and he knew it was over.

Martin looked at Aramas, who met his gaze with a sad smile.

And that was my journey. In his mind the images were still fresh. He saw Mojo who had been Beatrice and Julius. Then he thought about all the people he had killed while he was Cassius and then Marie.

"Anger moved me forward, but it was a shameful journey, and it caused great harm and suffering," Martin said.

"Yes, but all necessary. And it is no more."

I was the drowning child.

"But it seems that while Ashar, I was very close to liberation. Do souls go back?"

"Your spirit wanted the strength of total trust," Aramas said.

His heart echoed the words, and Ashar realized he was remembering instead of learning, and he could anticipate what his teacher would say next.

"Yes, Ashar. Trust comes from acceptance and oneness with God and creation. That's what you wanted to learn and the reason why you embarked on that journey."

He understood. Ashar understood and accepted. His heart seemed to know. All was the way it should be.

"What about Maria Lerna? She asked for my help but then wouldn't explain what she wanted. Please tell me."

Aramas looked sad.

"What will happen to her?" Martin's insides tightened.

Instead of answering, Aramas looked him in the eyes.

Martin saw past, present and future as one. In the past, he saw an older Maria Lerna watching him suffer through incarnations, crying for him.

She decided to help.

She came up with a plan, and decided to be with him in the lifetime when he was to become Martin. First, she prepared him so they both could emerge whole from that dark incarnation. She reached across to the future while he slept, when he was already Martin, to remind him who she was. She knew that once he recognized her, his love for her would propel him to help her and in the process of saving her he would save himself. She knew the risk involved. If Martin did not respond and become his real self, he wouldn't be able to help her; they both would stay lost for several miserable lifetimes. But she would do anything for him, so she assumed his state of consciousness and was once again, his wife.

"She is Jenny!"

"Yes, she is."

Martin saw Maria Lerna's face, smiling. His heart burst open with her image, and he felt like crying. *What a thing to do!*

Presently, Martin saw her as Jenny; and he saw that there were two possible paths for her. With his presence in her life her future was bright, and her soul became endowed with wisdom and devotion, her existence immersed in Spirit. She would become Maria Lerna once again. Without him, her future was dark, leading into despair, hatred and loneliness for what seemed like a long and painful journey.

Shaken, Martin sat transfixed.

"That's why she asked for my help, and then told me she couldn't explain, knowing that you would."

"Yes."

"So why exactly did you become involved?"

"I too wanted to help. Both of you."

Aramas seemed touched by what she had done. "She became trapped, but her spirit knows who she really is. And she knows that now you are safe. So she is asking you to help her."

"Help her re-awaken."

"Yes."

"But I'm not qualified—I have just begun to awaken myself. She needs you."

Aramas looked at him with affection. "Don't worry. Things will come to you when you need them. You will be helped. You alone can reach her, because at this point she won't recognize me. But she knows you."

Martin understood. They were destined to help one another. Everything had been carefully orchestrated. *But then, how would I remember who she is when I wake up back home?* His intention had been to divorce her.

"Ashar, don't fret. Your spirit is all-knowing. You are different. Trust that."

Yes, he was now very different. He felt a resolve grow inside. And he wanted to help Maria Lerna, and help Jenny.

Aramas raised his hand and waved it over his head. Then he held it there for a moment…as though blessing him, Martin thought.

"It will take a lot of wisdom and love to help her, but now you are well equipped for the challenge. And I, personally, will be very thankful to you."

Martin studied his teacher for a moment. "I guess this wasn't a routine intervention for you, was it?"

The Kahuna chuckled. "Each one has a special challenge, you might say."

They meditated together. Martin became Ashar and Ashar merged into Martin, and Martin meditated with his teacher. They remained this way for a long time, if there was still such a thing as time, for it seemed that eternity had opened up for him. And his soul soared.

Martin opened his eyes. He slowly stood up and bowed to the beloved.

Then he was gone.

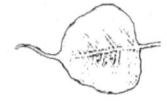

EPILOGUE

Isca is present-day Exeter. Much of the original Roman wall is still there, but the place I see in my mind's eye looks very different from the present city.

The Roman road in this novel is the Foss Way, in Roman times, "Via Fosa" which in Latin means "Canal Way."

The Seeker Colony was located in the area east of what is today's Glastonbury.

The ancient temple is Stonehenge.

Caledonia became today's Scotland. Back then the Scots lived in Hibernia, which is now Ireland.

Ambrosius was a real person who lived around the time the story took place, fought and won many battles against the Saxons and the Angles. Whether or not he was the real King Arthur, I don't know. Maybe. There is strong evidence that this part of Britain was not conquered for a long time, due to someone with a strong army.

I don't have any historical evidence that Maria Lerna was a real person. I personally believe she was.

I conducted the historical research for this novel after completing the first draft. At first, simply out of curiosity to see how much of what I had written was factual. Then, when I decided to publish, for the sake of authenticity. I thought the story and the characters deserved as much.

www.ingramcontent.com/pod-product-compliance
Lightning Source LLC
Chambersburg PA
CBHW050926120626
46552CB00001B/71